THE SCENE 4

Edited by
STANLEY NELSON

Special London Report by Ron Travis

THE SMITH–NEW EGYPT

(c) Copyright May, 1977 by The Smith. Volume IV, complete.
Published by The Smith under the New Egypt imprint as an activity of
The Generalist Association, 5 Beekman Street, N.Y. 10038.

Edited by Stanley Nelson

$5.00 per copy. The Scene, 5 Beekman Street, New York, N.Y. 10038.

Library of Congress Catalog Card Number 77-70415 ISBN: 0-912292-42-3

Copyright (c) by The Scene. First Printing, May, 1977

*Distributed by Horizon Press, 156 Fifth Ave., N.Y.C. 10010
& Drama Book Specialists, 150 West 52 Street, N.Y.C. 10019*

Contents

London's Fringe: Special Section

The London Fringe Scene   7
RON TRAVIS

Tsafendas   33
WILLIAM GARNET TANNER

When I Grow Too Old to Scream   64
I Shall Have To Surrender
STEWART PERMUTT

Honey From Yucatan   85
ALLAN BERRIE

The Vansittarts and the Bullworkers   129
ANTHONY SWERLING

Off-Off Broadway and the College Theatre   146

Slaughter   151
ALFONSO VALLEJO

Stage Directions   208
ISRAEL HOROVITZ

Gertrude's Easter   228
THOMAS TOLNAY

Paradise   237
STEVEN SHEA

288 Off-Off Broadway Theatres   256

Publisher: **Harry Smith**
Editor: **Stanley Nelson**
U.K. Editor: **Ron Travis**
Managing Editor: **Anne Heller**
Field Editors:
    Joseph Lazarus
    Tom Tolnay
    Seymour Reznitsky
Cover Design and Drawings: **Al Ingegno**
Frontispiece: **James H. Kay**
Special Consultant: **Virginia Kahn**
Photo Credits: **Alex Levac**—page 32;
                Nathaniel Tileston—page 238.

THE LONDON FRINGE SCENE

as observed by RON TRAVIS

The FRINGE is the universal term applied to the many alternative theatre ventures in London roughly equivalent to Off-Off Broadway in New York. As a midwesterner who has lived in London and worked in English theatre for the past four years as artistic director, actor, director, designer, writer and audience member, I maintain that the Fringe is the most exciting and rewarding theatre to be found in the British Isles. It has developed during the past nine years and has survived to become an established part of the English Theatre Scene—recognised by critics, theatre people, the Arts Council, the general public and (although grudgingly) the commercial theatre itself.

An example of the Fringe's influence and respectability can be seen in Harold Hobson's last review in *The Sunday Times* before his retirement. The review was entirely devoted to the Fringe or theatrical events that were spawned by the Fringe: 1) A *re*-review of *Weapons of Happiness* by Howard Brenton at the National Theatre. (Brenton's playwrighting teeth were cut on the Fringe.) 2) A performance by the Hull Truck Company at the Young Vic under the auspices of the National Theatre and in keeping with its policy to include the best from the itinerant groups and provincial repertory theatres in their seasons. 3) The King's Head production of *Elizabeth I* by Paul Foster. 4) A play written by a prisoner, George Thatcher (*The Only Way Out*), performed at the Theatre Upstairs, and 5) a tribute to Verity Bargate (Soho Poly) and Ed Berman (Almost Free) for the quality they have achieved in their work.

It seems to me that playwrights in the United Kingdom have an easier time of it than their colleagues in the States. Unlike television and radio in the States, which are almost entirely devoted to insipid series and screamer stations, the BBC and Independent television networks (there are 15) devote a large share of their programming to the production of plays. BBC Radio airs three or four hours a day of sound drama in new plays, readings and

7

classics. There are numerous itinerant theatre companies (Belt & Braces, 7:84, Hull Truck and Wakefield Tricycle Company, to name but four) that travel up and down the country in buses and vans presenting plays on one night stands in union halls, working men's clubs, university campuses and at festivals. Another important and growing outlet for the writer is the development and continued growth of Theatre in Education companies supported by local educational authorities and by regional repertory companies. TIE groups tour schools in a given area and perform in established venues throughout the country.

While all of these allow scope and work for playwrights, it is still the Fringe that attracts writers. Why? The Fringe provides a basic laboratory for writers to develop their ideas and technique under excellent conditions. Because of the status of the Fringe, well-known actors, directors and designers are willing to work for next to nothing. If a new play is presented in, say, the Soho Poly, the Bush, Almost Free, King's Head, or Theatre at New End, the playwright knows that—even with the inescapable economies of time, space and money imposed upon his production—it will be given more than fair chance to succeed. Many writers appreciate the feedback which is possible in a Fringe setting; audiences are not afraid to express opinions to anyone who is interested in listening. Thus benefits to the playwright include 1) a sounding board for his ideas and the way they have been expressed, 2) the opportunity of having his work seen and possibly picked up by radio or television, 3) an opportunity to be commissioned to write a specific play for a specific theatre or purpose, and 4) the possibility of the production and/or play to be picked up by another Fringe theatre, commercial management, regional theatre, or continental theatre.

One unfortunate element for the UK playwright is that no publication similar to THE SCENE exists in the United Kingdom. Although a few plays do become available through the new playscripts series issued by Methuen, Calder Boyars, Pluto Press, Davis-Poynter, and in the monthly *Plays & Players*, they usually appear (with the exception of *Plays & Players*) long after the initial excitement surrounding a production has died. Obviously, many of the plays which are excellent and merit further productions are lost and forgotten by all except those who wrote, appeared in, or worked on them.

1. FRINGE RELATIONSHIPS: CRITICS AND AUDIENCE.

The first thing one hopes for when working on the Fringe is a review—good or bad—in TIME OUT. TIME OUT is the weekly bible to those in London who seek alternatives to the establishment, and it can be seen in the furtive grasp of M.P.s, city businessmen and tourists, as well as in the society of the great unwashed. A review, when favorable, will swell the house for any Fringe play. An unfavourable review will provide marginal audience increase among those perverse readers who want to see if a play could really be as bad as TIME OUT claims. An ignored production—merely a listing of the time and place of the play—provides almost no response.

Established critics from the major papers are not reluctant to attend and review Fringe productions. Harold Hobson (The Sunday Times), Michael Billington (*Guardian*), Eric Shorter (*The Daily Telegraph*), Irving Wardle (The *Times*) and B.A. Young (*Financial Times*) have frequently been seen in a Fringe audience on opening day. Their criticisms are not offered as a milk sop; they are written with the same objectivity applied to a new commercial work. The value to an individual production receiving a good review from a major critic is difficult to assess; it appears their main function is to swell the scrapbooks of writers, actors, directors and designers with good notices for future reference.

One particular pheonomenon which has been developed by the Fringe is lunchtime theatre. The idea as initially developed and still naively held by some was to present short plays (45-50 minutes) at a time when people from shops and offices could leave their work and receive cultural entertainment while eating their lunch. While some of the people attending lunchtime productions could legitimately be said to come from these ranks, they are the minority. The greater part of any lunchtime audience (indeed of any Fringe audience) is composed of writers, tourists, students, friends of the cast, out-of-work actors, agents, casting directors, and a hard core group that religously criss-crosses the Fringe circuit on a daily basis. As most Fringe plays are given a limited run (2-3 weeks) and most Fringe houses are small (35-50, although some hold over 150) this clientele is enough to insure a healthy audience for most shows. Even when a play is a complete success it is rarely extended, although there are notable exceptions to that rule: *Kennedy's Children* by Robert Patrick had its run extended on several occasions before it transferred to the Arts Theatre Club in the West End and became the Fringe's longest running play (over two years); and *Hello Sailor* at the Soho Poly was revived by public demand.

2. FRINGE RELATIONSHIPS: WRITERS, ACTORS, DIRECTORS, DESIGNERS.

Fringe theatres serve both established and new writers. Last year the Fringe saw productions of new plays by Tom Stoppard, Edward Bond, Margaretta D'Arcy and John Arden, to name but a few. Because of the status the Fringe has achieved in its short life, well known writers do not consider it a poor relation; they are willing to contribute to it and challenge its audience with new ideas.

A work by an established playwright will not receive special treatment. A first play will be given the same planning and preparation applied to a script by a more established writer. But whether established or new, it is not always easy for a writer to get a play produced on the Fringe. The major Fringe theatres may receive upwards of 500 scripts for consideration during a year. They may be able to produce 2 or 25. The life of the playwright circulating scripts is also not easy. Barrie Keeffe accurately and humorously portrays the trials and tribulations of a Fringe playwright in an article recently published in *Drama*. (Barrie Keeffe, "Fundamentals," *Drama: The Quarterly Review*, No. 121, Summer 1976, p. 28.)

If a play is accepted for production, the Artistic Director will attempt to gather as strong a director and cast as possible. The vanguard of the Fringe (Soho Poly, King's Head, Almost Free, Theatre at New End and the Half Moon) are in a position to assemble star casts for their productions. It is not unusual to see actors and actresses in a lunchtime play who are also appearing evenings in the West End or working for the two large subsidised houses, the National and the Royal Shakespeare Company. By the same token actors and actresses are not reluctant to include Fringe work in their programme biographies. Those working in a long run in the West End, or connected with one of the subsidised companies, welcome the opportunity of working in a lunchtime show to keep their skills sharp and to cut the boredom which accompanies a long run.

This is not meant to imply that all Fringe is performed by actors who are bored. There is a central core of people who work almost exclusively on the Fringe. As directors get to know the work of certain actors and actresses they tend to call upon the same people to act in their productions, whether at the Soho Poly, Half Moon, King's Head or the Little. This inbreeding is not an unusual phenomenon in theatre; one only has to look at the Group Theatre after it disbanded to see certain names recurring in later productions by Clurman or Kazan.

In the early days, the Fringe used a curious mixture of amateurs, drama students and professionals. It has now evolved to where nearly all Fringe shows are performed by professionals. At the moment, Fringe payment to actors varies from a cut of the box-office to Equity minimum. (For two years there has been a committee within Equity investigating the Fringe and its rates of pay; what will happen is unclear.) Designers too, enjoy the challenge of the Fringe with its tight budget, but it is the easy working relationship that makes them return again and again.

The very nature of the Fringe, with its intimate facilities for the presentation of plays, breaks down the usual actor-audience relationship. Audience, actors and production staff mingle in the theatre after a show or adjourn to a nearby pub (if the theatre is not in one) to discuss the play. There is none of the abrasiveness associated with stage-door Johnnys and autograph hounds which so often mars actor/audience relationships in commercial theatre ventures.

3. FRINGE FINANCE:

The Fringe derives income from three major sources: a) memberships b) box office c) Arts Council of Great Britain subsidy.

a) MEMBERSHIPS: **Most Fringe theatres are theatre clubs which require membership. Prior to the Theatres Act of 1968 all plays had to be licensed by the Lord Chamberlain for public performance. A play could be refused a license for representing the Royal Family, a denunciation of God, opposition to the government, or obscenity. A play, native or foreign, which did not receive a license could be performed only by a membership society or club. In the 1890s, the first plays of Ibsen and Shaw to be presented in England were performed by J.T. Grein's Independent Theatre Society. During the 1960's the English Stage Society turned the Royal Court into a "club" theatre in order to present new plays by John Osborne and Edward Bond. Unity Theatre (founded 1936 and burned 1975) was a club theatre with an international reputation for productions of leftist political plays. Some of the plays produced at Unity and printed during its early days proudly declaimed "Banned by the Lord Chamberlain" on their covers.**

With the abolition of censorship, why do the Fringe theatres still maintain a club status? In some cases premises are not up to the standard of the building code. This does not mean that they are unsafe, but that a building's structure could not be altered without costly renovation to allow the public to attend performances. In other words, if you join a club and are injured it is your own fault, but if you are a member of the general public you can sue.

The most important reason for Fringe theatre memberships is the additional source of income. Subscriptions are annual and usually cost 50p (90 cents) or a £1.00 (1.80). Most Fringe theatres have reciprocal agreements with other theatres which will allow members of, say, the Soho Poly to attend performances at the Oval, Bush, Theatre at New End, the King's Head, etc., without having to be a member of each. A few theatres will allow one to purchase a temporary, one day membership, i.e. 15p (30 cents) to 25p (50 cents) on top of the ticket price which provides admission to a particular show. A few of the theatres will carry an annual membership of 2000 to 3000, which amounts to a considerable sum when planning and budgeting a forthcoming season.

b) BOX OFFICE: **The Fringe can guarantee a good show lunchtime or** evening at a reasonable price. Most lunchtime theatres charge 50p, with evening performances at around £1.00. But even with memberships and full houses a Fringe theatre cannot financially survive. A typical budget for a Fringe lunch-time show would be:

Expenses:	£
Sets and costumes:	50.00
1 director, 4 actors - 2 weeks rehearsal, 2 weeks playing at £15 a week each:	300.00
Playwright's royalty 7⅓% of gross box office:	22.50
Hire of theatre and payment of staff:	100.00
Publicity:	50.00
Miscellaneous (telephone, electricity etc.):	25.00
Total:	£547.00

Income:	£
12 performances - 50 seats @ 50p (600 seats):	300.00
20% new membership acquired during run (120 members at 50p):	60.00
Total income:	£360.00
Deficit:	£187.50

It could be argued that prices should be raised to make each theatre pay for itself, but then the Fringe could easily outprice itself and fold overnight. Therefore the option left open to a Fringe theatre is to apply to the Arts Council of Great Britain for a grant to assist its venture.

c) THE ARTS COUNCIL: Grants are given in three forms: direct grants to theatres production grants and new plays grants. Some theatres receive only one type of grant, while others apply for and receive two or all three.

Direct Grant:

The Arts Council reviews subsidised theatrical companies on a yearly basis and applies a direct grant to given theatres in various amounts. Grants range from over £1,000,000 to the

RSC and National, to less than £50 for individual productions on the Fringe. The vanguard of the Fringe receive from £8,000 to £30,000 a year, depending upon their previous successes and forthcoming productions.

Production Grants:

Every production of a new play, a neglected play (or, in some cases, the second production of a new play) are eligible to apply for a production grant. It must be shown that the production will be given whether a grant is received or not. The grant is of two types: either a set sum or a guarantee against losses of up to £250.00. Theatres usually submit proposals for every forthcoming production at least one month in advance.

New Plays Grants:

A specific grant guaranteeing a minimum royalty (290 for a one-act, 250 for full length) can be applied for in the case of a new work by a playwright who resides in the United Kingdom. Most theatres pay an additional $7\frac{1}{3}\%$ royalty on the gross box office to the playwright over and above the grant. The Arts Council also has a playwright-in-residence scheme. A small number of grants are awarded through the Council to provide theatres with playwrights-in-residence for six months or a year. If a such grant is given, it is over and above the theatre's general grant, and may be paid directly by the Arts Council to the playwright. In return, the recipient is usually required to produce one work for future production in the theatre, and to carry out such duties as agreed upon between the theatre and the playwright (literary manager).

The Arts Council and the commercial theatre recognise that the grant system is necessary for the survival of the Fringe. This system of grants allows enough flexibility for almost any new, worthwhile production to be given a fair showing without undue burdens being placed on the small incomes derived from memberships and box office. The Fringe respects these grants, and for the most part they are used wisely. Although there are cases in which production grants are misused or new playwrights' grants never reach the playwright, these are, thankfully, in the minority.

4. THE THEATRES:

The following is intended to serve as a guide to the Fringe for the prospective visitor to London, and for the writer who may wish to submit a play to a London Fringe theatre for possible production.

The theatres are as varied as the plays. Some are purpose-built, others are found in basements or lofts, and several are in pubs. There are theatres which produce only English and world premieres, others that are committed to social change; a few cater to the needs of ethnic communities. Of course, there are Fringe theatres with a more catholic approach which present anything they like. Still, Fringe theatres can be divided into three main groups: a) those that are aligned to the Fringe but are not b) the Fringe vanguard c) the Fringe second line.

a) THOSE ALIGNED TO THE FRINGE BUT NOT: **Four London theatres present certain types of plays to particular audiences and hope for the occasional West End transfer or American or Continental tour, coupled with a healthy Arts Council Grant. They are in a special category and operate with methods peculiar to themselves. Audiences found at the Theatre Upstairs, Hampstead Theatre Club, the Young Vic, and the Open Space tend to come from a younger, trendy middle-class which is slumming to see what the alternative theatre has to offer.**

> i) *Theatre Upstairs.* (Royal Court, Sloane Square SW1 Tel: 730-2554). The Theatre Upstairs was formed in 1969 as a natural extension to the Court's Sunday night productions of new plays. While not admitted by the Court, it serves the English Stage Company with production of new works by their "second string" of writers (Wilson John Haire, Richard O'Brien, Peter Gill, Heathcote Williams and Howard Brenton, for example). In 1975, the Theatre Upstairs closed due to financial pressures on the English Stage Company, but it reopened last spring to continue its work. Notable productions which have been first produced in the Theatre Upstairs include *AC/DC* by Heathcote Williams, *The Rocky Horror Show* by Richard O'Brien, *The Foursome* by E.A. Whitehead and *Roseman and Lena* by Athol Fugard.

ii) *Hampstead Theatre Club.* (Artistic Director: Michael Rud-man. Swiss Cottage Centre NW3 Tel: u22-9301). Founded in 1961 by James Roose-Evans. Receives substantial grants from the Arts Council and the London Borough of Camden in which it resides. Seats 157. Plays usually receive a month's run. Usually transfer one or two plays to the West End each year. Occasionally productions by outside companies, but most of the plays presented are their own presentations.

iii) *Young Vic.* (Artistic Director: Frank Dunlop. The Cut, Waterloo, SEI. Tel: 928-6363). Reformed in 1970 after 19 years under the wing of the National Theatre Company. Flew the nest in 1974. Two theatres in a former butcher's shop. Main auditorium seats over 400 in a flexible area, while the Studio theatre holds about 60. Produces classics and revivals of modern plays presented in a style designed to attract an au-dience of under 25s. Relies on tourists and middle-class to fill its theatre. Enjoys talking about its successful New York and West End seasons.

iv) *Open Space* (Co-Directors: Charles Marowitz and Thelma Holt. 32 Tottenham Court Road, W1 Tel: 580-4970). Marowitz, a New Yorker by birth, has made London his home. At one time an exponent of The Method, Marowitz worked with Peter Brook in his Theatre of Cruelty experi-ments in the early sixties. The diverse philosophies inherent in his direction make his production style unique. Par-ticularly noteworthy are Marowitz's adaptations of Shakespeare, *A Macbeth, An Othello, The Shrew, Measure for Measure.* While purists object to his interpretations, others find them exciting theatrical evenings. In its early days the Open Space experienced the transfer syndrome (*Fortune and Men's Eyes, The Bellow Plays*). Now it is content to work within its own space with a continental tour once or twice a year. The building housing the theatre is due for demolition, but a new theatre is planned in the redevelopment of the site.

b) THE FRINGE VANGUARD: Every movement is spearheaded by cer-tain groups which stand head and shoulders above the rest. The six theatres which lead the Fringe maintain their reputations by consistently presenting a high standard of work both in writing and production. Writers such as Steven Poliakoff, David Edgar, Snoo Wilson, Barrie Keeffe, Howard Benton, Andy Smith, Pam Gems and Chris Allen are but a few of the newer playwrights making their marks in the greater spectrum of English Theatre, but continuing to write plays specifically for these Fringe Theatres. The Soho Poly, Almost Free, Bush, King's Head, Theatre at New End and the Half Moon easily surpass the other Fringe theatres in the quality of work presented.

i) *Soho Poly* (Artistic Director, Verity Bargate. 16 Riding House Street, W1 Tel: 636-9050). The Poly was founded in 1968 by Frederick Proud and Verity Bargate. They moved into their present premises in 1972. Fred left the theatre last year and it is now completely under Verity's control. A basement space seating 50, the Soho Poly produces mainly lunch-time plays with occasional evening productions. It presents about 20 plays a year, usually for a two week run. Outstanding shows during the past year are many, but of particular note were: *Hello Sailor* by Eric Sutton; *And They Used to Star in Movies* by Campbell Black; *The Soul of The White Ant* by Snoo Wilson; a double bill, Campion's Interview by Brian Clark and Gotcha by Barrie Keeffe; and *The Project* by Pam Gems.

In addition to productions, the Poly has also contributed a playwrights' workshop to the Fringe scene. Held once a week and organised by George Byatt, playwright-in-residence, new plays are given a staged reading before an audience. The audience is composed of the theatre people and, surprisingly enough, members of the general public. The success of the venture is mirrored both in the size of the audience (rarely less than 40) and by the fact that several of the plays first read at the workshop have been performed during the year by other Fringe theatres.

ii) *The Almost Free Theatre* (Artistic Director: Ed Berman. Inter-Action Productions, 9 Rupert Street, W1 Tel: 485-6224). The Almost Free is but one segment of Inter-Action, formed in 1968 by Ed Berman, a former New Yorker now a citizen of the United Kingdom. Inter-Action is a curious mixture of theatre and community action work which is supported by the Arts Council, the London Borough of Camden, private companies and individuals. The community activities include the Fun Art Farm, a community advisory service, a community video unit, and a media van. Theatrically, Inter-Action runs the Almost Free, Dogg's Troupe (street theatre), the Fun Art Bus, O.A.T.S. (Old Age Theatre Society), and the Father Christmas Union. Each of the activities of Inter- Action merits discussion in its own right.

It is the Almost Free that provides Inter-Action with a voice on the Fringe. Formed in 1968, as the Ambiance (lunch-hour) Theatre Club, it began its work in London's Portobello Road market area. In 1971, Inter-Action acquired the premises for the Almost Free and moved Ambiance. As the name suggests, performances are almost free:

"You choose your own prices. In order that Inter-Action productions at the Almost Free Theatre are available to everyone, all members may determine both their membership fees and ticket prices from one pence upwards. Everyone who comes to the Almost Free theatre must become a member (no guests) which automatically includes membership in the Ambiance Theatre Club. Please pay as much, not as little, as you can." (Quoted from programme.)

Basically a lunchtime theatre, Almost Free's policy is to present British or world premieres by known and unknown authors. The Almost Free sometimes presents its plays in seasons: a season of gay plays, a season of plays by new British writers, or a season of specially commissioned new plays, The American Connection, marking "the 200th Anniversary of the American Revolt and the occasion of the Artistic Director of Inter-Action becoming a British Subject." The American Connection included new plays by Tom Stoppard, Margaretta D'Arcy, John Arden and two plays by Edward Bond.

18

Two productions at the Almost Free deserve mention from 1976 activity: *Tsafandas* by William Tanner and *The Non-Stop Connolly Cycle* by Margaretta D'Arcy and John Arden. *Tsafandas*—which appears in the SCENE—is the story of the assassin of Dr. Verwoerd, the South African Prime Minister, in 1966. Brechtian in style, it presents the picture of the man through extracts made known during his trial.

iii) *The Bush* (Artistic Director: Dusty Hughes. The Bush Hotel, Shepherd's Bush Green, W12 Tel: 743-5050). The Bush was formed in 1972 in a large room above a pub. Rather shaky at first, the theatre soon gathered momentum and steadily built a strong reputation on the Fringe. It produces its own plays and occasionally provides a home for various itinerant companies, including 7:84, Sal's Meat Market, the Wakefield Tricycle Company, and the Hull Truck Company. It is an open theatre plan with the audience (120) seated on two or three sides of the acting area. Performances at the Bush are in the evening, with only the occasional lunchtime production.

The theatre's most notable discovery to date is the young 23-year-old playwright, Steve Poliakoff, who has been appointed playwright-in-residence to the National Theatre. Poliakoff had his first play produced at the Traverse Theatre in Edinburgh in 1971 followed by *Clever Soldiers* at the Hampstead Theatre Club and *The Carnation Gang* at the Bush in 1974. While all three of the productions made their marks it was *Hitting Town* and *City Sugar* (published by Methuen) at the Bush in 1975 for which he received the Evening Standard's Playwrighting Award and rocketed to his present position. *City Sugar* transferred to the West End under a commercial management with a different cast early this year. While acclaimed, critics and theatregoers alike felt that the use of "stars" damaged the over-all impact the show had created at the Bush. It failed to achieve a long run and closed after six weeks.

iv) *The King's Head* (Artistic Director: Dan Crawford. 115

Upper Street, Islongton N1 Tel: 226-1916) The King's Head differs from other theatres in pubs in that the Crawfords control the bar as well as the theatre. Their policy is open ended; they present revivals, itinerant groups and new plays in rather random order, both at lunchtime and in the evening. The fortunes of the King's Head have been up and down throughout its history. A few years ago there was talk of the King's Head closing after a particularly rough patch. They decided to go ahead with a new play which caught everyone's attention. Its run was extended on several occasions. At one point it was necessary to book two weeks in advance. The play transferred to the Arts Theatre Club in the West End and became the Fringe's longest running play (over two years). *Kennedy's Children* by OOB playwright Robert Patrick indeed scored a hit in London. No wonder, when mentioned in front of Dan Crawford, a smile of pleasure creeps across his face.

Most evening productions at the King's Head run four to six weeks, lunchtime shows two to three weeks. Audiences for the evening performances have the option of arriving at the King's Head an hour before curtain and having a three-course meal before the play begins. The success of this dinner-theatre venture varies with the chef the King's Head may have at a given time, but it is the only Fringe theatre which provides the service.

v) *Theatre at New End* (Artistic Director: Robert Walker. 27 New End, Hampstead, NW3 Tel: 435 4949) Theatre at New End is the newest of the major Fringe theatres. Converted by Alec and Buddy Dalton from an old mortuary, it opened in 1974, closed in 1975, re-opened in 1975, almost closed in 1976, but continues to function. The initial conversion from mortuary to the best-equipped theatre on the Fringe used up capital initially set aside for production. Its first year was disastrous. Stories surrounding the ineptitude displayed by its former Artistic Director have become legendary. It should suffice to say that it opened with a tawdry play by Anouilh with eyes towards a West End transfer and closed ten months later after productions of *The Glass Menagerie* and a bill of Shaw one-acts. There was no surprise after its first year that the theatre did not receive the Arts Council grant it had anticipated.

Last October, the theatre reopened under the direction of Robert Walker, one of the best young directors in England. Since its reopening, Theatre at New End has played to full houses with new plays and plays which have been seen in the provinces but not in London. Unfortunately, the theatre is not in a position to make itself pay even though it charges the highest seat prices on the Fringe (£1.50). The Arts Council has provided an interim grant of £8000 which is expected to last for only three or four productions. What will become of the theatre remains to be seen; it can only be hoped that the Arts Council recognizes New End's work and provides a sufficient grant in the future to allow it to operate as it should.

vi) *The Half Moon* (Artistic Director: Pam Brighton. 23 Alie Street, E1. Tel: 480 6465). Situated in London's East End, the Half Moon functions as a service to the community in which it resides. It is the most politically motivated of the Fringe theatres. Many of its plays are re-written with an East End setting or written especially for it.

The Half Moon's playwrights have received marginally better support than most on the Fringe; some of their work has actually been printed! Steve Gooch's *Female Transport*, concerning the shipment of women prisoners to Australia in the 1800's, and *Will Wat, If Not, What Will*, about the Peasant's Revolt in the 13th century, have both been published by Pluto. Billy Colville and Dave Marston's *Fall In and Follow Me: A Play About The Children's Strike of 1911* was published in the History Workshop Pamphlet series issued by Ruskin College, Oxford.

The Half Moon has been attempting for several years to acquire the old Wilton's Music Hall in the East End docks for

the production of plays. To date they have pledges of
£100,000 but an additional £50,000 must still be found before
they can realise their aim.

c. THE FRINGE'S SECOND LINE: I do not intend this as a deroga-
tory category, but as a means of clearer understanding of the types
of theatres to be found on the Fringe, and of their methods of
operation. The majority of the Fringe can be found in this category: some because of their uniqueness, others because of their
location outside central London. A few cater to ethnic communities and, of course, a few do not attain a consistently high artistic
standard to merit classification with the Vanguard. The Little,
the ICA, Pentameters, the Oval House, and the Cockpit all operate
within the central London area. The Overground, Kingston-upon-
Thames, the Orange Tree in Richmond, The Combination at the
Albany Empire in Deptford, and the Warehouse in Rotherhithe
are outside the central London area. The Sugawn Kitchen, Teatro
Technis, and the Black Theatre of Brixton cater to ethnic seg-
ments of the London community.

i) *The Little Theatre* (Artistic Director: Ann Fenn 16/19 Upper St. Martin's Lane, WC2 Tel: 240 0660). Initially housed in
the fourth floor of an old sewing machine factory, the Little
moved to new and more spacious premises 50 yards up the
road in January, 1975. Its programme is easily the most ambitious of the Fringe, with some 165 productions each year. A recent programme is a typical example of the activity which
takes place at the Little: at lunch-time (1.15), *Katrina and
Petruchio*, an adaptation from Shakespeare's *The Taming of
the Shrew*; at tea-time (6.15), an experimental show with
music, mime and dance; in the evening (8.00), *And...* a new
play by Alan Passes; and late-night (11.00), *Robinson Crusin'*,
a gay cabaret. The Little mixes its own productions with outside companies and visiting groups. Because of the great
variety of times, styles and production techniques, the Little
suffers from the fact that audiences who have seen one bad
show are reluctant to return and actors, directors and
designers who have not had an easy time of it refuse to work
there again.

Though handicaps are many, the Little has produced several plays of merit. Arrabal's *The Car Factory* received its English language premiere in November under the direction of Ann Fenn. It was the first time that the Little had used the space allocated for the larger of its two theatres (seating 150); it hauled in junk vehicles to be incorporated into the set. Hobson, in his review of the production, included it in a small list of plays which showed that England had benefited from the elimination of censorship by the Lord Chamberlain in 1968. Also noteworthy was a lunch-time production of *Welcome to Buckhill* by Chris Allen. A slightly allegorical piece set in the not too distant future, it was the story of the take-over of a coal mine and village in the north of England which was turned into a holiday camp by an American leisure company. It was, perhaps, the best play on the Fringe last year which provided an ironic view of the state of Great Britain.

At the moment the work at the Little is spotty. If it is able to organize itself and assure a quality both in writing and production to go along with its quantity of work, it could easily become one of the Fringe's vanguard theatres.

ii) *The ICA* (Institute of Contemporary Art, The Mall, SW1 Tel: 839 5344). The ICA, as its full name suggests, was established as a base for all the Arts. Housed in a building designed by Nash, it has recently begun to strengthen its performing arts programme. It may offer a season of plays (recently there was a season by the Gay Sweatshop and four political plays), a venue for foreign companies or the odd outside company which has something special to offer (*Fanshen* by the Joint Stock Theatre Company, e.g.). Whether or not it is presenting a play, the ICA is always worth a visit for its latest exhibitions or a bite to eat in its cafe.

iii) *Pentameters* (Artistic Director: Leonie Scott-Mathews. The Three Horse-shoes Pub, Heath Street, Hampstead, NW3). Pentameters was formed in 1968 as a poetry society by Leonie Scott-Mathews. It assembles every Monday evening and has included such poets as Kingley Amis, Stephen Spender, Alan Sillitoe, Adrian Mitchell and Roger McGough. About two years ago Pentameters began using its space to present plays lunchtimes and evenings on weekends. Last year it produced three outstanding shows' *The Other Side of the Swamp* by Royce Ryton, *The Poetry Reading* by Stanley Nelson and *When I Grow Too Old To Scream I Shall Have to Surrender* by Stewart Permutt.

Stewart Permutt's *When I Grow Too Old To Scream I Shall Have To Surrender* is included in this volume. Let it suffice to say that the tradition of Pantomime in England is found nowhere else in the world. It is not to be believed. Almost every town of over 10,000 (and many smaller) has at least one professional Panto at Christmas. Some run until April. It is the time of year when every actor and actress can find work somewhere. There are many who only work in the Panto season. Most end up in a fourth rate show of the type Mr. Permutt has used as the background of his play.

In 1975, Stanley Nelson forwarded a copy of his play, *The Poetry Reading,* to London. Because of the primary function of Pentameters and the nature of the play it was given to Ms. Scott-Mathews for her consideration and was produced in March, 1976. The play was adapted from a New York to a London setting for the production. After its successful run it was returned by public demand for an additional weekend.

iv) *The Oval House* (54 Kennington Oval, SE11. Tel: 735 2786). The Oval House is a community centre for youth. It has two theatres: a studio theatre seating 50 and a larger, adaptable space which can hold up to 150. It relies mainly on outside companies to present plays on Friday, Saturday and Sunday evenings. Its weekend work provides the Fringe with its most experimental venue.

v) *The Overground Theatre Club* (Alan Bryce and Maria Ricco, co-directors. Opposite Kingston Station, Kingston-upon-Thames, Surrey. Tel: 549 5893). The Overground opened in 1974 as a lunch-time theatre in a room above a pub. The brewery closed the pub and gave the whole building to the theatre, which then began to present plays in the evening rather than at lunch-time. Its policy is to present "anything and everything worth doing." For the most part this means plays that could be found in a season by any community theatre in the States. As its name implies, it is not part of the "underground" scene; it's a respectable theatre in a rich suburban community.

vii) *The Orange Tree* (45 Kew Road, Richmond, Surrey. Tel: 940 3633). Another suburban theatre located in a room above a pub. Opened in 1971, it presents mainly lunchtime plays. Productions here regularly attract people out of central London to "catch a show at the Tree," and it is not unusual to have such a number turn up for a performance that a play will receive a second performance following the first to accommodate the overflow. It has a much more adventurous and exciting programme than its near neighbour in Kingston.

viii) *The Combination* (Artistic Director: Jenny Harris. The Albany Empire, Creek Road, Deptford, SE8. Tel: 692 0765). For several years the Brighton Combination was a leading itinerant group based in Brighton but travelling throughout the country combining music and media in their social-message plays. In 1972, they found a home in the Albany, a settlement house with an old theatre in the London Borough of Lewisham. While they still tour, most of their work is done at the Albany and in the Borough of Lewisham. Plays usually run for six weekends with a month's interval, during which time the theatre is completely dismantled and refitted for its next show. All shows are written collectively by the Combination and utilize their mixed approach to full advantage; some have a definite commitment to the problems of the people in the community—e.g., housing, inflation and urban development—while others are less localized and more universal.

ix) *The Warehouse* (Artistic Director: Ann Colthart. 99, Rotherhithe St., Elephant Lane, Rotherhithe SE16. Tel: 237

9443). Situated on the south side of the Thames in a depressed area of London's dockland, there is a theatre-cum-arts-centre-cum-community-centre being converted from an old warehouse. The theatre does not yet produce its own plays; it relies on groups like Belt & Braces, The Dockwhollopers, Red Brass, and Mayday to present plays and entertainment on the weekends. The building is still in the process of being converted and has the ever-present problem of money. It has built up a local reputation and is usually quite well-attended by a mixture of locals and people down to see productions that are not readily available in more central locations. It is a much needed venture in a neglected area of London.

x) *The Sugawn Theatre* (Artistic Director: Jerry O'Neill, The Sugawn Kitchen, Duke of Wellington Pub, Balls Pond Road, N1. Tel: 254 1458). The Sugawn Theatre caters to the large Irish community in London. Plays by Irish playwrights or with an Irish theme are presented by a dedicated group of amateur actors. They recently scooped the English professional theatre twice, first by giving the first production of Hugh Leonard's *Da* and then with an adaptation of *Finnegan's Wake*. From time to time, the theatre is let to professional companies. It also holds regular folk and poetry evenings.

xi) *Teatro Technis* (Artistic Director: George Eugeniou, Freightliners, York Way, N7). After fifteen years of itinerant existence, the Greek Arts Theatre converted an old building in a freightyard into a theatre. The theatre presents plays in Greek and English mainly for the Greek Cypriot community in North London. The repertory includes Greek classics, an international smattering of the classical and contemporary, and new plays by Greek nationals and immigrants. The theatre, happy with its new home, has recently found itself threatened with eviction to allow for redevelopment of the site. If the site is redeveloped and does not include plans for a theatre, the group will be forced into presenting occasional shows in town halls, pubs and churches once again.

xii) *The Black Theatre of Brixton* (Artistic Director: Jamal Ali, Longfield Hall, Knatchbull Rd., SE5. Tel: 673 4869). Formerly the Dark and Light Theatre Club, the theatre changed its name early in 1976. Productions are mainly for the Black West Indian communities, and rely heavily on the works of Black American writers such as Ed Bullins and Leroi Jones, although indigenous Black writers like Jamal Ali and Pauline Hutchins are beginning to emerge. The group uses its premises primarily as a rehearsal space and for workshops. It tends to take its productions out to other Fringe venues primarily the ICA, Soho Poly and the Little.

xiii) *Maximus Actors Arena* (Maximus Discotheque, 14 Leicester Sq. W2). Started as a novel idea to present lunchtime theatre in a space used as a disco at night. After initial in-fighting which left some of the founders on the outside, the theatre settled down and gave good quality productions for 15 months with several artistic successes. The premises were lost last July after a quarrel with the management about increased rent.

xiv) *The Roebuck* (32 Tottenham Court Road, W1). One of two new ventures that opened last summer. The Roebuck had a small lunchtime operation several years ago. Early this spring, the premises were to be taken over by the Women's Company which has since disbanded. It is now run by Daniel Makover and opened last July with its first production—a double bill by Anthony Swerling: *The Semi-Detached Cubicles* and *The Vansittarts and the Bull Workers* (included in this volume).

xv) *Square One* (The King's Arms Pub, Edgware Road). The second of the new theatres to open last summer. Situated in a pub, but different in that it is in a room below rather than above the pub. Three productions are planned before evaluating its success and continuing or disbanding.

The theatres discussed above provide a fairly comprehensive account of the Fringe, but it is by no means meant to be complete or all-inclusive. There are other groups to be found from time to time in church basements, pubs, community centres and shop fronts which could be mentioned, but space will not allow for their inclusion. Should you wish to pursue them on your own, check your current **TIME OUT** under "Fringe Theatre."

5. THEATRE WRITERS GROUP

For the most part, the Fringe has settled into a routine of presenting good productions of good plays. As implied, it is the writer who is the lifeblood of the Fringe, and only by a steady flow of new work can the Fringe continue to thrive.

The SCENE/3 pinpointed the revival syndrome that had plagued OOB. As yet, this syndrome has not reached the Fringe and, with the wealth of new material, is not likely to for some time. This does not mean that there aren't occasional productions of plays by Ionesco, Genet and Brecht, or the revival of a "lost play" like Henry Fielding's *Covent Garden Tragedy* or *The Wood Demon* by Ingmar Bergman. But these are in a minority and complement rather than detract from the Fringe scene as a whole.

Recently the playwrights themselves took steps to insure the Fringe's future. In November, 1975, about 20 playwrights assembled to share perspectives on their problems. From these initial meetings, the Theatre Writers Group has now developed into an organization of over 150 playwrights. Most of them have worked and continue to work on the Fringe. In its short life TWG has already made an impact on the British Theatre scene and has added a certain amount of dignity to the status of the playwright.

TWG members are exploring the possibilities of forming their own union, or of affiliating with Equity or the Writer's Guild, to provide themselves with a stronger base from which to work. Even unorganized, TWG's presence has been felt. It has brought pressure to bear on both the Arts Council and two of the large, subsidized companies— the Royal Court (English Stage Company) and the National—to examine their policies toward playwrights as individuals and as a group.

By creating an organisation which has made the situation of playwright known, TWG has already served a purpose. Whether the group will continue to function with the same efficiency shown during its infancy or whether it will destroy itself through committee work, remains to be seen. Members are optimistic that TWG will continue to gain strength and become a major force on the London theatre scene.

6. BITS AND PIECES: CONCLUSION

A matter that has been implied but not discussed so far is the degree of social commitment felt by writers of the Fringe. In what is, perhaps, a gross overestimation, it appears that the vast amount of writing on the Fringe is more committed than that found in its counterpart, OOB. Almost all of the plays mentioned in this essay create an atmosphere, as it were, for the betterment of Man. Plays such as *The Saliva Milkshake* by Howard Brenton, a fictionalised account of the assassination of a British Home Secretary; *My Girl* by Barrie Keeffe, which dramatically demonstrates the claustrophobic predicament of the tens of thousands in London who are forced to live and raise families in one room; and *On The Game* by Glenn Chandler, which portrays the tawdry world of the male homosexual porstitute, inherently include material that provokes questions and stimulates discussion—discussion which *could* lead to change.

It is the writer's ability to use society's ills and incorporate them into plots and character conflicts that is the hallmark of a successful Fringe playwright today. Through efforts by TWG and ventures similar the Poly Playwrights' Workshop, the strengths of commitment are being fostered and developed. The Fringe is playing an important role in creating a new theatre.

There are two possible problems which may lie ahead for the Fringe; inflation and unhealthy inbreeding. Either could destroy the Fringe as it now exists.

Infation is undoubtedly the more immediate of the two problems. Arts Council cuts and Equity minimum are subdivisions of it. *All*

29

costs in Great Britain are constantly escalating. Postal rates have gone up 150% in the last two years; electricity, actors' salaries, paper, building materials, etc., have all undergone similar or even greater increases. While the Arts Council has compensated to some extent by increasing grants for Fringe theatres, there is a fear that in the next fiscal year grants to all theatres may be cut or eliminated completely. Should that happen, venues will be forced to cut back production programmes severely or close altogether. If Equity should carry out a threat to demand its minimum for all performances on the Fringe, it would either cause the closure of those Fringe theatres that pay only expenses or force a cut of the Box Office for salary. At the same time, it would prevent actors and directors from working on experimental ventures which could never be made financially solvent on their own.

The matter of inbreeding that is starting to be seen could be the Fringe's own worst enemy, leading to slow death by strangulation. Theatres which present only the work of one playwright; actors, directors and writers who begin to form closed-shop networks— these in the long run could prove to be more fatal even than inflation.

Again, the dedication of those who work on the Fringe must stave off any threat that might be forthcoming either from without or within.

Feb. 1977

The following is a brief bibliography of material that should be available in bookstores or libraries for anyone who wishes to pursue the history of the Fringe or its current activity.

BOOKS:

Ansorage, Peter. *Disrupting the Spectacle: Five Years of Experimental and Fringe Theatre in Britain.* London and New York: Pitman Publications, 1975.

Browne, Terry. *Playwrights Theatre: The English Stage Company at the Royal Court.* London and New York: Pitman Publishing, 1975.

Findlater, Richard. *Banned! A Review of Theatrical Censorship in Britain.* London: Macgibbon & Kee, 1967.

Findlater, Richard. *Comic Cuts: A Bedside Sampler of Censorship in Action.* London: Andre Deutsch, 1970.

Itzin, Catherine, ed. *Alternative Theatre Handbook:* London: Theatre Quarterly Publications, 1976.

Roberts, Peter. *Theatre in Britain: A Playgoer's Guide.* 2nd edition. London and New York: Pitman Publishing, 1975.

PERIODICALS:

Drama: The Quarterly Review (quarterly)
Gambit (4-6 issues a year)
Plays and Players (monthly)
The Stage and Television Today (weekly)
Theatre Quarterly (quarterly)

OFFICIAL DOCUMENTS

The Arts Council of Great Britain Annual Reports
The Theatre Today in England and Wales. Published by the Arts Council in 1970.
Bruce, Ian Castillejo, David, et. al *Patronage of the Creative Artist.* London: Artists Now, 1974.

Tsafendas

WILLIAM GARNET TANNER

TSAFENDAS was first performed in the United Kingdom at Inter-Action's Almost Free Theatre, the Ambiance (Lunch Hour) Theatre Club in London, in February, 1976. It was directed by Tessa Marwick, and featured the following actors:

TSAFENDAS	Bill Flynn
CHAIRMAN	Glyn Jones
BEUKES	Frank Lazarus
MA	Evie Garratt
SYBIE	Yana Samson
DEREK	Alex Mavro
PA	Mel Oxley
LANDLADIES	Evie Garratt
ALEX	Alex Mavro
GEORGE	Martin Turner
MARY TSAFENDAS	Evie Garratt
JUDGE-PRESIDENT	Mel Oxley
POLICEMAN	Stefan Bubenzer

Approximate playing time: 60 minutes

1. Tsafendas delivers a message

First, the figure of DR. VERWOERD *is raised over the centre of the playing area. His voice, taken from the memorial recording of his speeches put out in South Africa shortly after his death, is heard outlining the principles of Separate Development. Or apartheid policy texts may be read out.*

Then TSAFENDAS *comes diagonally in to centre, unwraps a packet of raw meat and proceeds to devour it with his bare hands. He can be overheard muttering appeasingly to the "tapeworm" within him from time to time.*

The rest of the company move in a circle, chanting "Forget him," and "Why not indeed" etc., or something similar. They enclose Tsafendas.

CHAIRMAN: Tsafendas delivers a message. (*He begins to read from the Official Report.*) September the 6th, 1966, the 40th day of the first Session of the Third Nationalist Parliament of the Republic of South Africa, and Dr. Hendrik Frensch Verwoerd's 2,795th day as Prime Minister of South Africa, was a most important day as far as the House of Assembly and the public at large were concerned, since the Prime Minister was to speak on His Vote and was expected to make an extremely important statement in the House. Consequently, there were many visitors who wished to attend the Sitting in the building. Most of the Members of Parliament were also present. There was a great throng in the Lobby immediately before the House was due to go into Session. (*Division bells start ringing*) At about this moment, when the bells began to ring to indicate that the House was about to go into Session, Demetrio Tsafendas, then in his 37th day of employment as a Temporary Parliamentary Messenger, took from his Messenger's locker the two daggers which he had bought that morning. He secured them both on his person under his clothing. He intended to attack Dr. Verwoerd in the lobby but failed to draw one of the daggers from its sheath in time. When Dr. Verwoerd entered the Chamber, he therefore followed him. (*slight pause*) Also at this moment, when the bells began to ring at 2:10 pm on this day, Dr. Verwoerd's bodyguard, Lt. Col. Buytendag, hurried to his usual place in the Gallery, and the Chief Messenger, Mr. Beukes, who had not noticed Tsafendas in the Lobby, entered the Chamber and took up his position on the stairs so that he could overlook those present to ensure that there were no unauthorised persons or strangers present in the Chamber. All messengers were entitled, while the bells were still ringing and the House had therefore not yet gone into Session, to enter the Chamber if they had messages to deliver. (*bells stop ringing*) When Tsafendas reached Dr. Verwoerd's bench in the Chamber, he drew out one of the daggers. He leaned over Dr. Verwoerd as though he wanted to say something to him. He then gave Dr. Verwoerd the first stab in his chest on the left side. Dr. Verwoerd raised his hands as if to ward him off, but Tsafendas

34

dealt him three more stabs before several Members of Parliament overpowered him. Tsafendas put up a tremendous resistance, but the knife was taken away from him. In the struggle he was badly injured on the forehead and nose.

TSAFENDAS *falls to the ground. (A mute policeman was on hand in the Inter-Action production. He rang bells, was never far from Tsafendas, helped clear scenes, etc.)*

CHAIRMAN: Several Members of Parliament who were also medical doctors gave Dr. Verwoerd every possible treatment, but he was already dead.

TSAFENDAS *rises with bandage and plaster. He addresses the circle.*

TSAFENDAS: I am not a Communist. I am a Christian. I believe in the Bible. I did not think I could get away after murdering the Prime Minister. I did not care what happened to me.

CHAIRMAN: Demetrio Tsafendas—are you sorry for yourself?

TSAFENDAS: Yes.

CHAIRMAN: You regret what you have done?

TSAFENDAS: No. The whole affair is like a dream. I am the centre round which it all revolves. Lord, forgive me, I am a worm. I am a worm. Like Moses and the serpent you see, swallowing other serpents. This is how the Bible speaks of me—

CHAIRMAN: Did you see Dr. Verwoerd as Pharoah, and yourself as Moses?

TSAFENDAS: No.

CHAIRMAN: Then why—?

TSAFENDAS: The worm. It hypnotised me. Sometimes, I don't feel myself at all. I just don't feel my body. I am walking, and I just don't feel myself. I feel I am walking lightly as if I am floating on thin air. I do not remember a thing about stabbing Dr. Verwoerd. I could have stabbed him a thousand times without knowing it. I was stabbing him, who have never stabbed anyone before. If people had not stopped me, I would have been stabbing a corpse. I must feed the worm, you see. It is like a boa constrictor. When I feed it, it leaves off. It purrs. So, it corrupts me, this serpent. Here. If it wasn't for the serpent, I would live only for myself, only for myself. I struggle against this serpent, you see. Yes, have struggled. But it turns me into a twisted saint, the worm—(*breaks off,*

35

laughs) You know, I don't think I will be able to live in Cape Town after this. Because of the public opinion, you know. And if they ever offer me another job in the House of Assembly—I would not be able to face such a job again.

2. *Tsafendas makes an interview*

CHAIRMAN: Mr. Beukes, as Chief Messenger, you were responsible for the appointment of Demetrio Tsafendas as Temporary Messenger in the House of Assembly?

BEUKES: Yes, sir.

CHAIRMAN: Now tell me, when an applicant appears before you, what do you do in order to enable you to decide?

BEUKES: Sir, first when a person appears before me I always, at all times if possible, have two of my colleagues with me to watch his reactions, his behaviour, his appearance—but I ask No 1: "Are you a White South African?" and "What proof?" Upon which proof is produced. And I ask No 2: "Have you ever been prosecuted—have you ever been convicted of a crime, even a minor one?" Then I always make it very clear. I ask the men rather not to lie to me. If there is any lying to be done, they must leave it to me to lie for them— and also if they are really unemployed, their last employer and previous employers if they have not worked for a long time.

CHAIRMAN: Yes—anything else?

BEUKES: Sir, also—if they are young men I always want to know their school qualifications, and of course I ask their age, married or single—and those things one asks any person because he is only looking for work for a short time.

CHAIRMAN: Good. We shall now proceed to the special case of Tsafendas. How did you establish in his case that he was a White, and that he was a South African?

BEUKES: Sir, I accepted it—I asked him: Are you a White South African?

TSAFENDAS: Yes.

BEUKES: Where is your identity card?

TSAFENDAS: Sir, I haven't got my identity card. (*to audience*) I could not produce my identity card for him because I had handed it in for re-classification as

36

a Coloured person—Sir, I have not received my identity card, but here is the proof, my unemployment cards.

BEUKES: When he gave them, I saw—I think 1965 was the stamp on it—the Department of the Interior date stamp—and his Population Number, your identity number. I then did compare it with the other unemployment card which already had a 1962 date, and the two numbers agreed, and had the necessary "W" which we accept as White, and also said that he was a South African citizen.

CHAIRMAN: You simply accepted that he was a South African citizen because he said so?

BEUKES: No, the proof is your identity number, and on the unemployment card it also says that a White person is—

CHAIRMAN:(*growing steadily more impatient and angry*) Yes, but we are now talking about a South African citizen—not a White!

BEUKES: I accepted it. I accepted that he was now a South African citizen because there was his identity number, my lord, and—

CHAIRMAN: Were you not aware that aliens may also have identity numbers?

BEUKES: No, my lord, my knowledge did not go so far. If I made a mistake I must admit that I fell short there.

CHAIRMAN: The man had a foreign name, not so?

BEUKES: Yes, sir.

CHAIRMAN: Did you ask him where he was born?

BEUKES: Yes.

CHAIRMAN: What did he reply?

TSAFENDAS: Lourenco Marques.

CHAIRMAN: Well then, since that is in Portugese East Africa, why did you accept that he was a South African citizen? Did you not ask him whether he was naturalised? Or anything?

BEUKES: Sir, no. I asked him: Are you a South African citizen? And he said—

TSAFENDAS: Yes.

BEUKES: —and I accepted that, but his name—at the same moment I also happened to have a young boy who was born somewhere in England, which I also accepted. I accepted it here—

CHAIRMAN: I cannot understand why you accept that a person born abroad, if he says he is a South African citizen, why you accept that he is one. Why did you accept it?

BEUKES: Sir, if I slipped up there, I admit it.

CHAIRMAN: This was no small slip, Mr. Beukes. No small slip when we have subsequently discovered that this man was registered as an Alien on the 6th of March, 1964; that this man was placed on the Stop List as an undesirable immigrant on the 11th September, 1959; that this man was twice convicted for illegal entry into this country; that this man applied for Permanent Residence 7 times over the years and was 7 times refused; that this man had only temporary residence in this country and that there was a Removal Order on him the day Dr. Verwoerd was killed.

BEUKES: I admit it, sir. I slipped up there. But in good faith I took it that he was a South African citizen because he said so, and also because he showed me his number. So I failed there, sir.

CHAIRMAN: (*calm, a new tack*) Well, did you test him in both official languages?

BEUKES: Yes, sir.

CHAIRMAN: And—?

BEUKES: Sir, he speaks broken Afrikaans, but when I spoke Afrikaans in front of him to my two colleagues about his appearance and what I had found out— his knowledge—when I was saying to them that we could not let such a person do the humble work of messenger, then he understood it all and chipped in in Afrikaans—

TSAFENDAS: Ek verstaan wat U nou se, meneer. Maar ek het honger. Ek het geen werk. Ek sal bly wees om die nederige wek te doen—

BEUKES: —that he would be happy to do the humble work.

CHAIRMAN: Why did you think that this work was too humble for him?

BEUKES: Sir, he had—according to what he said—his knowledge. He had been a court interpreter and so on. But I added that he was capable of something much better—Maar jy kan iets veel beter doen?

TSAFENDAS: (*a last ditch appeal after scores of similar interviews*) MAAR NOU IS DIT VIR MY BROODNODIG! EK WIL DIE NEDERIGE POSISIE DOEN!

BEUKES: He needed to work desperately, right then. And I was so glad, for I thought—because I asked him whether his health was good and so on—I was so glad that such a—

CHAIRMAN: But did it not strike you that there was a man who was healthy, he was already 48 years of age, he had gone through life, and he was so broke that he was hungry?

TSAFENDAS: ASSEBLIEF! NET VIR DIE SESSIE! Hoe lank gaan U my die werk gee?!

BEUKES: So—yes—I said I would give him work for 2½ months. Tot in Oktober. And he was so grateful—

TSAFENDAS: (*genuine relief, and in good faith, quite without guile*) Meneer, U ek bedank. Ek sal my bes doen om U te help vir die hele Sessie!

TSAFENDAS *is now stripped, and dressed in his messenger's uniform for the rest of the scene. Various action as indicated and suggested by the text. He is put through his paces as a messenger at the beck and call of Parliament, "coming" and "going" when called for.*

CHAIRMAN: Mr. Beukes, you said he was one of the best. Why do you say so?

BEUKES: —of the loose, spineless, I'll call it. He was strong and healthy.

CHAIRMAN: How did you know he was strong and healthy?

BEUKES: I asked—

CHAIRMAN: Did you ask him when last he had seen a doctor?

The 2 nuns come forward. They hold down TSAFENDAS. *They apply electrodes to his temples.*

BEUKES: I asked him: Do you suffer from any ailment?

The nuns administer EST.

TSAFENDAS: (*screams*) NOOOAAAAAAAAAAAAAAAH!! (*then, quite calm, the convulsions over*) No.

BEUKES: His appearance was also to judge. He was temporary. He was good enough for the purpose.

CHAIRMAN: But you said of the loose, spineless applicants he was one of the best. What do you mean by that—the loose, spineless? What do you mean by that?

BEUKES: My lord, if you were to see the supply from which I have to get my people—as I always say, I have to scour the streets, because nobody wants to do the humble work, under the humble name of messenger, for a short time, and that is where I have to get my workers because for a young man there are no prospects. I have already lost all my good boys—

CHAIRMAN: But why did you call him one of the spineless people?

BEUKES: You see, because they have no steadiness. It is just a wrong expression we use here, but because there is such a great difference between a humble old man who has worked for 41 long years on the Railways where most of our people are given work, who has stability in life, and the people who come and go—

CHAIRMAN: You thought he was merely a rolling stone—a man who works for a while here, works for a while there—only to move on again to some other place?

BEUKES: Yes, my lord, exactly, because that is the source—

CHAIRMAN: The question is not because he came there he was from the same source. Did you know he was merely a rolling stone?

BEUKES: According to his unemployment card I took him to be one.

CHAIRMAN: Now I just want what he told you about being an interpreter.

BEUKES: He said he was an interpreter in Durban.

CHAIRMAN: Did you ask him why he left there? After all, according to you, it is a much better job than he was now seeking—

TSAFENDAS: I wanted to move to the Cape—

BEUKES: I could not swear to it but he pretended he was moving, that he was finding another job, but he could not find one temporarily.

CHAIRMAN: It is perhaps this unemployment card which shows—

BEUKES: Yes, sir, that is the card.

CHAIRMAN: And this is from City Engineering and Carron, Ltd?

BEUKES: Yes, it is from an engineering firm in Durban.

CHAIRMAN: No, it is from an engineering firm in Pretoria!

BEUKES: Or of Pretoria. I don't know. He was in too many places. But he worked in Durban as well. I mean, you can understand I have a lot to deal with. It is by chance that I—

CHAIRMAN: Well, yes Mr. Beukes, but we are now dealing with only this one thing. We shall not get very far if we continue like this. You say he had a testimonial?

BEUKES: He did show a testimonial, sir. I take no notice of testimonials—

CHAIRMAN: I see—you take no notice of testimonials!

BEUKES: I have reason—because of those sources with which we have to do daily—even from churches, sir.

CHAIRMAN: Now you saw on this thing that he had worked for City Engineering from 9th December '63 to the 3rd February '64. That is only about two months?

BEUKES: Yes.

CHAIRMAN: This, and other examples, indicated to you that he was certainly not a good worker.

BEUKES: Correct.

CHAIRMAN: Did you ask him what kind of work he had done at these places?

BEUKES: Yes, sir—but although one asks them—they just say they worked there—

CHAIRMAN: It does not make much difference what a man says?

BEUKES: No. You see, the purpose—excuse me, my lord—for which I need him: he must go when I say "go" and he must come when I say "come," and he must be honest and that is what I take notice of. My lord, he did not mention that he had worked on the Railways as well, but we do not always have the Railway records of many of the men who go to work there. So many of our older white men work on the Railways. He still fits into the picture and the source from which I get most of the supply—and younger people, too, on

41

whom we do concentrate, most of the time—I would almost say always—come from the Railways, or resign or the other way about. I at all times contacted a Railway detective when a youth had resigned from the Railways or had been discharged, who applied to me for work.

CHAIRMAN: That is as far a your enquiries went?

BEUKES: For youths, because when a—

CHAIRMAN: And old men? Did you make any enquiries about old men?

BEUKES: Old men, not pensioners. Never, because they have such a wonderful testimonial. When that Railway testimonial is placed in front of one, one is glad.

CHAIRMAN: Now, can you remember whether you asked him at all what he did between October 1965 and February 66.

TSAFENDAS: I was an interpreter. I just did casual work at other places in Natal.

CHAIRMAN: And then you left it at that?

BEUKES: Yes, my lord, I did—because that is how it is with all the other cases.

CHAIRMAN: But for all you knew, he might have been in jail all the rest of the time where there are gaps?

BEUKES: I could have known that too, and I can only watch and pray over the large number who work there—

CHAIRMAN: But as I say, for all you knew—

BEUKES: Yes, he might—my lord—actually, he might have—

CHAIRMAN: Now you have the special faculty, when you watch a man's face, and he lies, of knowing whether he is lying or not?

BEUKES: My lord, I have often made mistakes, but most of the time not really; what I looked out for, what I told my colleagues to watch out for in the men, because we need them only—

CHAIRMAN: What do you watch out for? That is what I should like to know!

BEUKES: My lord, do you mean when I talk to a person, or in his work?

CHAIRMAN: Yes!

BEUKES: Mostly for theft, in the sense of theft yes, because they are Members of

Parliament and so on we are working for, whose offices and their possessions are always open and we are more on the lookout for theft, because, my lord, we always simply accept the fact that a man who comes to work there as a temporary messenger, I mean to say is after all only a person whose old fingers would get up to mischief scratching in things where they shouldn't—

CHAIRMAN: Is that your approach—whether he looks like a thief?

BEUKES: Yes, and you know when a person is a good liar, one can't really judge, because you do not need the man for anything important.

CHAIRMAN: Now did it ever strike you that a Messenger is placed in a very favourable position to commit sabotage or murder in the House of Assembly? Or did it never strike you?

BEUKES: No, my lord, up to the 6th—never! I will put it this way: I could never have expected it.

CHAIRMAN: Now, looking back, do you realise in what a favourable position a Messenger is actually placed to do such a thing?

BEUKES: (*completely crushed*) Yes—as I am a weakling—I admit it.

TSAFENDAS *stands, dagger out.* TSAFENDAS *approaches the figure of Dr. Verwoerd. He goes through the motions of the stabbing. (The figure should not be violated in a vulgar or melodramatic fashion, but the extent of the wounds and the amount of blood involved should be indicated.) Meanwhile, the* CHAIRMAN *continues:*

CHAIRMAN: Tsafendas' attack on Dr. Verwoerd was savage. The longest of the four wounds about the chest and both shoulders was 4 cm. The stabbings penetrated both lungs and heart. The lungs were collapsed. The pleural cavity contained a total of 1750 cc. free blood. The pericardial sac contained approximately 25 cc. free blood. The heart wound penetrated through the entire thickness of the wall of the ventricle into the ventricular cavity. The minimum depth of this wound was 12 cm. The cause of death was established as "multiple stab wounds, one of which penetrated the left ventricle of the heart."

3. Tsafendas comes to Cape Town 28/8/65

MA *and* SYBIE *laying tea table.* SYBIE *drops a cup.*

MA: Sybie, now look what you have done! You stupid thing!

SYBIE: Sorry, ma.

MA: Ag, don't be sorry. Just clear up the pieces. There. Now get a grip on yourself—

SYBIE: Oh, ma—

MA: Sybie, stop trembling like that. Quiet. Get a grip on yourself. Read your Bible. (*pause*)

SYBIE: (*aloud*) No one, after lighting a lamp puts it in a cellar under a bushel, but on a stand, that those who enter may see the light. Your eye is the lamp of your body; when your eye is sound, your whole body is full of light; but when it is not sound, your whole body is full of darkness. Therefore, be careful lest the light in you be darkness—ag, ma, do I look alright?

MA: Sybie!

SYBIE: You sure he'll arrive today?

MA: You're a one! He said in the letter. Today or tomorrow.

SYBIE: Yes. (*She takes the letter from her Bible and reads it aloud.*)

> *Dear Miss Hendriks,*
>
> *I am most pleased to reply to your offer of marriage which shows the true spirit of yourself as a missionary in our Church, the Followers of Christ, following the receipt of my picture from our brother in Christ, my friend Theo Arendse in Benoni.*
>
> *So, I am coming to Cape Town on or around August 28th.*
>
> *As you know, my position is this. I am 47, and have been overseas since '41 when I joined the services. I only returned 2 years ago and the only thing I can do is interpret, translate and teach foreign languages. I therefore will kindly request for employment accordingly. I notice many tourists come here, but the employees can only speak English to them. I speak the other languages as I lived in those particular countries. I worked alongside these peoples, did business with them, etc.*
>
> *I speak German, Portugese, Spanish, Greek fluently.*
> *I speak French, Italian = Good*
> *Arabic, Changaan and Swedish = Fair*
> *I am sure I could be useful to you as a linguist.*
> *It took almost 5 years to learn each language,*
> *Sincerely Yours,*
> *Demitrio Tsafendas*

MA: Now, Sybie, tha's a well-educated man.

PA *and* DEREK *come in from work.*

DEREK: Hey, ma, what's this fancy tea?

MA: A new friend of Sybie's is coming.

DEREK: From the Church?

MA: Yes, a very clever man.

DEREK: A missionary like Sybie?

MA: I don't know. Sybie—?

SYBIE: He's coming all the way from P.E. to see me.

MA: She wrote to him—

SYBIE: Here's his picture. See—

DEREK: I see. And this? (*He grabs the letter and reads it quickly.*) Ag sissie, you'd better know what you are doing this time. He'll be a sponger, you'll see. Another sponger.

SYBIE: GIVE IT BACK TO ME! (*They tussle.*)

PA: DEREK!

Doorbell rings. TSAFENDAS *at door. He is shabbily dressed in a brown suit and a big hat. His jersey has a hole in it. Throughout this scene* TSAFENDAS *is child-like. His disorientation has a guileless quality about it. He does not remove his hat at any point.*

MA: Oh—Mr. Tsafendas?

TSAFENDAS: Good afternoon. I've come—

DEREK: We know—

TSAFENDAS: —from Port Elizabeth—

MA: —my husband—

TSAFENDAS: —to meet with—

DEREK: —we KNOW—

MA: —son Derek—

DEREK: OK.

MA: —my Daughter, Miss Sybie Hendriks.

TSAFENDAS: (*simultaneously*) —your daughter, Miss Sybie Hendricks.

SYBIE: (*shyly*) Hello. (*They shake hands.*)

MA: (*pause*) Did you have a good journey, Mr. Tsafendas?

TSAFENDAS: Yes. No. I don't know. One of my better journeys. Yes. (*He laughs suddenly. They all do so, nervously. Pause.*)

MA: Will you have some tea, Mr. Tsafendas?

DEREK: You haven't any luggage. Where's your luggage?

TSAFENDAS: At the station. Two cases. I left it at the station. A man gave me a lift. Then halfway I caught the train. I left it at the station.

MA: Oh Derek—you go down to the station and fetch Mr. Tsafendas' luggage?

DEREK: Ma!

PA: Now, go. NOW, Derek, (*Derek goes.*) Please sit at our table Mr. Tsafendas. You are welcome. (*They sit.*)

TSAFENDAS: (*as if saying grace*) Our Father who art in Heaven, hallowed be Thy Name, Thy Kingdom come, Thy Will Be Done, in Earth as it is in Heaven. Give us this day our Daily Bread—(*he breaks off distractedly and starts his tea. Vaguely alarmed, the others follow suit.* TSAFENDAS *grins engagingly. They follow. Tea is taken in silence.* TSAFENDAS *devotes his full attention to it. He drinks several cups of tea in quick succession which* MA *pours. He eats cakes immoderately. By formal standards his table manners leave a little to be desired. But do not exaggerate this.*)

SYBIE: (*handing over Bible. This is not a test, but what normally happens after tea.*) Now, Mr. Tsafendas, will you read us a passage, and give us a testimony perhaps?

TSAFENDAS: I will give you my favourite passage. But first, Mrs. Hendriks, have you got a piece of dry break?

MA: Of course.

She fetches it. Pause. TSAFENDAS, *wincing slightly at some inward pain, but smiling, contemplates* PA *and* SYBIE. MA *returns. Gives* TSAFENDAS *bread. He eats.*

TSAFENDAS: That's better. Now it's just me talking. (*He reads, with loving deliberation.*) Joshua, Chapter 15: "The lot for the tribe of the people of Judah according to their families reached southward to the boundary of Edom, to the wilderness of Zin at the farthest South. And their south boundary ran from—" I, who have crossed many boundaries in my time, know this. So, once when they were looking for me—looking for me for being in Canada—I crossed the St Croix River at night—walked right across it—because it was frozen—bone to the cold frozen, mind you. That is how I came into the United States. But that was in 1943. I think. "Then the boundary goes up by the valley of the son of Hinnom at the south shoulder of the Jebusite (that is, Jerusalem); and the boundary goes up to the top of the mountain that lies over against the valley of Hinnom, on the west, and at the northern end of the valley of Rephaim. Then the boundary extends from the top of the mountain to the spring of the Waters of Nephtoah, and from there to the cities—the cities are like sheep—the cities of Mount Ephron, then the boundary bends round to Baalah (that is Kiriathjearim)—" But because the cities are like sheep there are other ways of crossing, like writing letters, so that one time is got out and kept going when I wrote to her—the Queen of Greece, of the House of Glucksburg—when I was in Greece—and she gave me the passport because my own tribe was divided. The Lord in his wisdom has divided all the tribes—

DEREK: (*entering with cases*) What are you talking about?! Tribes! Bautustans!

MA *and* PA *are visibly upset. "Derek!" they remonstrate.*

TSAFENDAS: But the Lord Jesus Christ is our Saviour!

ALL: And the Lord Jesus Christ is our Saviour!

TSAFENDAS: And Caleb said: "Whoever smites Kiriath-sepher, and takes it, to him will I give Achsah, my daughter, as wife. And Othniel, the son of Kenaz, the brother of Caleb, took it; and he gave him Achsah his daughter as wife." When she came to him—now see what a good wife she was—she urged him to ask her father for a field, and while she herself was sitting on an ass, she farted, and Caleb her father said unto her: "What meanest thou by that dry and mighty fart?" And she said unto him: "Give me a present, since you have set me in the dry land of Negeb, give me also springs of water." And Caleb gave

47

her the upper springs and the lower springs— Now, you must love Achsah. She was sitting on her ass because in those days they travelled on an ass. It was before progress. But she knew her father gave her a dry inheritance, but he was a good man and when she asked him, because it was her marriage, he provided springs from the ground. My own father gave me a dry inheritance—of nothing. Thus, I was a bitter man. Now, I am no longer a bitter man because I have come to be saved in Our Lord Jesus Christ.

ALL: And the Lord Jesus Christ is our Saviour!

TSAFENDAS: And here I am among friends in the Church of Christ.

ALL: And the Lord Jesus Christ is our Saviour! And the Lord Jesus Christ is our Saviour!

TSAFENDAS: *(excited)* Here, let me show you—the best it is—let me show you my letter to the Prime Minister of England when I was there. It has a reply too— England, where I was not to stay either—

TSAFENDAS *has flung open and is rummaging in both cases. The contents fly out—from the one piles of dirty clothing, from the other pots and pans.* DEREK *laughs.* SYBIE *starts crying.*

MA: *(a delighted reproof)* Mr. Tsafendas, such dirty clothes. I see I shall have to look after you! Now let me take these and wash them for you!

TSAFENDAS: Yes, yes—do you have an aspirin? It is making me dizzy. Just an aspirin. An aspirin always helps.

MA: I'll get some. *(She goes.)*

DEREK: Sissie, you've done it again!

SYBIE: OOoh—

She retreats sobbing. DEREK *follows her out laughing.* TSAFENDAS *holds his head.* MA *returns with aspirins.* TSAFENDAS *gulps them down. He seems better.*

MA: Mr. Tsafendas, I'm sorry. I don't know what to say. The excitement, you know. She'll be alright in a minute, I'm sure. You must stay—in our house—as our guest—and as you are a gentleman and a member of the faith—you need not pay the—rent, only when—after you have found fit employment. As for my daughter—Sybie—well, well what happens is that that is up to you and her— she is old enough to know her own mind herself.

TSAFENDAS *(calming down instantly after drinking the aspirins):* Truly, you are good people. For before I was a wanderer, and now you have taken me in.

4. Tsafendas fails an interview

The cases are still open. The pots are still on the floor. TSAFENDAS *sits alone with* SYBIE. *He is reading to her from the Bible:*

TSAFENDAS: "But whatever any dare boast of—I speak as a fool—I also dare to boast of that. Are they Hebrews? So am I. Are they descendants of Abraham? So am I. Are they ministers of Christ? I am a better one—I speak as a fool. I am in labours more abundant, in stripes above measure, in prisons more frequent, in beatings more countless, and often near death. At the hands of the Jews five times have received the forty lashes less one. Three times have been beaten with rods; once I was stoned. Three times have I been shipwrecked; a night and a day have I been adrift at sea. On frequent journeys, in danger from rivers, danger from robbers, danger from my own people, danger from Gentiles, danger in the city, danger in the wilderness, danger at sea, danger from false brethren: In toil and hardship, through many a sleepless night, in hunger and thirst, often without food, cold and exposed. And, apart from other things, there is the daily pressure upon me of my anxiety for all the churches. Who is weak, and I am not weak? Who is made to fall, and I am not indignant? If I must boast, I will boast of the things that show my weakness. The God and Father of the Lord Jesus, he who is blessed forever, knows that I do not lie—" St. Paul! What a man, Sybie! What a leader! "Daily pressure upon me of my anxiety." Ah, but he was the strongest, hey? I'm strong, though not so strong. Don't you see that I am strong, Sybie? Hey, feel my arm—

SYBIE: Alright.

TSAFENDAS: You see! Now I also was condemned to travel like Paul. But he had no worm, as I have a worm. You know, Sybie, I would not have gone all over the world except for the murmers of the worm, except for its anguish and pains in my body, except for the heavy springs and coils it makes in front of my eyes. *(momentary distress. He indicates.)* Sybie, hey, do you believe me? You do believe me?

SYBIE: Yes.

TSAFENDAS: Yes, yes you do believe me. I see that. But Paul lived two years in

his own hired house in Rome. He was a Roman citizen, you see. They couldn't
touch him, oh no. But to be a citizen of your own country, that is the most difficult thing these days—

SYBIE: Why?

TSAFENDAS: Why what?

SYBIE: Why—I—why do you always keep your hat on?

TSAFENDAS: (*shyly*) If I took it off, who knows what might come out? (*takes off
hat*) There, do you like that?

SYBIE: Yes, better.

TSAFENDAS: (*gesturing cheekily, but he is also taking a risk for it might be his
worm popping out*) Pop, pop, pop, pop, pop, pop— (SYBIE *laughs slightly.*)You
like me? Dmitri? You like Dmitri?

SYBIE: I—don't—know. No, PLEASE don't touch me—yet.

TSAFENDAS: (*playful and serious by turns, and on the brink of the abyss near the
end of his speech*) Yes, yes. Even though I have fallen far short of Paul in my
own life, I am not to be mocked. No! I am strong like Paul and was in many of
the same countries, so that I too was in Asia Minor and Turkey where I got
this silver tooth. Look. And in Turkey there they have special hot baths with
little windows in the round white roofs like skulls. And these little windows
catch a small square of the blue sky. You can be in the water and in Heaven at
the same time. It burns you clean. It makes it all fall away from inside. But I
didn't catch anything. (*pause*) That was how I came to boil my head. I
BOILED MY HEAD! Put it right under. Sizzle. SIZZLE! I—BOILED—MY
—HEAD. And I swallowed the water because of the mineral salts in the water
which I thought would kill the white worm. But the worm liked the hot
mineral salts and got even bigger. I felt it choking up in my throat, and I felt it
writhing round inside me as I feel it writhing round—inside—me—all—the—
time, and — making — little — gnashing — sounds— because —of — its —tiny —
teeth — and — it — is — picking — my — stomach — because — it — is —
sometimes —like — a — serrated — sword — with — serried — edges — that —
prick —and — rub — (*recovers, laughs*) But, you see, that is why I must go on.
Always. To be strong. And to keep it happy so that it purrs—purrs so I can
hear it in my brain like a little velvet head. (*pause*) Did I tell you the time they
brainwashed me in Portugal—?

50

SYBIE: Yes, Dmitri, you did. But—

TSAFENDAS: —Which has made me now in voluntary exile until such time as I am sure which way the wind blows. In Portugal there I always carried my Bible and I told them I was a Christian, but they wanted to punish me for not being Roman Catholic, and for these reasons too I was refused military service, but things got very tense and they kept me in a small cell for a year. They questioned me. They were trying to change my brain. In a hospital they finally did it—they finally gave me treatment—

SYBIE: Poor Dmitri—

TSAFENDAS: —in the form of hammer blows on the head—MARTELLADAS INA CABECO!—BAP, BAP, BAP by those nuns with crawling white fingers and pinched little monkey faces putting electrical injunctions through my head. ZAP, ZAP, ZAP—AAAAAAAAAH! (*suddenly quite calm again*) You see, my real feeling was that I did not want to serve a dictatorship like Portugal—So, you see, I have survived. I am strong and you will need me for you—

SYBIE: Dmitri, I want to ask you—

TSAFENDAS: What is it? Why don't you like me? You don't like me!

SYBIE: Dmitri, listen—

TSAFENDAS: YOU DON'T LIKE ME!

SYBIE: I—do. I—don't KNOW!

TSAFENDAS: (*eagerly*) Oh, you think I don't know what to do? You think I am not a man? You think I don't know all what it is between a man and a woman?

SYBIE: It's not that—

TSAFENDAS: Listen. I tell you, I know. I know. I know because my stepmother —not my real mother, no, who was a Royal Princess—because my stepmother made them. She made them—of my own family—come and show it over me. Afterwards it was grey and sticky. Here. A grey, sticky worm on my stomach. Now it is dry. But I know. And I loved my sister too. And you are very lucky for I wanted to marry another woman in South Africa and they refused me—(*lunges for suitcase*) Look, it's all here in a letter I sent to Pretoria from Athens—

51

SYBIE: Please, please—

TSAFENDAS: (angry) You don't want to hear my letter! You don't want to hear my letter!

SYBIE: If you wish. Dmitri—

TSAFENDAS: (appeased) I knew you would. I knew you would. It's to Pretoria, like I said. From P.O. box 80, Central Post Office, Athens, Greece. 12th April, 1949.

Dear Sirs,

With reference to your rejection of my application to re-enter the country I was brought up in and the country of my mother Amelia William.

Will the authorities concerned provide me with information as to why I was refused permission to re-enter my country. I did war-work in Johannesburg 1940 till 1942. For the British Mining Supply Co, Ltd.

I left the above Co. and did more important work, when I joined the merchant navy voluntarily and risked my life in submarine-infested seas all over the South and North Atlantic, leaving my soft jobs behind in Johannesburg. I am still working for the Allies under the Marshall Plan. To make life safe for you people and my family in Southern Africa to live in.

But the difference is that I have been away from home since 1942, more than 7 years. Away from my father, my stepmother, my three sisters and brother, who is a blueprint expert at the Iscor Iron and Steel Corp., Pretoria.

I made the mistake of not taking out my Citizenship papers before I went to serve, due to my young age then and inexperience, thinking I was automatically a South African Citizen. Will you please consider the above and let me return to my home, and to the girl I was brought up with, to whom I want to marry, as we have so much in common. I am here a man without a country. Living in strange lands, with people who have different ways of living and customs, and languages. Please help me get back to my country. It is not a small mistake, the difference is between the North Pole and the South Pole.

I have a lot more to mention, but cannot put it into writing.

Remain yours,

James Demetrios Tsafendakis.

The trouble was, if they ever replied, I had already had to leave Athens for some reason or other. I don't remember what now, and—

SYBIE: Dmitri, I know you are proud of your travels. I know you have suffered much. And even though you are a member of our faith, even with all this I would have to ask you—I—no—Dmitri, Dmitri, it can never be—between—us—

TSAFENDAS: Sybie, why—?

SYBIE: Because—because my brother says you are White. You are a WHITE man!

5. Tsafendas has to move

TSAFENDAS *is finishing two or three pounds of T-bone steak, eggs, tomatoes and onions with his bare hands.* PA *and* DEREK *watch.*

TSAFENDAS: Derek, I am making a pig of myself.

DEREK: I can see that.

TSAFENDAS: I have to feed the worms.

DEREK: God!

PA: Derek, that's not necessary.

MA: (*entering*) DEREK! Here, I've done your washing again for you, Mr. Tsafendas. (*exits*)

DEREK: God alive!

PA: Stop it, I tell you. Stop that blaspheming. It's not necessary!

DEREK: OK, Pa, YOU tell him.

PA: Not now.

DEREK: Pa, you TELL him. You tell him now—or I will!

PA: Dmitri—this is difficult—you know we would never turn away a brother in need. I know you are having difficulty in gaining employment—there is nothing wrong in that—you could stay here as our guest—but you have had so many jobs in the past two months—the thing is—you just lie in bed all day—

TSAFENDAS: I don't think I have done too badly for a poor Portugese boy born in Lourenco Marques. (DEREK *sucks in his breath.*) What you say is true. I try.

53

Applications. But my worm is restless. 6 ft. of it has come down already, but the head is still behind. It's a dull white, a dull white every segment, and it's two inches wide, I tell you. Two inches wide. If I could only get the head, the head—(*pathetic*) It robs me of energy. In spite of my big body, it makes me tired. It affects me in many ways so my finances are always low—

DEREK: Jesus Christ!

TSAFENDAS: And the Lord Jesus Christ is our Saviour.

ALL: And the Lord Jesus Christ is our Saviour.

DEREK: For fuck's sake—

PA: Now look here, boy—!

DEREK: I CAN'T STAND ANY MORE OF THIS! Tsafendas—I tell you, this snake is a thing of the mind.

TSAFENDAS: Derek, I am disappointed—

DEREK: I tell you candidly that you should get your mind above matter. This worm is a figment of your imagination.

TSAFENDAS: Derek, I am most disappointed—

DEREK: There's NO WORM! YOU IMAGINE THE WHOLE THING!

TSAFENDAS: Derek, you are just like the doctors. Now your mother—at least your mother is sympathetic—

DEREK: LEAVE MY MOTHER OUT OF THIS!

PA: DEREK, BE QUIET! Actually, Dmitri, there are other things—about the Church of Christ. Some members at the meetings feel—you are—not in the true spirit. We pray in our hearts, but against the teachings of Our Lord you have said aloud prayers. This is not what we do in our sect—

DEREK: You say when you were baptised in Greece you were put under the water three times—

PA: This is not what we do in our sect—

DEREK: And there is another thing—

PA: Which is really to do with Sybie—

DEREK: And with your living here—

PA: Because you live among us—

DEREK: And she is not interested in you—

PA: —mainly for the reasons we have just been through—

DEREK: She absolutely cannot be interested in you for—

PA: —but mostly because we have accepted you as a Coloured man—

DEREK: —and you are white. WHITE. WHITE. WHITE!

PA: Our doctrine is peace, love, humility and subjection to all laws—

DEREK: Do you believe this? Do you believe this?

TSAFENDAS: I believe that our doctrine is peace, love, humility and subjection to all laws.

PA: (*quietly, almost as if reiterating it for his own elucidation*) Then, if you are a Coloured man, it is right for you to stay in a Coloured home, but if you are a White man you must go to a White man's home. If you are a Coloured man, you can attend services in a Coloured home, but if you are a White man then you must go to services in a White home.

TSAFENDAS: I am a blank. My card is blank. But now I prefer to be Coloured, so I have sent it in to be reclassified Coloured. I am not accepted among White people, but when I am made a Coloured officially, Sybie will accept me.

DEREK: She will never accept you. She will never even like you because— because whatever else you are, you are also silly—SILLY IN THE HEAD! That's it—SILLY! She will NEVER like you!

TSAFENDAS: (*with great dignity*) Then, I must go.

As he has done so often before, he puts the neat, clean washing in the one case. He shuts both cases. He takes them up. He goes.

6. Tsafendas keeps moving

Before each dismissal, a doorbell is heard and TSAFENDAS *reopens and shuts his cases—a bit like a door-to-door salesman hawking his worldly existence.*

LANDLADY 1: Mr. Tsafendas, I must give you notice forthwith because the other tenants complain that when you fetch water in the kitchen for shaving, you spill it all over the floor.

LANDLADY 2: Mr. Tsafendas, I must give you notice forthwith because of your general slovenliness and because you lie on your bed on my nice clean quilt with your dirty shoes on.

LANDLADY 3: Mr. Tsafendas, I must give you notice forthwith because of your bragging and because you have left on my electric kettle in the kitchen and burnt it right out to a frazzle.

LANDLADY 4: Mr. Tsafendas, I must give you notice forthwith because there is a widowed daughter in the house and though you mean nothing to her, there will always be gossip.

LANDLADY 5: Mr. Tsafendas, I must give you notice forthwith because you turned the garden hose on my fowls one afternoon when you said they were too hot.

LANDLADY 6: Mr. Tsafendas, I must give you notice forthwith because you are lazy and childish and your table manners are bad.

LANDLADY 7: Mr. Tsafendas, I must give you notice forthwith because you clap your hands suddenly and frighten the other tenants by jumping up and down.

LANDLADY 8: (*in tears*) Mr. Tsafendas, I must give you notice forthwith because I am a decent, hardworking woman and you are my first tenant—and I assure you you will be the last.

7. Tsafendas does a deal

Aboard the "Eleni" in the Cape Town docks during August, 1966.

ALEX: They insult us. They insult the Greek nation. They insult our manhood. I am a man, am I not, Sissie?

TSAFENDAS: (*drinking from a bottle of Buchu brandy before him*) Yes, Alex.

ALEX: Well, if I am a man, a man can fuck who he wants when he wants, where he wants. Two months stuck in this harbour and I only get to fuck standing up in back streets. It's not civilised. I tell you, Sissie, they're the best girls in Cape Town, the dark girls. Isn't that right? They make my balls ache. My balls scream out. But you wouldn't know. Not interested in it, hey Sissie. Too old, Sissie?

GEORGE: Leave him alone, Alex. It's not his fault—

ALEX: I know. Alright. But hell, it's not right. The Captain caught me sneaking one up again late last night. "Get her off here," he says. "Think I can't see her in the dark? The police can see her in the dark too." Yes, Captain, but we're Greek. "You'll obey the local laws if you want to get out in one piece, my boy. I didn't make them. Verwoerd made them." Shit on Dr. Verwoerd then, I say. (*He makes that most insulting of Greek gestures whereby the tips of the five fingers are touched, the fist clenched, and the fingers splayed palm out as if in the face of Verwoerd.*) Shit on all his five senses! I'd like to kill him. What do you say to that, Sissie?

TSAFENDAS: (*a bit drunk*) It's the Coloureds, I tell you. Dr. Verwoerd is a clever man. He holds the right position. It is the Department of Coloured Affairs. They do too much for the Coloureds. They leave us Poor Whites—

GEORGE: Sissie, you're all mixed up. It *is* Verwoerd. He organised it all. All the laws.

ALEX: Then he's the one that's got to go. (*He is trying on the suit* TSAFENDAS *is trying to sell him.*)

TSAFENDAS: You know, down over there on the other side of the docks where they have the big pipes for cooling the water. Forty foot underground. Like a torture chamber—a big castle dripping with water, cold, dirty, dark—it stinks. I was working down there for nothing, for 120 Rand a month. Not enough to make ends meet—and any Coloured skollie—the Coloured girls belong to him—he can have them any day. Yes, you know what they should do? You know what Verwoerd should do. He should put them all down there—the Coloured—and open the big metal doors and drown the lot.

ALEX: All the Coloured men, yes. But not the Coloured girls. Leave them for me. I'd have them all.

GEORGE: Put Verwoerd down there first—

ALEX: So this is the suit you are trying to sell me, Sissie?

TSAFENDAS: Yes. You like it? Nice grey. You can have this mauve shirt to go with it too.

GEORGE: How much commission you take, Sissie?

TSAFENDAS: Not much. I have to live too—and you know I wanted to be a Col-

57

oured. I've applied to be a Coloured because nothing is done for the Poor White. They are all employed like me by the Government or on the Railways. For fuck-all. It's all just one big family pittance. Poor Whites, Unite. No, there's no hope there. But on the other side, that's where the advantages are. A coloured man can still get ahead of himself. The Government helps them more, not like the bastard Portugese—

ALEX: How much this suit?

TSAFENDAS: Fifty Rand. With the shirt—and the tie to match.

ALEX: I'll think about it.

TSAFENDAS: Fifty Rand, the lot. I'm not cheating you. I'm not taking a big commission. I'm not. Down at the Houses of Parliament, carrying cups of tea and coffee, fetching newspapers, up and down the stairs, up and down all day and they only pay me R170 a month. A man must live—

GEORGE: Say, Sissie, you see Verwoerd in the Houses of Parliament?

TSAFENDAS: Sometimes. In the distance. Not so close. He's got white hair. We can't go in when they are in Session.

GEORGE: If you were a man you'd go in there—and kill him!

ALEX: (*laughs*) Here, I'll give you this gun. (*serious*) Hey, what about a deal. This gun for the suit?

TSAFENDAS: What is it? The make?

ALEX: A Beretta. A real Beretta. Isn't that so, George?

GEORGE: Sure. That's right, Sissie.

TSAFENDAS: (*taking it*) This could be useful. For protection. A man needs a gun nowadays.

GEORGE: Now you look like a man, Sissie!

TSAFENDAS: Don't say I'm not strong! Don't say it! I've fought for myself. I'm Greek like you. One Greek is worth fifty kaffirs. I don't take any cheeky talk from kaffirs, or Coloureds. I was in a fight in Natal with my foreman. He called me a "Commie Bastard" because I told him Salazar is a dictator. I attacked him with my bare hands. He cut me with a knife in the stomach. Here—(*indicates*) And across the arm. Right here. I should have had this gun then. I would have killed him. Then I wouldn't have lost in Court either.

ALEX: Sissie, I'll do a deal. This suit and the shirt and the tie for that gun. OK?

TSAFENDAS: I don't know—

GEORGE: It's worth the same. At least.

ALEX: What do you say, Sissie? It's a bargain?

TSAFENDAS: I'll take it. Yes.

GEORGE: Good boy!

TSAFENDAS: Pow! Those Kaffirs better watch out now, hey!

8. Tsafendas loses his temper

TSAFENDAS: This is not fair! You have made a fool of me! This is not a Beretta—or even a gun. It is a useless gas pistol, a useless thing. A child's toy.

ALEX: Too late, Sissie. You did the deal. George here is my witness.

TSAFENDAS: I WANT A GUN! A REAL GUN!

GEORGE: What are you going to do, big man? Shoot the Prime Minister? (*laughs*)

ALEX: (*laughs*) You're a simple, hey Sissie, a simple? NOW BUGGER OFF!

TSAFENDAS: Give me the money then. Or give me the clothes back. I'm a poor man. You cheat and take advantage of a poor man.

The company, led by the boys, dance round TSAFENDAS, *laughing and chanting at him:* "Poor man, dumb man, Sissie man—we got you! Big man, simple man, Sissie man—we got you!"

GEORGE: Now bugger off! And don't cause trouble.

The company push TSAFENDAS *to the figure of Verwoerd. Freeze.*

TSAFENDAS: I see there will be no satisfaction for me here. And now I cannot go anywhere else yet. I now have a job to do before I go anywhere.

9. Tsafendas goes to town

TSAFENDAS: (*to the audience: a quiet, deliberate, flat monotone till near the end*) I went to the Captain to protest, but as I saw I could get nothing and did not want to cause a scandal, I gave up and left. I returned to my room in Rondebosch. The next thing is that I decided to use a knife to stab the Prime Minister in the House of Assembly. I never discussed my plans with anybody. The shops were closed over the weekend and on the following Monday, which was a public holiday. I started work at 7.45 a.m. on Tuesday the 6th of September. I started work early in order to do my work and then go out and buy the knives. I went to town at about 9 a.m. to buy the knives. I did not get permission to go to town to buy the knives. (*pause*) I bought one knife from the first shop which was open. This shop is known as City Guns. I went to another shop further down the road and bought another knife. Both shops were closed when I arrived. I walked up and down the pavement waiting for the shops to open. I cannot remember whether I spoke to a man or woman in either of the shops. (*pause*) I entered City Guns first and purchased a dagger. I paid R3.30 for this dagger. I then went to the other shop where I bought the other dagger—the one with the aluminium handle. It was more like a stiletto. I bought two weapons in order to make certain of the job which I had in mind. I thought that something might be wrong and that one weapon might be taken away from me. Both weapons were wrapped up in brown paper. *(pause)* After I bought the weapons I returned to the House of Assembly. There I removed the brown paper wrapping from the weapons and left the daggers in my locker. I then went to the first floor to serve coffee and tea. I waited for the lights to go on, indicating which offices were calling for coffee and tea. I was doing this until about 2 p.m. that afternoon. (*pause*) A few minutes before the assembly bells began to ring (*the bells are again heard*) I went to my locker to fetch the knives. I put them into the sheaths inside my pants and went into the Lobby to wait for the Prime Minister—

(*shouting*) WHAT DO YOU WANT?
WHAT SENSE DID I WANT?
DO YOU WANT WHAT I SENSED?
IS THERE ANY SENSE IN WHAT WE WANT—
OR WHAT WE DO?

10. Tsafendas is judged

JUDGE-PRESIDENT: The court does not like to sit back and allow a man who has committed a grievous crime to get away on a plea in an enquiry of this nature. It is clear, however, that there can be no doubt whatever that the man before me is a schizophrenic. He has not got the makings of a rational mind. Such a man can perform no legal act. He cannot plead. (*pause*) I have before me a sick man, mentally sick and irresponsible, with a diseased mind subject to delusion, so betrammelled, if not guided by irrational forces, that obviously I cannot begin to find whether he is guilty or not guilty. The process cannot even start. I can as little try a man who has not at least the makings of a rational mind, as I could try a dog or an inert implement. The case of the State vs Demetrio Tsafendas is complete for the present, and probably for all time. As far as the legal aspect is concerned this is just another murder case. If the court were to put a man to death without acting according to the law, it would be murder. (*pause*) We are a law-abiding people. I fully understand that the people of this country have deep feelings about this case. I fully understand when people ask: How can it be that a meaningless creature could have done what he did do? I know too that the first reaction of any community through the ages is a feeling of revenge, of retribution. I share that feeling. If the law does not attend to this feeling of revenge, then the community feels that it should do so. But when people trust that legal action will be taken, one does not get these feelings. This is one of the reasons why we have not had an example of lynch law in this country. (*pause*) I am fully aware of these feelings, but one must try to understand these things a bit more deeply. If this man were to pay with his life for what he has done, it would do nothing for us. It would make no difference to our loss. If the court were to disregard the law, he will indeed have done greater damage to the continuation of our nation than he has already done. By giving up his life he will have shaken the foundations of our society and we would give this creature an importance which does not become him. He would thereby do a greater damage than he has already succeeded in doing. (*pause*) To tell the truth, people come and go, but if this nation should lose its trust in its legal institutions and the bench, we should indeed bring about humiliation and shame which would be an irreparable blot on this country. So great a statesman as Dr. Verwoerd, would without any doubt have wished it no other way. (*slight pause*) We must go forward in the deepest knowledge that by giving this man the best legal medical assistance he can have, and by the order I am forced to make, the honour, prestige, and good name of our land remains untarnished and the foundations on which we are building remain unshaken and undamaged. (*pause*) I can expect a certain amount of dissatisfaction and shock among certain people, but I am sure they will realise that it could not be otherwise and that it is not humane, or Christian, to condemn mentally ill people. When the law says he is not responsible for his actions, it is not only legally right, but humanely right too. It is my duty to order that this person, Demetrio Tsafendas, be taken from here to a jail and held there at the State President's pleasure.

11. Tsafendas now

TSAFENDAS, *in prison and flanked by a policeman, sits directly beneath the effigy of* VERWOERD. *He can be overheard reading from the Bible the endless catalogue of the division of the land for the tribes in Joshua 15.*

MARY TSAFENDAS: Demetrio was two years old when I married his father and I accepted him and learned to love him as my own son. I treated him as I treated my other children. He was not especially naughty but he did get regular spankings for normal boy's mischief. (*pause*) I brought up Demetrio as a Christian boy. He was a normal child. He was, as I knew him, a man of gentle nature and I could never believe he would be responsible for such a terrible deed. I am broken-hearted now and want nothing more to do with him. He has never contacted me since the assassination and I will not contact him. I wish the Government had deported him from the country in time. It would have saved South Africa a lot of pain and saved me from feeling so terrible. (*pause*) I brought him up as a Christian because I am a Christian and I believe he will receive judgement from the Almighty for what he has done, the killing of that great man, Dr. Verwoerd. (*pause*) I am particularly sorry for Mrs. Verwoerd and I cannot express how I have suffered since the unfortunate day. This is in spite of the fact that people have been so good to me—particularly Government officials and the police.

CHAIRMAN: Political assassinations are not exactly rare. Dr. Verwoerd is said to be the 13th statesman murdered in 1966. Demetrio Tsafendas remains detained in the Pretoria Central prison and is under continuous psychiatric treatment. Mr. W. M. van den Berg, Attorney-General of the Western Cape has declared:

"Up to this stage I have heard absolutely nothing from the psychiatrists treating Tsafendas and I have therefore to assume that he is still too mentally deranged to stand trial. However, the minute he is pronounced fit by psychiatrists to stand trial, I will have him arrested and brought to court to stand trial on a charge of murder. I have said this before and I say it again."

Furthermore, it is suggested that the names and particulars of all persons who are receiving—or who have received—treatment for a mental disorder in any hospital or mental institution, or who are mentally disordered but are not in an institution, should be sent to the Commissioner for Mental Health so that the latter should compile a list of such persons, and that any psychiatrist or psychologist who is consulted by the Security Police in connection with a Security investigation should be entitled to ascertain from the said Commissioner whether the person concerned appears on such a list, as well as particulars he may have at his disposal. Finally, it is noted in this official report of the Commission of Enquiry into the circumstances of the late Dr. the Honourable Hendrik Frensch Verwoerd that the doctor who carried out the post-mortem examination declared that there were no grounds for the rumour that the wounds were inflicted by an expert stabber. He describes them as "quite ordinary."

END

When I Grow Too Old to Scream
I Shall Have to Surrender

STEWART PERMUTT

WHEN I GROW TOO OLD TO SCREAM I SHALL HAVE TO SUR-
RENDER was originally produced at Pentameters, London, in May, 1976.
The play was produced by Leonie Scott-Mathews, directed by Royce Ryton,
and featured Evie Garratt, Morar Kennedy, Andrew Quiney and Ivan Vander
in the cast. The characters are as follows:

KENNY BAINES . . . . *The Producer*
DUGGIE CHARLTON . . . . *The Dame*
ETHEL WATERS . . . . *The Comedy Fairy*
TRICIA PETERS . . . . *The Principal Boy*

Approximate playing time: 25 minutes

Scene: on stage and the green-room of a small provincial theatre.

*The tabs open to reveal what looks like the green room of a small provincial
theatre. A few chairs are scattered here and there, plus one or two theatrical
posters on the wall.* DUGGIE—*the Dame—a man in his late sixties, is discovered
sipping a cup of tea. He wears a dressing gown over his dame attire. Next to
him sits* ETHEL WATERS, *once a diminutive Soubrette, now a comedy fairy of
over sixty, wearing a rather tatty fairy's crinoline. During the Green Room
scene, sounds of laughter and music can be heard at various intervals coming
from the show on-stage.*

DUGGIE: Of course the opening's all wrong if you ask me.

ETHEL: We used to always open "Dick Whittington" with a full chorus and
production number.

DUGGIE: Ray comes on just after the girls have gone off and then me following
on straight after.

ETHEL: Then if I was playing Cat I'd jump up from behind one of the chorus
girls.

DUGGIE: The audience have scarcely had an opportunity of settling down.

64

ETHEL: The children loved it.

DUGGIE: This afternoon I had to stop a minute to give them a chance to sit down; I slipped in that gag of mine about you better get in quick as the one and nine's are full; always gets a laugh.

ETHEL: One and nine! I should like to be able to go anywhere for under five pounds. People can't afford todays prices. Simply wicked.

DUGGIE: You don't have to tell me. Wicked! But Roy's opening—no timing whatsoever. He just races through all those gags, it's a wonder anyone can understand a word he's saying.

ETHEL: I went to elocution classes from the age of five.

DUGGIE: I've told him till I'm blue in the face about that gag at the beginning of the shop scene, but he kills it stone dead.

ETHEL: He's so terribly young of course, Duggie. When I was his age . . .

DUGGIE: Youngsters ought to learn the hard way, like we had to. All those one night stands up and down the country.

ETHEL: And freezing cold digs.

DUGGIE: I remember once I was in Panto in the Midlands.

ETHEL: I made my debut in the fol de rols in Crewe.

DUGGIE: Playing Wishee Washee I was, that was before I started doing Dame. I was staying in a place round the corner from the theatre: ordinary place, but not a bad little room. They had one of those outside lavatories that was cleaned by the Council every three weeks.

ETHEL: You were lucky to have a loo dear. At Bangor we had to use the convenience in the High Street. Very inconvenient it could be. I remember one night—little Doris—

DUGGIE: When I got down there it must have been the twentieth day, the state it was in! You've no idea. So I used to go to the theatre. Anyway, I'd been there about a week when I came in one night for my tea, in between shows, and the old girl said to me "Are you alright?" "Yes thank you, I think I've got everything I need." "No, I don't mean that," she said, "You've been here since Sunday and I've never seen you go out the back once." *(Duggie laughs)*

ETHEL: *(Politely)* Yes dear. They're a dying race, landladies.

DUGGIE: It's just cheap flatlets or those awful commercial hotels now.

ETHEL: And the prices they charge!

DUGGIE: They wanted four pounds fifty a night down the road. And you should have seen the size of the room, you couldn't even swing a cat in it.

ETHEL: I remember my first job as a student at the Gaiety. We found a quaint little place to stay: twenty two and six a week.

DUGGIE: Yes, and you got as much as you could eat in between houses.

ETHEL: In those days you started off in a No. 2 or 3.

DUGGIE: These youngsters wouldn't know what a No. 2 or 3 are.

ETHEL: Equity's stopped all that. I think it's ridiculous paying some of these youngsters thirty pounds a week, when they know absolutely nothing. You may not have been paid very much in the old days, but you did learn your trade.

DUGGIE: The managements can't afford to keep apace with today's prices. Years ago it would have been unheard of to put on a pantomime without full chorus and orchestra.

ETHEL: I do miss not have a "Curry's waterfall" in the Neptune scene. I always used to—you know.

DUGGIE: And Heaven knows what they're paying Roy.

ETHEL: I had twenty-five shillings a week for my first engagement, you considered yourself rich if you were earning more than thirty.

DUGGIE: They think he's a name to pull people in. Well, if he's such a big attraction why aren't we playing to packed houses.

ETHEL: I had to look after all the properties and costumes, and first house each Saturday I was allowed on to make up the numbers in the ballroom scene.

DUGGIE: He's done the odd television appearance and they've billed him as a star. I had to work damn hard to get where I am I can tell you that. I had no manager to pull strings for me.

ETHEL: George was in the other night from the pavilion.

DUGGIE: He loves my Dame, said what a change it was to get a Dame who could really act, thought Roy still had a lot to learn of course. He said to me though, "Duggie, I think your billing is disgusting! I've never known the Dame being billed smaller than the second principal girl."

ETHEL: Even the printer's name is bigger than mine on the poster.

DUGGIE: And there wasn't even a mention of me in any of the papers, it was some kind of conspiracy, everyone was mentioned right down to the Cat, but not me, I'm not in the Show.

ETHEL: No respect is shown for the more experienced artiste these days. I was sitting in my dressing-room, nobody came round to tell me that there was a phot-call.

DUGGIE: And what annoys me, is the way these youngsters walk straight into a West End Show, without so much as a by your leave.

ETHEL: I've been offered the odd West End Show, but I'll only take it if the part's right.

DUGGIE: We are touring a musical comedy just before the war for Howard Brent.

ETHEL: Now I flatly refuse to tour. I've too many commitments at home.

DUGGIE: Nice little show, it was. I was playing the footman and understudying Bobby Howes. Then a fortnight before we were due to open in Town, the manager called me into his office and said "I'm awfully sorry Duggie, but I'm afraid I'll have to let you go." The Producer's brother-in-law had been engaged to play my part in Town. That's all very well I said, but people will think I'm no damn good.

ETHEL: When I played Goose at Scarborough—just after the war, the Director insisted I came down last in the finale.

DUGGIE: I think it's a disgrace me going on third from last in this production.

ETHEL: Of course, if you are any performer at all you can steal the show in an animal part. I used to do a little scene when I came on drunk and I used to talk through the quacks. I was known as the original talking goose. I've still got my own skin you know, worth at least two hundred pounds. It's made of real goose feathers.

DUGGIE: Not like the goose I had last year—biggest Goose I ever had. You should have seen the size of her. Must have stood about six foot eight inches, I had to look right up at her all the time. These managements won't realise that the goose in Mother Goose is important. They will leave everything to the last minute.

ETHEL: I should have been playing Goose this year at the Palace, but that stupid agent went and put someone else up for it when the management has specifically asked for me if you please.

DUGGIE: These agents are all the same. I was booked in for the wrong act last year at Penzance. Expected me to perform with seals.

ETHEL: They put Vera in because she could fly. Well, I flatly refused to fly— not at my age dear. If it isn't done properly it can look just like a bundle of washing, not artistic at all. But whenever Vera and I are up for a job, she always tries to underbid me. She'll go anywhere for silly money and whenever I play Goose I won't go outside London; if they want me they can jolly well pay.

DUGGIE: Performing seals! I never cared for animals at the best of times. If they can afford to pay these pop groups a thousand pounds a week just to sing one number in the shipwreck scene like last year, then they can afford to pay us a living wage. Times are getting hard, I've got to make my money stretch. You never know when your next job's going to come along. I've been offered that tour of course.

ETHEL: You mean the one Kenny's doing?

DUGGIE: About that actress.

ETHEL: Sarah Siddons.

DUGGIE: That's right.

ETHEL: They wanted me to play the comedy dresser, the one who has a fit in the second act and goes mad in the third. But I'm not sure I could manage that.

DUGGIE: They offered me the footman. Said it was a nice, little character part, but have you seen the script? There isn't a part there.

ETHEL: It's twenty seven weeks. Tibbles could never bear to be away from me so long. He'd pine to death.

DUGGIE: *(3 entrances and a soft-shoe shuffle)* I won't go on tour unless I'm billed above the title.

ETHEL: And then I promised to go with dear old Elsie to Bognor again this summer. She looks forward to it so, not being able to get about much. It's a wonder they don't offer it to Vera. She usually takes my cast-offs. I remember one year we both went up at the Royal and, unbeknown to me at the time she underbid me twenty-five pounds, and then after telling the management she's got her own skin, she has the nerve to phone me up that same night and ask if she can borrow mine. You see Vera can't do comedy work, which is so important for Goose; she only does skin work and nothing else.

DUGGIE: I don't like Vera—never have. I swore blind I'd never work with her again, after she tried to trip me up on my entrance in Mablethorpe. Only left the wicked fairy's broomstick right by the door of my cottage, and you know how short-sighted I am.

ETHEL: Now, little Jean's always phoning me up asking if there's anything I don't want.

DUGGIE: What, little Jean Pritchard. Nice artiste. Bit on the short side.

ETHEL: I'd never hesitate to recommend her, I'm usually offered at least three or four parts each year. Jean's a nice, little artiste. I taught her that mock-ballet routine I do when I join on a line of girls and how to talk through her quacks; she's always billed as "Jean Pritchard, one of Ethel Waters' original talking Geese."

DUGGIE: Now I don't think an animal in pantomime should talk.

ETHEL: I believe she's at Cleethorpes this year with Frankie. I've also trained cats.

DUGGIE: I wish you'd teach our one a thing or two. No sense of discipline whatsoever.

ETHEL: If you're playing Cat, then you've got to be a cat. Now I understand them. They always used to send them to me for their training.

DUGGIE: He crouches on the stage with his hand on his knee.

ETHEL: You'd never see a cat do that.

DUGGIE: And you never see any reaction in that shop scene when Dick gets the job. "For goodness sake" I said "jump up and down and show some sign of enjoyment, instead of just sitting there like one o'clock waiting to strike."

ETHEL: You can't just put on a skin and walk across a stage. You've got to make that skin live.

DUGGIE: Tricia's late off.

ETHEL: Has she done her number yet?

DUGGIE: No, you can always tell by the patter of tiny feet rushing to the toilet while she's doing her spot.

ETHEL: I think she finds it difficult hearing the orchestra dear.

DUGGIE: You've got to be able to reach the high notes comfortably. I wouldn't say this to anyone but you. I'm very fond of Tricia, but she's getting past playing principal boys, and that's a fact.

ETHEL: We're all getting past it. I miss my home. I shall be looking forward to seeing Tibbles again. He'll be waiting for me at the doorstep, frisking his whiskers; he knows when his old mum's coming home.

The tabs close as TRICIA PETERS *enters in traditional principal boy attire. She is tall and attractive and with typical thigh slapping panto approach. She is perhaps forty and her age is beginning to show.*

TRICIA: Tommy! Tommy! Tommy! *(to audience)* have you seen Tommy? You haven't? that means I'm all alone and I'm so cold and hungry, and what's more I've been called a thief. Yes, a thief! You don't think I'm a thief, do you? No, of course you don't. You're my friends. *(pause)* I wonder what fate holds in store for me? *(pause)* There must be someone who can help me! *(pause)* Oh for a kind fairy! *(*ETHEL *enters, mop in hand.)*

ETHEL: Late again dear, like British Rail. Oh dear, I've forgotten my wand! *(exits, then re-enters smartly with wand)* Now what was I going to say dear?

TRICIA: A word of good cheer I hope, kind fairy.

ETHEL: Ah yes, that's right! A word of good cheer. But are you ready to receive it dear?

TRICIA: Ready and waiting, madam.

ETHEL: Now let's see if I can remember it. I tied a knot in one of my bellstrings.

Ah yes! Cheer up, young Whittington, for at the end of all these gloomy prospects here, there lies a path of beauty, hope, faith and cheer. Oh dear! I must away, I can no longer stay, for I shall miss the 8.15 to Whitby Bay. *(She exits).*

TRICIA: Have faith. But how can I have faith! I'm just a poor, lonely orphan boy. Now cheer up Whittington. You're going to go aboard the "Saucy Sal." Perhaps I might even meet Alice on the Quayside before the ship sails. You know I think Miss Alice still has faith in me, don't you? *(going)* Come on Tommy, wherever you are.

TRICIA *exits, still looking for the cat, and* DUGGIE *rushes on with an enormous handbag.*

DUGGIE: Have you seen that cat? You just wait till I get hold of him. Do you know what he's done? I had a lovely piece of fish for my dinner and that blasted creature went and stole it. Well I'll tell you what I'm going to do when I see him—give him some of my walloper. *(He waves his handbag)* That'll cure him of his tricks. But never mind him. I nearly forgot what I came on to tell you—oh yes of course—there's so much plot in this pantomime I never know where I am. . . . Well, boys and girls, Christmas time is story time and I've got a lovely, little story to tell you today—all about the Three Bears. You would like to hear it, wouldn't you? Well, once upon a time there was a Mummy Bear, a Daddy Bear and a Baby Bear, and they all went ice-skating on the lake, when all of a sudden, well all of a couple of suddens, the ice broke and they fell into icy water. Aah! *(Wait for audience's reaction)* All fell into the icy cold water. That's better. And little Mummy Bear, sitting on her piece of ice said, "When I get home, I'm going to have a tale to tell!" And Daddy Bear, sitting on his piece of ice, said "When I get home, I'm going to have a tale to tell!" And little Baby Bear, sitting on his piece of ice, said "My tale's told." *(pause)* Well I can't stand here talking to you all day. I've got to make the Alderman's tea.

Tabs re-open on Green Room. TRICIA *enters immediately, flops into a chair exhausted and kicks off her heels.* KENNY *enters.*

KENNY: Martin King's out front and he thinks you're absolutely magic.

TRICIA: How sweet!

KENNY: Actually it looked super tonight, darling.

TRICIA: It ought to be after all that work I've put into it. That damn cat was

71

late on again, and I wanted tonight to be especially good—with Martin being in as well.

KENNY: You're a real pro. Trish, you managed the scene wonderfully. Nobody would have known.

TRICIA: Course, when he's on, he's never really concentrating. He feels frustrated I think, not being allowed to sing, but you can't very well have a singing cat!

KENNY: No, of course not darling.

TRICIA: He waves to the kids while I'm trying to do a straight number. You know darling, that it's hard enough work trying to put over a straight number to all those brats without someone deliberately working against it. That's very naughty. That endless rush backward and forward to the loo, especially during "Please don't go" And I wish Roy wouldn't ad-lib in that scene when I'm trying to be a bit sad after I've been accused of the theft. You've got to have a little bit of pathos though God knows I'd prefer to do comedy.

KENNY *is about to go.*

Kenny!

KENNY: Yes darling.

TRICIA: I was wondering if I couldn't just have a quick word with you. That's if you're not going to dash off madly somewhere and do something frightfully important.

KENNY: Why of course, sweetheart. But I mustn't be too long. This is the last performance. Still, for you . . .

TRICIA: I just want to say it's been such a lovely season Kenny, enjoyed every minute of it.

KENNY: Thank you Trish, you've been a treasure.

TRICIA: Thank you darling.

KENNY: Really super.

TRICIA: I love Panto. It's such fun.

KENNY: It's just a little bit of magic.

TRICIA: That's just it darling. You don't really find it elsewhere in the business. Of course I love doing straight plays and tours of musicals, they're heaven, but Panto's always been my game.

KENNY: Give me an experienced pro any day darling.

TRICIA: You've just got to have that experience to play Boy.

KENNY: Martin still thinks you're one of the best in the business.

TRICIA: Does he?

KENNY: He remembers your Aladdin in Llandudno.

TRICIA: Really, with Mickie Fields as Wishee. He was super to work with.

KENNY: Mickie Fields? Wasn't he killed in that disaster in the fifties?

TRICIA: Such a tragedy. It was my first boy part. I couldn't have been more than seventeen at the time. They were really pantomimes in those days. I came on with a chorus of twenty-four, full orchestra and sets . . . not that I'm saying anything against your production, Kenny. I think you and the boys have simply done wonders with so little. Anybody can put on a good show with pots of money, but you've given us a nicely thought out, well balanced panto.

KENNY: Quite.

TRICIA: Martin must come round for a drink after the show. It'll be lovely seeing him again.

KENNY: 'Fraid he's got to tear off . . . work.

TRICIA: Work! He must be doing rather well.

KENNY: Just been appointed entertainments officer on Jersey.

TRICIA: That's wonderful. And I knew him when he used to pick up the—never mind. Give him my love when you go round.

KENNY: Of course. I must dash. *(about to go)*

TRICIA: Kenny.

KENNY: Yes?

TRICIA: About that little conversation we had the other evening over at Ernie's flat . . . *(awkward pause)* Well, I must know one way or the other pretty quickly. I've got so many irons in the fire at the moment, and you know my Agent's terribly fussy about money, not that it bothers me, especially when it comes to working with friends. We're like one big happy family here.

KENNY: All I can remember is drinking rather too much wine and nearly collapsing on the floor.

TRICIA: You were talking about the new musical based on the life of Sarah Siddons. You said you had a No. 1 tour planned for it and then possibly the West End.

KENNY: It's not definitely fixed.

TRICIA: But you are going to do it?

KENNY: It's all very tentative at the moment, you understand.

TRICIA: Of course, with my divorce coming up, I shall have to stay in London for a while. You can always ring my agent.

KENNY: The casting's not up to me, but naturally I'll put in a good word for you.

TRICIA: I wouldn't even have mentioned it, but you said what a splendid Evdokia I'd make.

KENNY: Evdokia?

TRICIA: Sarah's confidante, a kind of glam. duenna role. Very me, you said. Had a big number in the second half with a pair of castenets and orchestra playing off stage.

KENNY: I said all that? *(incredulous)*

TRICIA: And more. You said you had a big telly name to play Sarah. . . . Patricia Paul.

KENNY: That's strictly confidential.

TRICIA: And how great we'd be together, kind of like Rita Hayworth and Joan Blondell.

KENNY: And I meant it Trish but I honestly don't have anything to do with the casting. *(He exits)*

TRICIA: How bloody humiliating! How bloody, bloody humiliating! If they don't want me, why don't they just say so.

Spotlight on DUGGIE

DUGGIE: *(Singing)* Some like a cuddle in the morning, Some like a cuddle late at night, Some like a cuddle in a haystack, And some prefer a flat, But give me a cuddle with a nice young man On Ilkley Moor Bar Tat. . . .

Now here's a nice little song for you, and you're all going to learn it before you go home for your tea. And we won't let you go until you can sing it nice and loud, so the quicker you learn it, the quicker you can go home. Everyone's got to sing including the mums and dads. Remember when you come to the pantomime, you're all really children at heart.

Lights back on the Green-Room. ETHEL *bustles in.*

ETHEL: You'll be late dear. I've just gone under the sea to meet Neptune. The nymphs were off again.

TRICIA: *(In a sudden outburst)* The whole pantomime's off if you ask me. I'm sick to death of doing these tatty little panto's in God forsaken seaside towns with about three worn backcloths, a two-piece unharmonious band and chorus consisting of four local girls who can't do point work. I bet Martin King's having a bloody good laugh in the stalls. Done alright for himself with a house and two kids, one of each naturally, and some neat little wife. And to think I knew him when he was some spotty little Vizier with bad diction.

Spotlight on DUGGIE

DUGGIE: Shall I bring Dick on to help me out? Well, shall I? Come on Dick, come and help your Auntie Sarah.

TRICIA *enters.*

TRICIA: Hello boys and girls.

DUGGIE: Now, we're going to have a competition to see which side can sing the loudest. And remember, when we get to the line about give me a cuddle with a nice young man, all the little girls sing that, but the little boys sing nice young girl instead, because if you don't, people will think you're most peculiar. Won't they Dick?

TRICIA: I'll say.

DUGGIE: Now you take that side Dick, and I'll take this.

They go to opposite sides of the stage.

75

TRICIA: I'll bet my side can sing loudest, can't we?

DUGGIE: Oh no you can't.

TRICIA: Oh yes we can.

DUGGIE: Well we'll see. Come on my side, sing for your Auntie Sarah.

Repeat of song.

TRICIA: We can do better than that, can't we children?

DUGGIE: It wasn't fair anyway.

TRICIA: What wasn't fair?

DUGGIE: There was a woman in the front row, nudged her husband and said "Sing if you dare."

TRICIA: Come on my side, we'll show them. *(Repeat of song)* We won! We won!

DUGGIE: I think—taking into consideration the size of the house—it was about equal.

TRICIA: Yes, about equal.

DUGGIE: Both sides won. Now we'll have it just one more time and really raise the roof. It's not ours so we don't mind what you do to it.

Repat of song. Exit of DUGGIE *and* TRICIA *as tabs open.* ETHEL *is fixing a crown on her head as* DUGGIE *enters the Green Room.*

DUGGIE: Friendly lot out there tonight. Nice class of people. All the better sort are in tonight; nice middle-class family audience.

ETHEL: This has been the first audience up here that have understood my song about the fairy.

DUGGIE: They're less dirty-minded than some of the others we've had, that's why they're not laughing so much at Roy tonight. Have you noticed?

ETHEL: We had a terrible comic one year at Eastbourne.

DUGGIE: Such a nice class of town—Eastbourne.

ETHEL: The filth that came out of that man's mouth was unthinkable and of course it doesn't do for every kind of audience. It may be alright for the working mens' clubs, but summer season is different.

DUGGIE: I was at Eastbourne with the "Frolics Review," we made a mint. Never asked us the following year though.

ETHEL: I had to follow him. People used to say it was like a breath of fresh air when I came on.

DUGGIE: I had the same trouble last year when Reg produced—they had every three-handed gag in the book.

ETHEL: They will do that old gag about the "sticks." If it hasn't been done once it's been done twenty times.

DUGGIE: He didn't want me to do my Women's Lib gag about burning bras. He said the kids didn't want to hear about bras. And only three scenes later Simple Simon comes on with that wretched feed they had—God only knows where they got him—and cracks the gag about the woman next door having five babies—a black one, a brown one, a yellow one and a red one . . . she's been taking Smarties . . . if that isn't smut, I don't know what is.

ETHEL: Nice panto was it though Duggie?

DUGGIE: Well it was and it wasn't and have you heard the language of some of the kids today? I was doing the song sheet one year in Aladdin, so I said to the children "you will sing won't you" and one little kiddie said "anything for you Wankey." He couldn't have been more than six.

ETHEL: Last year at the Palace, we had that awful rock-and-roll star as the comic. He had no idea of timing and a pair of left feet. He never could keep still.

DUGGIE: Why do they always engage these pop stars who know absolutely nothing about anything. Bunny nearly had a breakdown trying to produce the show at The Empire. She said some of them couldn't even walk across the stage.

ETHEL: Being on television is totally different. They've had no real experience of live theatre. I was the only one that could really work with him.

DUGGIE: I'm up for that part of the elder statesman in that new television series on famous historical figures.

ETHEL: I used to come on and do a little spot with him, which I'd taught him

77

and every time I'd try to do anything he'd be cavorting all over the place.

DUGGIE: My agent thinks I'm a sure winner for it. It's between me and Joey Miles—and he drinks.

ETHEL: They've pinched some of my material for this year. They were expecting me—I think they're half hoping that Vera will trip over a wire and I'll be called in—she'll never be able to cope with Eddie.

DUGGIE: I had trouble with a young comic one year when we did Little Red Riding Hood. He only wanted to use my gags.

ETHEL: I was never a great lover of Little Red Riding Hood.

DUGGIE: The trouble all started when I fell foul of the producer, he wanted my part.

ETHEL: It's a pretty pantomime but there's no real story to it. So difficult to introduce any comedy.

DUGGIE: If the stairs could have opened and swallowed me up, he'd have been delighted. But there wasn't even a part there! I had only one schoolroom scene and my spesh and that was it. I like to be produced properly if I'm doing Dame. I know some comics like to just come on and do their own front cloths, but I like to be part of the story.

ETHEL: The children love a good pantomime story. Some of the little ones used to be in floods of tears when I did my big scene with Mother Goose.

DUGGIE: Do you know, in the third week of the run they had the nerve to come and say we're running over-time and would I cut my spesh. I said to this producer, if my spesh goes so do I. He said "Right Mr. Charlton—you'll be paid at the end of the month." "I'm not having that. I'm paid weekly, in both senses of the word," always the great comic me—I went up to the management, told them straight I didn't want to be paid for nothing. The producer can damn well do the part himself. "Of course" they said "Duggie your spesh can't go." Always got my own way in the end with these people. . . .

ETHEL: I always say if they want me, they can damn well pay.

DUGGIE: We had endless trouble with the babes.

ETHEL: Sea nymphs are the same.

DUGGIE: Stan and Max were playing the Robbers—anyway they had this scene with the kids—they were called the Doncaster Delights. They were all dressed up as fruit in plastic.

ETHEL: You can never be too careful with plastic.

DUGGIE: The curtain was just about to go up when the matron rushed on stage and screamed "you can't go on" "why ever not" said Stan. "The little apricot's shit himself." It couldn't have been the bunch of grapes could it? it had to be the apricot.

ETHEL: I thought it was the little tangerine.

DUGGIE: No the apricot.

KENNY *enters.*

KENNY: Your number was really super tonight Ethel.

ETHEL: That's a genuine, Victorian sea-lament. My father taught it to me. Trouble is, modern-day audiences miss the subtlety of it.

DUGGIE: I never use anything later than mid-Edwardian.

KENNY: I've just had head office on the phone about "Sarah Siddons." They're leaving the entire production in my hands. You know we've booked Patricia Paul for the lead.

ETHEL: The girl who's all the rage in that series—Mother married a Major?

DUGGIE: Always struck me as a bit vulgar.

KENNY: She'll bring them in. Now darlings, head office are anxious to complete the casting by Monday. We begin rehearsals in a fortnight. It's going to be an absolutely magic production. Super cossies, and Brian's designing the set. All pink with heaps of slashing. The offer still holds for both of you. I'm a man of my word. You'd be simply wonderful as the eccentric dresser Ethel, with a huge blonde wig and lots of kiss-curls.

ETHEL: It's twenty-seven weeks?

KENNY: Marvelous, isn't it? Possibly longer.

ETHEL: Oh dear!

KENNY: And we've had a nibble from Australia. Pat's all the rage there.

ETHEL: Oh it would be unsettling going out on tour. And Australia too. The odd pantomime's one thing, but all that time . . . and things are so different to-day.

KENNY: We're paying well above the minimum.

ETHEL: Tibbles would pine to death without me. You see he doesn't mix very much with the neighbourhood cats. He likes his Mum. And there's my job at the Social Security. I know they'll be behind without me. Besides, I've made some new friends. And of course, Elsie is relying on me to take her down to Bognor. She's my only near relative and she can't get about much—

KENNY: You'll be missing a wonderful opportunity.

DUGGIE: That's just it Kenny. I'm up for a new television series. I do a very good line in elder statesmen and grand dukes . . . it's my deportment. You know what they say at the Centre—if you want a grand duke—ring for Duggie.

KENNY: That's your decision then. I don't know what the office is going to say. I thought you would have been glad of a year's work at least. *(he exits)*

ETHEL: I'm glad that's settled.

DUGGIE: I mustn't miss that television opportunity.

TRICIA *enters.*

TRICIA: It's only your spesh Duggie and then the finale thank God, and that'll be the end of the pantomime for this year.

DUGGIE: I hate last nights. I keep wondering, especially at my age, whether I'll ever do another.

TRICIA: I know the feeling.

DUGGIE: Naturally it would break my heart if I didn't, but it wouldn't be the end of the world. We can't expect to go on for ever. I've got two bookings for the week after I get back to London, and I have to be on the end of the phone in case the odd television comes up—that's why I turned down Kenny's tour.

TRICIA: Kenny's tour?

DUGGIE: Nice part I was offered, the male lead's father. A big scene with the leading lady, rather like La Traviata.

ETHEL: I won't go on tour again. Not at my age dear—and when he talked of Australia and a year . . .

TRICIA: Australia?

DUGGIE: I've got a commercial coming on next month. I play an arch-duke who mistakes a plate of cheap marg. for butter.

ETHEL: That's lovely Duggie.

DUGGIE: I expect you're all fixed up, Trish?

TRICIA: Oh of course darling—I've got a super engagement, only I don't want to say too much just at the moment. You never know what might happen.

KENNY *re-enters.*

KENNY: Oh Duggie, do you think you can cut your gag about the twin sisters?

DUGGIE: It always gets a good laugh.

KENNY: I know, but we've got the Mayor in tonight and he might consider it a bit risque—you know what these people are like.

ETHEL: I expect the Mayor will come up and give us a nice speech. I hope he won't go on too long, my finale crown can get so heavy.

KENNY: I'd just like to thank you all again for being such a super company, real pros all of you.

DUGGIE: That's what comes of being in the business for so long.

KENNY: Who knows when we might . . .

DUGGIE: Have you made any plans for next year yet? I know your people generally come here.

KENNY: Nothing definite. I'd like to do Jack and the Beanstalk but . . .

DUGGIE: I nearly did the Dame in that this year in Bradford.

ETHEL: Lovely old theatre.

DUGGIE: He half promised it to me, then they decided they wanted a broader comic for up there. I'm a more motherly type of Dame. Children like it. Mustn't be late on. *(He exits.)*

ETHEL: Just got that crown adjusted. I thought Kenny—seeing as the Mayor is in—I might put a bit of ivy round the top.

KENNY: Super darling.

ETHEL: Adds a little something for the last night. I feel sorry for Duggie, it's a hard business trying to do comedy and Roy hasn't been very helpful to him. He was terribly upset about the twin sister gag.

KENNY: I didn't want the Mayor to go away thinking that that was the standard of the patter. That gag always dies a death. *(He exits.)*

TRICIA: Sometimes even though it may seem kind of hard you've just got to re-think your own material. I know when my mother died, I became much less exhuberant, and things that used to work for me just didn't any more. Then some friends told me to re-think my whole approach. I rely on glamour while I still can—with a touch of comedy thrown in. I shan't be here for the next time. You know what he can do with his duenna and her castenets!

ETHEL: I was just reading in the obituary column of The Stage that poor old Lilly Ford died in her dressing-room at Scunthorpe. Well you know what they say about Scunthorpe. People come there to die on both sides of the curtain. She was eighty one you know. Found dead with a stick of make-up in her hand.

TRICIA: Died in harness so to speak.

ETHEL: I kept telling her to be like me and give things a rest. There's a lovely old people's home in Cheshire would have suited her to the ground.

TRICIA: Home?

ETHEL: Most of my friends are there. Lovely grounds, quite like old times when I go there on a visit. But Lilly would go on till she dropped.

TRICIA: Perhaps she was happy.

ETHEL: She wasn't at her best in later years. The old voice could be shaky especially on the top notes. The secret is to retire gracefully while they've still got happy memories of you. I'm past sixty and quite content doing the odd lit-tle bit. After all there's my garden and Tibbles.

TRICIA: Well I haven't got a garden and I don't like cats, and I'm not sixty and when I am I shall still be treading those old boards, whether its Scunthorpe or the Old Vic. It's the only life I know, it's in my blood. I may not be able to have a home with lots of children, but I've got my career. *(Music is heard off)* There's our cue for the finale.

Lights fade. Spotlight on DUGGIE.

DUGGIE: *(singing)* I need seeing to in all the old familiar places. . . . Oh what a day I've had today. I don't know what day it is, but I've certainly had it! And what do you think of the price of things today girls! It's wicked. I went into the pet shop and it had Chunky Meat for Dogs 50p. I said to the assistant—50p for dog food, that's right madam, it's for pedigree dogs. I said my dog's a mongrel and I'll have a tin for twenty-five *(pause)* No, don't tell him lady, let him work it out for himself. And you'll never guess what happened when I went into Boots, I said to the woman behind the counter—I'll have a jar of that face cream, so she said I've been using it for years and I may be over forty but I've got a complexion like a peach. I said that's as may be, but have you ever seen a forty year old peach—oh, that reminds me of when I was young and beautiful—what do you mean, I was young and beautiful—and just to prove it to you I'll tell you about my boyfriend, he was a woodworker, but he wouldn't. One night I came home and said to him, well tonight's the night! and he turned round and said to me it's lent! so I said when you get it back let me know.

DUGGIE: Then I had a boyfriend who was a meteorologist—you know what that is don't you? That's a chap who can look into a girl's eyes and tell weather! Thank you for that burst of heavy breathing. I've been married three times, yes, I'm a thricer. My first husband was a doctor, my second was a tailor and my third was a sailor. I've one on the panel, one on the flannel and one on the channel. I was only saying to a girlfriend of mine the other day, just before she was about to embark on matrimonial bliss. I said always leave something to the imagination, it makes you more desirable. One night her husband turns round to her and said does insanity run in your family, because you've been going to bed for three weeks without taking your hat off. But I can't stand here all day talking to you, we've still got some more programme to get through. And now I'd like to sing you a little song I learnt at my mother's knee, or some other low joint; called when I grow too old to scream I shall have to surrender. Thank you Ernie!

DUGGIE *then lauches into an Old Tyme Music Hall song, not necessarily one suggested by the title; when this is finished, full lights up as the cast take their bow in character—joined a second later by* KENNY.

END.

Honey from Yucatan

ALLAN BERRIE

Approximate playing time: 60 minutes

SCENE ONE:

A large Victorian room, curtains drawn, hanging down to one side on broken rail. The windows look out onto the street. The room, once obviously elegantly furnished, has now fallen into squalid neglect; everything appears to be on its last legs; even the carpet has gone in places exposing naked floorboards. An unshaded bulb hangs from the centre of the ceiling.

(The only props that affect the actual action are mentioned here: a bureau with a pull-down top; a cupboard, door slightly ajar revealing chaos: empty jam jars, bottles, old biscuit tins, etc., etc. A sofa with a heap of blankets and an old fur coat used as an eiderdown. In a corner an old wind-up gramophone, half-hidden under junk and a pile of old records in brown dust jackets.)

The muffled sound of demolition machinery working up the street.

A woman of about sixty, dressed in housecoat over nightdress, her hair dyed blond and disheveled, face still heavy from sleep, sits at a table that's as cluttered and disorderly as herself and the rest of the room. She pours herself a cup of what appears to be tea but is in fact whisky from a China teapot. The woman's name is Karin-Marie—hereafter referred to as 'Marie'.

The door opens and a younger woman, in her late thirties, enters, wearing good winter clothes and carrying two expensive-looking pieces of matching luggage. The woman, a natural blond, her hair worn long, would be described as very attractive, if not to say beautiful. Her face shows us clearly that the flare of life has long since been extinguished; and yet even this obvious manifestation of despair perversely adds to her compelling attraction. The woman's name is Karin.

When she enters, the older woman is just lowering the cup from her lips and the sudden shock of seeing her causes her to drop the cup noisily to the saucer; and her lips tremble but she can't utter a sound for a few seconds. The younger woman puts her luggage down, closes the door, leans against it.

MARIE: (*face bursts into a guilty smile*) Karin?! (*pause*) Karin, it's you?! Did I leave the front door—Karin! It's you!

KARIN: (*eyes close and open slowly; nods her head wearily*) And it's you.

MARIE: (*Smiles afresh; a skeletal smile*) After all these years it's you! (*eyes closed, shakes her head and giggles nervously*) I can't believe it! Honestly! And look at the state of me, the state of everything. (*laughs*) Come and sit down! Let me look at you! You're beautiful! You've really grown into a very beautiful woman . . . (*Nervously, she finishes off her cup of whisky, pulls a face*) Aaah! Cold! I'll make some fresh.

KARIN: Not for me.

MARIE: No? (*pause*) Well . . . I've so much to tell you—

KARIN: Have you? And I've so much to hear from you.

MARIE: (*averts her eyes*) I—And I'm sure you've a lot to tell me.

KARIN: No.

MARIE: Why didn't you keep in touch—now don't get me wrong, I'm not reproaching you, it's just that I often worry—

KARIN: (*snaps*) WHAT?!

MARIE: (*swallows*) I often wondered what had become of you . . .

KARIN: Why didn't YOU keep in touch?

MARIE: I didn't know where you were. You must have known I'd still be here, otherwise you wouldn't be here now.

KARIN: I wrote to you.

MARIE: (*points to herself incredulously*) Me?!

KARIN: I wrote twice.

MARIE: Oh Karin! st, st, st . . . (*goes to the bureau, pulls down the flap, unopened letters spill all over the place. She laughs nervously*) I really must try to —I am sorry, Karin . . . it's just that . . . (*shakes her head, comes back and sits

86

down) What must you think of me?!

KARIN: They were foolish letters; they weren't letters at all in fact; they were questionnaires. I was trying to find out—

MARIE: Never mind! You're here now! You look lovely, no, BEAUTIFUL, but —a trifle sad.

KARIN: I—

MARIE:When you were a tiny little girl and you looked like something had hurt you—

KARIN: What sort of thing?

MARIE: Oh, I don't know—

KARIN: You never asked?

MARIE: (*forced laugh*) Do you know what I'd do? I used to go straight to the cupboard, bring out the honey and spread it thickly on a slice of bread and—ha ha ha—you loved it! You'd gobble it all up like a hungry wolf. Sometimes I thought you were going to eat your fingers too! (*gets up and goes to the cupboard: rummages amongst the chaos*) But it did the trick!

KARIN: The trick . . .

MARIE: (*whirls about with a jar of honey in her hand*) Look! (*looks at the label*) Honey from Yucatan! (*comes back, takes out a sliced loaf from amongst the clutter on the table and shakily spreads it with honey*) Here, that will put the smile of life back into your eyes.

KARIN: No thank you.

MARIE: Go on—eat it!

KARIN *shakes her head—almost imperceptibly—to herself. She reaches out and takes it, looks strangely at it, and then at the woman who averts her eyes. She takes a bite.*

MARIE: Well? . . . What does it taste like?

KARIN: (*puts it aside. Takes a crumpled kleenex from her pocket and wipes her mouth and hands*) Honey . . . from Yucatan.

MARIE: Don't leave it Dar—Karin . . . eat it all up, it's—

KARIN: Good for me.

MARIE: I love honey too . . . when you were a child you went through jars of it.

KARIN: Tell me something—

MARIE: Why don't you call me—(*their eyes meet and fix intensely for a couple of seconds and then avert*) M—My name is Karin too y'know, I just thought . . . my second name is Marie . . . perhaps you could call me by . . . by that . . .

KARIN: Tell me something, Marie—

MARIE: (*visibly trembles at the sound of the name; speaks quickly through her*) Do you know, Karin? I knew you were coming today! I, I had a dream about you last night! Honestly! I saw you almost exactly as you are now. In the dream I asked you—no! PLEADED with you—to stay . . . but you wouldn't! You said you were just passing through. (*nervous laugh*) Imagine . . .

KARIN: Do you dream a lot, Marie?

MARIE: Me? No—I nev—yes! but I, well I forget most of them. Not this one though. I could remember it all. And then something told me this morning that you'd come. Was it this morning? It's the afternoon now, isn't it? Is it? Clocks don't work anymore. I suppose I should draw the curtains. It's winter, isn't it? Is it? Can't tell in this street anymore. Did you notice the houses on the other side have been replaced by skyscrapers or whatevertheycallthem. This side is being demolished. The Grant's house has gone, so has the Simpson's, the Keir's, the Morgan's and most of the others. Listen! You can hear the demolition machinery, Karin. They asked me to go ages ago, but I won't. Knock the damn place down, I said, but I won't budge, I'll go with it. (*pause*) Can't tell what time it is, what season it is, with those big ugly monsters across the road behind us—yes! behind too, in Chesterfield Street—keeping the light out! The sun out! (*She gets up and pulls the curtains back, they fall down.*) Even the wretched curtains know it's all over! (*She points out the window.*) Over there on the corner where the Ogdens used to live, they've made a gambling club! Imagine, a Casino in a district like this! It's called the BLUE BELL, I think. At night a huge blue neon light goes on and off, on and off, and even with the curtains drawn the terrible blue light keeps crashing in and out of the room like the big iron ball on the swinging chain they use to smash down the street. (*sits down with a sigh*) Oh to hell, I went once to the Blue whatyoumay-call it. No—I went twice. I only went because the damn light going on and off nearly drove me—anyway I went. (*forced, giggling laughter*) Oh stop me, Karin, don't let me go on like this—ha ha ha—I haven't seen you for—for a life-time and here I go on and on about my petty little troubles!

She reaches for the pot, hesitates, hands trembling, withdraws quickly; Karin's vacant eyes following her every movement, only adds to her agitation; she picks up the empty cup and pretends to drink from it.

KARIN: May I have a cigarette?

MARIE: (*burst of relief*) Of course you may! (*runs her hand through her hair, looking wildly about her*) Now then, honestly, I must get some order—where did I—

KARIN: The packet is next to the TEAPOT.

MARIE: (*reaching for it, her hand momentarily freezes at Karin's emphasis on the word TEAPOT*) Here! You can have anything you wish! Anything I've got! See, I haven't changed, I always gave you everything you asked for!

KARIN: Like honey?

MARIE: Oh, you absolutely adored honey! (*looks quickly towards the window; forced laugh*) Don't suppose you're any good at odd-jobbing, Karin? Couldn't fix the—

KARIN: Did I really eat such a lot of honey?

MARIE: (*rubs the back of her neck*) Yes, I told you . . . you ate pots of it . . . as a matter of fact, you drank it, too.

KARIN: How did I drink it?

MARIE: In hot milk at night to make you—How about a nice cup of tea?

KARIN: To—make—me—sleepy?

MARIE: (*sits down uneasily*) Well, all children have hot drinks at night, what's so special . . .

KARIN: So I couldn't sleep?

MARIE: (*about to reach for the teapot, hand withdraws*) Well you—

KARIN *picks up a tea cup, blows the dust out of it, picks up the teapot, pours herself a full cup of whisky.*

KARIN: You don't mind me helping myself to your cold tea, do you?

MARIE: (*trembling all over*) N-No . . .

KARIN, *holding her eyes, gestures a refill.*

MARIE: (*swallows. Averts her eyes*) Please . . .

KARIN: Milk?

MARIE: (*almost a whisper*) N-No thank you . . .

KARIN: Sugar?

MARIE: (*almost a whisper*) N-No thank you . . .   *Pause.* KARIN *gulps her whisky and refills it.*

KARIN: So . . . I couldn't sleep?

MARIE: Why, you were always a highly strung child.

KARIN: What did I do instead? I must have done something. Did I just toss and turn in bed? Did I go for long walks? Did I—

MARIE: (*grabs her forehead*) I can't remember—

KARIN: Cheers!

MARIE: (*dazed*) Mm?

KARIN: I said: Cheers!

MARIE: Oh? (*looks at her cup; raises it slowly*) Cheers . . .

KARIN: How old was I when my strings became highly strung?

MARIE: Oh, you were always a difficult-

KARIN: (*mouths the words*) D-i-f-f-i-c-u-l-t?

MARIE: (*quickly*) Y-You were never a good sleeper. (*gulps her whisky*)

KARIN: And you can't remember what I did instead?

MARIE: N-No. (*swallows*) I found you once outs—(*suddenly looks terrified*)

KARIN: Where? (*pause*) where did you find me once?

MARIE: (*quickly*) In the kitchen! Yes, drinking milk and eating-

KARIN: You said you found me once outs-outside? The front door? The back door? (*pause*) Outside where? (*voice rises*) Outside your bedroom door?

MARIE: (*gasps*) What's that supposed to—

KARIN: Listening perhaps? But listening to what?

MARIE: (*almost a shout*) How the hell should I know?!

KARIN: Because you were in the room!

MARIE: (*puts hand over eyes. Pause. Tries to calm herself*) . . . it's good to see you again, Karin, I really mean that . . . but for God's sake let's forget the past; the past is over and done with, finished . . .

KARIN: How right you are, Karin-Marie! (*raises her cup*) To hell with the past!

MARIE: (*raises her cup; hand jerks at the way she pronounces her first name*) To (*forces laugh*) yes: to hell with the past! (*They drink.*)

KARIN: And judging by the speed and height of those buildings going up—to heaven with the future!

MARIE: (*laughs and drinks*) To heaven with the future! (*Pause. Jokingly*) What must God think of us I wonder-ha ha ha . . .

KARIN: He doesn't. He's turned his back on us.

MARIE: (*pulls a face; laughs and sings*) We're just poor little lambs, Lost in the snow-bah! bah! bah! (*Pause. Shaking her head, smiling to herself*) Will he never face us again?

KARIN: (*drinks*) He might, if we were to wake up, to recognize our evil, to stamp it out and destroy it. (*Pause*)

MARIE: Cigarette?

KARIN: I am smoking, so are you.

MARIE: (*looks stupidly at the cigarette between her fingers, pulls a face, stubs it out and immediately lights another. Coughs*) I believe in God—ha ha ha—God is omnipresent. God owns this street. God owns this very house we're sitting in. God is THE UNITED NORTH WESTERN BUILDING SOCIETY, and— (*giggles*) And such is my faith in God that I have two thirds of my capital invested in him. (*pause. Looks at her cigarette and pulls a face*) How is the cigarette, Karin? It's a new brand I'm trying. They give gift coupons. I've saved thousands of them. (*looks vaguely about the chaos. Waves her arms limply*) They're all there—somewhere. I must try to get some—(*pause. Exaggerated study of the cigarette*) A bit . . . a bit dry . . . (*looks stealthily at Karin*) Would you . . . would you say they taste a bit dry, Karin? A bit hot and dry to the mouth?

KARIN: (*lifts her cup*) Not if you wash the cancerous clouds back with whisky. (*She drinks.*)

MARIE: (*nervous laugh. Exaggerated puffing and tasting of the cigarette*) I don't like them anymore . . . I think I'll change my brand.

KARIN: (*opens her handbag and takes out a packet of French cigarettes*) Here, try one of these.

MARIE: (*takes and lights a French cigarette, stubbing out her own; looks at the packet with distaste*) Eughhhhh . . .

KARIN: Wait till you try it before making a judgement.

MARIE: (*puffs*) Anything for a quiet life.

KARIN: (*looks up slowly, strangely*) What did you say?

MARIE: (*averts her eyes*) I . . . I just said—(*Skeletal smile*) Ha ha ha— I'll try anything once—

KARIN: You said: anything for a quiet life.

MARIE: (*swallows*) So?

KARIN: I've heard that before.

MARIE: It's a saying, a cliche, just . . . just a saying. Why must you take me up on it?

KARIN: Did you use that SAYING a lot when I was a child?

MARIE: (*looks agitated*) I . . . I don't know, oh for heaven's sake—

KARIN: What does it mean?

MARIE: OH KARIN!

KARIN: What does it mean? Did you lead a quiet life?

MARIE: Quiet? Well, I . . . I lived just—Karin, have you no memory?

Very long pause: KARIN *looks vacantly at her;* MARIE *holds her gaze for a time and then quickly averts her eyes.*

KARIN: (*almost a whisper*) No.

MARIE: (*tries to hide her relief. Long pause*) None?

KARIN: A little. (*pause*) Just for the immediate past.

MARIE: But . . . but you can't remember . . . remember the past . . . us, I mean . . . us in the past?

KARIN: (*long pause. Looks strangely at her*) No.

MARIE: (*swallows*) Your memory has just . . . just gone?

KARIN: Gone.

MARIE: An accident?

KARIN: Me?

MARIE: I meant—

KARIN: Can you remember me as a little girl?

MARIE: (*big nervous smile*) Of course!

KARIN: As a baby?

MARIE: (*pours a drink. Smile collapses*) As a baby too!

KARIN: (*pours a cupful*) Have you any photographs of me as a baby?

MARIE: No—yes! Somewhere . . .

93

KARIN: And (*pause*) as a little girl?

MARIE: HE took pictures of you. HE, HE, was always—

KARIN: Did he?

MARIE: (*quickly*) I did too!

KARIN: But the photographs are no more?

MARIE: (*laughs*) We had a cat, Karin, a beautiful black and white cat, long-haired—ha ha ha—I called it Sue, because it was so pretty I was sure it was a she, but when I took HER to the vet I discovered SHE was a HE—ha ha ha—

KARIN: What has that got to do—

MARIE: Oh yes! I had a camera, a big Kodak box camera and I was forever trying to take some snaps of Sue-Cat, ha ha ha—would he stay still, ha ha ha—not on your life!

KARIN: Do you have any snaps of Sue-Cat?

MARIE: (*jumps up*) Yes! (*goes to the bureau and opens the bottom drawer*) There was a beauty I got one day when he was looking up into a tree at a big juicy woodpigeon . . . (*She lifts up a framed photo, suddenly hesitates, places it back slowly in the drawer and closes it. She turns to face* KARIN, *a nervous guilty grimace meant as a smile. Shakes her head*) No . . . no I can't find it.

KARIN: Maybe if you looked more thoroughly you might find it. You might even find some of me.

MARIE: No! (*coughs, hand to mouth. Comes back and sits down nervously*) No, there's nothing in the drawer but . . . junk, bits and pieces of God knows what. (*laughs*) Someday I'm going to have a bonfire and get rid of all this rubbish . . . (*laughs*) Yes, the flames will lick the empty heavens—ha ha ha . . . (*pause. Both drink*)

KARIN: Could you find some more cold tea?

MARIE: (*holds her forehead*) Some more what?

KARIN: (*lifts the lid of the pot and rattles it noisily*) We're running out of cold tea, Karin-Marie.

MARIE: Oh! (*swallows*) Yes, I . . . (*gets up dazed; looks about her*) I have a little— (*Clicks her fingers*) The kitchen! Of course the kitchen. (*goes unsteadily out through the door*) Won't be long . . .

Hear her walking unsteadily down the hallway; she talks all the time but we can't hear what she says.

KARIN *gets up and goes to the drawer of the bureau opens it and takes out the framed photo of the cat.*

From the kitchen a crash of glass, and MARIE's *voice swearing and audible:* "Bloody hell!" *. . . . and her inaudible monologue continues.*

KARIN *takes the photograph back and puts it on the table, leaning against the teapot, and gazes at it.*

MARIE: *comes back carrying a full bottle of whisky.*

MARIE: (*breathless as she had run a great distance*) I managed to find . . . a whole bottle. Did you hear the crash? I knocked all the damn crockery off the draining board. No, I mean the damned draining board collapsed—oh, never mind. (*takes top off bottle*) Shall I top you up, Karin?

KARIN: Aren't you going to put it in the pot and let it stand for a while?

MARIE: The pot?

KARIN: The TEAPOT.

MARIE: Oh, the—

She sees the photograph; nearly drops the bottle; lifts the top off pot and pours the entire contents of bottle into it—photo falls flat on its face—she replaces lid, pours two drinks, goes back and sits down.

KARIN: (*picks up photo*) I found this when you were in the kitchen.

MARIE: You found it?! Did you REALLY find it?! (*looks about her wildly*) Now where did I put my—what have I done with my spectacles? (*gets up and wanders about the room knocking things off surfaces like a blind woman*) Can never find anything when I—so you REALLY found it—

KARIN: It was just lying on the top of the things in that drawer you opened in the bureau.

MARIE: No?! st, st, st . . . can't see a thing without my spectacles . . . (*puts her hands in her housecoat and takes out a spectacle case. Puts on colour-tinted specs. Sits down again*) Now then— ha ha ha—after all that—

KARIN: May I see your specs?

MARIE: (*looks terrified*) See them? Why do you want to—

KARIN: (*hands outstretched across the table*) May I?

MARIE *involuntarily, slowly, takes them off and shakily passes them to her.*

KARIN: (*deliberate inspection*) Pretty frames . . .

MARIE: (*coughs nervously*) Cost a pretty penny!

KARIN: And the lenses are slightly tinted . . .

MARIE: Yes, the, the . . . (*swallows*) The light hurts my eyes . . . they were fitted at the doctor's . . . at . . . he suggested it.

KARIN: (*holding them at arm's length*) Are you long or short sighted?

MARIE: I . . . I'm (*scratches her head and laughs*) Blowed if I know . . . long, short . . . I, I just can't—

KARIN: May I try them on?

MARIE: (*pause. Just looks pathetically at her; pleading with her not to*) Try them . . . why if . . .

KARIN: May I?

MARIE: (*closes her eyes and nods her head*) All right, but . . .

KARIN: (*puts them on*) Everything looks mauve.

MARIE: (*feebly*) Does it?

KARIN: Don't you know? These are yours?

MARIE: Yes I—

KARIN: Everything . . . no, not everything. Your hair looks mauve, but the shadows under your eyes look blue. Everything in the light looks mauve and in

96

the shadows blue. Pretty, very pretty, but the lenses don't appear to magnify at all.

MARIE: Well they're—

KARIN: They're plain glass!

MARIE: (*quickly*) They help me! They help me! I went to one of the best eye men in the country and he suggested them! I get such terrible headaches when I read—

KARIN: (*looks around the place for books: there are none*) Read? What?

MARIE: Just, just looking gives me—

KARIN: (*takes them off and hands them back*) PRETTY frames, Karin- Marie.

MARIE: (*puts them on*) I'm so pleased you found that photo of Sue . . . may I have a look . . . (KARIN *passes her the photo*) ahhhhh (*giggles*) I remember the day I took it as if it were just yesterday . . . (*sugary voice*) Look at Sue . . . Suecat . . . (*smiles aloud; baby voice*) Naughty Suecat looking up at big, fat, juicy woodpigeon . . . (*face suddenly sad*) Karin, do you know what happened to poor—

KARIN: You remember the day so clearly?

MARIE: Oh yes, I remember it because that day I managed to take the first snap of Suecat . . . I remember it as if it were just yesterday . . . it was a glorious day . . . the sun was shining, the grass, the flowers, all that sort of thing. (*laughs*) Anyway, I got so excited by getting Suecat sitting still for a change that I used the whole roll of film on him. (*smiles aloud*) But this was the only one that came out . . . I did something wrong with the twisting thing, the knob or whateveryoucallit . . .

KARIN: Where was I on that glorious summer day that you remember as if it were just yesterday?

MARIE: (*starts*) You?!

KARIN: Yes, ME. Where was I?

MARIE: (*gets up slowly and tries to be matter-of-fact. Boozey smile. Chàrming persona. Points to ceiling*) The sun . . . (*holds her forehead*)

KARIN: (*points to the floor*) The grass, flowers, THINGS LIKE THAT.

MARIE: (*points*) The grass, the flowers, the beech, or was it birch? or elm? (*points*) The tree . . .

KARIN: (*points*) Suecat . . .

MARIE: (*laughs*) Yes . . . dear ol' Suecat . . . (*Points*) Just there . . .

KARIN: And you?

MARIE: (*stumbles backwards*) About here . . . (*She goes right back and comes forward again on tip-toe. Whispers*) I had to come up very slowly, very quietly. I stood like this . . . (*mimes camera to eye*) and CLICK! CLICK! CLICK!—ha ha ha—CLICK! until—

KARIN: (*voice loud and cold*) WHERE WAS I?

MARIE: (*waves her arms, laughs*) You were everywhere . . . you were like Suecat, always everywhere — ha ha ha you were—ha ha ha— you were probably up the tree with the woodpigeons—ha ha ha . . .

KARIN: PROBABLY! You remember the day as clearly as if it were yesterday yet you don't remember where I was—

MARIE: YES, I DO!

KARIN: Where?

MARIE: (*points blindly at the corner of the room; voice tremulous*) There! There! You were there! Look! There! There! There!

KARIN: What was I doing there yesterday?

MARIE: (*hand to forehead*) Yesterday? Oh, I see what you—you—(*swallows eerie laugh*) You were making a daisy chain! You adored making daisy chains! I, I, I taught you myself—

KARIN: Squatting on the grass?

MARIE: (*nods her head feverishly*) Y—Yes, that's it, squatting on the grass—

KARIN: Wearing a pretty little frock?

MARIE: Yes, you had beautiful clothes, Karin, really beautiful—I loved buying you—Nanny never shopped—I always insisted on—.

KARIN: Pink? Or blue? Or perhaps it was yellow?

MARIE: Pink or?—oh, I see—yellow! Yes, it was yellow!

KARIN: With a ribbon in my hair?

MARIE: A ribbon? Yes, a yellow ribbon, with a bow as big as your little blond head—ha ha ha—you looked a picture, Karin, you really looked a picture . . .

KARIN: But a *picture* not inspiring enough to be taken by your precious camera!

MARIE: (*goes back and literally collapses into her seat*) But I did!

KARIN: You just said you used the whole roll on Suecat—

MARIE: I — I had more than one roll—

KARIN: And did it come out all blurred?

MARIE: It . . . (*drinks and catches her breath*) No. It came out all right . . . (*quickly*) HE was for ever taking your picture . . . HE had pictures of you all over his room — (*points to the ceiling*)

KARIN: (*snaps*) THAT'S THE SUN!

MARIE: (*voice breaks; almost in tears*) That's NOT the sun! I'm talking about the house now! Stop trying to confuse me!

KARIN: "HIS ROOM"?

MARIE: Yes. His, his room . . .

KARIN: Her room, and HIS room! You only could have been married a few years and yet you didn't share the same room, the—

MARIE: (*pulls off her spectacles*) KARIN!

KARIN: THE SAME BED!

MARIE: Things were different in those days.

KARIN: DID YOU?

MARIE: I won't be questioned like this! I won't be—

KARIN: (*leaning over the table, almost shouting*) DID YOU?

MARIE: (*hands to her temples*) STOP IT, KARIN!

KARIN: DID YOU? DID YOU? DID YOU?

MARIE: (*both hands slamming the table, knocking things all over the place*) NO! NO! NOOOOOOOO!

MARIE *falls into folded arms on table and weeps silently.* KARIN *falls back in her chair, her head drops forward like a broken rag doll; her long blond hair veils her face. After a time,* MARIE *sits up slowly, sniffing back tears.* KARIN *raises her head slowly and looks over at* MARIE. *There is no pity in her vacant eyes.*

MARIE: (*raises spectacles, rubs her eyes with the back of her hand, replaces them*) This . . . this is not how I imagined it Karin . . . (*pause . . . sniffs*) It . . . it wasn't like this in the dream.

KARIN: (*monotonously*) Oh yes; THAT DREAM.

MARIE: I told you I dreamt about you?

KARIN: You told me.

MARIE: Can't remember when it was now, but I dreamt about you . . .

KARIN: (*looks at her luggage*) I was just passing through.

MARIE: That's what you said in the dream . . . your exact words . . . I'm just passing through . . . (*Pause*)

KARIN: (*looks strangely at her*) But you PLEADED with me to stay.

MARIE: (*drinks, dries her eyes again*) Yes, I said, PLEASE stay, Karin . . .

KARIN: But I refused.

MARIE: (*sniffs*) Yes, you sat like you are now, dressed like you are now coat on like you are now . . . (*looks at her luggage*) Your luggage beside you as it is now . . . ready to—

KARIN: Pass through.

MARIE: Ready to—yes. (*pause*) But in the dream it was different.

KARIN: How different?

MARIE: We sat at this table, that bit was the same, but . . . but we didn't quarrel, we . . . we talked about all those lost years and (*sobs*) I wasn't crying, Karin, I was . . . I was roaring with laughter . . .

KARIN: What made you roar with laughter in this dream you had?

MARIE: I . . . I can't remember . . . it had something to do with what you were telling me . . . stories from your past.

KARIN: (*shakes her head slowly. Bitterly*) AND YOU LAUGHED!

MARIE: (*almost childishly*) Yes . . . (*smiles aloud*) I laughed as I've never laughed before.

KARIN: And when you finished laughing, I took up my cases and— passed through . . .

MARIE: (*vaguely*) Mm . . . that's it . . . that's the way it was in the dream . . . (*pause*)

KARIN: (*reaching*) May I have another one of your cigarettes?

MARIE: Karin, you can take anything you want. You could always take anything you wanted. That's the way it was with us, and is, oh yes! AND IS!

KARIN: (*lights cigarette. Sotto voce*) Us . . .

MARIE: US . . . You and Me, Karin.

KARIN: Inseparable . . . (*long pause*)

MARIE: Karin?

KARIN: Yes?

MARIE: I'm . . . (*swallows*) I'm so glad you came.

KARIN: Are you?

MARIE: Yes, yes, honestly I am . . . (*pause*) But . . . (*averts her eyes*) Why did you come?

KARIN: I had to.

MARIE: (*looks frightened*) Had to?

KARIN: I tried all the other places.

MARIE: What other places?

KARIN: (*theatrically*) The white north; the yellow south; the red east; the golden west.

MARIE: (*unctious*) Everywhere! You've been everywhere!

KARIN: (*sotto voce*) Yes . . . nowhere . . .

MARIE: Have you spent all the money he left you? (*ingratiating laugh*) Don't worry, Karin, I've still got lots, I don't need it, I don't go anywhere, don't spend anything; you can have as much as you want; it's going to be yours anyway! (*hopefully*) Is that it, Karin? Are you broke?

KARIN: (*wistful, but hard laugh*) Broke . . .

MARIE: Karin, I'll write you a —

KARIN: I don't need YOUR money!

MARIE: I just thought —

KARIN: (*raises her voice*) I DON'T NEED YOUR MONEY!

MARIE: (*swallows. Unctious*) Karin, tell me all about your travels, I bet you've been to all the famous galleries and museums . . . you've seen the great works of antiquity, the magnificent art treasures . . . it must have been a great experience! It must have moved and excited you like —

KARIN: It made me sick!

MARIE *almost recoils, looks utterly lost.*

KARIN: SICK! (*They look strangely at each other; both avert eyes*) I saw stone, marble, wood bronze gold and silver . . . peeling canvases, crumbling architecture. When a sign said: 'Don't touch' I touched even at the risk of prosecution — no, NOT EVEN—BECAUSE of the risk of prosecution! (*pause*) I felt nothing . . . I felt NOTHING. I had phantasies of being dragged away by the police who shouted at me in a foreign tongue, to a dank, pissy cell and being ill-treated, abused, even violated, for touching a piece of nothing that a sign proclaimed immortal — I — m — m — o — r — t — a — l!

MARIE: I . . . (*swallows*) I, I thought if I could get a bit of order into things, I might go to Venice next year —

KARIN: I wanted to take a knife and rip a canvas to shreds; a hammer and

102

smash a piece of stone to powder; put a bomb beneath the high alter of an ancient chapel; throw petrol all over the floor of a library and set it alight!

MARIE: (*drinks; tops it up*) One has to be in a certain frame of mind, a certain mood, to to . . . appreciate the arts . . . it's as if you said to yourself: Who the devil do they think they're conning? This is all just a great hoax, nothing whatsoever to do with *real* life. (*pleased with herself*) That's it, isn't it?

KARIN: Huh . . .

MARIE: I know the feeling only too well. You really musn't get morbid over this loss of memory business, I mean . . . (*takes a cigarette, taps it hard on the box before putting it in her mouth and lighting it*) How many people do you know, who can really and truly remember much about their past?

KARIN: I don't know any people.

MARIE: Oh Karin, of course you do! Everybody knows people!

KARIN: Do they?

MARIE: Of course they do . . . I'm sure you have lots of, of friends . . .

KARIN: No.

MARIE: (*swallows*) No? Well, acquaintances then.

KARIN: I don't know any people.

MARIE: (*frightened*) You don't . . . none?

KARIN: None.

MARIE: But, look at you, you're young—

KARIN: I'm nearly forty.

MARIE: Attractive, no BEAUTIFUL is the word! You're a very beautiful woman, Karin, I'm sure lots of people would want to know you; I'm sure lots of men—(*A sudden flare in Karin's eyes silences her. Long pause.*) Did you . . . did you ever marry?

KARIN: Yes.

MARIE: It didn't—

KARIN: No.

MARIE: (*swallows*) I'm sorry . . .

KARIN: (*sniggers*) Sorry . . .

MARIE: You musn't blame yourself, Karin. I mean, nowadays marriages—

KARIN: (*almost spits the words*) DON'T TALK TO ME LIKE THAT!

MARIE: (*head shaking, drinks; and drinks. Gets up slowly, cup in hand, goes to the window and looks out into the street.*) This used to be a beautiful street, Karin. Before the war. (*drinks*) The Ogdens lived over there where that hideous nightclub is now. The Grants, the Morgans, the Simpsons and the Keirs were our neighbours. It was a beautiful street. And this was a beautiful house. Our garden at the back ran right up to the back gardens of Chesterfield Street. We had a small orchard and grass and things . . . and there was Suecat and . . . there was you . . . and me (*pause, bitterly*) First they came and flattened out that side. Machinery going day and night. Everybody left of course. (*pause*) They offered me a small fortune for my lease which had less than a year to go anyway. To hell with them . . . (*drinks*) I'll be sitting at that table the day the big iron ball swings and crashes through the wall . . . (*laughs boozily; cups hands to mouth and shouts*) Come and get me BARBARIANS! Come and get me! (*drops her arms limply to her sides; shrugs her shoulders. Pause*) Then up goes another row of those concrete and glass monsters . . . (*pause*)

KARIN: What was the house like in those days?

MARIE: Like?

KARIN: What went on?

MARIE: (*smiles aloud*) Oh, you know . . . living . . .

KARIN: Did you entertain a lot?

MARIE: No—yes. Sometimes . . . entertained out quite a lot . . .

KARIN: So the house was empty most of the time.

MARIE: Yes—well no, it was . . . (*runs her hand through her hair*) Just like any other house really. Sometimes I went out and sometimes I didn't.

KARIN: YOU?

MARIE: Mmmm?

KARIN: You said: Sometimes *I* went out and sometimes *I* didn't.

MARIE: (*quickly*) We! I meant to say WE.

KARIN: HIM and YOU?

MARIE: (*swallows; pause*) Him and . . . me.

KARIN: I'd be with a nanny I suppose?

KARIN: Yes, but I, we—didn't go out all that often.

KARIN: You're contradicting yourself again, Karin-Marie.

MARIE: (*swings round*) I'm drunk! Do you understand? I'm drunk! Of course I'm contradicting myself, because, because . . . because I'm drunk! And I was drunk yesterday! (*sobs, shouts*) And I'll be bloody well drunk again tomorrow! So what? So what the bloody hell . . . (*turns back slowly to the window*)

KARIN: Why?

MARIE: Because . . . (*pause*) Because they've destroyed my beautiful street! (*sobs*) My beautiful street . . . my beautiful house . . .

KARIN: The street you loved.

MARIE: Yes, loved.

KARIN: The house you loved.

MARIE: The house I loved!

KARIN: The house you loved so much that you had to leave it for—the street you loved so much that you had to leave it for—what?

MARIE: (*laughs and sobs*) Mrs. Ogden had a lisp, I remember she used to say, Isn't it tweet to hear the birds twitter in the twees—ha ha ha— that's what she used to say, isn't it tweet to hear—(*pause. Finishes cup. Goes awkwardly back to the table and refills cup, about to sit down, hesitates, gives Karin a stealthy look, goes back to the window. Laughs quietly.*) Mr. Ogden had a chauffeur named Bruce, who was, as the saying went, fond of his beer—

KARIN: What was HE like?

MARIE: (*Pause*) Who? Oh . . . He was . . . he was rather sweet. (*drinks noisily to kill the silence*) Sweet person really. He . . . (*pause. Shakes her head sadly from side to side*) He was sweet. (*pause. Wistful laugh*) He used to describe himself contemptuously as, 'The reluctant usurer'. . . (*wistful laugh to herself*) . . . The reluctant usurer . . . (*pause*) When his father died he took over his chair in the merchant bank, but he loathed banking . . . (*drinks*) He was donnish. Loved his books, his library. You . . . you are very like him in many ways.

KARIN: What ways?

MARIE: Well . . . you were a bit of a bookworm, and he had that, that serious sort of look that you have now . . .

KARIN: A 'trifle' sad, as you put it earlier.

MARIE: (*starts*) He, he . . . perhaps a trifle sad—(*quickly*) but only in looks, not in actual fact!

KARIN: As if something had hurt him . . .

MARIE: (*edge on her voice*) I don't know what you're talking about!

KARIN: What hurt him?

MARIE: Who said anything hurt him? (*swings to face her*) I didn't hurt him!

KARIN: When he looked at you like that, did you give him a slice of bread and honey from Yucatan?

MARIE: How dare you!

MARIE *swings back to the window, trembling all over.* KARIN, *now just as unsteady on her feet, brings the teapot over to her.*

KARIN: More tea?

MARIE: (*hand shaking*) Thank you. (*She swallows it all off.*) And, and again please.

KARIN: Say when.

MARIE: When . . . (*pause. Turns slowly to face* KARIN) It wasn't like you . . . (*shakes her head*) Honestly, Karin, it wasn't . . .

KARIN: I have to know.

MARIE: (*almost a whisper*) Is it all so important to you, Karin?

KARIN: It's ALL that's important to me.

MARIE: Why Karin, why? (*sobs*) We're both drunk . . . too much drink on an empty stomach makes people morose and . . . can't we talk about it some other time . . .

KARIN: No, Karin-Marie, we talk about it now. There won't be another time: I'm just passing through—remember?

MARIE: Is this the real reason you came?

KARIN: Yes; the only reason.

MARIE: (*half laughing and crying*) And vain bloody creature that I am, I thought you'd come, come to . . . to see me.

KARIN: You are the only living person who can answer the questions.

MARIE: YOU'VE done nothing else but question me since you came this afternoon. Like a detective. (*drinks, spilling the whisky down her face*) Besides having no memory have you no feelings?

KARIN: No. (*goes back and sits down*)

MARIE: I should have known you'd turn out like this . . .

KARIN: Like what?

MARIE: (*swings around; points at her; shouts*) Like that! A COLD CRUEL HEARTLESS BITCH! (*her head shaking, turns away quickly to the window and drinks. Long Pause.*) Suecat was missing. For a whole day, then two, then three . . . I combed the neighborhood; I told the police; I advertised in the local paper; I pinned cards up on trees along all the next street and up at the park. But no Suecat. (*sobs*) No Suecat ever again. The man who did the garden found him some time afterwards, at the back of the garden shed behind a pile of junk with his head crushed in . . . (*puts her hand in her mouth*) His head . . . all crushed in . . . (*long pause. Sucks her drink*) I thought at the time a girl named Austin did it out of spite because I gave her the sack for neglecting you

107

while I was away for Christmas with—anyway I sacked her—(*pause*) I thought she did it.

KARIN: While you were away for Chritmas I was put in the charge of this strange girl—

MARIE: (*still looking out of the window, speaks with an eerie calm*) YOU did it, didn't you?

KARIN: (*speaks through her*) Who neglected me and was named Austin . . .

MARIE: (*swings around; stumbles over to her; shouts.*) YOU MURDERED SUECAT, DIDN'T YOU?

KARIN: (*pause; hold each other's eyes*) Maybe . . . yes, maybe I did.

MARIE: Why would you do such a terrible . . . (*averts her eyes; goes back and sits down*) Suecat was the only living thing I ever . . .

KARIN: The only living thing you ever? (*long pause*)

MARIE: Karin?

KARIN: What?

MARIE: (*pause*) You . . . You didn't do it. Did you, Karin? (*pause*) You weren't like that . . . you never played with Suecat. I once saw you push him away when he came up for cuddles . . . but that's different . . . I think you had an allergy . . . you had asthma and most people with asthma can't stand cats, but . . . (*shakes her head*) No, no you wouldn't have done that . . . you were too gentle. I'm certain you didn't do it . . . it was that awful whatshername. Forgive me, Karin, whatever possessed me to say such a vile thing. (*long pause*)

KARIN: Did HE like me?

MARIE: (*head bowed*) Yes . . . he . . . he liked you . . .

KARIN: When you went away did HE stay with me?

MARIE: I never—(*swallows*) I only went away now and again . . .

KARIN: (*coldly, relentlessly*) When you went away did HE stay with me?

MARIE: Yes.

KARIN: Did HE hold me in his arms when I was little?

MARIE: (*shakes her head but means the affirmative*) Y-Yes . . .

KARIN: When you were away and I looked like him, sort of serious, sort of hurt, would HE give me bread and honey?

MARIE: I didn't—HE was—HE was a shy man. Shy with children. Shy with everybody.

KARIN: What does 'shy' mean?

MARIE: Shy? It just means . . . (*shrugs*) shy.

KARIN: But HE wasn't too shy to hold me in his arms?

MARIE: (*lights a cigarette*) HE was a very busy man. In the bank all day . . . in his study all night . . .

KARIN: Did I ever go into his study and sit with him; squat at his feet perhaps while he read his books and wrote his papers?

MARIE: No one ever went into his study. The door was always . . . no one ever went into his—study.

KARIN: I couldn't have seen very much of him.

MARIE: Oh yes! When he came home in the evenings he always went looking for you . . .

KARIN: To photograph me?

MARIE: (*looks strangely at her; averts her eyes*) To . . . just to see you.

KARIN: And then he'd lift me up and kiss me?

MARIE: (*nods. Swallows. Looks to the floor*) Yes . . .

KARIN: You'd be standing with him, smiling lovingly at the beautiful sight of a returning man kissing the little pink cheeks of his baby girl.

MARIE: (*sobs*) Oh Karin . . .

KARIN: Was it like that?

MARIE: I . . . I don't know . . . I —

KARIN: You weren't with him . . . YOU weren't there?

MARIE: I . . . (*pause*) I didn't see much of him.

KARIN: So you can't tell whether or not HE came looking for me in the evenings.

MARIE: HE did!

KARIN: How do you know?

MARIE: I—I just know!

KARIN: It's just a guess, isn't it?

MARIE: I—

KARIN: Maybe when he came back he went straight to his library.

KARIE: HE wouldn't do that—not straight—HE'D—

KARIN: Why did he lock the door?

MARIE: HE . . . HE didn't like to be disturbed.

KARIN: (*takes a cigarette, lights it*) By you? (*pause*) By me?

MARIE: By anybody.

KARIN: Yet he was always taking photographs of me.

MARIE: Oh yes, HE . . . HE took lots of photographs of you, Karin—

KARIN: Had them all over the walls of HIS room.

MARIE: Yes . . . yes, all over the place.

KARIN: (*stands up unsteadily*) Could we go up and have a look at them now?

MARIE: (*starts*) Now?

KARIN: I'd like to look at them. I'd like to look at his room and her room. I'd like to imagine what it was like for that little girl, making the journey each night to her room. I'd like to see HIS study too, the door no longer locked, the

110

shy man no longer hiding behind his books . . . the shy man, the serious man, the sort of hurt-looking man no longer, no longer . . .

MARIE: Sit down, Karin.

KARIN: Why can't I see? (*pause*)

MARIE: (*eyes closed*) There's nothing to see.

KARIN: (*sits down slowly*) Nothing?

MARIE: (*runs her hand through her hair*) For God's sake, Karin, you talk about it all as if it were just yesterday . . . can't you realise that time consumes everything . . . you're talking about things that happened over a quarter of a century ago.

KARIN: (*looks strangely about the room*) Over a quarter of a century ago . . .

MARIE: (*nods her head; eyes closed*) The house is . . . is falling apart. I . . . I only use this room and the kitchen . . . I sleep over there on the sofa . . . don't you understand, Karin, it's all . . . it's all over . . .

KARIN: But surely you brought some of the things from upstairs down here?

MARIE: Yes.

KARIN: You cleared out your own room, I suppose?

MARIE: Yes. I . . . I just left the bed . . .

KARIN: And HIS room?

MARIE: No . . . No I never touched it after he . . . I never disturbed anything . . .

KARIN: Well then, all those photographs will still be on the walls.

MARIE: (*swallows*) The . . . the photographs . . .

KARIN: (*struggles to her feet*) I must see that room, I must see those photographs — (*staggers to the door*) You don't have to come, it's got very little to do with you anyway, this is between HIM and ME. (*She exits.*)

MARIE: (*sobbing, face in hands*) Don't Karin, don't . . .

Fade down lights. End of scene.

SCENE TWO:

Fade up to:

MARIE *is sitting slouched over the table.*

KARIN, *looking very drunk, is framed in the doorway. Her hair dishevelled, dust all over her clothes, her face smudged. She has fallen down the stairs in the dusty dark. They stay in these tableau-like attitudes for a time. Outside, darkness is falling quickly. Lights go on in the big block of flats opposite.*

MARIE: I heard you falling . . .

KARIN: Did I scream?

MARIE: (*shakes her head*) No . . . (*pause*)

KARIN: I went upstairs. (MARIE *lets her head fall into her arms.*) It's growing dark early now, but I could see through the dusty gloom. Only just. I fell.

MARIE: (*hoarse whisper, without looking up*) I told you not to go, Karin.

KARIN: No carpets, the stairs are naked, splintered, broken timber. The walls are falling to pieces—just ribs. I inhaled deeply and smelt an anonymous dry dust. I went to the first landing. The walls, the floors the same, dry, crumbling, splintering. I went from empty room to empty room: no furniture, no drapes, no carpets, just that anonymous dusty smell. And further up even it ceased to exist. I looked for the room with the bed, but it wasn't there. I looked for the room that had never been disturbed, with all the photographs of the baby girl in the yellow frock with a ribbon in her hair tied in a bow bigger than her little blond head, but it wasn't there. I looked for the room of books where the shy, serious man ensconced himself and hid his hurt and fear from the whole world, but it wasn't there. I tried to find something, anything, a glove, an old sock, a button, a broken comb, a hair clip, a hair even, but no, there was nothing there. I looked out the back window on the very top storey for a birch, beech, chestnut or elm that might have given sanctuary to a big, fat, juicy woodpigeon fleeing from the claws of a tom named Suecat who was battered to death by Nemesis. There was no such tree, no orchard. I came back the way I'd come, from empty landing to empty landing. This is not a dead house, I thought; to be dead it would have first had to live. This house never lived. This house never existed. I reached out to touch the wall, but there was no wall; my other hand reached out to touch the banister, but there was no

112

banister; I raised my foot to strike the splintering stairway, but there was no stairway—I fell.

MARIE: (*struggles up onto her elbow, excited and agitated*) You've got it all w-wrong, Karin . . . this was a beautiful house! A very beautiful house! Life pulsated through the carpeted corridors, stairways, rooms of this house, even as fiery blood pulsated through the arteries of the happy young woman who was its mistress!

KARIN: (*staggers*) There's no smell of death about this house; there are no ghosts haunting the rooms of this house. Nothing to see, smell, hear, why is that?

MARIE: (*gets up quickly, awkwardly*) I could show you things that would prove to you that this house was once . . . people were always calling here, for no other reason than just to be here. We had a big iron table out in the back garden under a chestnut tree, and on summer evenings we all sat around it sipping cool drinks, talking and laughing . . . (*holds her head*) When was that? Nineteen . . . Oh, I don't know, nineteenthirtysomething. I could show you things that would—

KARIN: There are no things in this house! (*comes forward and falls into her chair*) What happened to your bed? What happened to HIS books? What happened to the furniture, the carpets, the drapes?

MARIE: I, I, I just got rid of everything!

KARIN: Why?

MARIE: Because . . . (*swallows*) I told you: the whole street is being demolished.

KARIN: Did you give it away? Did you sell it? Did you destroy it?

MARIE: I, I, I just . . . gave it all away . . .

KARIN: How long ago did you give it all away?

MARIE: Does it matter?

KARIN: (*pours a drink, shrugs wearily*) No . . . (*Pause*) What about the photographs?

MARIE: The—(*looks wildly about the room*) They're . . . somewhere . . .

KARIN: You said you never disturbed HIS room.

MARIE: I could show you things that would prove—

KARIN: So far, the only thing you've proved is that you are a liar; an abjectly stupid, bloody liar!

MARIE: Karin! (*sobs*) Don't say that! Please let me—

KARIN: And what makes it even more pathetic, you don't even know you are a liar!

MARIE: (*goes around the room wildly, opening drawers, tossing things all over the place, looking for something, she knows not what herself*) I'll show you, Karin . . . just you wait and see—(*stops, looks around stupidly at her*) I, I did show you the picture of Suecat, didn't I?

KARIN: (*sighs*) Yes!

MARIE: (*takes out a book in a blue leather cover*) L—Look, Karin! A book. (*staggers over to her and drops it in front of her*) See, I told you, didn't I? I wasn't lying, Karin, that was one of HIS books!

KARIN: (*pulls her head up and looks at it boozily; opens it, reads out inscription on first page*) 'For Karry to read to Socrates, and perhaps teach him how to laugh. Love: Reggie St. Norman.'—huh! (*turns page*) 'Nonsense verse by Edward Lear.'

MARIE: (*puts hand to forehead; forces a laugh*) Dear ol' Reggie—ha ha ha— Oh, Karin, you would have loved dear Reggie, he was . . . he was a real good sort, an absolute darling, mad as a hatter of course, he'd . . . he'd do anything for a wager—

KARIN: And the allusion to humorless Socrates?

MARIE: (*laughs*) He was only a boy—ha ha ha—he meant no . . . he was only eighteen or so at the time . . . and I . . . I was only a girl, only just past twenty . . . Reggie was—

KARIN: A real good sort.

MARIE: Oh yes, he . . . (*swallows*) He was killed in the battle of Britain . . . most of them were killed later . . . (*shakes her head sadly*) The finest group of young men you could ever hope to meet . . . the cream of their generation . . . Reggie, Alex Thompson, Dickie Forsythe, Hughie Rawlings . . . I've forgotten most of their names now . . . But that was later . . . (*laughs*) Then it was a beautiful gay house, I'll show you, Karin. (*goes back to her frantic rummaging; now drawers fall to the floor, contents heaping up all over the place. She gets to her hands and knees*) Look, Karin! A postcard from Alex Thompson . . . (*laughs*) He went to Florence with Lavinia Swain . . . She was a girl, Lavinia . . . my best friend . . . mad as a—(*looks into envelopes, packages, boxes, her back to* KARIN *whose head has now fallen into her arms on the table*) See all this . . . this is history, Karin . . . all this is history . . . proof . . . proof that this was once a living house . . . a living vital house. (*Sobs*) This was a . . . (*sniffs back tears. In a corner she finds an old wind-up gramophone and a pile of records.*) Look, Karin! (*laughter that sounds more like anguished crying*) The old gramaphone . . . HE bought it for me—ha ha ha—and there are still some records left . . . (*picks up record in dusty brown papaer jacket. Blows dust off. Winds up player and puts on record: a cliche pop song of the period. Speaks above music*) Listen Karin! Karin! Are you listening? (*hums the tune for a while, and after punctuates monologue with humming. Tears streaming down her face all the while: the effect is macabre*) That's proof, eh? That's proof of how this house used to be . . . (*laughs*) I remember this . . . la la di la la la di da—Oh how I remember this—la la di da—on summer's evenings, music and laughter floated all through the house—la la di da— all the windows open, all the doors open . . . the sweet smell of summer, laughter . . . music—la la di da—the house swelling with joy and excitement . . . (*covers her face with her hands and weeps bitterly*) Karin . . . listen . . . close your eyes and imagine . . . isn't it proof . . . isn't it, Karin . . . Karin . . . isn't it . . .

The record ends, the needle scratches out an ugly rhythm in the almost silent room. Up the street a shrill whistle: the muffled sound of pounding machinery comes to a halt. A long pause. MARIE *sniffs back tears; dries her eyes with the back of her hand.*

MARIE: Karin? . . . Are you still there?

KARIN: I'm imagining . . .

MARIE: (*Almost a whisper*) You are?!

KARIN: Yes.

MARIE: *(climbs to her feet awkwardly, excitedly)* YOU ARE! *(pulls a chair close to* KARIN*)* You DO believe me. YOU DO! Oh, Karin! Tell me what you are imagining?

KARIN: *(voice, as always, cold, monotonous)* It's the sweet-smelling summer of nineteenthirtysomething, a group of young men and women, all good sorts, all mad as hatters of course, sit around an iron table under a chestnut tree, sipping cool drinks and listening to a record popular at the time. A young beautiful woman, with long blond hair tied in a yellow ribbon, wearing a light yellow dress, rushes from one person to the next, pouring drinks and laughing, as if competing with the gramophone; her voice, her laughter, increasing in volume as her anxiety increases lest the gramophone should silence her; she's also afraid the record will come to an end for she hasn't even got confidence in her own ability to sustain a continuous clamour. Suppose the record should stop? Suppose her voice should suddenly fail? Suppose her friends—could she really trust them?—should fall silent? What then?

Opens her eyes; lifts her head to look up at MARIE. MARIE *shakes her head, puzzled, bewildered.*

MARIE: What's . . . what's going on?

KARIN *drinks, closes her eyes.* MARIE *gulps her drink, most of it flowing down her face, mingling with, and washing away, her cosmetic mask. Now* MARIE *looks more than her age; she looks ugly; her voice is just a tremulous whisper.*

KARIN: Now she's dancing on the grass. Her feet, as feverish as her tongue, pound to paste the daisies that she'd used earlier to make a chain, to bind the boneless limbs of a little girl, also wearing a yellow dress, a yellow ribbon in her blond hair, so that she couldn't move from her corner somewhere over there; so that she couldn't approach the iron table and maybe cause the laughter, the dancing, even the very music to cease, for although she was barely born, her huge eyes had an uncanny opaqueness even in the brilliant sun that made others blink and use their hands as shades; that told of an early blindness brought about by seeing too much and all at once.

MARIE: What in the name of God are you talking about?

116

KARIN: And if that should happen—

MARIE: (*shakes her head feverishly*) You're drunk, Karin, you're—

KARIN: And if that should happen, then the blond woman and all her gay guests would be frozen to sobriety by the deathly screams coming from a room on the first floor of that living vital house.

MARIE: Screams? What screams? (*leans over and looks into Karin's face, whose eyes remain closed*) What the hell is going on in there, Karin?! (*Yells*) WHAT THE HELL'S GOING ON? I SAID?!

KARIN: (*same cold monotonous voice*) On this sweet-smelling summer's day of nineteenthirtysomething the sun floods the room on the first floor, with the long windows overlooking the elms in the backgardens of elegant Chesterfield Street. The room is without furniture, carpets, drapes, books. The walls are in rags, just ribs and dried-up gut hanging down between them. The door is locked from the outside. The solitary figure of a man stands in the recess of the window. It's HIM. And although he stands directly in the sun's rays he casts no shadow. From the back HE looks young. But from the front his pallid flesh is creased, cadaverous, jaws concave, eyes lost in sockets, lips lost in fold over toothless gums. And although his toothless mouth never opens—he screams!

MARIE: (*her whole body trembling, her head shaking so violently that she has to rush her hands to her temples to steady it*) Eyeless! Lipless! Toothless! Oh for God's sake stop it! Why is he screaming? How can he scream if he doesn't open his—Who is he?

KARIN: He screams because yesterday he was just a boy, free in the illusory way all boys and men are free; but today he is an old man, a prisoner; and worse: tomorrow he knows the sentence will be carried out—

MARIE: Sentence? (*hand over mouth*) What happens to him?

KARIN: (*raises her head and stares at her*) Don't you know?

MARIE: (*hand slips up to hide her eyes*) No.

KARIN: I'll tell you. (*pause*) Tomorrow he suffers the absolute penalty: violent bloody death!

MARIE: Why? (*gasps*)

KARIN *gets up and goes to one of her suitcases, opens it, takes out a two-hundred carton of French cigarettes. Takes out a packet; takes out a cigarette —all her movements awkward—throws the carton across the room on top of all the other rubbish; staggers back and falls into her chair. She lights a cigarette and smokes noisily for a while.*

KARIN: To understand the crime, you must understand the criminal—

MARIE: I don't understand *anything* anymore . . . (*drinks*) No . . . I don't know WHAT you're talking about . . . (*ruffles her hair*) I need a cigarette, I need a drink . . . (*She takes one of Karin's cigarettes, lights it, coughs, throws the match over her shoulder.*)

KARIN: The boy—man was sensitive: too, too sensitive; his nature was more suited to poetry than banking—

MARIE: (*gasps*) You're talking about HIM!

KARIN: HE had a highly developed intellect, but he never allowed it to rule him from his own body; he thought of it as an equal to his little finger, his arms, his legs, just a part of the whole; and the whole owed its very existence to the soul that lived before flesh and would go on after it. So thought the man. He met a woman. He married her for love. To him it was meaningless to talk about 'Till death do us part'. To him the union was of body and soul; death didn't come into it. Banker though he was, the soul was not negotiable, but could only be given once and to one person; and since the body was also of the soul, it too was not negotiable and could only be given once and to one person. Imagine his horror when one morning he found his body lying in a bed beside the body of a strange woman. To him this was not just an offence of carnal adultery— Oh no! It was a complete and absolute betrayal of the soul! (*pause*) The man believed he was God, he believed that all men were God. It was as the God of wrath that he sat in judgement on himself. God found him guilty and sentenced him to life imprisonment; but after one day, which was a lifetime, God felt dissatisfied with the punishment and reversed the sentence to death.

MARIE: (*head wavering, looks strangely at her*) What's all this about . . . this is supposed to be an alleg-alleg—damn it, I can't even pronounce the—an allegory . . . this is supposed to be an allegory, isn't it?

KARIN: (*pause. Sips drink. She's also finding it difficult to keep her head up.*)

You asked me: What do you see? What are you imagining?

MARIE: (*points stupidly at herself*) Me? I—

KARIN: YOU! You asked me. I told you.

MARIE: (*suddenly jumps up, knocking chair over; still holding cup, she staggers dangerously across the room to the window*) BELIEVE ME . . . please BELIEVE ME, I don't understand a word you're saying . . . I—

KARIN: (*sotto voce*) You understand all right.

MARIE: (*shouts*) Am I not allowed to say what I understand and what I don't understand? I'm not HIM, I'm no intellectual, I'm ME . . . just . . . just me . . .

KARIN: (*swings around; thumps herself violently on the chest, shouting and sobbing*) ME! ME! ME! (*slowly faces the window again*)

KARIN: What happened to HIM? (*long pause.* MARIE *sucks her drink noisily. Sniffs back tears.*) What happened to him, Karin-Marie?

MARIE: I . . . I don't know . . .

KARIN: You DO know. (*long pause*)

MARIE: Karin?

KARIN: Yes? (*pause*)

MARIE: I didn't tell you before . . . I didn't want to upset you . . . (*pause*) I'm . . . I'm a sick woman, Karin—

KARIN: I know . . . we're all sick, Karin-Marie.

MARIE: No, no, you don't understand, I'm . . . I'm a very sick woman . . . I should be in hospital . . . I've got CANCER, Karin, I didn't want to tell you, I didn't want to worry you, seeing as how you were just passing through, but the specialist said I hadn't long to—

KARIN: (*suddenly jerks upright and literally screams at her*) WHAT HAPPENED TO HIM?

MARIE: (*starts. Gasping sob. Drops cup. Rushes hands to her face*) I don't know, I . . . (*tries to shout but can't*) I don't know! I don't know! I don't know! (*She picks up cup shakily; goes to the table shakily; pours another drink shakily; and shakily returns to the window without once meeting the other's eyes. She gazes out silently for a while.*)

KARIN: (*pours herself another drink; she's now very drunk; with great difficulty she lights another cigarette; she props her head up with her hand and looks over at Marie*). I know what happened to him.—

MAIRE: (*almost a whisper*) Then why do you persist in asking questions?

KARIN: HE was executed. What I want to know is how?

MARIE: (*drinks*) More riddles . . .

KARIN: How was the sentence carried out?

MARIE: (*runs her hand through her hair*) I should be . . . I should be in hospital. I'm a very sick woman . . . (*pause*)

KARIN: How?

MARIE: Your poor mind is in a terrible mess, Karin . . . you should be in hospital too . . .

KARIN: I've been in and out of hospitals for the past ten years.

MARIE: Couldn't they help you?

KARIN: No. They didn't understand the questions.

MARIE: Well, what hope have I got then, a sick woman, if the professional couldn't—

KARIN: It came late to me, but it came, that the answers were all here; all here in this squalid room.

MARIE: Executions and God knows what . . . (*She trembles all over as she hears* KARIN's *chair move; as she hears* KARIN's *unsteady legs move towards her back. Stammering; not turning*) What do you want? (*long pause.* KARIN *stands just a yard behind her back*) W—What do you—

KARIN: (*coldly*) ANSWERS!

MARIE: I can't—

KARIN: (*voice rises to a shout at the last word*) You can and you bloody well WILL!

MARIE: (*without turning; shouts*) WHAT?! ASK ME! AND THEN FOR GOD'S SAKE LEAVE ME! LEAVE ME!

KARIN: How did HE execute himself?

MARIE: Must you use such—

KARIN: ANSWERS!

MARIE: (*swings around, suddenly shocked by the proximity of* KARIN's *eyes; stumbles back against the window like a cornered, hunted animal*) He . . . his car skidded . . . across a road into a wall . . . he was going too fast . . . much too fast they said . . . it was in the country . . . somewhere, there was no one else involved . . . no witnesses . . . no one will ever know exactly what happened . . . I was asked to identify the body . . . but I couldn't be sure it was him . . . I told them I wasn't sure . . . but a dentist said it was him from a filling he'd done in one of his teeth . . . I didn't want to go to the morgue . . . I . . . I didn't want to go, but they said I had to . . .

KARIN: (*closes her eyes*) So that's how he did it.

MARIE: (*looks at her furtively, guiltily, for just a second*) It . . . it was an accident . . .

Long pause. They stand, both very drunk, opposite each other. The older woman holds her head down; the younger woman inspects her from head to toe to head.

KARIN: Who are you?

MARIE *closes her eyes, shakes her head.*

KARIN: (*almost a whisper*) Look up please.

MARIE: (*almost a whisper*) Go now . . . in the dream you were just passing

121

through. Go now . . . soon this house will be no more, even as I will be no more . . . say good-bye and go . . .

KARIN: Look up . . . (*pause; shouts*) LOOK UP!

MARIE *starts. Head jerks up with a gasp.*

KARIN: WHO ARE YOU?

MARIE *looks wildly about her for a means of escape; she staggers away from* KARIN *to the right towards the door.* KARIN *staggers after, falling over a heap of junk, she scrambles to her feet and meets up with* MARIE *who has also fallen, also risen, and now she squashes herself into a corner next to the door. This short burst of activity has winded both women.*

KARIN: (*facing* MARIE. *Swallows to catch her breath*) Answer me, woman!

MARIE: PLEASE . . .

KARIN: WHO ARE YOU?

MARIE: Leave me alone!

KARIN: (*almost a whisper*) Answer me. (*shouts*) ANSWER ME! (*Again* MARIE *rushes past her, again falling and again dragging herself to her feet. Finding herself trapped in another corner as* KARIN *approaches, staggering, stumbling, falling, pulling herself up*) GO! JUST GO! (*As* KARIN *approaches she rushes again, falls again, but now exhausted, she just squats on the floor among the rubbish, head bowed, breathing stertorously.* KARIN *has also fallen a few yards away from her. She drags herself right up to* KARIN MARIE.) Leave me . . . leave me alone . . .

KARIN: Who are you?

MARIE: Leave me . . .

KARIN: (*shouts through clenched teeth*) WHO ARE YOU?

MARIE: (*screams*) I DON'T KNOW! I DON'T KNOW! I DON'T KNOW! (*breaks down completely*) I . . . I don't know . . .

Long pause. KARIN *just looks at the sobbing heap of* MARIE *with cold vacant eyes.*

KARIN: I want to touch you —

MARIE: (*starts. Head jerks up for just a second*) NO!

KARIN *reaches out her trembling hand slowly;* MARIE *drags herself away along the floor;* KARIN *follows her in the same fashion. Once again they come to a halt.*

KARIN: (*reaches out her trembling hand*) I want to touch you.

MARIE: (*tries to make herself smaller*) NO!

KARIN: (*through clenched teeth*) I HAVE to touch you!

MARIE: (*face buried in her hands*) NOOOOOO . . .

KARIN: (*touches her shoulder, hand trails down and cups her breast*) Nothing . . . Nothing . . . Nothing . . .

MARIE: Nothing . . .

Long pause. Both women squatting amongst the junk. MARIE, *head bowed, sobbing quietly now;* KARIN, *head bowed, looking strangely at the hand that has just touched* MARIE.

MARIE: The man God lay with nothing. In his dream HE had dreamt a woman and he lay between her thighs, hot as fire, wet as water, free as air, solid as earth. He was asleep in pure love, holy love; and at the height of his ecstasy he ejaculated; and some nine months later, nothing presented God with nothing. God named nothing Karin. In unconscious collusion with the woman of his wet dream HE allowed nothing to wander the earth disguised as a beautiful girl named Karin, causing chaos, confusion, pain, suffering, and eventually murder.

MARIE: (*looks up with a start. Averts her eyes*) Murder?

KARIN *nods her bowed head.*

MARIE: Did you . . . did you hate him?

KARIN: No. (*pause*)

MARIE: Did he hate you?

123

KARIN: No. He loved me, but LOVED me. (*pause*) He asked: Will you marry me? I thought: No! Never! Go away beautiful child, go away before I destroy you! I said: Yes. Early in the day, his love was powerful, like a great bursting river in spring, that I could conceal my nothingness in its spray. He said: I love you! I love you! I love you! The flame in his eyes was so intense it forced reflection on my opaqueness. He was an innocent, beautiful boy. He saw only what he wanted to see: my eyes aflame with reciprocal love. Even then early in the day, I knew that his fate was related to that of Narcissus. How could it be otherwise, when unbeknown to himself, second by second, he was falling more and more in love with the reflection of his own love. He asked: do you love me, Karin? I thought: there's still time to save yourself, beautiful child; GO, FOR GOD'S SAKE GO! I said: yes. He asked: do you truly love me, Karin? I thought: I have no truth. I said: yes, I truly love you. And once he said: We'll have children, Karin, many, many beautiful children. I thought: We'll have no children; I have no blood. I said: yes, we'll have children. He said, with persistence and excitement: BUT MANY, MANY, BEAUTIFUL CHILDREN! I said: yes, many, many, beautiful children.

MARIE: (*almost a whisper*) Did the blood never come, Karin? (*pause*) No, the blood never came. (*pause*). In the afternoon of his love, the flame in his eyes cooled, even as his body grew more feverish. He pleaded: KARIN, DO YOU LOVE ME?! And: KARIN, DID YOU COME, DID YOU?! DID YOU, KARIN?! DID YOU COME?! I thought: what's he talking about? What does he mean by COME? I said: Yes, yes, I've come. He tried hopelessly to keep the truth behind him; but the truth was with him, so that when he turned this way, there it was in front of his eyes: he'd quickly turn the other way only to find it still there. My head lay heavily in the pillow, I used my long hair as a drape to hide my eyes from the light of the candle he'd brought in a desperate effort to infuse mystery and passion into our cooling bed. I said: Will you do something for me? He said: ANYTHING, Karin, I will do ANYTHING for you; why can't I make you happy? Oh, why can't I make you happy, Karin? I said: WHIP ME, WHIP ME UNTIL I BLEED!

MARIE: (*gasps*) NO! KARIN! . . . OH GOD . . .

KARIN: (*speaks through her*) He turned away from me and wept. Towards the night of his love, he added alcohol to candlelight in a hopeless attempt to keep the frost from our bed, He said: KARIN, I'LL WHIP YOU! I'LL WHIP YOU UNTIL YOU BLEED! He whipped me, and the only blood that flowed,

flowed from his own mutilated soul. In the evening of his sick, sad love, I thought the only way to save him was to make him hate me so he'd leave. He was a painter. A week before an exhibition of his work I went into his studio and ripped his canvases to shreds—

MAIRE: (*gasps*) NO!

KARIN: Later he sat amongst the chaos, head in hands, just sobbing and whispering over and over: But Karin, why? I love you, I love you, I love you . . .

(*Now the big blue neon sign of the 'Blue Bell' goes on: flashing on and off at intervals, flooding the dimly lit chaotic room with an incongruously gay light; adding to it's gloominess when it's on: adding to its eeriness when It withdraws. The muffled sounds of a jazz band playing an arranged version of a pop ballad floats in from across the street.*)

KARIN: Just before the midnight of his lost love he came to the frozen bed with a young whore he'd picked up in some nightclub. They were both drunk. He undressed her in front of me. I was sitting up in bed reading a book. They laughed all the time, he told her what a mad perverted frigid bitch he'd married.

MARIE: (*sobs. Shakes her head*) Poor you—

KARIN: (*snaps*) POOR HIM! (*pause*) Leaving all the lights on they both got into bed beside me and—as polite people would say—'made love' but in fact they fucked in the same frantic, feverish way as two drowning people maul each-other, knowing no one is coming to their rescue; knowing that they have only each other to cling to; and again knowing that neither of them can swim . . . and they continue to grapple until they reach the heavy depths where they are finally torn apart and crushed to eternal silence. (*Pause*).

MARIE: Didn't you leave?

KARIN: No.

MARIE: But . . . but what happened? (*pause*)

KARIN: He threw her out of the bed, screamed abuse at her and followed her as she snatched up her clothes and backed out of the room. (*pause*) Then he caught her by the hair and beat her up so violently that she couldn't even scream for help.

MARIE: And you . . . just . . . just watched?

KARIN: Yes. He threw her and her cheap rags out into the street. (*pause*) He came back and stood in the doorway, naked, his head bowed, his body stained with the whore's blood, and he raised his head to face me. He tried to say something . . . his eyes welled with tears, his black hair disheveled, his face calm for his final confession, he looked the beautiful child again. He shook his head, then turned and walked to his empty studio; empty because he hadn't painted since his temple had been desecrated by the barbarian. I got out of bed and followed him, for I knew what he had to do; but I also knew what I had to do. In the drawer of his desk he had a luger pistol brought back from the war by his late father. Although he was by nature a passive man who couldn't kill a fly, he kept that weapon in perfect working order. I don't know why. Perhaps in some uncanny way he always knew his destiny . . . (*pause*) I came into the studio to face his naked back, the luger raised and pressed to his temple. I called his name. (*pause*) He made no reply. (*pause*) He just stood trembling, never turning, never seeing me again. (*pause*) I pulled the trigger and he was released from my sin. (*long pause*)

MARIE: (*head still bowed and holding her hands to her face, sobs. Whispers*) Oh God, I need something . . .

KARIN: (*without looking up*) Try a slice of bread and honey from Yucatan . . . (*pause*)

MARIE: Karin?

KARIN: Yes?

MARIE: It was I who squashed his foot on the accelerator of the car; it was I who grabbed the steering wheel from his hands and swung it crashing through the rough-rocked country wall . . . I . . . I murdered too, Karin . . . (*pause*)

KARIN: Yes, you murdered, Karin-Marie, but not two, you murdered THREE. (*pause*)

MARIE: (*shakes her head*) THREE? . . . did I? . . . did I, Karin? (*pause*)

KARIN: You murdered HIM; you murdered yourself; you murdered me.

Long pause. They just squat on the floor, heads bowed tableau-like amongst the heap of junk. The blue light flashing on and off at intervals. Footsteps coming up the front steps. A loud knocking on the frontdoor. The women act as if they'd heard nothing, but remain in the same attitudes during the following off-set dialogue.

FIRST MAN:(*Cockney*) Karin-Marie! (MARIE *puts on her spectacles. He whistles.*) Karin-Marie!

SECOND MAN:(*Cockney*) She aint in.

FIRST MAN: The light's on.

SECOND MAN: The ol' cow always keeps the light on, she's as scared as shit of her own shadow.

FIRST MAN: (*kicks the door*) MARIE! KARIN MARIE! ARE YOU IN THERE?! I KNOW YOU'RE IN THERE! IT'S ME, TEDDY FROM THE 'BLUE BELL'. THAT CHEQUE YOU CASHED HAS BOUNCED BACK!

SECOND MAN:(*lower voice*) How much was it for anyway?

FIRST MAN: 'Undred nicker.

SECOND MAN: On the tables I suppose?

FIRST MAN: She lives on the bloody tables.

SECOND MAN: (*anxiously*) Ay, Ted, watch it for Christ's sake, don't climb up on those railings; you'll
　　　　　FIRST MAN: What are we goin' to tell the govenor?

SECOND MAN: She wasn't in.

FIRST MAN: Soon find out . . .

SECOND MAN: What are you doin'?

FIRST MAN: If you hear a scream she's in, if you don't she's out . . .

A brick comes crashing through the window; neither of the women react.

FIRST MAN:She's out.

SECOND MAN: Come on.

FIRST MAN: What the 'Ell are we goin' to tell the governor?

Footsteps fade away. The two women raise their heads simultaneously; they stare at each other.

KARIN: *(softly)* I can't see you with those coloured spectacles on.(MARIE *raises a shaking hand to her specs, her hand hesitates for a few seconds as she touches them*) Let me see you, Karin-Marie . . . (MARIE *takes the specs off slowly and averts her eyes. Pause. Slowly she looks up and their eyes meet and hold for a time.*) I see you now.

MARIE:(*closes her eyes briefly; nods her head*) I . . . I see you now . . . *(pause)*

KARIN: During my search, I came across many wise men, I can't remember their names or half of what they said . . . but one of them—I think he was a Russian—said something that's made an impression on what's left of my mind.

MARIE: What? What did he say to you, Karin?

KARIN: He said: Nothingness is immanent evil . . . *(pause)*

MARIE: *(swallows, head bowed)* Nothingness . . . nothingness is immanent . . . evil . . . *(pause)*

KARIN: Would you agree with that, Karin-Marie?

MARIE: *(nods her head)* I think . . . I—yes . . . *(pause)*

KARIN: Do you remember when we spoke earlier about evil? About recognizing evil?

MARIE: Yes, I remember . . .

KARIN: And when we recognize it, what should we do about it, Karin-Marie? *(pause)*

MARIE:(*swallows. Looks up at* KARIN; *their eyes hold*) Stamp it out . . .

KARIN: *(through clenched teeth; yet almost a whisper)* DESTROY IT!

MARIE:(*nods her head. Softly*) Yes . . . destroy it . . .

They stare searchingly at each other as the curtain falls slowly.

The Vansittarts and the Bullworkers

ANTHONY SWERLING

THE VANSITTARTS AND THE BULLWORKERS was first presented at The Roebuck theatre on London's Fringe, during July, 1976. It was produced by Louina Beaballa, directed by Kate Crutchley, and featured the following actors:

JONATHAN *(industrialist in his early fifties)* .... David Gant
JANE *(his wife, late thirties)* .... Anne Robson

Approximate playing time: 30 minutes

A simple and elegant room. A dark winter morning. Covered by coats, curtains and a table cloth, JONATHAN *and* JANE *are lying fully clothed in a makeshift bed on the carpet.* JONATHAN *is clearly awake.* JANE *is asleep. He lights a cigarette which suddenly wakes her. She gets up, turns on the light, walks to the window presumably overlooking a garden, and looks out.*

JANE: So many unexploded bombs in the garden that we could open a munitions boutique.

JONATHAN: Not another overnight attempt to blow us up?

JANE: Afraid so.

JONATHAN: They've failed again.

JANE: No room for complacency.

JONATHAN: We really ought to go to the police this time.

JANE: The police . . . they won't do anything. Our safety's no longer their concern.

JONATHAN: We might at least report . . .

JANE: What's the use? We're not the only ones. Anyway the duty officers demand U.S. dollars and jewellery before filing a complaint.

JONATHAN: A few earrings and bracelets can buy a great deal in terms of security.

JANE: Not necessarily.

JONATHAN: I sometimes wonder whose side the police are on.

JANE: Certainly not ours.

JONATHAN: *(getting up, putting his shoes on)* We've been stuck in here too long. I'm getting claustrophobia. Got to go for a walk. It's a lot safer in the morning.

JANE: Don't go out, Jonathan. Don't leave me alone—not with the Bullworkers in the bathroom. Besides, the garden path's probably mined.

JONATHAN: Thank God they didn't come down in the night.

JANE: They probably did.

JONATHAN: I would have heard them. The Bullworkers don't tread softly.

JANE: Have a good sleep?

JONATHAN: Not all that bad, considering.

JANE: To think we were too frightened to go to our own bedroom in our own home. *(pause) You* were frightened. Not me. You're the coward in the family.

JONATHAN: I dare you to go to the bathroom now. I dare you to invite the Bullworkers down for breakfast.

JANE: Bugger the Bullworkers and bugger the bathroom.

JONATHAN: You're just as scared as me.

JANE: Funny couple, the Bullworkers.

JONATHAN: To say the least.

JANE: How long have they been upstairs?

JONATHAN: *(looking at his watch)* About thirteen hours.

JANE: Maybe they've fallen asleep—or sick.

JONATHAN: Wishful thinking. Just before you woke up . . .

JANE: *(interrupting)* You woke me up with your smoking.

JONATHAN: About half an hour ago I could hear them splashing about in the bath with the overflow pipe gushing down the wall like Niagara Falls. They were singing revolutionary songs—and whistling like nobody's business. I'm glad they didn't wake you up.

JANE: Smoke wakes me up, not songs. *(Pause)* No one's ever taken a bath in this house without asking my permission—not even you.

JONATHAN: Wonder why they don't come downstairs.

JANE: It's not shyness, that's for sure.

JONATHAN: Hope they washed the bath and tidied up a bit.

JANE: That's the least of our worries.

JONATHAN: Let's forget about them for the time being—and enjoy this period of non-confrontation.

JANE: I can't get them out of my mind—and dread the horror of finding that Iris and Manfred Bullworker have left their hairs in the bath, tarnished the new taps with their breath, defiled the tiles, filthied the bidet, used our towels, toothbrush and paste. Makes me ill to think that Iris is or has been rubbing my face cream into her wrinkles.

JONATHAN: She didn't have all that many.

JANE: A few round the eyes.

JONATHAN: She's so coarse. Probably thinks my aftershave's some kind of scent. I can visualise her using my best *eau de cologne* to deodorise her groin—and my razor to shave it.

JANE: Sponging her armpits and behind with my face flannel—the bitch, powdering herself from top to bottom with my talc.

JONATHAN: They're quiet enough now.

JANE: For how long?

JONATHAN: Maybe they'll come down and say something like, "Sorry we decided to take a bath. We won't stay for breakfast. God bless you both." And then get the hell out of our lives.

JANE: As if . . .

JONATHAN: If only . . .

JANE: Odd details keep coming back to me. The way they were more interested in talking to each other than to us . . .

JONATHAN: Open the window. Freshen the atmosphere a bit.

JANE: Opening windows is a man's job.

JONATHAN: *(trying to open)* It's stuck, jammed.

JANE: What about the door?

JONATHAN: Let's leave it closed. For safety's sake.

JANE: We're powerless to stand up to them. What with our beautiful manners and self-control.

JONATHAN: It's not only that. They've weakened us somehow.

JANE: And we can't throw in our lot with them.

JONATHAN: They disdain us through and through.

JANE: We're going to lose out.

JONATHAN: They're going to hit us hard.

JANE: Perhaps to the extent of a death sentence.

JONATHAN: Perhaps worse.

JANE: What's worse?

JONATHAN: Taking possession of our souls.

JANE: They can take my soul—as long as they leave me my body. *(Pause)* It seems ages since I went for a walk, with my rib-cage, pelvis, spine and limbs all moving to a coordinated rhythm. I miss my steady pace of three miles an hour.

JONATHAN: It was your idea to invite them in.

JANE: I didn't invite them. They banged on the door demanding shelter. You've forgotten how wet it was last night.

JONATHAN: We should have let them rot in the rain.

JANE: I didn't ask them to stay indefinitely.

JONATHAN: With people like that you've got to set a time limit beforehand.

JANE: We seem to attract the hooligan element.

JONATHAN: *(nervously blurting out)* Mention them again—and I'll leave you.

JANE: And our bargaining unit will be left with a single voice. Besides, you'll have nowhere to go.

JONATHAN: All's quiet.

JANE: For the time being. Their silence worries me. I'd give anything to know what they're up to.

The sound of breaking crockery comes from upstairs.

JANE: Not my collection of China.

JONATHAN: Maybe an accident.

JANE: Or the beginning of the demolition. *(Sound of a vacuum cleaner.)* Probably drying their hair with a vacuum cleaner, ignorant bastards.

JONATHAN: Can't remember the last time I wasn't on edge.

JANE: Why bother to remember? At times like this memories are unnecessary luxuries.

JONATHAN: Which I can't do without. *(Pause)* Last week I saw a former Cabinet Minister trying to pass himself off as a chimney sweep.

JANE: We didn't go out last week.

JONATHAN: Must have been the week before.

Sounds of furniture being moved come from upstairs.

JANE: Already rearranging our furniture.

JONATHAN: Prior to a takeover. *(Slamming of a door)*

JANE: Sounds like the big wardrobe door.

JONATHAN: They're after our bedding and clothing.

JANE: The way they insisted on second helpings of supper, thumping the cutlery on the table.

JONATHAN: No more flashbacks please. *(Pause)* We're so vulnerable with a thatched roof instead of corrugated asbestos.

JANE: Reinforced concrete's better still.

JONATHAN: Staying here's a form of self-punishment.

JANE: Grim determination.

JONATHAN: Let's get out of here and go it alone.

JANE: That's no solution. The streets are full of Bullworkers and their brethren.

JONATHAN: I'd so much like to dissolve in mirth and say, "Ha, ha, they're up there, and we're down here. Isn't it funny?" But I can't.

JANE: They're not a bundle of giggles. *(She turns her fingers upwards and outwards in a classic gesture of despair.)*

JONATHAN: Maybe we're like England, losing every battle but the last.

JANE: Didn't know there was an optimistic flair in you.

Noise of moving, drilling and banging can be heard.

JONATHAN: They're redoubling their efforts.

JANE: Sounds like they're re-wiring the house.

JONATHAN: Trust the Bullworkers to come up with something daringly different.

JANE: They're philosophers, all right.

JONATHAN: Them? Philosophers? You're kidding. And what might their philosophy be, perchance?

JANE: The grand old revolutionary one of instant gratification, of getting what you can while you can.

JONATHAN: I hope we'll qualify for a roll of muffled drums and a few strains of the Last Post.

JANE: Don't count on it. *(Pause)* I want to use the bathroom.

JONATHAN: Share it with the Bullworkers?

JANE: I'm bursting.

JONATHAN: What for?

JANE: To pee.

JONATHAN: Go into the garden.

JANE: I'm frightened.

JONATHAN: Go into the kitchen, then, and do it in the sink or a pan.

Exit Jane nervously. JONATHAN *hides his head in his hands but straightens up when* JANE *returns. Before she has time to sit down the morning paper is thrust through the letterbox. She picks it up and hands it to* JONATHAN.

JONATHAN: Thank heaven there are still newspapers. Fewer pages and the ink's not as black as before but papers all the same. *(Reading newspaper)* There are rabid dogs at large, causing annoyance to passers-by and danger to residents, spreading sheep-pox and cattle-plague, swine fever and fowl-pest.

JANE: *(yawning)* I dreamt that half the year's rain had fallen this week and most on me. *(Pause)* We're reduced to our own frothy salivering.

JONATHAN: How's your angelic body?

JANE: Though my breathing's getting quicker, I feel dull and lazy. No appetite. I feel like a sow who's been over-serviced by a boar.

JONATHAN: The things that come into your mind and out of your mouth.

JANE: I was perfectly demur until I married you.

JONATHAN: You needed fattening.

JANE: And now I need milking.

JONATHAN: *(getting up)* I hate Mr. and Mrs. Bullworker so much that I can hardly stand up.

JANE: Sit down then.

JONATHAN: I can't—'cause when I sit down I seem to see their snake-like heads even more vividly. *(Pause)* I'll have to lie horizontal, supine or prone, parallel to the skies. *(This he does for most of the play, now on his back, now on his stomach.)*

JANE: I wonder if all this animal disease affects the health and comfort of the workers.

JONATHAN: It must be detrimental. I suppose it seriously impairs their amenities. They lose a lot of money as well. Some of them are fond of their animals, and the *Times* says that the funerals they're arranging are causing undue traffic congestion.

JANE: Anyway the plague's keeping the farm labourers off the streets and out of mischief.

JONATHAN: To think that the Revolution has come with his minor form of plague, hand in glove with it.

JANE: Plague and revolution always go together. Each is an outgrowth of the other.

JONATHAN: I don't see how there could be a tangible connection between the animal and vegetable and the abstract and doctrinal.

JANE: There's nothing even vaguely abstract in this revolution. You know that as well as I do.

JONATHAN: Petrol bombs, sand-filled bottles, stones and sticks are adding to the confusion. Several people have been seriously and curiously injured in this district alone. I don't know whether it's frustration or greed.

JANE: A bit of both, I'd say.

JONATHAN: There's grief and agony too.

JANE: All revolutions begin by being a nuisance and end by being a terror. It's a battle for safety. The poor are flocking into the big cities while the rich are heading for the hills.

JONATHAN: There's safety in numbers.

JANE: There are only two of us at the moment.

JONATHAN: Can't we make peace with . . . the enemy?

JANE: They won't make peace with us since they clamped down on the army.

JONATHAN: They cracked down on them long ago, crippled them with their stranglehold. So much for our peace of mind. *(Pause)* Mrs. Bullworker's not all that bad. If I forced myself . . . There were those evening exercises of hers, the flamboyant, flamingo-like movements. If she hadn't been so obviously born to bread and cheese, she could have been almost anything. She's ambitious, that's for sure.

JANE: There's too much vigour and intensity in her. Her movements aren't healthy. And although her husband didn't—perhaps couldn't—utter a word, he seemed riddled with hypocrisy and cant. Even his silence seemed imitative.

JONATHAN: His virtues elude me.

JANE: I knew our foursome wouldn't be a harmless frolic when Mr. Bullworker tripped me up while you were out of the room. He didn't say a thing, just chuckled, and I crumbled inside.

JONATHAN: You've not breathed a word about this before.

JANE: I didn't want to upset you. (Pause) It's strange, Jonathan, that hideous couple are bringing us closer together. Tension and suspense normally make us fall apart.

JONATHAN: I'm dreading the moment we're face to face with them again, mind to mind, words to words.

JANE: The revolutionary powers-that-be have chosen an ideal time for their uprising, while our best troops are fighting in the Americas.

JONATHAN: Did Mr. Bullworker *have* to write "Thanks for your hospitality" all over our bedroom walls?

JANE: Did he?

JONATHAN: Yes.

JANE: How do you know it was him and not her?

JONATHAN: She never went to the bathroom despite drinking huge quantities of our tea. She never went upstairs until they both rushed up together. (Pause) Goodness knows how we managed to get them out of here. (Pause) He's not as simple as he looks. His soul is encased in a multitude of forms. He's a wise fool. His "Thanks for your hospitality" was more . . . than writing on the wall.

JANE: What did he write with?

JONATHAN: A ball-point pen. (Pause) Another thing I didn't tell you about was that he stuck a passage from St. Matthew's Gospel to the dressing-table-mirror, and wrote it over the walls: "For unto everyone that hath shall be given, and he shall have abundance; but from him that hath not shall be taken away even that which he hath."

JANE: There's still time for a happier land to emerge.

JONATHAN: But not for us to salvage ourselves.

JANE: Mr. Bullworker was the more frightening of the two. His silence seemed to militate against our generosity. It was as if his silence were screaming at us—"I cry shame on you."

JONATHAN: The malign silence of decay with its paralysing force . . . We musn't let them bring chaos into our home. Things are bad enough outside. *(Pause)* They've got the brains of buffaloes and could leave our minds lacerated, rotten, reduced to a pulp. Jane—we've forgotten the strangest thing about them. He had eight arms and his hands were clawed like those Indian statues, whereas she had two arms but never seemed to use them. She just dipped her face into the cup and drank her tea, lapping it up like a cat.

JANE: Fancy our forgetting a thing like that.

JONATHAN: How could we have forgotten such strange details?

JANE: I felt as helpless as a pancake.

JONATHAN: What makes you think pancakes are helpless?

JANE: Don't take me up on everything I say. I'm not in a very literal mood.

JONATHAN: Their pockets seemed to bulge with hand grenades! *(Pause)* I thought it very strange when she said, "Why don't you call your house the leaning Tower of Pisa?"

JANE: She asked it out of the blue, without warning, without any preparation whatsoever. Her talent for improvisation is quite alarming.

JONATHAN: Why do you think Bullworker's got eight arms?

JANE: If he had seven, I'd say each one represented one of the seven deadly sins: pride, covetousness, lust, anger, gluttony, envy and sloth. But that theory leaves one arm unaccounted for.

JONATHAN: Maybe there's an eighth sin we don't know about.

JANE: There's either a judgment on him or he's a freak. *(Pause)* Who are these creatures, the Bullworkers?

JONATHAN: They're like locust plagues which occur in cycles.

JANE: It's our fault for relaxing our vigilance.

JONATHAN: But this is green, fertile Great Britain, not the hungry landmass of Africa or Asia.

JANE: Now that the Bullworker-Bullfrogs are almost upon us again, I can't help thinking of how we finally manoeuvred them upstairs and Mr. Bullfrog's puzzling need to have every one of his hands shaken. As if going upstairs was going on a journey a long way away . . .

JONATHAN: So that between us we spent half an hour shaking hands with him.

JANE: As they left the room, there was a slight earth tremor.

JONATHAN: They were a strain, an enormous pressure on the earth, generating electric fields into the air. It was as if the earth's crust were reacting against them.

JANE: You seemed to notice more than me, Jonathan. I was too shattered to be aware of anything. I must have kept my eyes shut for a long time after they'd left us alone.

JONATHAN: They created high voltages and shock waves fanned out through the room.

Suddenly the electric lights go off.

JANE: How annoying, just when we need all the light and all the music we can get—organ duets, sea-shanties, drinking songs, catches, a sacred service, double oboe concertos, preludes and fugues. I want to hear music playing in my bones.

JONATHAN: It's all right. There are plenty of candles. It's only a power failure or a fuse or something. But I'm not in the mood to attend to it. Maybe another power plant's been flooded.

JONATHAN *lights a couple of candles. The rest of the play takes place in candlelight.*

JONATHAN: You kept nudging me and kicking me and whispering to me not to voice disapproval.

140

JANE: I didn't want a showdown. I didn't want to turn our newly-decorated house into a combat zone with Mr. Bullworker up in arms, with all his limbs coordinating, tearing me limb from limb, separating the layers of my skin, cutting me to shreds. *(Pause)* They're after us, and they want us to have the begging bowls. Iris said something about "Claridges will be littered with begging bowls."

JONATHAN: Until they came—I mean, all my life—I've always thought that the future was just a question of potluck as to which way you choose. But they seem to have been imposed upon us.

JANE: They've probably come to avenge the death of Trotsky.

JONATHAN: That was ages ago. Anyway, what's Trosky's death got to do with us?

JANE: There's a confusion of realms.

JONATHAN: Still, they'll want a hot drink when they come down and there's no electricity. We'd better use a candle and start now.

JANE: It's no use. They'll be here long before the water's even tepid. Let's just wait and see what happens. A hot drink isn't going to make all that difference.

JONATHAN: Jane. Let's try, let's make an effort—let's try and talk about something other than the Bullworkers—I mean the Leapfrogs. Let's play a game. The first to mention the Leapfrogs must give the other a pound.

JANE: All right. Here we go. Did you hear the joke about the tramp who managed to get onto the stage while a distinguished musician was playing the piano? The tramp faced the audience and said: "Tonight I'm going to play the piano." *(Stuttering)* I—I—I've forgotten how the jokes ends.

JONATHAN: I could have done with an explosion of laughter. There's something foul about a bad joke or a joke which can't get off the ground.

JANE: This conversation is almost as painful as talking about the Bullworkers.

JONATHAN: You've lost.

JANE: Lost what?

JONATHAN: You were the first to mention the Bullworkers.

JANE: Funny that we should be so helpless and forlorn in our own neighbourhood while our warships are shelling San Francisco and our proud navy is cruising the seven seas. *(Pause)* I'd better put my wooly on. It's getting rather chilly. *(She dons a pullover.)* We'll have to try and stop worrying about them. Too much worry can give you a nervous breakdown. You know what happened to Oscar Rappton, don't you?

JONATHAN: Even if we kept on worrying at this rate, it would take us at least a week before we contracted a nervous breakdown. If only we could take leave of our senses.

JANE: You're wrong. We must try to remain alert, and in control of the situation. *(Pause)* Are you sure we didn't—inadvertently—invite them to stay here for as long as they liked?

JONATHAN: I'm not sure if we did or we didn't. I'm not sure of anything now.

JANE: Yesterday, it seemed so natural to invite them to stay for supper. While you were doing the washing-up, Iris Bullworker said they'd come especially to see us, but were intending to make a day of it. So I suggested they stay for supper.

JONATHAN: You don't think they'll spend too long in the bathroom and give us an excuse for having no more to do with them?

JANE: I should have sent them for supper elsewhere, to the Mercury Restaurant, for example.

JONATHAN: Never heard of it.

JANE: I didn't tell you—just after dawn our self-styled benefactor rang us again.

JONATHAN: So I wasn't the only one to wake you up. *(Pause)* I didn't hear a thing. *(Pause)* What did he say?

JANE: The usual. His panting voice kept repeating that passing an electric current through water breaks it down into hydrogen and oxygen.

JONATHAN: I can't understand it. There's still a breatheable atmosphere. Maybe he thinks he's helping with his unnecessary tips.

JANE: He's not got the kind of voice to reassure us and bolster us up.

JONATHAN: Maybe they're using him to break down our morale—in the guise of benevolence. *(Pause)* Iris Bullworker seemed to be a virtuoso in vice, avid for rapture like those anxious dandies of the last century. Jane, I wouldn't mind doing battle with her. She ignites my turbulent fancy.

JANE: So you're becoming attuned to her?

JONATHAN: Attuned to her with helmet, shield and spear.

JANE: It would be easier if we weren't on speaking terms with them.

JONATHAN: Are we?

JANE: Iris had the alert eye of the pigeon and the swift movements of the vulture.

JONATHAN: And her husband kept repeating to himself: "My name is Mumbo-Jumbo and I'm an elephant."

JANE: Jonathan, you don't realise what you've just said. You've just remembered that Bullworker did in fact say something. *(Pause)* Come to think of it, he said quite a lot. His words came out by installments, as if he were paying off a debt to language.

JONATHAN: He kept calling me Charlie, although he knows my name's Jonathan.

JANE: How could we have thought that he kept silent?

JONATHAN: Especially as my face is still aching after all the defensive smiling I did.

Suddenly there is a loud banging on the ceiling. JANE *holds a candle over her watch to make sure of the time.*

JONATHAN: Maybe it's not them.

JANE: Who else could it be?

A brick is flung through the window and the VANSITTARTS *are covered in glass splinters.* JONATHAN *is evidently struck by a splinter.*

JANE: *(screaming)* Jonathan, are you badly hurt? Oh, Jonathan, I'll never say to you again "Do this, do that, don't go here, don't go there."

JONATHAN: *(wiping the blood off his face)* I've not got an ounce of strength left.

An old tin can is flung through the broken pane.

143

JANE: Someone's adding insult to injury. *(Pause)* The ordeal's been too much for me. I think I may have gone blind, gone blind, blind because we've sinned against the light. I can't see any more. Let the Bullfrogs come. We're outwitted before we start.

JONATHAN: Don't let's give them the satisfaction of an easy victory. *(Pause)* How *did* we manage to get them upstairs?

JANE: I don't think we manoeuvred them. They manoeuvred themselves. Iris asked: "Do you mind if we go to the bathroom? We've both got a little pain." You said, "No, please go ahead."

JONATHAN: What else could I have said? You can't refuse the use of your lavatory. It's a question of humanity and compassion. If only we had an outside toilet instead of an upstairs one.

JANE: *(whispering)* Don't let them notice I'm blind. Don't let them notice I'm afraid. They're like animals who can sense fear and can smell it. We musn't let them think twice. Jonathan, let's think of a better future and let's—let's sing.

JONATHAN: I can't sing. I'm finished, Jane.

JANE: Do your best. *(Begins)*
　　Greensleeves, you do me wrong
　　To cast me off discourteously
　　For I have loved you so long
　　Delighting in your company.

JONATHAN: Maybe I should have laughed at his jokes.

JANE: It's still not too late.

JONATHAN *forces himself to laugh loudly, directing his voice to where the bathroom is presumably situated.*

JONATHAN: It's just not done for two people to go to the bathroom together even if they both have a little pain. And even if they are husband and wife—particularly in someone else's home.

JANE: The bathroom is a vantage point in this house. Once you control the bathroom, you control the house, even the street. They're probably listening to us now. The walls are wafer-thin. Their "little pain" was their pretext.

JONATHAN: For what?

JANE: Did you leave his writing on the wall last night? *(Pause)* Well, did you tamper with it?

JONATHAN: I rubbed it off with a wet rag.

JANE: That's bound to have upset them. *(Pause)* It's difficult to get ballpoint ink off a wall even with a wet rag.

JONATHAN: I was fibbing. It wasn't a ballpoint ink. It was blood.

Suddenly IRIS BULLWORKER *shouts from upstairs.*

VOICE OF IRIS: Hello, can you hear me? We've locked ourselves in the bathroom by mistake. Do you mind letting us out?

JANE: Jonathan, there's no lock on the bathroom. There's never been a lock. In fact, I've always intended to put one on. And even if there were a lock, how could *we* help from the outside. *(Screams out to the Bullworkers:)* Break down the door, then.

VOICE OF IRIS: We can't. Please help.

JONATHAN: I think I'd better go and see what they've got up to. *(He drags himself out of his chair and slowly leaves the room. After a moment:)*

JANE: *(shouting)* What's the matter with the door? *(pause)*

JONATHAN: *(screaming)* Jane! They've ambushed me. They won't let me go. They're holding me hostage.

VOICE OF IRIS: Mrs Vansittart? *(Pause)* Jane? We'd like to invite you to join your husband. Are you ready? Like to come upstairs?

JANE: *(howling)* No! No!

VOICE OF IRIS: *(with authority)* The Bullworkers don't take no for answer.

VOICE OF JONATHAN: Jane, I love you, Jane.

The blind Jane gropes and stumblingly feels her way out of the room—and upstairs.

The stage is empty.

SLOW CURTAIN

Off-Off Broadway
& The College Theatre

In a controlled sampling of college and university theatre programs across the United States, *The Scene* found vigorous interest in Off-Off Broadway.

"An intriguing thing has happened to Off-Off Broadway. With the end of the 'revolution', it exploded from the geographical confines of New York to become what might be called the non-geography of an idea, now expanded throughout the country. Future activity may well find university theatre at the center of creative theatre. Certainly it is now beginning to exhibit the same excitement that characterized OOB in the 60's and early 70's."

This provocative response came from the Department of Theatre Arts at the University of Kentucky in Lexington, as *The Scene* surveyed 16 drama department heads. All but four described their OOB "I.Q." as at least "fair," while precisely half of those queried indicated an intense interest.

The State University of New York at Binghamton, for instance, responded that "many students and staff members regularly see productions in the Off-Off."

Those who described their knowledge as merely fair typically revealed desire to learn more. At Carroll College's Youman's Little Theatre in Wankasha, Wis., David Molthen described available information as being limited to *Variety-New York Times*-type coverage and drama anthologies "all lacking depthy examination."

At the theatre department of the University of Michigan in Flint, Alfred J. Loup described himself as "slightly less than fairly" well informed about OOB and not familiar—"but I would like to be"—with OOB publications. Indeed only six of the 16 professors were familiar with such literature of the field.

25 percent deemed their students very knowledgeable about OOB, while another four thought their students fairly familiar with the scene.

45 percent of the theatre programs have produced plays by Off-Off Broadway playwrights; one indicated, however, that this is a rare occurrence. The drama department at the College of the Pacific in Stockton, California, for example, reported "the pleasure of doing several, including a European tour which in-

cluded a play by Benjamin Bradford,'' a playwright published in *The Scene*. Another program, which has not yet presented such works, replied that it at least has considered some. SUNY Binghamton reported having presented many, and at least five of the departments were mounting such productions on a continuing basis.

Seven of the colleges surveyed—interestingly not necessarily those who considered themselves *au courant* on OOB—said that OOB groups has been invited to perform on their campuses. Negative response to this question on inviting groups, however, did not necessarily indicate lack of interest. Two respondents mentioned insufficient budget for such events, while SUNY Binghamton said "almost never because those that tour are certainly no better than our own avant garde student productions, therefore not worth spending resources for them in a time of budget cutback." At Carleton College in Northfield, Minnesota, a professor who admitted unfamiliarity with OOB plays and publications reported that OOB touring had nonetheless reached there.

Here are capsule profiles of the programs surveyed.

Carleton College. Liberal arts undergraduate college, no drama major. Five major productions in arena theatre. Student studio productions in lab theatre (no definite number) and student-produced musicals (three).

College of the Pacific. 5 major productions: two dramatic, two comedy, one musical, on average. Also one Readers Theatre production and evenings of one act plays out of directing class. Moving into new facilities; current setup is proscenium thrust stage in house seating 456, of which 142 are balcony.

Dowling College. Loft Theatre, Oakdale, New York. Two stage facilities, the "Loft" and the Performing Arts Center. Does mostly experimental plays and some classics, Ned Bobkoff reports.

Carroll College. Youman's Little Theatre, Wankasha, Wisconsin. Small modified proscenium stage; 247 seat house. New mainstage and studio facility planned for 1977. Three mainstage productions; several original one acts; one or two touring productions yearly. Two majors in theatre—Professional, and Theatre Education. 24 students, two professors.

Columbus College. Columbus, Georgia. Offers B.A. in speech and drama, with concentration in drama. Three mainstage productions yearly. 25 majors, three faculty members, one costumer. Two theatres, mainstage seating 600 and experimental theatre seating 50 to. In 75-6 produced Tango, a Polish

147

play by Slawomir Mrozek, and Camelot. Answered "No!" to all questions on awareness and receptivity to OOB.

Long Beach City College. Long Beach, California. Total of 250 students taking theatre classes; eight acting courses offered; two performance classes. Seven major productions per year, 12 or 13 experimental plays a year; 250-seat flexible theatre; full technical support.

North Carolina School of the Arts. School of Drama, Winston-Salem. Four-year professional undergraduate training leading to a B.F.A. or certificate of proficiency. Three mainstage productions; 200-seat house; six or seven well-dressed workshop productions in OOB scale 70-seat house. Variety of touring.

Indiana University-Purdue University. Fort Wayne, Indiana. B.A. in theatre; one stage, a 70′ by 346′ room, four to six productions yearly, two of them musicals.

Rio Hondo College. Theatre Arts Department, Whittier, California. Community college, 327-seat facility; three or four productions. Performs original plays and always interested in receiving scripts.

Southern Connecticut State College. Theatre department, New Haven. Full undergraduate major in theatre; enrollment 70; five full-time, five part-time faculty. Undergraduate production company; five major productions a year, three faculty-directed, one bill of student-directed one act plays, one faculty-directed children's show; 1650 seat auditorium, thrust stage; 100-200 seat flexible laboratory theatre.

Southwest Texas State University. Department of speech and drama, San Marcos. M.A., B.A., B.S. in theatre, 1971 theatre building; two theatres, proscenium and a thrust-arena. 140 majors, faculty of 11. Five major productions, five summer, ten student-directed productions.

Sperlman College. Department of Drama, Atlanta, Georgia. 350-seat proscenium theatre, fully equipped with showers, costume, property stage, costume shop, counterweight system, hub lighting board, backstage shop, dressing rooms. Four majors a year, productions varying from classical, modern, expressionistic to musicals.

SUNY. Binghamton, New York. Offers M.A. in theatre history, criticism, directing and acting; MBA in arts administration. Now accepting applications for a proposed certificate program in voice and body technique for the actor;

Ph.D. program awaiting implementation. Fine Arts Building houses Don A. Watters Theatre with 650-seat capacity; two 150-seat experimental theatres; all theatres have sophisticated sound and lighting systems. Facilities include rehearsal rooms, dance studio, modern shop facilities.

University of Kentucky. Department of Theatre Arts, Lexington. Offers B.A., M.A. Interaction with OOB: "will participate in the discovery of new plays and playwrights, innovative interpretations of the classics, contemporary approaches to informal theatre." Many productions.

University of Sciences and Arts of Oklahoma. Drama department, Chickasha. Four plays a year: one children show, one drama, one comedy, one musical. Little theatre houses 330; large auditorium 1500.

Thus *The Scene*'s rundown shows programs large, middling and small from all regions.

Obviously size and regional situation are no longer limiting factors to the spread of experimental drama.

Slaughter

ALFONSO VALLEJO

translated from the Spanish by Susan Meredith

Approximate playing time: 60 minutes

1.

On the right hand side, men's toilets. On the left, the ladies'. Both are separated by a partition through which communication is possible. The toilets on both sides are visible. RODRIGUEZ, *a thin, pale, sober-looking individual, racked by a cough, arrives on the scene. He glances behind him repeatedly, his face distorted with fear. He walks into the men's toilets, sits down on the lavatory seat, wipes the sweat from his brow and removes his false beard, hat and glasses. Shortly afterwards,* DOROTHY, *a young woman in her early twenties, arrives. She goes into the ladies' lavatory, kicks off her shoes, takes off her blouse, gets onto a chair, takes a bottle of wine out of the cistern, sprawls on the floor, lights a cigarette, fans herself and taking a radio out of her bag, tunes into a classical music programme.*

RODRIGUEZ: *(knocking on the partition)* Excuse me . . .

DOROTHY: *(Turning down the radio)* What do you want?

RODRIGUEZ: Excuse me, but I must make a confession to you. They're after me. They mean to kill me.

DOROTHY: Who's after you?

RODRIGUEZ: Wolves . . . snakes, monkeys . . . flies, mosquitoes, men . . .

DOROTHY: Carry on, I'm listening.

RODRIGUEZ: Are you sure I'm not making a nuisance of myself? My words are full of sorrow . . .

DOROTHY: I'm tough and I've plenty of time.

RODRIGUEZ: Well . . . to tell the truth . . . I don't quite know how to begin. You come here fairly often, don't you?

DOROTHY: Every day.

151

RODRIGUEZ: Have you . . . have you got an upset stomach?

DOROTHY: Well, you see . . . smoking's not allowed inside . . . I like it here. I smoke, drink, listen to music . . . This library's nothing like what it used to be.

RODRIGUEZ: It's very cool in summer . . . I like it too. Haven't you . . . haven't you a home to go to?

DOROTHY: Yes, I have, but I've got awful problems at home. I prefer being here. It's hell at home.

RODRIQUEZ: Same here.

DOROTHY: My father's a real Hitler . . . he's incredibly cruel. He forces my mother to play tennis for hours on end until she finally collapses on the court, exhausted, practically in coma . . . There are no limits to his cruelty. When he feels like it, he goes to bed with the maid and stays there for hours while my poor mother plays tennis in the garden on her own, against an unseen enemy, running from one side of the court to the other, hitting back the useless balls just to prolong the concubinage . . . balls . . . over and over again . . . Oh God!

RODRIGUEZ: How dreadful!

DOROTHY: On top of that, if she ever is unfortunate enough to miss the ball, even if she simply trips, my father gets out of bed, takes hold of the leather strap and doesn't stop beating her until she falls down unconscious. . . . Then, triumphantly, he gets into bed with another of our maids. . . . My life's meaningless. I'm not a skeptical young person, believe me. I'm living amid sorrow and desperation. It's only here that I find I can forget my existence.

RODRIGUEZ: I know you sometimes spend the night here . . . right there on that toilet which isn't intended to be a bed or a chair. You lean back against the wall with your neck twisted. . . . You'll end up with piles, you know. . . .

DOROTHY: I've made this into a little flat for myself.

RODRIGUEZ: I sometimes hear you singing a strange tune very late at night. My office is right next door. . . .

DOROTHY: I know you're listening to me.

RODRIGUEZ: Pardon?

DOROTHY: I know you're there until the early hours of the morning, deep in your calculations. . . . Professor . . . I'm in love with you. I know each one of your steps, I can tell your voice miles away . . . years away . . . light years. . . . Your voice is a logarithmic well deep inside me . . . a well of lustful exaltation . . . It's all because of you that I'm here, in these toilets, shut up for ever, as if I were in a cloister.

RODRIGUEZ: So you know me?

DOROTHY: I'm one of your students. I'm studying astronomy.

RODRIGUEZ: Dorothy. . . . Oh! I love you too.

DOROTHY: Really!

RODRIGUEZ: I've loved you for years . . . for 15 to 20 years. I've known you since you were a child, but I never dared tell you. I know your father. You're the deacon's daughter.

DOROTHY: Professor!

RODRIGUEZ: You're a revolutionary!

DOROTHY: A true revolutionary!

RODRIGUEZ: I knew you before, a long time before you went onto the streets.

DOROTHY: That was a relatively short time ago. . . . I give everything I have for the Cause.

RODRIGUEZ: I know your father's father . . . your mother's father . . . your father's mother and your mother's mother.

DOROTHY: In that case . . . you know practically all of us. The rest died burnt to a cinder. . . . They all threw stones at me. Sometimes they'd cut my hair to nothing and put me on show, naked, at the fairs. They were disgusting, bourgeois pigs . . . junkies, psychopaths. . . .

RODRIGUEZ: Dorothy . . .

DOROTHY: For God's sake, Professor, don't mate with me. I'd hate to think what the outcome would be . . . perhaps a snake.

The sound of running footsteps and barking is heard nearby. They remain silent.

RODRIGUEZ: I'm frightened, Dorothy. They're after me. . . .

DOROTHY: I was there when the bomb exploded.

RODRIGUEZ: They're talking about large-scale aggravation, medieval torture. . . . They're talking of killing me and smashing up my theories.

DOROTHY: Rest assured. They'll never succeed. The entire University is behind you . . . the whole country, Europe, Africa. . . . We're all with you.

RODRIGUEZ: I've had anonymous letters. . . . They talk . . . they walk about cutting my balls off.

DOROTHY: We'd never allow it! You're our mental beacon, our leader. Your defense of freedom, your steadfast loyalty, your amazing capacity for revulsion . . .

RODRIGUEZ: Dorothy!

DOROTHY: You've been our guiding star. . . . Now we don't even believe in Pelayo.

RODRIGUEZ: Come now, it's not . . . Why don't you believe in Pelayo?

DOROTHY: Beside you, Pelayo was just nobody. . . . Professor . . . I feel so excited at the thought of you being here, on the other side of this leafy wall, alive, palpitating, speaking, quivering . . . with your little glasses and your stupid face. . . . Come here. I want to kiss you! (RODRIGUEZ *moves closer to her.* DOROTHY *kisses the wall.*) You really are a true revolutionary!

RODRIGUEZ: Kiss me once more, once more!

DOROTHY: *(kissing him again)* You deserve everything.

RODRIGUEZ: Take me in your arms! I'm frightened! Protect me!

DOROTHY: *(embracing the wall)* Would you dedicate a copy of your book to me?

RODRIGUEZ: I haven't any copies with me . . .

DOROTHY: *(throwing a book over the partition to him)* I've got one here. Sign it. I've been devouring it passionately. What a fantastic book! It's been a resounding success, a number one hit! It's revolutionised half our civilisation.

RODRIGUEZ: *(returning the signed copy to her)* Oh! I didn't intend . . .

DOROTHY: What do you mean . . . ?

RODRIGUEZ: O.K., well, it's a book of Physics . . . a theory . . .

DOROTHY: A general theory! A conception of life! An attempt to destroy the structure of our culture! "The variability of physical constants in a deed . . . The constancy of the constants cannot be guaranteed. The constants may become inconstant at any time." . . . Well!

RODRIGUEZ: One mustn't jump to rash conclusions.

DOROTHY: What about Planck! What have you done with Planck! Ha, ha, ha! You've smashed him to pieces! You've wiped him out completely!

RODRIGUEZ: Planck's constant . . .

DOROTHY: *(interrupting him)* It's really inconstant. It's constant that it may become inconstant. Antiphysics . . . Antiastronomy, they've just been born. All depends on fate. Everything's hanging on a thread. The very structure of the Universe is in the process of evolution, as is life itself. Professor . . . this might be the end of hunger . . . of thirst . . . of lechery. . . . Nobody understands anything any more. . . . Everything's in confusion . . . it's all a mystery.

RODRIGUEZ: Exactly . . . ! You've seen the light. I feel like crying . . . Kiss me again. I need it.

DOROTHY: Come in here. I'll kiss you with pleasure. Your voice for me is like . . .

RODRIGUEZ: *(clambering up the partition clumsily)* I know, I know. *(He's on top of the partition, his suit completely smudged with plaster.)*

DOROTHY: It would have been easier to have come in through the door.

RODRIGUEZ: They're keeping a close watch on me. I've already told you that once.

DOROTHY: Let me kiss your feet.

RODRIGUEZ: Don't pull me about too much, I beg of you. I'm about to fall down any minute now.

The partition begins to crack.

DOROTHY: Come on! Make an end to the whole building. Put an end to this factory . . .

RODRIGUEZ: *(preparing to go down)* May I blow you a kiss from here?

155

DOROTHY: You can forget about kisses! *(She undoes her blouse.)* Look. . . . *(She holds out a breast for him.)*

RODRIGUEZ: What's this? What are you doing? Have you gone mad?

DOROTHY: Does it meet with your approval?

RODRIGUEZ: Does it . . . it looks like a little lemon . . .

DOROTHY: It's for you! A present from me! It's at your disposition whenever you want it. I won't cut it off and wrap it up for you because it's physically impossible for me to live without it. . . . But don't overlook the fact that many other women would do absolutely anything for you. Fifty out of the hundred pupils of yours have gone onto the streets. . . . You're a pimp! Your theories send women onto the streets and that, as far as I'm concerned, is something very positive indeed.

RODRIGUEZ: And . . . the other one?

DOROTHY: It's where it should be according to biological law. I'm keeping the other one for myself.

RODRIGUEZ: Have you some friend in mind?

DOROTHY: A whole tribe of them.

RODRIGUEZ: Why don't you help me to get down? My legs are going to sleep.

RODRIGUEZ *tries to get down. Part of the partition falls away. He emerges from the debris and they embrace.*

DOROTHY: Professor . . .

RODRIGUEZ: Let's stay and make our home here!

DOROTHY: Yes!

RODRIGUEZ: Let's run away together. . . .

DOROTHY: What's it to be then?

RODRIGUEZ: I don't know what I'm saying. I'm overwrought.

DOROTHY: I'm sorry we have to meet here. . . . It smells . . .

RODRIGUEZ: I would have liked something better for you.

DOROTHY: I don't care! I love you very, very, very much.

RODRIGUEZ: You're not starting to stutter by any chance, are you?

DOROTHY: I hope to God no! Now that I've found happiness.

RODRIGUEZ: I'm deliriously happy! I don't think I can stand it . . . Oh Dorothy!

He stands on the toilet seat, jumps onto the top of the door, wobbles, loses his balance and falls outside. At that moment a peculiar individual wearing a faded overcoat goes by.

MAN: Aren't you the man from this afternoon's lecture?

RODRIGUEZ: Well . . . *(realising he had removed his disguise)* not exactly . . .

MAN: You're Rodriguez. . . . There's no doubt about that. . . .

RODRIGUEZ: I bear quite a strong resemblance to him.

MAN: What a bombshell, eh? You've turned half the University upside down!

RODRIGUEZ: It wasn't me, honestly . . . I merely spoke about the variability of the constants . . . , the transient nature of political existence . . . and the end of hunger. . . . It wasn't a bombshell. It was a short circuit.

MAN: Don't you feel embarrassed being in the ladies' toilets? Are you a queer?

RODRIGUEZ: For God's sake, no! You see . . . I came in to look for my sister.

MAN: Have you found her?

RODRIGUEZ: Not yet, no.

MAN: That's tough.

RODRIGUEZ: Thanks.

MAN: But don't go breaking a leg. I want you alive.

RODRIGUEZ: I hope I won't.

MAN: Is she small?

RODRIGUEZ: About the size of a fingernail, not much bigger.

MAN: Good luck.

He shakes hands and disappears. RODRIQUEZ, *looking very pale, goes into the lavatory again.*

RODRIGUEZ: We're being closely watched.

DOROTHY: By whom?

RODRIGUEZ: Out there . . . Vultures, serpents, soldiers, machines . . . everyone's turned against me. They say that the Miguel Servet affair will be nothing compared to this. *(Steps are heard on the wooden floor.)*

DOROTHY: Shush . . . ! Keep quiet. Someone's coming . . .

They squat down, huddled together, panic-stricken.

MAN: *(knocking imperiously on the door)* Have you finished yet?

DOROTHY: Who . . . who is it?

MAN: I am Death.

RODRIGUEZ: What . . . what did you say?

MAN: I said I am Death. I have a message for you both.

DOROTHY: Tell us what it is in a low voice. We're not deaf.

MAN: I must go to the toilet too . . . I'm feeling slightly loose.

DOROTHY: Go into the one next to this.

MAN: I'm a lady. I couldn't . . .

RODRIGUEZ *puts on a pair of sunglasses, a moustache, a cap, he clasps* DOROTHY's *waist as if he were ill.* DOROTHY *opens the door. The* MAN *stands looking at them both.*

MAN: What are you doing here?

RODRIGUEZ: I feel slightly sick . . . I was having my forehead bathed with water . . .

MAN: *(removing his moustache)* Cut jokes out, sir. . . . Don't lie, you might get pimples on your tongue. . . .

RODRIGUEZ: A stone, a huge stone has fallen on my foot. . . . I'm holding on to this young lady because I can hardly walk, honestly . . .

MAN: *(pulling one of his ears)* I don't want any lechery or sinfulness here! Death is always on the watch. . . . Besides . . . I don't happen to like your theories at all. *(He snatches his cap off.)*

DOROTHY: Don't keep on at him. He's not feeling at all well.

MAN: This is what I came to tell you . . . the Miguel Servet affair won't be anything . . .

DOROTHY *places her head between* RODRIGUEZ*'s legs and lifts him up onto her shoulder.*

DOROTHY: Can't you see he's got a splinter in his foot?

MAN: Where? Let's see . . . I'll call a car . . . an ambulance . . . this is my domain.

DOROTHY: You can forget about the car. Revolution!

MAN: What?

DOROTHY: Revolution! We're sick to death of cars!

RODRIGUEZ: I feel sick . . . I've got a splinter in my foot . . . Please, Madam.

MAN: It seems you're being carried out in a very triumphant fashion, on her shoulders, and you've not accomplished any feat to deserve this.

RODRIGUEZ: Don't be like that. . . .

DOROTHY: I intend to take him to Stockholm.

RODRIGUEZ: Quite honestly, my theories are only theories when all's said and done. *(They begin to move away.)*

MAN: I came to announce to you the end of everything . . . the end of all the systems of all the equations . . . The final insult . . . is coming . . .

DOROTHY: Go to hell, you clown! Revolution! Down with cars! Love!

RODRIGUEZ: I'm very ill, very tired . . . Allow me . . .

MAN: And in the ladies' lavatory too . . . ! You wretch! I'll never forgive you for this! When you're least expecting it, I'll cut your balls off, just like that!

RODRIGUEZ: That was him. He was the one, Dorothy . . . Get a move on . . . for your own sake . . . quick . . .

RODRIGUEZ *disappears through a side door and very shortly returns on stage with different lighting. He is still on* DOROTHY*'s shoulders. They go up to a door.*

RODRIGUEZ: Here it is.

The door opens and MARY, RODRIGUEZ's *wife, a multicoloured, insane-looking woman with a palid face, appears.*

MARY: What can I do for you, young lady? Who are you? Why have you got two legs hanging over your shoulders? Are they some type of ornament? Answer me! You think I'm short-sighted, but you're wrong. I wear glasses to avoid seeing such depressing sights as this. I knew straightaway who that useless article you're carrying was. . . .

RODRIGUEZ: Mary . . .

MARY: Look carefully, young lady. *(She takes off her glasses and throws them away.)* There you are! I can do without glasses. They're of no use to me. . . . And you . . . get down right now! *(She grabs hold of* RODRIGUEZ's *leg and hurls him to the ground.)* Adulterer! *(She slaps him across the face.)* Pansy! Fornicator!

DOROTHY: Madam, I forbit you . . . !

MARY: Shut up! . . . Shut up, you fool! You don't know what kind of man this is. . . . I could tell you a thing or two. . . . Every afternoon, fifteen or twenty children here . . . his children, along with their maids, nurses, neighbours . . . wanting chocolate and buns . . . mothers asking for coffee, asking about the father of their children . . . And here am I, covering up for him, defending him, telling them he's very busy. . . . me, a monarchist, a traditionalist! What a disgrace!

DOROTHY: He's within his rights! He's a man and a man is highly entitled to satisfy his sexual appetite. . . .

RODRIGUEZ: Listen, Mary . . . this is different. . . . I'm being accused of some dreadful things. They're after me, they want to arrest me . . . dogs are after me. . . . I must get away. . . . Death is coming for me.

MARY: What are you accused of?

RODRIGUEZ: Corruption, derision, cynicism . . . anarchy . . . and . . .

DOROTHY: And wanting to put an end to everything . . . They say he's a magician, that . . .

RODRIGUEZ: I must go. I came to collect my things.

160

MARY: What about her?

RODRIGUEZ: She's a very useful element, my dear. She knows a great deal about physics . . . and apart from that, she's got very strong shoulders. . . .

DOROTHY: He's in good hands, don't you worry. I'll keep his feet warm at night. I'll be his hot water bottle.

MARY: I'm horrified. . . . I've been humiliated and ill-treated to such an extent that I'm going to close the door for the very last time.

DOROTHY: Madam . . .

MARY: I'm falling into a void, I'm going to pieces . . . God, oh God! Get out, you're damned! Now, my life will become an eternal period of mourning. I shall speak; but my words will be black, desperate. Oh Lord, why have you forsaken me? *(falls on her knees.)*

RODRIGUEZ: Mary . . .

MARY: Keep away from me, monster! *(She starts to cry.)*

RODRIGUEZ: I'll soon be back.

DOROTHY: Straightaway . . . you'll hardly notice . . .

MARY: Are you going with her?

RODRIGUEZ: Yes.

MARY: Where do you plan to go?

RODRIGUEZ: To the Himalayas! We need some fresh air.

MARY: Do you intend to carry him all the way on your shoulders.

DOROTHY: With all my love . . .

MARY: What shall I do with your letters?

RODRIGUEZ: Make paper aeroplanes with them.

MARY: Shall I get some food ready for you, some pasties, for example?

(Silence.)

RODRIGUEZ: We'll buy some sandwiches on the way.

DOROTHY: Get on my back. (RODRIGUEZ *gets onto* DOROTHY's *back.)*

161

RODRIGUEZ: Gee up!

MARY: I bless you in the name of the Father, the Son and the Holy Spirit. *(singing out of tune)* Glooo . . . ooooo . . . riaaaa . . *.(pulls off* RODRIGUEZ's *wig and with intense hatred tears it into little pieces.)* You should really get an aeroplane. She won't get very far. She's not very strong. Did you know he was almost completely bald?

DOROTHY: We're sick of planes.

RODRIGUEZ: Hear, hear!

MARY: No, no! I shan't allow it! I'll use the ecclesiastic privelege!

She grabs hold of the back of RODRIGUEZ's *shirt.* DOROTHY *starts to move forward, knocks* MARY *onto the floor and drags her along.*

RODRIGUEZ: Let go of me, woman! You're causing a scandal. . . .

MARY: I'm going with you . . . No . . . my God . . . she's a strong brute. Tell her to stop!

RODRIGUEZ: Whoa . . . !

ANTON, *a solid, impressive looking individual with a bishop-like face appears, dressed in blue.*

ANTON: Very nice too! . . . I guessed you were here. *(to* DOROTHY*)* Put him down this minute!

DOROTHY: No, I won't! No one will ever come between us.

She continues to walk dragging MARY *along with her.* ANTON *takes out a gun, crouches down and points it at her.*

ANTON: Don't move or I'll fill your head with lead.

RODRIGUEZ: Deacon . . . I . . .

ANTON: Shut up! *(to* DOROTHY*)* My daughter or not, I'll expel you from the University! I'll send you into exile!

DOROTHY: Father . . . !

ANTON: Don't call me father!

MARY: They were going to the Himalayas. . . .

ANTON: So you planned to go to the Himalayas, did you? *(He hits her.)* You trollop! You're not designed to be a beast of burden. If he wants to go travelling he can buy himself a motorbike!

RODRIGUEZ: Well, you see, I've got a splinter in my foot. . . .

ANTON: Rubbish! Who do you take me for? In the event of something like that happening, one asks for a pair of tweezers and one takes the splinter out, even though it hurts. . . .

RODRIGUEZ: It was . . . a splinter. . . .

DOROTHY: The fact is . . . we're in love. . . .

ANTON: A splinter? Rubbish! You just wanted to sit up there comfortably with your testicles hanging down this lady's neck, with . . . with your pubic hair on display . . . like a muffler open at the neck . . .

DOROTHY: I love him!

ANTON: *(firing into the air)* That's enough, you wretch! From tomorrow morning on you can get your tennis racquet and go and play with your mother.

DOROTHY: *(spitting in his face)* Swine! That's a sight your eyes will never get to see. I'm going to go with him, for your information. . . .

RODRIGUEZ: Dorothy . . .

DOROTHY: Yes, I'm going. I'll give up my studies. And my genitals will always be at his disposal. . . .

MARY: This is outrageous. . . . I wish I were dead. I wish I could suffocate myself, or explode.

DOROTHY: *(attempting to take hold of RODRIGUEZ)* Come on, get on . . . open your legs.

RODRIGUEZ: Wait, child . . . your father is looking at us. . . . I feel a bit embarrassed. . . .

ANTON: Go on . . . get on if you're man enough. . . .

RODRIGUEZ: So you think I'm incapable of doing it?

ANTON: No.

RODRIGUEZ: Close your eyes. . . . You'll see. . . .

DOROTHY: Don't hesitate any longer. We've no time to lose.

RODRIGUEZ *gets onto her shoulders, mistrustfully. Silence. They exchange glances.*

ANTON: Well, what now?

RODRIGUEZ: *(with a burst of energy)* Gee up, yaa!

ANTON: *(grabbing* RODRIGUEZ*'s neck)* Don't move! Get down or I'll wring your neck just like I would a hen.

DOROTHY: Take no notice of him! Spit in his face! That's what hurts him most.

Silence. RODRIGUEZ *shyly spits at him, like a small child.* ANTON *knocks him off with one swipe and stamps on his stomach.*

ANTON: Microbe! *(to* DOROTHY*)* You stupid creature, don't you realise you're liable to get pregnant any day. He's like an animal where sex is concerned. . . . Sometimes it just takes a look. . . . He's got 150 kids.

DOROTHY: That many?

MARY: No, more . . . a lot more. . . . Call in one afternoon. . . . It's worse than a candy store. . . . 200, 300 . . . it's impossible to tell. . . . Believe me, young woman . . . I'm only telling you for your own good. He'll pull his trousers down, just like that, as soon as you get round the corner, even before you get up the street. He's . . . he's like a streak of lightning, like a snake, like an electric shock. He'll get on top of you and bang! Say goodbye to the Himalayas, he's off after another woman! . . . Can't you see, I know this story off by heart now.

DOROTHY: *(to* RODRIGUEZ*)* Is it true?

RODRIGUEZ: Me. . . . *(to* DOROTHY*)* It sounds like a pack of lies. Nonsense.

ANTON: Be quiet!

RODRIGUEZ: Dorothy . . .

ANTON: Shush! That's enough! Of course it's true. . . . Tell me . . . has he kissed you?

DOROTHY: Yes!

MARY: Oh no! That's it then. . . .

ANTON: You'll never escape now.

MARY: I'll expect you at home any time now, young lady.

RODRIGUEZ: It's all slander. . . . I'm a poor, innocent devil. . . . I'm a simple physicist, that's all . . . an astronomer, to be exact. . . .

ANTON: *(producing an X-ray)* Look . . . he's got tuberculosis. All this is completely hollow. *(He points to the lung.)*

DOROTHY: All that?

ANTON: All of it. He's hardly any lung left. . . . Rodriguez is the typical poor rascal, one of those subproducts from the outskirts of town. . . . A cigarette one day, another the next, then another, then a small cigar, then a big one! The worm sets in and soon the lungs disappear.

MARY: *(to DOROTHY)* He smokes like a chimney, pipes, tipped cigarettes. . . .

ANTON: The doctors have written him off as a hopeless case. Believe me. You wouldn't get far. . . . He'd drop dead on your shoulders. Apart from that, he hasn't got a passport. He's got a criminal record. They wouldn't let him out of the country. He's not been vaccinated against smallpox either. . . . Isn't that so, Rodriquez?

RODRIGUEZ: I can't quite remember.

ANTON: See what I mean. He can't remember. If he'd been vaccinated, would he be likely to forget it? Of course not! You don't forget things like that!

MARY: He's in the pub all day long, playing whist and dominoes, drinking anisette and huge quantities of red and white wine, mixed together. When he gets home he sometimes goes to bed with one of the neighbours thinking she's me and in the morning he calls her Mary, instead of Mathilda, her real name. . . . Imagine what my life with him is like!

ANTON: Don't think I'm trying to disillusion you, my girl. You know when you decided to become a prostitute, I put no obstacles in your path, in spite of my religious beliefs. I didn't want to interrupt the development of your personality. But, take a piece of fatherly advice now. Keep right away from him, go away!

DOROTHY: But where? I've nowhere to go.

ANTON: Go home to your mother. Adopt her love of tennis. . . .

DOROTHY: Try as I might . . .

ANTON: I don't know . . . do something. . . . Go out with your friends . . . sing. . . . How should I know! Study, damn it! Study something for once, even if it's only sewing!

DOROTHY: Sewing bores me. Everything bores me. . . . My life's an empty shell . . . a void . . . a hole . . . a gap . . . a . . . a . . .

ANTON: That's enough! We know now what your life's like. Off you go now. For God's sake, go.

DOROTHY: But where, father? I love him. . . . I love him very much. . . .

ANTON: Get stuffed, girl! You're beginning to make me mad. *(He pushes her off-stage.)*

MARY: What an annoying woman!

DOROTHY: *(re-entering)* I love him, I love him. . . . I love him very much. . . .

ANTON *takes out his gun and squatting down, fires. Silence. Shortly afterwards a duck, riddled with pellets, drops down from the top of the stage.*

RODRIGUEZ: You ought to have come out with a pack of hounds . . . Deacon.

ANTON: Wise cracks, eh? Stand up! Get inside *(They go into the house.)* Sit down there. *(They sit facing each other.)* Do you know my curriculum?

RODRIGUEZ: Yes, Deacon.

ANTON: It doesn't matter. I'll tell you all the same.

MARY, *interested, sits down.*

ANTON: Into the kitchen with you, my good lady. I'm warning you, I'm staying to dinner and I'll possibly be sleeping here with the pair of you.

MARY: I'm a lady! I'm a decent woman!

ANTON: What the hell! I'm the Grand Rector of the University. I beg you not to forget it.

MARY: Sir!

ANTON: *(going toward her)* Give me your hands.

MARY: What are you going to do?

166

ANTON: Hold tight. *(ANTON begins to swing her round and round until her feet come away from the floor, like an iceskater.)* Can you see how strong I am?

MARY: I'm going . . . I feel sick . . . You've put an end to me, Deacon. You devil!

ANTON: *(sits down)* Are you aware that I obtained no less than seventy awards while I was studying Medicine?

RODRIGUEZ: Lies! You were a duffer. . . . I know from very reliable sources. . . .

ANTON: So it's a lie is it? I suppose it's also a lie that I'm an authority on surgery?

RODRIGUEZ: You pompous ass. . . . you . . .

ANTON: And it's a lie is it that I'm shortly to be awarded the Nobel Prize for Medicine? My candidature has been accepted. You know that. You know perfectly well that I've carried out 26 liver transplants. You know I'm a world authority and that I've the greatest success record in the world, better than the one in Minnesota!

RODRIGUEZ: How many of your patients are still alive?

ANTON: Shut up, fool! Big mouth! Whom did they send for when they suspected the need for a transplant on the son of the Capo. . . . Il Cap Di Tutti Capi, the big chief. . . . Who? You? No, of course not! Me, my dear friend. While the dog's liver that I transplanted on him gradually becomes accepted by his system, you can rest assured that the Nobel won't slip through my fingers. . . . Furthermore, for your information, I am an animal as regards sex! Even worse than you! I'm slicker than you, more of a man. . . . Beside me you're just a snivelling idiot, a greenhorn, a little nobody . . .

RODRIGUEZ: Anything else?

ANTON: But of course. . . . *(He takes out a piece of paper.)* I'm carrying an order from the Senate to expel you from the University and, if possible, from the country itself. Once you became a mortal enemy of this society which pro-tects you . . . once you began to sew systematic doubt and revolution . . . once you attacked the established truth and the very foundations of Physics, that Physics that protects and feeds you . . . by God! Invested with the powers con-ferred upon me by my office, I declare you outside the law, I declare your pants and your trousers illegal, I excommunicate your waistcoat and your flies.

I declare you impotent, by Act of Parliament. Your career is over. You're finished.

RODRIGUEZ: Get out of this house!

ANTON: *(flushing him into the armchair)* Fool . . . ! I've treated you like my own son. I've rocked you in your moments of endogenic depression. . . . I've kissed you and kisses don't deceive. . . . I've sung to you. . . . I've even carried you home in my arms, when you had no means of transport, so your feet wouldn't get wet. . . . And now, this! How dare you raise your voice to me!

RODRIGUEZ: You're a repulsive swine . . . a traitor . . . a slanderer . . . dirt!

ANTON: They've destroyed seats, blackboards, the entire University. This morning's affair was no campus lecture, as you stated. It was an angry outburst . . . before the Senate, before the highest civil, academic and ecclesiastical authority, before the intellectual cream.

RODRIGUEZ: That's right, yes.

ANTON: The students all rose up together, held hands, kissed each other. . . . You were saying that at any moment everything could become unstable and fall down, all the truths, laws, hunger, thirst . . . everything could go wrong . . . and then . . . bang . . . a terrible bombshell . . .

RODRIGUEZ: A short circuit!

ANTON: Broken arms and legs, heads cut off . . .

RODRIGUEZ: Slander!

ANTON: You're a hardened revolutionary, an anarchist. . . . I'm quite aware of that.

RODRIGUEZ: No, I'm not, but I'm going to become one. You haven't the slightest idea. You're just nothing. Your transplants are a load of rubbish.

ANTON: Don't get on my nerves. I'm warning you. . . .

RODRIGUEZ: You play around with other people's lives, all you're after is some gory publicity. . . . You're a pig . . . a . . .

ANTON: *(grabbing hold of his jacket)* I've come to debase you, stupid! *(He pulls his jacket off.)* I've an order to annihilate you . . . to wipe you out, to leave you here with your scrawny, ridiculous chest bare. . . . *(He pulls his jacket off and*

168

tears it into pieces with his mouth.) I know all about you Rodriguez. We've been having you watched for a long time now. *(He pulls off his trousers and ears them to pieces.)* I know all the ins and outs of your life. . . . All of them! Even the filthy dreams you're plagued with! *(He leaves him in underpants.)* And now! Just look at you, cachetic, dying. . . . Look what your theories lead to. . . . You're dying, Rodriguez. I've come to tell you so.

RODRIGUEZ: Oh, my God!

ANTON: Stop being so affected! Get down on your knees! *(He gets hold of his nose and forces him onto his knees.)* Take everything back!

RODRIGUEZ: This is all quite comical. Let me go.

ANTON: Impossible. . . . The students were after my blood. They've asked for my resignation. . . . They've gone around shouting their mouths off and now the workers want me to resign. They all want me to resign. They wanted to kill me. . . . I'm the only one who isn't demanding my resignation. No, I won't give way! . . . Take back everything, every idea that the Devil's put into your head! One . . . two . . . two and a half . . .

RODRIGUEZ: I only spoke of freedom. I . . . don't believe in violence. . . . I believe in man. . . .

ANTON: Lies.

RODRIGUEZ: You're hurting me . . .

ANTON: Firstly, Copernicus . . . then Galileo . . . now you, all attempting to destroy everything! . . . Take it all back! Deny your entire system! Sign here! Say it's all a lie. *(He produces an enormous document, ready for signature.)*

RODRIGUEZ: What's that?

ANTON: Cross your arms! Sign! *(He twists his nose around. An expression of pain crosses RODRIGUEZ's face.)* You're no modern physicist, Rodriguez, and don't you forget it . . . a physicist like those at Yale, good grief, no! You're nothing but a medieval alchemist . . . sign, idiot! It's for your own good.

RODRIGUEZ: I refuse.

ANTON: *(gripping him in a lock)* Sign or I'll break your neck.

RODRIGUEZ: No. I can't sign.

ANTON: Why not?

RODRIGUEZ: I haven't got a pen.

ANTON: Here you are.

RODRIGUEZ: It's run out of ink.

ANTON: *(throwing away the pen, beside himself with rage)* Of course it hasn't! *(grabs hold of his ear and rips it off)* You fool! You don't want it to work, do you? Oh, Rodriguez, you don't know how much damage you're doing me.

RODRIGUEZ *starts to cry while attempting to check the bleeding.*

ANTON: But just how far do you intend going? Look what I'd brought for you . . .two air tickets. . . .

Sudden entrance of MITCHUM, *a cold, calculating character with a scar across his face. A mad expression on his face.*

MITCHUM: Everybody stand still! Don't move! You're all under arrest!

ANTON: This is Rodriguez, Mr. Mitchum . . .

MITCHUM: Everything has ground to a halt . . . completely suspended . . . without remission or possibility of salvation. This is the end of your chances to cultivate your gardens or raise chickens!

RODRIGUEZ I've had an ear ripped off. I've been unjustly mutilated. . . . I . . .

MITCHUM: I said be quiet! Not a sound! Understand that everything you say from now on will be used against you. Do you know whom you are speaking to? You don't, do you? You are speaking to Mitchum . . . Undersecretary of State, Minister of Justice, the country's highest intellectual authority, stockbroker, wine grower, ascetic. I order you to surrender your arms before the articles of the code are brought to bear upon you in all their strength . . . . Speak, say something. *(holds a microphone in front of him)*

RODRIGUEZ: I've . . . I've nothing to say. . . . I . . .

MITCHUM: I, what? Do you stutter?

RODRIGUEZ: What do you expect me to say? I hardly know you. . . . We've just made each other's acquaintance, so to speak. . . .

MITCHUM: It doesn't really matter. It wouldn't have helped you anyway.

170

You're a hopeless case. You've some exceptionally serious accusations to answer to, friend. . . . You've succeeded in terrorising the people. . . . That's a very serious charge, friend. . . .

RODRIGUEZ: I'm terribly sorry. . . .

MITCHUM: It's too late now! The damage has been done . . . Astronomic cataclysms . . . exploding stars, shifting nebulace. . . Bloody Hell! The world's been going round since the beginning of time and nothing's happened so far. And now this bombshell! This nuclear explosion! This . . . this earthquake!

RODRIGUEZ: Oh, for God's sake. It was only a short circuit, a mere spark.

MITCHUM: It's no good bringing God into this, stupid! You should have thought about that before! They've rebelled against us! They've barricaded themselves in. . . . They want to make an end of us. It's all your fault! You weren't like this before, Rodriguez. You were perfectly normal. What have you been reading? What's got into you?

RODRIGUEZ: I only said . . .

MITCHUM: I'm perfectly aware of what you said! Another Black Death, that's what you'd like. . . . You'd like the Earth in one revolution to come away from the sun . . . to go to Hell, drifting solitarily through space. . . .

RODRIGUEZ: Exactly, sir . . . that's just what I think may happen. Hunger . . . lechery . . . may come to an end. I believe that Physics, like Biology, has its evolution. . . . I'm going to bleed to death, sir. They've pulled off one of my ears. . . . A bandage . . .

MITCHUM: (*turning towards* ANTON) I came for you as a matter of fact, my good fellow. (*Seizes hold of his tie and pulls it off.*)

ANTON: You've no right . . .

MITCHUM: I am the Right . . . The Right and the Left. I am the Legislation. I am . . . (*silence*) Five days ago you carried out the transplant of a dog's liver on the son of the Capo . . . Il Capo Di Tutti Cap.

ANTON: That's right.

MITCHUM: On Raimundo, the son of the Supreme Leader, the son of the President of everything . . . the BIG BOSS IN CAPITAL LETTERS . . .

ANTON: That's so. A dog with a brilliant pedigree.

171

MITCHUM: This morning . . . he began to bark.

ANTON: What? What did you say? Who began to bark?

MITCHUM: Raimundo, you fool. . . . He'd agreed to do a television interview . . . . When asked about the country's future . . . woof! Woof! At that very moment . . . Most embarrassing! Not one bark, several. Woof, woof, woof! And then, he sprang at the interviewer and bit him in the neck. There's been an absolutely dreadful scandal!

ANTON: (*sits down, looking pale*) This is the end. . . . Oh, my God. . . .

MITCHUM: You're no surgeon! You're a butcher! A . . . he's said to have rabies!

ANTON: You don't mean that!

MITCHUM: They've had to shut him in a kennel. . . . The son of the All- Powerful and he cooks his leg up to spend a penny. Alas! This is the end of the Mafia, of politics, of morals . . . of political morals, of the political and moral Mafia.

RODRIGUEZ: Look here . . .

MITCHUM: Shut your mouth! Cover yourself up, you brazen fellow!

RODRIGUEZ: I'm bleeding to death . . . May I go to the hospital?

MITCHUM: No, not yet! I couldn't give a damn about your ear. (*turning towards* ANTON) I've come to humiliate you on the lowest scale of naturalistic biology. . . . I think you should know that before they were able to detain him, the boy got his fiancee pregnant . . . If the offspring turns out to be a mongrel be prepared. . . . I've a galley waiting in the nearest port just for you.

ANTON: Does it belong to Colombus?

MITCHUM: That's right, yes. . . . Put your hand out. . . .

ANTON: Why?

MITCHUM: Put it out, I said. (*gets out a ruler and wacks him as hard as he can*) Next, time, you can stick this little hand of yours right up your arse. (*Takes a stamp out of his pocket, dips it in ink and stamps it on his forehead.*) Now you're branded! (*goes up to* RODRIGUEZ) You too!

RODRIGUEZ: Why me?

MITCHUM: (*twisting his nipple*) You're crap, Rodriguez. You deserve the very worst, you . . . are a . . . (*turning to* ANTON) I'll give you two minutes to come up with a solution . . .

ANTON: Do you know . . . Do you know, minister, why liver transplants don't take? Well, they don't take because we mess around with all sorts of filthy things, like dogs, horses . . . dead creatures . . . corpses. . . . Yuck! They don't take because we use dry, dead, revolting entrails. . . . If we want organs to adapt to other bodies, we should take them from a living body!

MITCHUM: Legal horror! Anathema!

ANTON: Be reasonable. . . . Can the liver of a stray dog transplanted on a human being really be expected to take?

RODRIGUEZ: (*to* ANTON) Will you let me have my ear, please.

ANTON: How the hell should I know where I've put your ear! I'm talking to this gentleman!

MITCHUM: (*stamps him again*) Things look bad, friend. . . . That's two now . . . . On the third one . . .

Telephone rings. MITCHUM *answers.*

MITCHUM: Don't any of you move. . . . Hello! . . . yes . . . I . . . yes . . . what!? He's escaped? He's bitten several of the State Council. Yes . . . yes . . . I understand. Of course, yes. . . . Well! What can we do? (*hangs up, stands looking at* ANTON) He's only got one thought in his head . . . to put an end to you. Raimundo's making his way over here. . . . Have you got any anti-rabies vaccine?

ANTON: (*beside himself*) I . . . I don't know if there's any left.

In the street there is an uproar of people, barking and shouts of help can be heard.

ANTON: This just isn't possible . . . Something must be done.

RODRIGUEZ: (RODRIGUEZ *has started to get dressed.*) Will you let me have those two tickets?

ANTON: Leave me, leave me alone. I'm feeling very worried. (*Closes doors and windows. There is barking at the door.*)

MARY: (*who has gone to the door*) Who is it?

173

ANTON: Give me a bone, for God's sake, give me a bone!

MARY: Wait, I'm going to open the door. Someone's knocking.

ANTON: Give me a bone, you fool! Don't open the door!

MARY *brings him an enormous bone. Dreadful noise of barking.*

ANTON: (From inside.) Little boy . . . babykins . . . (*the sound of barking*)

MITCHUM: Listen to the voice he's got! (*looking at* RODRIGUEZ) What do you make of all this?

RODRIGUEZ: Things look very black, very black indeed.

MITCHUM: Well, if the bone's juicy . . .

ANTON: I'm sorry . . . little Raimundito. You had incurable cirrhosis. . . . The alcohol . . . (*the sound of growling, scratching at the door.*)

MITCHUM: Face the situation like a man. (*looking out of the window*) People are getting frightened. He's bitten several of them. They're coming armed with sticks and shotguns!

ANTON *opens the door suddenly and goes out, closing it behind him. Barking, growling and shouting can be heard.* ANTON *comes in again bleeding and bitten in various places, his suit torn. A shot rings out in the street.* ANTON *goes to the window.*

ANTON: Keep calm! We don't want any violence! Raimundo is in good hands. I've just given him a wonderful bone . . . a beef bone. . . . He's told me he won't bite anyone else and is going to be good and obedient. No shooting! . . . Furthermore, I think you should know that tomorrow morning, I, the giant of surgery, having transplanted hens', lizards', rats' and frogs' livers and even flowers . . . I, for the first time ever, will attempt the transplant from one living human being to another. . . . The organs must be taken out of the living person and transplanted from human to human, live entrails, red, throbbing guts . . . We mustn't turn our backs on reality. We need martyrs to shape history. . . . History is built on the sacrifice of the few . . . yes! Now, an exceptional man, a wizard . . . a man like the rest of you, a thin, sober, dark, long-suffering man has offered his liver voluntarily in order to remedy this situation! Tomorrow, dear people, a completely normal Raimundo will be restored to you. Go home now. . . . have dinner peacefully and watch television. The country's future has been saved. *(Closes the door. They stand looking at each other.)*

MITCHUM: Well, what now?

ANTON: Now . . . we must go in search of that fresh . . . living . . . throbbing red liver.

They stand looking at RODRIGUEZ *who has his case ready.*

RODRIGUEZ: Hey . . . that's enough of your jokes. . . . I must go. They're waiting for me.

ANTON: *(slapping him on the back)* You know, I'm very fond of you, Rodriguez . . . . The small differences in our respective ideologies mustn't spoil our friendship.

MITCHUM: Of course not. Shake hands.

RODRIGUEZ: Sirs . . . I'll withdraw anything you wish. . . . I . . .

ANTON: No . . . afterwards you'll say we didn't care about you . . . but escapism at a time like this when your country needs you, is a serious offence.

MITCHUM: A very serious offence indeed. . . .

MARY: I don't understand what's going on . . .

ANTON: That lung of yours must be removed. . . . You can't go around con-taminating your fellow citizens. . . . You understand, we must perform an emergency operation on you. . . . You're dangerous.

MARY: Very dangerous indeed. . . .

ANTON *produces a bottle of chloroform, tips some into a handkerchief and goes over to him.*

RODRIGUEZ: *(recoiling)* That's enough! No more joking! Keep away from me!

MARY: They won't hurt you, darling. . . . You're in good hands. . . . You have the Mafia's protection.

ANTON: *(hurling himself onto him)* Come on! Let's get on with it! You can't take all the time, you've got to give sometimes!

RODRIGUEZ: *(A shout as he tries to escape.)* This is . . . an affront . . . this

175

. . . no, no please . . . let me go. I must go . . . they're waiting for me . . . they're waiting for me. *(He slumps down, unconscious.)*

ANTON: He's acted like a real man.

MITCHUM: I would never have believed it. It was a truly moving act which just goes to show that civic virtues are a long way from disappearing, as some people say. . . .

MARY: What will you give him in place of the liver?

ANTON: A plastic bag.

MARY: What for?

ANTON: You do ask some weird questions! We've got to give him something . . . . His bile's got to go somewhere. . . .

MARY: Ah . . . if you put a plastic bag inside him so that he can get rid of his bile, then . . . that's all right. The only problem would be if the bile dropped down into his stomach and gradually corroded his insides. . . .

ANTON: We won't allow that to happen. You can be sure of that! We're not heartless.

Darkness.

2.

A door opens at the back of the stage. ANTON *appears covered in blood from head to foot. He is wearing his operating dress, gloves and a mask. He takes off his cap, and sits down defiantly in a black armchair, facing the audience.*

ANTON: Ladies and gentlemen, the first man to man, human to human liver transplant has just taken place. *(bright light on* ANTON, *flashes, loud noises)* Keep calm, please. We are in the anteroom of the operating theatre. Do not destroy the serenity of this place. I will willingly answer all your questions . . . . Excuse me if I appear a little shaky. I am under the effects of the chloroform and the blood.

INTERVIEWER: *(Voice on tapercorder)* Deacon . . . has the operation been successful?

ANTON: A complete success.

176

INTERVIEWER: Do you always leave the operating theatre with so many blood-stains on your clothes?

ANTON: What an absurd question!

INTERVIEWER: It looks as if you've just fought in the bullring. . . .

ANTON: Don't pester me, young man, I beg you. I'm still rather agitated.

INTERVIEWER: Whose is all this blood? Raimundito's or Rodriguez's?

ANTON: It belongs to both really. They have both taken part in a wonderful surgical experience . . . stomachs opened . . . cut into pieces, elbow to elbow . . . both palpitating . . . one the receiver, the other the donor. . . .

INTERVIEWER: Don't you consider it has been rather a bloody operation?

ANTON: You're an idiot!

INTERVIEWER: Have there been any immoral dealings in this matter? Have you transgressed article 20 of the Penal Code? Answer me! Have you committed a grave deontological mistake?

ANTON: Young man . . . I'm no moralist!

INTERVIEWER: Speak up! We are listening to you. We need to justify ourselves in the face of History.

ANTON: You've got poisoned guts, young man. Your questions are inspired by hate . . . . You belong to a lost generation. . . . Man is more . . . more than that unit of impulses . . .

INTERVIEWER: How disgraceful!

ANTON: Man is one jump forward, a metaphysical structure . . . What use was Rodriguez's liver to him?

INTERVIEWER: What are you asking me for?

ANTON: Just to let him act the fool!

INTERVIEWER: What?

ANTON: It was no use to him whatsoever! It was an utterly wasted, functionless liver, an idle organ, an absurd liver in an absurd abdomen. . . . Victims are inevitable, sir, I'm not a moralist but I must say that ever since Man has been on the Earth, society has called for martyrs in its universal evolution. . . .

177

INTERVIEWER: Answer this question without any previous meditation! Would you call Rodriguez a martyr?

ANTON: He's an ascetic . . . a thin, sober, long-suffering individual. . . .

INTERVIEWER: A Christian . . .

ANTON: Yes, definitely, yes! A Christian, and a good one at that! You're right, he is a martyr!

INTERVIEWER: What kind of future can he look forward to?

ANTON: A miserable life, perhaps a life without hope . . . by the side of his bed, keeping himself warm with numerous blankets . . . in a village in the Steppes, near his ancestors.

INTERVIEWER: Has he got long to live?

ANTON: No. . . . It's a question of minutes. He's lived a life of vice and ruin.

INTERVIEWER: Vice?

ANTON: Wandering around, wine, sex and orgies, the high life . . . That's about it. I don't think he'll last long. He's killed himself.

INTERVIEWER: Don't you think that abroad they will look upon this mutilation process as . . .?

ANTON: Look here!

INTERVIEWER: . . . this civil massacre, as first degree murder . . .?

ANTON: Everything has gone against him.

INTERVIEWER: The sea, the waves, the wind, people . . .

ANTON: Everything. He's been unlucky.

INTERVIEWER: Downright unlucky . . .

ANTON: Plain, rotten unlucky.

INTERVIEWER: They say he had an understanding, a relationship with your daughter . . . .

ANTON: I forbid you. . . .

INTERVIEWER: They say they met in the toilets, like savages, and there they indulged in dreadful sexual aberrations, with goats, wolves, bears and even snakes.

ANTON: It's a lie! A fairy tale!

INTERVIEWER: Some people say she's not yours . . .

ANTON: Come into the light! Don't hide! Sit down at the negotiating table with me.

INTERVIEWER: They say he carried her to his house each day on his shoulders and that she placed her genitals on that man's neck with immense pleasure, and that sometimes she pissed all over him and he smiled like a child. . . .

ANTON: Hold on a minute . . . who are you? For whom are you conducting this interview?

INTERVIEWER: I'm a historian. An embittered historian and a poisonous interviewer. I've been made to suffer immensely, sir. I consider that society is the monstrous oppressor of the individual. . . .

ANTON: I don't have to put up with you . . .! I'm weary! I've just performed a surgical feat. . . .

INTERVIEWER: You'll never escape. It's useless to try. Rodriguez is one of us. His ghost will stop you from sleeping. It will follow you around, perched on your tongue, its head thrust into your throat, making you cough at your slightest attempt to communicate. . . .

ANTON: That man has been laughing at the whole world, if you must know!

INTERVIEWER: He's a good father, that I do know. A model citizen. . . .

ANTON: An anarchist! A revolutionary! . . . How does that grab you! You don't know anything about him at all! He was an utterly subversive character.

INTERVIEWER: He was the typical taxpayer, a flawless character, the silent gentleman. . . .

ANTON: You're wrong! You're completely out of touch with everything. You cretin. (gets up, walks up and down in agitation) Everyone had accepted the physical parameters that govern the Earth's rotation in the Heavenly Cosmos . . . even the backward accepted it! Starting with Galileo and Copernicus . . . . Good! A step forward! Then Newton mathematically establishes how this huge astronomic machine works. Fine! Let's carry on!. . . . However, when Planck . . . when Planck himself . . . Planck, who racked his brains to find his constant, which is why it is referred to as Planck's constant . . . Planck . . . where was I?. . . . Well, anyway, this whippersnapper arrives on the scene . . . and says that it's all false, that it's all a question of chance and that at any moment the constants may cease to be constant!

INTERVIEWER: So what?

ANTON: What do you mean, so what? You'll drive us insane!

INTERVIEWER: You brute . . .

ANTON: We've had enough innovations for the time being! You're going to abolish Planck's constant, as well! No, sir! On to the bonfire like Miguel Servet! To blazes with the lot of you! Let us live in peace. But don't take that too far. The world's fine as it is.

INTERVIEWER: Revolution!

ANTON: You too, you crackpot?

INTERVIEWER: All this must fall to pieces. . . . The whole of humanity will have to rise up and cry out against abuse thousands and thousands of times until this civilisation comes crumbling down . . .

ANTON: You make me laugh, you poor deluded little penny of an interviewer.

INTERVIEWER: What have you given him in place of a liver?

ANTON; A plastic bag.

INTERVIEWER: What for?

ANTON: What do you expect me to give him? A cabbage?

INTERVIEWER: What did you give the others?

ANTON: What do you mean by that? What are you insinuating?

INTERVIEWER: It's a well-known fact that you've got a long string of corpses behind you. . . .

ANTON: This is a fine interview, this is!

INTERVIEWER: It's also common knowledge that not one of the 26 livers you've transplanted has been accepted. Some people have exploded, others have sprouted flowers.

ANTON: *(walking round the room)* If I ever come across you again, my little journalist friend . . . *(He gnaws his fist in rage.)*

INTERVIEWER: When you transplanted a hen's liver into a horse, the horse laid an egg. . . .

ANTON: So what?

INTERVIEWER: Where did it lay it?

ANTON: What has that to do with you?

INTERVIEWER: What did you do with the egg?

ANTON: I ate it! What did you expect me to do with it?

INTERVIEWER: What did it taste of, horse or hen?

ANTON: Powdered soup, you idiot! I'm beginning to get sick of you now!

INTERVIEWER: If a horse has laid an egg, could Raimundo now lay one?

ANTON: That's enough! Go and make fun of your mother!

INTERVIEWER: Please let him lay an egg, Deacon, just one. . . .

ANTON: This interview is over! Woof, woof!

INTERVIEWER: *(in fits of laughter)* Keep barking! You've got rabies! You've finally got rabies!

ANTON: *(slobbering)* I'm healthier than a dog! I'm capable of taking a huge leap! I'm wild! *(lifts the armchair into the air)* I'm a wolf! I'm a professional success! I'm a giant of surgery! Woof, woof! Grrrr! *(Terrible barking can now be heard inside.)* Oh!

ANTON: Oh no! . . . What's happened?

The door at the far end opens. A bed appears. MITCHUM *holds onto it.*

MITCHUM: That's it! You're all under arrest! Look, you fool! He's bitten me!

ANTON: You too? This boy's a wolf!

RAIMUNDO: *(from the bed)* Woof, woof! Grrrr!

ANTON: Don't bark . . . my beauty . . . that's all in the past now. . . . The whole

181

nation's listening to you. . . . Don't let's start fighting. . . .

RAIMUNDO: *(louder and louder)* Wow, bow wow!

MITCHUM: This is dreadful, terrible! Biting each other like animals . . . in front of the entire nation . . .

ANTON: Smile, dearest . . . they're looking at us. . . .

RAIMUNDO *sits up in bed. He is identical in appearance to* RODRIGUEZ.

MITCHUM: Oh, God, no! You've altered his face! The liver, the liver!

ANTON: What a miracle!

MITCHUM: Come off it! You idiot! It's all your fault . . . you and your transplants!

ANTON: Raimundo . . . most mighty one . . . what . . . what is your opinion of the present situation . . . of inflation . . .?

RAIMUNDO: I think everything is inconstant.

INTERVIEWER: Inconstant!

RAIMUNDO: I think life is a result of fate . . . and that only Divine Providence can explain why this whole astronomical work hasn't gone to blazes. . . . I . . .

ANTON: *(putting his hand over his mouth)* And now all this!

INTERVIEWER: Murderer! Let him go! Let him speak! Speak, all of you! The whole nation is listening!

ANTON: You crap interviewer!

MITCHUM: Cut it, cut it! This is scandalous. . . . *(breaks the taperecorder.)*

ANTON: Listen . . . talk about something else . . . leave philosophy alone. Something lighter . . .

RAIMUNDO: I do not believe in the State, or in Morals, or in the Mafia . . . or . . .

MITCHUM: Good God, where is this going to end?

RAIMUNDO: I believe only in Revolution.

ANTON: Well!

RAIMUNDO: I believe in the freedom of man, above all else. . . .

MITCHUM: *(to* ANTON*)* Look what you've done, you stupid idiot! It was all in the liver. Bloody Hell, you could have given him an ear transplant.

ANTON: Let's have a little song. This is no time for holding a discussion. He's just coming out of the anaesthetic. . . . He's still not coordinating well.

RAIMUNDO: Ay, poor wretch that I am!

ANTON: Oh not that, for God's sake! I can't stand it! A light song! You won't discover anything. I'm getting sick of you! *(takes hold of his lapels and shakes him vigorously.)*

RAIMUNDO: *(holding out his arms)* I don't do a thing. Hit me. There will be other after me, strong, dark men. . . .

MITCHUM: *(firing into the air)* Silence! I beg you to think this over. You are carrying a terrible responsibility. You cannot continue to rant and rave. The Stock Exchange is crumbling. Capitalisation is falling.

RAIMUNDO: I foresee great catastrophes, mass disasters . . . let me carry on, Mitchum.

MITCHUM: Speak up. What's bugging you?

RAIMUNDO: I fear for my virility.

ANTON: Well, I'm blowed! We are in a fine state!

MITCHUM: Listen to me, lad. . . .

RAIMUNDO: Mitchum, I've got an itchy bottom. . . . It's driving me mad.

MITCHUM: You must have worms. . . . You've no reason to worry. . . .

RAIMUNDO: I fear for Humanity, dearest.

ANTON: This Rodriguez fellow . . . this Rodriguez . . .

MITCHUM: Don't let the maggot of torment and evil get inside you, Raimundo . . . . Remember what befell Hamlet.

RAIMUNDO: Hamlet didn't suffer from an itchy bottom.

ANTON: This child . . .

MITCHUM: Who knows . . . Don't don't make a mountain out of a molehill. Perhaps you'll be all right tomorrow.

RAIMUNDO: I'm suffering dreadfully. I'm suffering for man and for his fate on Earth. I feel a terrible anxiety. I'm surrounded by clouds of dust, and lizards, snakes, rats and hens are crawling all over my chest.

MITCHUM: What's happened to you, lad?

RAIMUNDO: *(very effeminate)* Oh dear, my metabolism's undergone a radical change. I think I'm suffering from an excess of hormones. *(Gets up and begins to walk unsteadily. Looks at them, his neck in an extremely twisted pose. Smooths his hair down, humming a tune.)*

MITCHUM: Can you see what you've done. You've gone and converted a pure human being into an existentialist.

RAIMUNDO: Father . . . father . . .

IL CAPO: *(over loudspeaker)* Son. *(sound of shifting clouds, a storm.)*

RAIMUNDO: I've got a bullet wound in one side . . .

IL CAPO: A bullet wound? . . . Speak, you dogs, how did the operation go? . . . Is it a very large bullet, son?

RAIMUNDO: It's like a drainpipe, father.

IL CAPO: A small vein . . .

RAIMUNDO: No . . . a big vein . . . a . . . pipe, father, shooting across my back.

IL CAPO: What will your fiancee think, son?

RAIMUNDO: She's the last thing I feel like now. Oh!

IL CAPO: You swine . . . what have you done to my son?

RAIMUNDO: Father, I've an awful feeling that I've sinned. . . . I'm very unhappy.

IL CAPO: Who gave the boy the Kierkegaard book? Come on, tell me!

MITCHUM: Oh mighty, meet one, much loved ruler, we've done what we could . . .

RAIMUNDO: Let's flee father. Power lies with the people.

IL CAPO: *(hurling down a thunderbolt)* Silence! This is heresy!

RAIMUNDO: Let's bring this system to an end. Let's give man back what is his by right.

IL CAPO: My only son . . . a revolutionary and a terrorist . . . Oh my God. *(weeps)* You wretches, what have you done? *(thunder and lightning)* My anger will know no bounds. I'll destroy or deport you, you traitors. . . . A whole string of thieves wiped out in a moment! I preferred him when he was a senseless alcoholic! I preferred him when he barked . . .! He spent the afternoon quite happily with a bone!

RAIMUNDO: Down with the Mafia! Long live the inconstant Revolution.

MITCHUM: You can't have assimilated all that rubbish, lad . . . keep quiet! You've got it all wrong!

RAIMUNDO: To arms! Let the traitors die!

IL CAPO: I'll have the three of you shot like rats . . . Grrrrr . . .

MITCHUM: Woof, woof!

IL CAPO: Who dared to bark at me? Who?

MITCHUM: We've got to remove that liver from him, somehow. Our lives depend on it. It's a bad, infected liver. . . .

ANTON: That's child's play. It's as easy as getting rid of a wart. *(tips some chloroform into a handkerchief.)*

RAIMUNDO: Hold it! Don't come any nearer!

ANTON: *(following him)* It's perfume from Paris. I've had it smuggled in for you.

RAIMUNDO: *(climbing up to the window)* Don't move, you fascist! I'll denounce you to the People's Commission!

RODRIGUEZ *comes crawling out of the door at the back of the stage, half-naked. He disappears into the wings, leaving behind him a trail of blood. Nobody notices his presence. He is dying.*

MITCHUM: I implore you, if anything were to happen to you . . . your father would kill us. . . . You might fall. . . .

185

ANTON: After him!

RAIMUNDO: I'll jump out! I swear I will!

ANTON: Be reasonable. . . . You won't feel a thing. We'll give you a pig's liver. You'll produce delicious ham and salami sausage every year and many poor people in the country will feed off your excellently prepared and garnished ear.

RAIMUNDO: *(starting to sneeze)* I must have caught a cold . . . aaaaachew! *(looses his balance and falls into the air. They rush up to the window.)*

MITCHUM: Oh, my God!

ANTON: His arms and legs have parted company with him.

MITCHUM: All that's left of him is the trunk. . . . He looks like a dwarf.

IL CAPO: *(over the loudspeaker)* What's happened? Where are those screams coming from? Where's my son?

MITCHUM: He's here, sir. Safe and sound.

ANTON: He's caught a cold.

IL CAPO: He didn't catch colds like this before. . . . I don't know . . . something funny is going on. It all smells very fishy to me. . . . If something were to happen to him . . . If you don't bring him back to me alive . . .

ANTON: *(to* MITCHUM*)* What a bore!

IL CAPO: I'm going to send you a snowstorm, you wretches. . . . with electrical equipment.

ANTON:This is quite unbearable!

They run for shelter. Thunder and lightning, snow falls. They get up numb with cold.

MITCHUM: What do we do now?

ANTON: There's only one thing we can do. Go down and perform an emergency operation on him. We'll remove his liver and substitute a donkey's liver. Then we'll tear Rodriguez's arms and legs off and transplant them onto Raimundo. Then we'll put a soaking wet cap over his ears, some sunglasses on his nose, and say he's been the victim of an attack.

MITCHUM: Do you think you'll get away with it?

ANTON: No problem.

MITCHUM: Let's get going then! Our lives depend upon your surgical skill.

ANTON: Come on. *(They go inside to look for* RODRIGUEZ.*)*

MITCHUM: *(grabbing his arm)* What if he starts braying?

ANTON: If he brays, we'll just have to give him some straw and become revolutionaries.

MITCHUM: That's what I was thinking.

They go in and, shortly afterwards, come out.

ANTON: He's run away! The rotter . . . And just after his operation.

MITCHUM: This way . . . Woof! Woof! Let's follow this trail.

ANTON: I won't have you bark at me, understand?

MITCHUM: Woof!

ANTON: Bow wow!

MITCHUM: What a Deacon! It's disgraceful, barking like a common criminal . . . .

ANTON: You know what? I'm beginning to feel like biting you.

MITCHUM: Give you a race.

ANTON: O.K. All fours?

MITCHUM: Of course. Let's see who gets to Rodriguez first. *(They go down on all fours.)*

ANTON: Hang on a moment. *(goes to the wall, cocks his leg up and urinates.)*

MITCHUM: Ready, steady. . . . go!

They rush out on all fours. RODRIGUEZ *is seen sitting on the lavatory checking his haemorrhage with a newspaper. He is half naked and dying.* DOROTHY *arrives and goes into the toilet next door.*

DOROTHY: *(banging on the wall)* Hey . . .

RODRIGUEZ: What do you want?

DOROTHY: I've been sitting here waiting for you day and night. I've got piles. Where have you been?

RODRIGUEZ: Dorothy, darling . . . come in. I'm dying.

DOROTHY *goes out. Just as she is about to open the door of the men's lavatory the* MAN *appears.*

MAN: This is the men's lavatory, young lady. That is the ladies'.

DOROTHY: It's . . . half demolished. The wall's collapsed.

MAN: That's not true. I've rebuilt it, brick by brick. I've also put up a metal support so that you can both climb up.

DOROTHY: Sir . . . I entreat you . . . I beg you . . . I beseech you . . .

MAN: What?

DOROTHY: It's so little to ask. He's nothing but a bag of bones. He's suffered a great deal. . . .

MAN: Nothing can be done. Nobody can do anything for him, it's absolutely impossible. This is inevitable . . . believe me. *(knocks on the door.)*

RODRIGUEZ: *(in a barely audible voice)* Who is it?

MAN: Will you be long?

RODRIGUEZ: My bowels are a bit loose. . . . To tell the truth, I've only just started . . . apart from that I've got to clean my teeth and wash my hair. . . .

MAN: Don't talk so much. Save your energy. You're very weak. *(A trickle of blood flows under the door. To* DOROTHY) Look, he hasn't got diarrhea. He's dying. Go in and see to him. Don't let him get excited. Tell him to start reciting all the prayers he knows. *(banging hard on the door)* I'll give you a quarter of an hour. Then I'll come back and if you're still here I'll kick the door down.

RODRIGUEZ: Hey, listen, please. . . .

MAN: It's no good.

RODRIGUEZ: I don't want to die.

MAN: Don't waste your breath.

RODRIGUEZ: I've got to live.

MAN: Useless words.

DOROTHY: Oh, please. . . .

MAN: Twleve minutes and not a second more. It's the end. It's the beginning of a disaster. It's . . . death. *(silence)* I'll let you have any relevant information straightaway. Don't worry. I'll keep you informed. *(to DOROTHY)* Go in and attend to him. He needs your help now more than ever.

DOROTHY: Leave him alone . . . please. I love him very much, very much indeed.

MAN: You're completely useless, young lady.

DOROTHY: But . . .

MAN: I've heard this story a hundred times.

DOROTHY: I'll give you everything I've got. *(gets out a few cents)* I haven't . . . any more. . . . Would you like to see one of my breasts?

MAN: I'm not interested in breasts.

DOROTHY: What . . . what are you interested in? Tell me.

He begins to walk away. DOROTHY *grabs his arm.*

MAN: I'm interested in skulls, maggots . . . decomposition. Now, let me go. Let me go or I'll break your arm.

DOROTHY: *(weeping, lets go of him)* I love him, I love him, I love him . . .

MAN: Don't waste your tears. You'll never manage to melt this heart of mine. *(sielnce; he looks at her.)* Come now, dry your tears. *(puts his hand on her shoulder)* Go to him.

DOROTHY: Oh, my God!

MAN: It's only a giddy turn, so go to him. I'll be around.

Exit MAN, into the wings. DOROTHY *goes into the lavatory, nervously pulls up one of the paving stones and, still weeping, hauls* RODRIGUEZ *into the hole, replaces the stone.* ANTON *and* MITCHUM *appear, panting, running on all fours.*

ANTON: Here. *(smells the floor.)* I smell blood. *(goes into the cubicle.)*

MITCHUM: There's nobody here!

ANTON: But that's impossible!

The MAN *appears and stands staring at them.*

MAN: What are you doing in the ladies' lavatory?

ANTON: Listen here, I'm the Deacon. . . .

MAN: *(interrupting him)* I've heard some very bad reports about you. *(takes hold of one of his ears)* Your operations are extremely insufficient. You have a long string of corpses to your name.

MITCHUM: I order you to . . .

MAN: Keep quiet! You've only a few minutes left! Set your conscience at rights.

ANTON: What right have you to . . . ? !

MAN: *(tearing off his white coat)* Save your energy. Don't waste it in the lavatory, go out into the country and play with the children.

MITCHUM: This is absurd! I'm the Law here!

MAN: Get ready to die. . . . Very soon, these pockets and articles of clothing *(he tears off one of* MITCHUM*'s lapels)* will be of no further use to you. *(He produces a pair of scissors and leaves them both stark naked. Silence.)* Here you are, under here. Lift this stone up. Carry on. It is written that this should take place.

ANTON *and* MITCHUM *lift up the paving stone and get into the hole. They soon appear through another hole energetically pulling legs and arms. Cries of pain. They pull them off.*

ANTON: He was a tough fellow. I'd never have credited it.

MITCHUM: We've no time to lose. Let's get going.

ANTON: Would you like to see me beat you again?

MITCHUM: On your mark . . . get set . . . go!

They rush off with RODRIGUEZ*'s arms and legs. Shortly afterwards the* MAN *pears with* MARY, *in tears, on his arm.*

MARY: What are those shouts?

MAN: Some relative, perhaps. One can't be sure. Go on, go down, it's getting late and a strange, night wind is beginning to blow. . . . Go down. . . . *(taking hold of her cheek)* But don't be too long. Put your thoughts in order.

MARY: Your hand is absolutely freezing.

MAN: I spend many hours working outside.

MARY: You're a strange fellow.

MAN: So my friends say. Come on, I'll help you down.

MARY *goes into the hole.* DOROTHY *comes out of the other end. She is carrying* RODRIGUEZ's *head which she lays on the floor. The actor will be firmly fixed onto the stage, with only his bloody head in evidence. The* MAN *slides the water closet on top of the entrance hole. He takes out a hammer and some nails and starts to nail up the other exit. Inside, cries for help can be heard.*

DOROTHY: There's someone inside.

MAN: I'm not sure. . . . I don't think so.

DOROTHY: What are those screams then?

MAN: They're distant screams coming from near the centre of the earth. They're digging galleries, like moles. They're trying to get away.

RODRIGUEZ: Son of a bitch . . . Son of a bitch. . . .

MAN: Is he still alive? What vitality? Let's see. . . . *(He gets out a stethoscope and sounds his chest.* RODRIGUEZ *bites his head.)* No. *(thumping him on the head)* Don't bite me. . . . Why are you so ill-natured?

RODRIGUEZ: Take your hands off me. I don't want you to sound my chest.

MAN: I thought you were dead. . . . I've never seen a case like this before. Just a head on its own . . . no stomach, no lungs . . . and it can think and speak. This indicates that the spirit is situated in the head. Don't you agree? *(silence.)*

DOROTHY: We're planning a trip . . .

MAN: Yes, I know, to the Himalayas.

DOROTHY: Now he needs to recover . . . He needs fresh air and good food.

MAN: You'll have to carry him in a basket and not on your shoulders, as you intended doing.

RODRIGUEZ: Listen here . . . I'm really very, very tired. I beg you to have a little sympathy. . . . My situation's desperate, as you are well aware. Leave me alone.

191

MAN: Why have you got this idea into your head that you must make a stand? Against whom? Against me? It's pointless . . . let yourself go. . . . Make my job a little easier. . . . I'm not as bad as you think. But I must perform my duty. *(He takes hold of his hair.)* Come on. You'll hardly feel a thing.Come on. Close your eyes.

RODRIGUEZ: *(biting his hand; crimson with rage, his eyes bulging out of their sockets)* Son of a bitch . . . Son of a bitch.

MAN: *(to DOROTHY)* Put your hand over his mouth so that he can't insult me again. Put a plaster over his mouth and don't try to take it off.

DOROTHY *covers his mouth over with her hand. The* MAN *stands looking at them.*

MAN: These simple village fellows . . . talk about play you up! You can't finish them off just like that. . . . *(smiles)* Look at him, crimson with rage, in the face of Death. It's funny. It's nice. It's moving. What a will to live. *(He takes out an enormous hammer, and brings it down with an almighty effort onto* RODRIGUEZ*'s head. There is a loud explosion and smoke. When it clears.* RODRIGUEZ *is more entrenched than before, but alive. His head remains above ground, the rest covered in cement.)*

RODRIGUEZ: Help! Help! Police!

DOROTHY: Don't you feel any pity?

MAN: *(smiling)* How sweet. Here he is, alive and kicking. So tiny and unimportant. Who would have credited it.

RODRIGUEZ: Dorothy, get me out of here, I'm getting my mouth full of earth!

DOROTHY *squats down.*

MAN: Keep still! Don't try anything.

The MAN *places his foot on* RODRIGUEZ*'s forehead and begins to press it down.* RODRIGUEZ *begins to sink downwards.*

MAN: I'm sorry but it's my duty.

RODRIGUEZ *furiously bites his shoe.*

DOROTHY: No . . . not that way. Give us a few minutes. I must confess him. He has been a great sinner. *(silence.)*

MAN: *(grabbing hold of* RODRIGUEZ's *nose)* All right then. Ten more minutes. Then . . . *(to* DOROTHY*)* I'm only doing this for you, you know.

The MAN *disappears into the wings.* DOROTHY *lies down by the side of* RODRIGUEZ. *She wipes his face. They look at each other.*

DOROTHY: I'll save you. . . . I'll give you transfusions, suppositories, the best of everything. . . . Don't you worry. We'll go into hiding. He'll never find us . . . but, what's the matter? Are you crying? . . . Yes, you are. *(She dries his tears.)* I'll give you my liver, my sternum. . . . I'll buy you a cap . . . some glasses. . . . He won't find us. Come on. Don't cry . . . cheer up. Better times aren't far off. . . . They can't take much more away from you. You've hardly got anything left as it is. You haven't really got any cause to worry, as it were. . . . He won't do you any harm, you'll see. And if anything were to happen to you, I'm sure some part of you would always linger here, some flying particle. . . . Come on, let's go. Stop crying.

Darkness. ANTON *can be seen sitting in a chair, pale and frothing at the mouth, occasionally barking and emitting a deep growl like that of a mad dog. He takes hold of a newspaper and tears it into shreds with his teeth. He bites his hand in an attempt to control himself. He is wearing a cap, mask and surgical gloves. He is covered in blood.* MITCHUM *enters with a parcel.*

MITCHUM: Are you all right?

ANTON: Yes, I'm fine! Why?

MITCHUM: You've left the operating theatre.

ANTON: *(with unusual aggressiveness)* I left because it was time for me to leave, because my surgical mission had come to an end . . . because my assistants have also got to operate . . . because I felt like it. I'm one of the giants of surgery. I'm highly talented. Don't you forget it. I'm getting fed up with you. You're getting on my nerves.

MITCHUM: Was it successful?

ANTON: A resounding success. Nothing like it had been done in the history of medicine. Woof! Woof!

MITCHUM: What are you barking for?

ANTON: It helps me to relax, any objections?

MITCHUM: Nobel Prizewinners don't bark.

ANTON: I'll be the first one that does. No one will be surprised. Some of them have nervous tics, others play golf and I bark! I bark because I feel like it! *(He starts dribbling.)*

MITCHUM: The Swedish Academy have sent us this parcel for you. *(He gives it to him.* ANTON *opens it, and takes out a dunce's cap.)*

ANTON: This . . . this is outrageous! It was an unparalleled feat! A . . . a surgical cataclysm . . . it . . .

A stretcher comes wheeling in on its own. Silence. RAIMUNDO *gets up. He is in a disastrous state, emaciated and jaundiced, his feet apart. He begins to walk around like a drunkard.*

ANTON: They've put his shoes on the wrong feet!

MITCHUM: You fool! You've grafted his legs on the wrong way! You've put the left leg where the right leg should be and the right leg where the left leg should be! Look at him! You've turned him into a grotesque monster!

ANTON: It's impossible! I'm sure . . . !

MITCHUM: Look at your work of art! He looks drunk! During the operation something fell into his stomach and now, when he moves, it sounds like a rattle! *(He shakes* RAIMUNDO. *Noise like a giant rattle.)*

ANTON: Woof! Woof!

MITCHUM: That's enough woof, woofing! That's your answer to everything. Now what am I going to tell the boss? Have you any idea what will happen to us?

ANTON: *(moving up to Raimundo)* How do you feel, lad?

RAIMUNDO: *(a stupid grin on his face)* I don't know. . . . These arms . . . don't seem to work properly. I feel really miserable.

ANTON: You've just come from the operating theatre. You're still under the effects of the anaesthetic. . . .

RAIMUNDO: I think I'm dying.

MITCHUM: I beg you . . .

RAIMUNDO: Nothing in the heavenly sphere has any importance. I predict grave spatial catastrophes. . . .

MITCHUM: Cast aside those obsessions, my child. Go to sleep. Relax.

RAIMUNDO: No, I must go. I've only a few minutes left . . . I can no longer have a fiancee and get married like all the other boys in the world.

ANTON: For Heaven's sake. I think you're looking fine . . . sturdy and upright like a poppy. In your eyes an inner light burns . . . illuminating the whole nation. . . . I think you look marvelous, elegant, very attractive . . . fragrant and charming, honestly I do. Now . . . go to sleep. Don't worry any more about . . .

RAIMUNDO: I'm going . . . I must get away. They're waiting impatiently for me. The constants are calling me, one by one. . . .

ANTON: There he goes again!

RAIMUNDO *begins to walk. Weird movements with legs completely stiff. He moves forward jerkingly.* ANTON *begins to laugh with loud, uncontrollable guffaws.*

MITCHUM: *(to* ANTON*)* Fool! Murderer!

ANTON: It looks as if you've shitted yourself, Raimundo, ha! ha, ha!

RAIMUNDO: If I have, it'll be on you, swine. Wow wow!

ANTON: *(curling up with laughter)* Would you like me to give you a chicken liver transplant? Ha, ha, ha! A chicken liver "a la Molinera" and a cucumber, ha, ha, ha!

MITCHUM: Take no notice of him. He's sick. He's showing unmistakeable symptoms of rabies.

ANTON: *(putting on the dunce's hat and running round the stage laughing, barking and somersaulting)* Rabies, rabies! Woof, woof! Ignore that fellow, Raimundo. He's an idiot, take it from me. I know him well. Ha, ha, ha!

MITCHUM: You're under arrest.

RAIMUNDO: Watch it!

ANTON, *slobbering, remains staring into* MITCHUM's *eyes. He hurls himself onto him and bites his arm. He tears his jacket off.*

IL CAPO: *(over loudspeaker)* What have you done with my son? How is he?

ANTON: In a terrible state. Ha, ha, ha! He's only got a few minutes left. . . .

IL CAPO: How dare you? You will feel the full weight of my anger, wretch!

ANTON: Degenerate! Imbecile! I'm fed up to the back teeth! Long live anarchy!

IL CAPO: Consider yourself a dead man.

ANTON: Raimundo . . . let's form a republic! I'll elect you President.

IL CAPO: *(sound of a thunberbolt)* My fury has burst its bounds.

ANTON: *(takes out a bomb, removes the percussion cap, and hurls it in the direction of the voice)* Scarecrow! It's all over! Down with oppression!

MITCHUM: You've just signed your death warrant. . . .

ANTON: Grrrrr . . .

RAIMUNDO: Don't you think . . . I look rather comical . . . for a President . . . with this rattling inside.

ANTON: What the Hell! If you're no good as President, I'll make you director of a circus. . . . I'll make you a plaster corset.

RAIMUNDO: Oh no! I won't even let you cut my nails!

ANTON: Er . . . let's put the past behind us. Let's shake hands on it lad. Don't bear grudges. *(They shake hands and* RAIMUNDO's *arm remains in his hand, having come effortlessly from his body.)*

MITCHUM: Oh my God! This man's falling to pieces!

RAIMUNDO: You really fixed it well for me, didn't you! You wretch . . .

ANTON: What a small number of us there are. . . . Human nature is so fragile. The human condition is so wretched. . . . Oh dear . . . *(He detaches* RAIMUNDO's *other arm which falls to the ground and smashes like glass. Silence. Everyone stands staring at him in surprise.)*

RAIMUNDO: What did you stick them on with? Cellotape?

ANTON: Ha, ha, ha! Now you'll have to hang your watch over your ear.

MITCHUM: How dreadful!

RAIMUNDO: Let's hope I don't lose anything else.

ANTON: We'll just have to hope you don't. . . .

MITCHUM: What a masterpiece!

The MAN *appears. He looks at them and begins to pick up the pieces of arm and put them into a bag.*

MAN: Excuse me, one moment . . .

ANTON: Who are you?

MAN: Would you let me have that arm back?

ANTON: *(still holding the arm)* What do you want this rubbish for?

MAN: I'm writing a biography of you. . . . I need all the details. They must all be numbered and labelled.

ANTON: You will, of course, have the grace to send me a copy.

MAN: Naturally, I'll bring it to you in person. If you are in agreement, we can dance together for a while, cheek to cheek, like two lovers. . . . A wonderful, final dance, believe me.

MITCHUM: What a strange fellow!

ANTON: What line are you in?

MAN: I go around collecting and storing information.

RAIMUNDO: Information about me too?

MAN: Naturally.

RAIMUNDO: Do you think anything else will drop off me?

MAN: It could do. . . .

ANTON: Don't worry about that. I'll fix you up with a pair of artificial limbs.

MAN: It's a waste of time. He's dying.

RAIMUNDO: How . . . how do you know?

ANTON: You seem to know a lot of things . . .

MAN: *(to* RAIMUNDO*)* Open your mouth . . . *(to* ANTON*)* Look . . . can't you see death?

197

ANTON: That? Is that death?

MAN: It is.

ANTON: That black . . . that delicate, sensual shape . . . that . . .

MAN: In the roof of his mouth . . .

MITCHUM: Would you look at mine . . . I'm intrigued. (MITCHUM *opens his mouth.*)

MAN: Yours is different. You're a fool, that's your trouble.

ANTON: Exactly. You can see that a mile off. . . .

MITCHUM: I'll have none of your jokes, sir. Do you realize who you are talking to?

RAIMUNDO: Listen . . . um . . . how long do you estimate I could live for?

MAN: You're decomposing. You've only got a minute or two left, at the most.

RAIMUNDO: I'd like to confess myself . . .

MAN: I don't think you'll have time. . . .

RAIMUNDO: (*crying*) Will I go to Heaven? I've been good.

MITCHUM: You've been good . . . I'll second that. I'm the highest ecclesiastical authority in this country.

ANTON: I thought you were a lawyer . . . or a draughtsman. . . .

MITCHUM: So I am . . . but I'm also a bishop. Didn't you realize, you fool?

RAIMUNDO: In that case, what do you advise me to do? Speak up. . . .

MAN: Get into bed and await death calmly.

ANTON: In luxury . . .

RAIMUNDO: What will my father say when he sees me like this?

ANTON: He'll think you're drunk. Put a pair of dark glasses on and a raincoat over your shoulders. That way he won't notice. . . .

RAIMUNDO: Goodbye. . . . (*kisses each of them on the cheek.*)

MAN: Get moving or you won't get there in time—any moment now, you . . . Cut the kisses out and say a prayer for your soul.

RAIMUNDO: Oh Lord . . . Lord . . . please don't let anything else come away from me. . . .

RAIMUNDO *rushes out, soon afterwards, there is a sound of wood breaking, something falls onto the floor. Silence. They look at each other. A little later the head comes rolling onto the stage. Silence.*

ANTON: *(picking it up)* How disgraceful! It's hollow! What a disgusting substitute material *(smashes it)* . . . dust . . . air . . . nothing, nothing at all.

MITCHUM: Poor devil . . . dying in the street like a tramp . . . without confession. *(telephone rings; MITCHUM answers it.)* Yes? What? It can't be true! . . . Okay! . . . All right . . . We'll arrange everything. *(turning to ANTON)* Rodriguez has been awarded the Nobel Prize for Physics. His theory regarding the variability of the constants has been universally accepted. . . . They say he's got to receive the prize. . . . and . . . and he's got to go to Sweden to collect it.

ANTON: There's going to be a proper uproar now. He'll have to receive it . . . in his mouth . . .

MAN: Give me that head, idiot.

ANTON: You want everything. You don't leave anything for us.

MAN: This doesn't belong to you. *(puts it in a bag)* It's the property of the people. It's part of the National Heritage. I'm convinced you intended to make money out of it.

MITCHUM: Let's go. We've got to tell Rodriguez the news.

MAN: Let's make a move. I'd like to go along witth you.

ANTON: Nobody's invited you. . . .

MAN: Open your mouth. *(to MITCHUM)* Look . . . he's suffering from rabies. He's very ill indeed.

MITCHUM: What's that on the right?

MAN: A decayed tooth.

MITCHUM: Behind it, at the back . . .

MAN: A beetle . . . or a rat perhaps. It's hard to say.

MITCHUM: How revolting! I'd never have thought . . .

MAN: Shall we go then?

MITCHUM: Yes, let's go.

MAN: Don't you want to go to the toilet first?

MITCHUM: Well . . . yes, I do actually. How did you know?

MAN: I knew all right. You can see it in your eyes. In you go. We'll wait for you.

MITCHUM *goes into the lavatory. The* MAN *nails the door up from the outside.*

MAN: *(to* ANTON*)* He was unbearably conceited . . . don't you agree?

ANTON: Yes. Do you intend to keep him shut in indefinitely?

MAN: He needs to do some serious thinking. He needs to be alone in order to find his true self. That's the best place for him.

ANTON: Will you bring him food? Nothing at all?

MAN: He's overeaten. He needs to fast for a while.

ANTON: But . . . he'll die of loneliness . . . all on his own, in there. . . .

MAN: Chastity, a divine treasure . . .

ANTON: His wails will go up to heaven.

MAN: Let's get going right away. He'll soon start kicking the door and making an unbearable row.

ANTON: Why have you shut him in?

MAN: He's been wicked. *(silence)* He's played around with human life.

ANTON: Do you think my rat problem will turn out to be serious? Won't it eat my throat?

MAN: Not if you keep fairly still . . . and don't talk for the sake of talking . . . and don't irritate it.

ANTON: But . . . that's impossible. I depend on my powers of oratory for my living.

200

MAN: In that case, there's no possible way of saving you. It will eat your throat and destroy your muscles, tendons, carotid artery and jugular vein. At the least movement, your head will become detached from your body.

ANTON: Couldn't I possibly get hold of it? I'm very skilled with my hands. . . . Perhaps with a pair of tweezers or forceps. . . . You could help me.

MAN: I don't know if I'd be able to. I was a nurse once . . . but that was a long time ago. . . . It's up to you. . . .

ANTON: You see . . . my throat's beginning to hurt. I've got a sort of jerking movement there which won't let me breathe. . . . *(begins to slobber, with clenched jaws.)*

MAN: It's rabies, there's no doubt about it. You must take care of yourself. Keep your head covered when you go out into the sun, that's very important.

ANTON: Get this creature out of my throat—it's burning . . . I'm going mad. . . .

MAN: Keep right out of the sun. Understand? Plenty of shade. Don't eat anything hot or spicy and no strong drink. . . .

ANTON: That's for ulcers.

MAN: The treatment's similar.

ANTON: Get rid of this for me, I beg you. I can hardly breathe. . . . If not, I'll bite you. . . .

MAN: Whatever you say. . . .

ANTON: I haven't any instruments here. . . .

MAN: I'll get some. *(produces a huge pair of forceps.)*

ANTON: You certainly came prepared.

MAN: Even for sewing buttons on. . . . Open your mouth. . . . *(opens ANTON's mouth.)* I'll have to cut the raw flesh. There's no other way. *(introduces the forceps into ANTON's mouth and grips hold.)* Does that hurt?

ANTON: Slightly.

MAN: Shall I pull it out?

ANTON: By its roots. Oh God, I can't stand the pain. . . . .

201

MAN: It's going to be painful. . . . It may be a tumour.

ANTON: Take it out, quickly. I can't bear it any more. *(He gives a tug and AN-TON collapses.)*

MAN: I'm a disastrous surgeon. . . . Fancy getting hold of his heart. . . . I should have consulted a good specialist. *(throws the body over his shoulder and goes out).*

DOROTHY *can be seen sitting on a low, folding chair, fanning herself. She is wearing a very full skirt. She looks to right and left. Next to her, a basket and a knapsack.*

RODRIGUEZ: *(from under the chair)* Is it much further?

DOROTHY: *(lifting up her skirt and looking underneath it)* Much further? Do you think the Himalayas are right on our doorstep?

RODRIGUEZ: This is awful. I'm getting a mouthful of ants!

DOROTHY: Keep quiet and hide! There are people coming. *(Still fanning herself, she smiles as if someone were walking past.)*

RODRIGUEZ: A potato beetle!

DOROTHY: *(in a whisper)* Quiet or they'll find us.

RORDIGUEZ: A hen! Serpents, snakes, flies! I'm stifling! Air, quickly! Lift your skirt up.

DOROTHY: *(beating on the floor with her fan, frightening off the animals)* Cluck, cluck, cluck . . .

RODRIGUEZ: When a hen! It looks like a bull! A cat! A dog! It's licking my face. Down boy!

DOROTHY: You're hysterical. They're not doing anything. Calm down and make friends with them so they don't see you're frightened.

RODRIGUEZ: Get lost, you bastards.

DOROTHY: Take your tablet.

RODRIGUEZ: Forget about tablets! A helicopter! A tower! They're eating me.

DOROTHY: *(smiling at another passer-by)* Hallo . . . how are you? I'm fine. . . . -

Just taking a breath of fresh air.

RODRIGUEZ: My eye's stinging. I've got a bit of dust in it. Another hen! A cock! There's nothinng but cocks and hens here! What a place!

DOROTHY: Temper, temper! For Goodness' sake, dear, we won't get anywhere like this. You must try to be brave.. Animals don't do anything unless attacked. You have nightmares . . . you wet the bed. . . . We can't go on like this. . . .

RODRIGUEZ: Help . . . help . . . a wasp! A huge wasp! It's stinging me! Air! You bastards!

DOROTHY: No! *(A passer-by stops and stares at them.)*

PASSER-BY: Is anything the matter?

DORorhy: *(speaking under the seat)* I've told you a thousand times, Lewis! Don't say bad words! Your tongue will drop off. *(to the passer-by)* Children!

PASSER-BY: *(looking under the seat)* He's quite grown up.

RODRIGUEZ: Bastard!

PASSER-BY: What a voice he's got! It's like a man's!

DOROTHY: He's a heavy smoker, one cigar after another.

PASSER-BY: *(taking hold of his ear)* Don't say such wicked words, my boy.

DOROTHY: He's got a dreadful temper . . .

PASSER-BY: You're a maid, aren't you?

DOROTHY: A serving girl, sir. . . . I have to take him out every afternoon. He had a very difficult labour. Look how he's turned out.

PASSER-BY: *(putting his hand up her skirt)* I'm a soldier.

DOROTHY: But you're not in uniform.

PASSER-BY: I know, but I feel like a soldier.

DOROTHY: A habit doesn't make a monk.

PASSER-BY: Exactly. *(referring to RODRIGUEZ)* Does he like sweets?

DOROTHY: Oh, er, sweets . . . sweets . . . no, not much!

PASSER-BY: Or chewing gum?

RODRIGUEZ: Fuck off. Bloody Hell . . .

PASSER-BY: He has got a temper, hasn't he? *(raps him on the head)* Behave yourself or I'll give you one. . . . On the other hand, if he's only got a head . . .

DOROTHY: He's a real bighead.

PASSER-BY: What about his hands . . .

DOROTHY: They cut them off at school.

PASSER-BY: He won't be able to do his military service then. . . . What would he shoot with?

DOROTHY: He'll be written off as useless.

PASSER-BY: He's got a very narrow chest, hasn't he?

DOROTHY: Very narrow . . . on top of that, the cigars he gets through!

PASSER-BY: Why don't you give him his dummy and then come with me behind those bushes?

RODRIGUEZ: Behind what bushes? What for?

PASSER-BY: *(slapping him)* Listen, youngster . . . sshh! Daddy's talking.

DOROTHY: Some other time, sir. Don't take offence but you're wearing such thick glasses . . .

PASSER-BY: I'm dreadfully short-sighted. I'm sorry. I didn't realize you only liked sharp-eyed men.

DOROTHY: I'm afraid so.

PASSER-BY: Goodbye, miss.

DOROTHY: Goodbye.

PASSER-BY: He wouldn't be your child by any chance, would he?

DOROTHY: Well . . . yes. I didn't want to tell you. He's mine and I'm an unmarried mother.

PASSER-BY: In that case, we shan't be seeing each other again. You could ruin my military career.

DOROTHY: Better luck next time.

PASSER-BY: I hope so.

He disappears. RODRIGUEZ *is heard crying.*

DOROTHY: Not again? What's the matter now?

RODRIGUEZ: My nose's running . . . my nose's running. . . . I can't wipe it. . . .
My face itches, sweat is running into my eyes. I can't do a thing about it. It's
no good. We'll never get to the Himalayas. Dorothy, I want to die.

DOROTHY: Keep quiet. Don't say such things.

RODRIGUEZ: The sun's beating down on the back of my neck. . . .

DOROTHY: I'll buy you a cap, a mask, anything you want. I'll be your
secretary. . . .

RODRIGUEZ: Oh my God. . . . Oh my God. . . *(continues to cry)*
Approaching steps can be heard.

MAN: Hallo . . . Fanning yourself?

DOROTHY: I can't bear this heat.

MAN: I'm looking for Rodriguez. Have you seen him?

DOROTHY: I haven't seen him for ages. With him being so small, one almost has
to get down on one's hands and knees . . . No, definitely not. I haven't a clue
where he could be.

MAN: You wouldn't be lying, by any chance?

DOROTHY: Search me. . . . If you like we could go behind those bushes there
and you could search me thoroughly. Then you won't need to bother me
again.

MAN: You might get pregnant though.

DOROTHY: Don't worry . . . I can take care of myself.

MAN: What's in that basket?

DOROTHY: He's not there. How can I convince you?

MAN: What about inside the haversack?

DOROTHY: He's not there either. It's a folding chair. . . . I often use it. The doctor told me that if I remained standing for any length of time, my womb could
drop.

205

MAN: It could even fall out and break into a thousand pieces.

DOROTHY: Understand?

MAN: *(sitting down beside her)* By the looks of things, you've taken quite a liking to mountaineering.

DOROTHY: Yes.

MAN: Don't go to the Himalayas, young lady. I work there a lot. I'm telling you in all sincerity. One slip, one avalanche . . . one storm . . . and it could be fatal. . . . To tell the truth, I wouldn't like anything to happen to you. . . . Do you know what it is I like about you? You've got such a soft voice and it comforts me. . . . I'm tired, very tired indeed. This is a hard, exhausting profession. People think that Death never gets tired. . . . If only you knew! Looking everywhere . . . under tables, under chairs. . . . Give me your hand.

DOROTHY: You're a romantic.

MAN: No, I'm an idealist.

DOROTHY: Oh!

MAN: And that's why, when I see someone cling on so determinedly to life . . . When I see such vitality, such exuberance . . . my task becomes very miserable indeed. I suffer greatly, believe me. *(Silence. They sit quite still, absorbed in the sounds of the country.)* There are many hens in this area, aren't there?

RODRIGUEZ: Yes, there are.

MAN: What did you say?

DOROTHY: I said yes, yes there are. Loads of them. There are loads of hens here.

Sound of mighty explosion. Everything remains in darkness. A long, yellowish candle carried by the MAN *is lit. Silence.*

DOROTHY: What's happened?

MAN: Do you know what? Planck's constant has exploded.

DOROTHY: You don't say.

MAN: It's become inconstant.

DOROTHY: When someone is awarded the Nobel Prize . . .

MAN: *(rising)* There's generally a reason. . . .

DOROTHY: Are you off?

MAN: I'm just going to stretch my legs. I feel sad and I can't work when I'm sad.

DOROTHY: Won't you stay and have tea with me? I've some cheese with live maggots inside. I think you'll like it.

MAN: How revolting! Where can I get a nice ham sandwich?

DOROTHY: That's just what I was thinking.

MAN: *(shakes hands with her)* Cheerio.

DOROTHY: What cold hands you've got.

MAN: Perhaps in the Himalayas . . .

DOROTHY: Who knows . . . *(The* MAN *begins to walk away.)* Hey. . . . when will daylight return?

MAN: It won't. The Earth has just lost the sun and has just come out of its orbit. The equations have all just exploded. . . . Now Earth is condemned to wander in darkness throughout space.

DOROTHY: How awful! How do we . . . get about and . . .

MAN: *(giving her the candle)* Here you are. It's a present you're going to need. You've a long way to go.

DOROTHY: What about you?

MAN: Don't worry about me. I'm used to walking in darkness. *(Exits into wings. Silence.)*

DOROTHY: He's gone. He's left. Are you happy now?

RODRIGUEZ: *(with a loud scream)* Bastards!

DOROTHY: Can't you say anything else?

RODRIGUEZ: Bastards!

DOROTHY: A fine journey I've got in store for me!

CURTAIN

Stage Directions

ISRAEL HOROVITZ

THE PEOPLE OF THE PLAY

RICHARD; A thin, hawklike man, forties.
RUTH; A thin, hawklike woman, thirties.
RUBY; A small, wrenlike woman, twenties.

THE TIME OF THE PLAY

Late afternoon, fall

THE PLACE OF THE PLAY

Living room, New England home,
overlooking Lake Quannapowitt, Wakefield, Mass.

N.B. The people of the play will speak only words that describe their activities and, on occasion, emotions. No other words or sounds are permitted. By definition, then, all activity and conveyed emotion must be born of spoken stage directions.

STAGE DIRECTIONS had its first public performance on May 31, 1976, at The Actors Studio, New York. It was directed by J. Ranelli and featured the following actors:

Richard .... Lenny Baker
Ruth .... Laura Esterman
Ruby .... Nancy Mett

Approximate playing time: 30 minutes
(The play is performed without an intermission.)

Lights fade up.
Sofa, slightly Right of room's Center.
Bar wagon and liquor, Upstage Right.
Overstuffed chairs, Right and Left of sofa, slightly Down-stage.
Large framed mirror, 24" x 36", draped in black fabric,
Upstage Left wall.
Equal sized framed photograph, draped in black fabric as well, opposite wall,
Upstage of Center of sofa.
China cabinet filled with bric-a-brac, wall beside Upstage chair. (optional.)
Single door to room, Upstage Right wall.
Copious bookshelves and books, wherever space permits.
General feeling wanted that room belongs to bookish person.
Small desk Downstage Right. Writing stand, memo pad, stationery, on same.
Wastebasket at Upstage front foot. Oriental carpet, subdued tones, under all
of above.

RICHARD: (*Enters.*) Richard enters, quietly. Looks about room to see if he is alone. Certain he is, closes door. Pauses, inhales, turns and leans his back against door, exhales, sobs once. He wipes his eyes on his cuff, notices black armband, which he removes and into which he blows his nose. He then stuffs armband into pocket of his overcoat which he then removes and folds somewhat fastidiously over back of sofa. He pauses, looking about room, taking a private moment: possibly adjusting his underwear and then discovering and dealing with a day-old insect bite in the pit behind his knee. A fly buzzes past his nose, breaking into his thoughts. He swats at fly carelessly, but somehow manages to capture same in hand, which he brings down and then up close to his eye. He opens hand ever so slightly, watching fly awhile. Although it appears certain that he will open hand allowing fly her freedom, he suddenly smashes hands together, finishing fly and causing clap to sound in room. He walks to desk and using slip of memo paper from pad, he scrapes fly from palm and into wastebasket at foot of desk. He inspects stain on palm, lowers hand to side, pauses, returns to chair, sobs once, sits, bows head, notices shoe, removes same, places single shoe in his lap, sobs again, searches for and finds lightly plaided handkerchief into which he blows nose enthusiastically, unclogging same and producing substantial honking sound in room. He settles back in chair, stares vacantly up at ceiling.

RUTH: (*Enters.*) Ruth enters, quietly, closing door with her heel. She looks cautiously about room to see if she is alone, sees Richard sitting in chair.

210

RICHARD: Richard quickly bows his head and assumes somewhat grave look on his face, rather a studied vacant stare at his black-stockinged foot.

RUTH: Ruth smiles, as though she has been acknowledged.

RICHARD: Richard flashes a quick look at Ruth, to be certain it is she who has entered.

RUTH: Ruth catches Richard's glance and smiles again.

RICHARD: Richard is forced to return her smile and does. He then returns to former position in chair, head-bowed, eyes vacant, staring down toward black-stockinged foot.

RUTH: Ruth leans her back against door, exhales.

RICHARD: Richard adjusts his underwear, discreetly.

RUTH: Ruth sighs.

RICHARD: Richard wipes the palm of his hand behind the knee of his trouser-leg, accomplishing both a wipe and a rub of the day-old insect bite.

RUTH: Ruth touches her black armband to be certain it has not been lost, sighs again.

RICHARD: Richard glances at his hand to be certain now that fly stain has been completely removed. Satisfied, nonetheless, he wipes his hand on his trouser-leg again.

RUTH: Ruth pretends to be removing her overcoat while never removing her stare from the back of Richard's head. She slips her hand inside her coat and discreetly adjusts her brassiere . . .

RICHARD: . . . just as Richard turns to her . . .

RUTH: She recoils quickly, pulling her hand from her coat.

RICHARD: Seeing that he has startled her, he turns away, reviving his former position, head bowed, vacantly staring at his black-stockinged foot.

RUTH: Ruth pauses a moment and then moves directly to bar and surveys liquor supply atop same.

211

RICHARD: Richard senses her presence at the bar and turns to look disapprovingly at her.

RUTH: Ruth, sensing his disapproval, quickly pours an inch of bourbon, which she downs in a gulp.

RICHARD: He continues his disapproving stare, while unconsciously touching his nose.

RUTH: She raises her glass toward him, nods: blatantly hostile. She smiles, unconsciously touching her nose as well.

RICHARD: She is smiling, deliberately handling her nose . . .

RUTH: He turns away, pompously . . . She clears her throat, attempting to regain his attention, but he remains unmoved, disapproving . . . She pulls open her coat and adjusts her brassiere . .

RICHARD: Raising his hip and thigh, slightly and quickly, he adjusts his briefs, scratches his day-old insect bite and then spits directly on to his palm and fly-stain, wipes his hand on his trouser knee, smiles . . . He turns now and faces her directly, but she is pretending not to notice, not to be paying attention to him. She searches for and finds a rather gaudy orange nylon handkerchief, into which she indelicately honks her hooked nose . . .

RUTH: He removes his sock and pulls at toes, playing with same . . .

RICHARD: She flings her coat sloppily over back of sofa . . . His other shoe off now and . . .

RUTH: (N.B. Words and actions overlap competitively.) Ruth removes her gloves . . . and hat . . .

RICHARD: (overlapping.) . . . placing it precisely beside his first shoe . . .

RUTH: (overlapping.) . . . tossing them in a heap on the sofa . . .

RICHARD: (overlapping.) . . . He then peels off his other sock . . .

RUTH: (overlapping.) . . . She then hoists her skirt and unhitches her stocking-top from the front and back garters on her garter-belt . . .

RICHARD: (overlapping) Richard averts his eyes!

RUTH: Ruth stares at the back of Richard's head, directly. The affect should be one of deep hostility. She is, however, surprised to notice that she is weeping.

RICHARD: . . . as is Richard.

RUTH: There is a moment of absolute silence. (*five count.*)

RUTH: There is a moment of absolute silence.

RICHARD: Sock clenched in fist, Richard will pound the arm of his chair, three times. He stares straight ahead, eyes unblinking. Three . . . dull . . . thuds . . . . And then silence. (*five count.*)

RUTH: Ruth approaches Ruby's chair, stands behind it a moment, pauses.

RICHARD: Richard turns to her and their eyes quietly meet.

RUTH: Ruth is the first to turn away.

RICHARD: Richard bows his head.

RUTH: Ruth walks quickly to the bar wagon and liquor supply, pours two inches of bourbon this time, tosses bottle cap on to floor and then returns to Ruby's chair.

RICHARD: Richard does not look up. He picks at a loose thread on his trouser-knee.

RUTH: Ruth sits, crosses legs, removes shoes, floors them.

RICHARD: Richard turns his body away from her, staring off vacantly.

RUTH: Ruth notices now she wears one stocking pulled taut, the other dangling loose by her knee. She removes first stocking and allows it to stay on floor near her foot. She reaches under her skirt and unhitches other stocking from her garter-belt.

RICHARD: Richard glances at her, discreetly touching his nose.

RUTH: She senses his glance, but neither looks up nor acknowledges same. She instead removes stocking which she crunches and holds in same hand with glass of bourbon.

RICHARD: Richard suddenly stands, floors shoes, crosses room to bar.

RUTH: Ruth watches him, unconsciously touching her nose.

RICHARD: Richard searches for and finds small clear bottle of club soda, which he neatly uncaps, pouring liquid into small clear glass. He recaps bottle, replacing same precisely where it was found. Taking glass in hand, returns to chair, sits, sips.

RUTH: Ruth sips her bourbon and notices stocking crunched in hand. She reaches down and finds other stocking, joining both in loose knot, which she flings on to sofa seat.

RICHARD: Richard stares at her disapprovingly.

RUTH: Ruth remembers armband on coat. She stands, goes to it.

RICHARD: Richard stares after her.

RUTH: Ruth begins to remove armband, but thinks better of it, returns to chair, begins to sit, thinks better of it, drains glass of its bourbon, returns to bar, pours three inches of fresh bourbon into same glass.

RICHARD: Richard turns away from her.

RUTH: Ruth glances at back of Richard's head.

RICHARD: Richard rubs his knee.

RUTH: Ruth tosses bottle, now empty, into wastebasket.

RICHARD: The sound startles Richard, who turns suddenly . . .

RUTH: . . . startling Ruth, who recoils, spilling her drink . . . on the rug.

RICHARD: Richard stares at stain . . . on the rug.

RUTH: Ruth rubs stain with her toe.

RICHARD: Richard turns away.

RUTH: Ruth turns, cupping her forehead in the palm of her right hand. She then moves her hand down over her nose and mouth and sobs.

RICHARD: There is a moment of silence, which Richard breaks first by dropping his glass on to floor.

214

RUTH: Ruth looks quickly in direction of sound.

RICHARD: Richard is amazed. He grabs his nose.

RUTH: Ruth smiles.

RICHARD: Richard leans forward and picks up glass.

RUTH: Ruth drains her glass of its remaining bourbon, one gulp.

RICHARD: Richard wipes his stain on rug with his socks, never leaving his chair, but instead leaning forward to his stain.

RUTH: Ruth, for the first time, notices his body, now stretched forward. Her smile is gone.

RICHARD: Richard seems perplexed. He pulls at his earlobe.

RUTH: Ruth places glass atop bar. She searches for and finds dish towel, which she aims and pitches on to floor near Richard's stain.

RICHARD: Richard looks first at dish towel, then at Ruth, disapprovingly. He then picks up dish towel and covers his stain with same.

RUTH: Ruth crosses to Ruby's chair, sits. She is weeping.

RICHARD: Richard, too, is weeping.

RUBY: (*Enters.*) Ruby enters, somewhat noisily, clumsily.

RUTH: Ruth turns to her from chair, smiles.

RUBY: Ruby returns the smile.

RUTH: Ruth looks away.

RUBY: Ruby looks about the room until her eyes meet Richard's.

RICHARD: His expression is cold, the muscles of his face taut, his mouth thin-lipped, angry.

RUBY: Ruby nods to Richard.

RICHARD: Richard turns away, fists clenched on knees.

RUBY: Ruby closes door, bracing back against same.

RUTH: She has Richard's enormous Tel Avivian nose . . .

RICHARD: . . . Ruth's hawklike eyes, her hopelessly flat chest . . .

RUTH: . . . Richard's studied pompousity: his gravity . . .

RICHARD: . . . Ruth's unfathomable lack of courage . . .

RUTH: . . . Richard's incomprehensible lack of feeling . . .

RICHARD: . . . Ruth's self-consciously-correct posture . . .

RUBY: Rich girl's shoulders.

RICHARD: Richard loathes Ruby.

RUTH: As does Ruth.

RICHARD: Evident now in his stern glance.

RUTH: As in Ruth's sudden snap from warmth to disapproval: from passion to ice.

RUBY: Ruby moves four steps to center of room and then stops, suddenly, somewhat squashed by their staring.

The following speeches are to be spoken as though interruptions, often over-lapping, as often blending. No considerable movement wanted during this section.

RICHARD: N.B. Richard was first to hear news of father's death . . .

RUTH: N.B. Ruth heard news of plane crash and mother's death from Richard.

RUBY: N.B. Ruby was last to hear news of plane crash and mother's death . . .

RICHARD: . . . Mother's call put through by Betsy—the secretary—Mrs. Betsy Day, the secretary—Conference room, cigar smoke thick, business trouble, no time, distractions impossible . . .

RUTH: . . . Richard's phone call, Asian Studies Office, University of Vermont, town of Manchester, employed as nobody, researching nothing, touching no one . . .

216

RUBY: . . . Read news in Chicago *Sun-Times*. Heard same on FM station, midst of news, interrupting Bach's *Concerto in D Minor for 3*, harpsicords and orchestra, *Alla Siciliana*, my name, them famous, now dead, now famous death . . .

RICHARD: . . . Father's body must be gotten. Died in Hot Springs, Arkansas, getting cured . . .

RUTH: . . . Ruth had not known her father had died . . .

RUBY: . . . Flew from O'Hare International to Logan International, United Air Lines, 707, morning flight, a clot of double-knit polyester leisure-suited businessmen, whispering loudly. Her second flight only, entire lifetime . . .

RICHARD: . . . Arranged for mother to fly to Hot Springs, Arkansas, to collect father's body, fly it home . . .

RUTH: . . . Ruth had not even known her father had been ill . . .

RUBY: . . . Her first flight was three years prior, visited father, first news of illness . . .

RICHARD: . . . Had reserved and paid for American Airlines First Class ticket. Had ticket hand-delivered to mother two days prior . . .

RUTH: . . . Had years ago conquered fear of air travel. Had flown to and from all continents of the earth . . .

RUBY: . . . Met with doctors, disease incurable, all hope lost . . .

RICHARD: . . . Had summoned surviving siblings to family home, New England September, all chill . . .

RUTH: . . . Had preferred Asia to all others. Had preferred living in countries possessing languages she could neither read nor speak . . .

RUBY: Brother Robert, gone as well, same disease, spared no pain, three years prior, family . . . curse . . .

RICHARD: . . . Had not spoken even one word to Ruth in four years' time, since her third divorce . . .

217

RUTH: . . . Had preferred most of all living within Cantonese dialect, Northern China, most difficult, words impossible to separate, blend together, word as din . . .

RUBY: . . . Missed brother Robert's funeral, fear of airplanes, trains too slow, Jewish custom, grave by sundown, arrived during night . . .

RICHARD: . . . Had not spoken even one word to Ruby in four years' time, since her first divorce . . .

RUTH: . . . Had stayed in room once, one full month, three years prior, Northern China, never straying, never speaking, not one word, not aloud, voice postponed . . .

RUBY: . . . Jewish Law, beat the sundown. Only mirrors, covered, her absence . . . All else saw . . .

RICHARD: . . . Had not spoken even one word to father in five years' time, since news of father's irreversible disease . . .

RUTH: . . . Ruth had loved her brother, Robert, deeply . . .

RUBY: . . . Family shocked by Ruby's absence, never forgiven, never heard . . .

RICHARD: . . . Richard was first to hear news of plane crash, second half of ticket, both together, Ozark Mountains, hillbillies found them, picked their clothing clean of money, pried their teeth clean of gold . . .

RUTH: . . . Mourned brother Robert's death, deeply, endlessly, silently . . .

RUBY: . . . Ruby, youngest, most degrees, PhD, Modern British, Joyce and Woolf her favored pair . . .

RICHARD: . . . Pried their teeth clean of gold . . .

RUTH: . . . Never forgiven parents' not reaching her in time. Never said "Goodbye" to Robert . . .

RUBY: . . . One brief marriage, to a surgeon . . .

RICHARD: . . . Mother's death . . .

RUTH: . . . Never reached her . . .

RUBY: . . . Engendered nothing, born barren, ovaries broken at birth . . .

RICHARD: . . . Richard feels responsible . . .

RUTH: . . . Ruth feels angry . . .

RUBY: . . . Ruby left husband; her, first to door, first to street, first to forget . . .

RICHARD: . . . Richard feels responsible . . .

RUTH: . . . Ruth feels angry . . .

RUBY: . . . Lived with friends, always male . . .

RICHARD: . . . Richard feels responsible . . .

RUTH: . . .Ruth feels angry . . .

RUBY: . . . Loved her brother, Robert, deeply. Mourned his death, not forgotten. Parents and siblings never forgiven, they never forgave . . .

RICHARD: . . . Richard feels responsible for his parents' death . . .

RUTH: . . . Ruth feels angry at her parents' death . . .

RUBY: . . . Jet from Chicago, late as usual, missed their funeral, struck again. Ruby still stunned, unable to weep . . .

RICHARD: . . . Richard feels responsible for the death of his parents . . .

RUTH: . . . Ruth feels angry at the death of her parents . . .

RUBY: . . . Ruby is unable to weep at the death of her parents . . .

RICHARD: N.B. All of above.

RUTH: N.B. All of above.

RUBY: N.B. All of above.

RICHARD: Richard glances at Ruby.

RUTH: Richard smiles, seeing Ruby's pain . . .

RICHARD: As does Ruth.

RUBY: Ruby regains her strength. She moves to the sofa where she flings her black coat, after tossing small Vuitton weekend case to the floor beside sofa.

RICHARD: Richard is contemptuous of her gesture . . .

RUTH: As is Ruth, who is, however, somewhat amused at the same time and is surprised to find herself smiling. She adjusts her skirt.

RUBY: Ruby adjusts her skirt, re-tucks her blouse into skirt by reaching under skirt, pulls down blouse-ends from bottom, straightening blouse perfectly into skirt and, at the same time, pulling blouse tightly over her breasts.

RICHARD: Richard studies her breasts, certain there is no brassiere supporting them.

RUTH: Ruth studies her breasts, certain there is no brassiere supporting them.

RUBY: Ruby adjusts her brassiere.

RUTH: Ruth adjusts her brassiere.

RICHARD: Richard scratches his chest and coughs.

RUBY: Ruby moves to bar and pours glass full with ginger ale. She lifts brandy decanter from shelf, holds and studies same, somewhat lovingly.

RICHARD: Richard glances at dish towel . . . on his stain . . . on rug . . . near his foot.

RUTH: Ruth looks cautiously at her own stain.

RUBY: Ruby drops decanter . . . accidently. It crashes down on bar top, causing loud noise to sound sharply in room.

RICHARD: Richard turns quickly to see what Ruby has done.

RUTH: As does Ruth.

RUBY: Ruby is amazed by what she has done. She takes the bar-towel and feverishly wipes the spilled liquid.

RICHARD: Richard bows his head. He removes wallet from pocket, studies photograph of daughters and ex-wife, replaces wallet in pocket.

RUTH: Ruth bows her head. She pauses. She quietly slips from her chair and removes black veil from mirror. She studies her own image.

RUBY: Ruby moves discreetly behind Ruth, so that she is now able to see her own image in mirror as well.

RUTH: Ruth sees Ruby seeing herself and moves away from mirror, turning directly to face Ruby . . .

RUBY: . . . who is unable to meet the stare and turns her face downward, to the floor.

RUTH: Ruth smiles, crosses to sofa; sits.

RICHARD: Richard stands and walks directly to the mirror. He avoids looking at his reflected image, but instead recovers mirror with black fabric veil, moves to Ruby's chair; sits.

RUTH: Ruth crosses to Richard's chair and sits.

RUBY: Ruby clenches eyes closed, three count.

RICHARD: Richard adjusts his underwear.

RUTH: Ruth adjusts her underwear.

RUBY: Ruby crosses to what appears to be second veiled mirror and removes black fabric from it.

RICHARD: Richard averts his eyes from image . . .

RUTH: As does Ruth.

RUBY: Ruby exposes 24-by-36 inch tinted photograph of their parents, posed, taken on occasion of their 40th wedding anniversary. Ruby stares at photograph.

RICHARD: Richard is weeping. He silently mouths the word "Mama."

RUTH: As does Ruth.

RUBY: Ruby continues to stare at photograph a moment before taking two odd steps backwards, stiffly. She stops. She silently mouths the word "Papa."

RICHARD & RUTH: Silently: Mama.

RUBY: Silently. Papa.

RUTH: Ruth glances at photograph and then at Ruby. She faces Richard, three count. She is openly contemptuous of her sister and brother.

RUBY: Ruby looks first at Richard and then at Ruth. She replaces veil over photograph. She moves to bar . . .

RICHARD: Richard follows her with his eyes, openly staring . . .

RUBY: . . . Ruby leans against bar, somewhat slumped, anguished . . .

RICHARD: . . . Richard coughs, turns away . . .

RUBY: . . . Ruby covers her eyes with palm of left hand. Right hand slides discreetly across stomach to waistband of skirt. She's adjusting and turning same.

RUTH: . . . Ruth remains silent, staring at stain on rug, lost in a memory . . .

RICHARD: . . . Richard strokes a tear from his cheek.

RUTH: Ruth stands, moves toward Ruby, tentatively: painfully slow, frightened. She plans to embrace her sister, but will not have the courage to do so.

RUBY: Ruby senses Ruth approaching, turns, faces her, smiles.

RUTH: Ruth is suddenly stopped.

RUBY: Ruby spies bottle-cap on floor, scoops it up, bending quickly, tosses same easily into wastebasket, leg of desk. Ruby turns, suddenly facing Richard . . .

RICHARD . . . who has been discreetly admiring Ruby's upper thigh, made quite visible during her rapid bend and scoop . . .

RUBY: . . . Ruby giggles . . .

RICHARD: Richard turns quickly away from her, outraged.

RUBY: Ruby contrives a serious stare in his direction, but giggles again.

RUTH: Ruth is now holding her hand to her mouth, attempting unsuccessfully to contain a chortle.

RUBY: Ruby chortles openly.

RUTH: Ruth looks across stage to Ruby . . .

RUBY: . . . who looks across to Ruth.

RUTH: Ruth takes a step again in Ruby's direction.

RICHARD: Richard produces a wailing sound, suddenly, burying his face in his lap.

RUTH: Ruth turns to him and watches him awhile . . .

RICHARD: Richard is sobbing.

RUBY: Ruby walks to the back of Richard's chair, stops, reaches forward and allows her hand to rest a moment atop Richard's bowed head.

RUTH: Ruth watches, quietly, disapprovingly.

RICHARD: Richard seems unable to move. He neither turns toward Ruby nor away from her: he is instead frozen. His sobbing is now controlled: stopped, quenched.

RUBY: Ruby is embarrassed, sorry she negotiated the touching of Richard's head. She steps back now, three odd steps, stiffly; stops.

RUTH: Ruth stands staring at Ruby.

RUBY: Ruby looks directly at Ruth now. The sisters' eyes meet and hold an absolutely fixed stare.

RUTH: Ruth neither looks away, nor does she smile.

RUBY: Nor Ruby.

RICHARD: Richard stands and moves directly to veiled photograph . . .

RUBY: . . . Ruby does not break her stare at Ruth . . .

RICHARD: . . . He pauses a moment, touching black fabric with the back of his hand . . .

RUTH: . . . Nor does Ruth break her stare at Ruby . . .

RICHARD: . . . Richard carefully, silently, removes black fabric veil from photograph, allowing fabric to fall to floor beside his feet.

RUTH: Ruth is the first to break the stare between the sisters. She turns now to watch Richard.

223

RUBY: As does Ruby.

RICHARD: Richard stares intently at the photograph, reaching his left hand up and forward, touching the cheek of the man in the photograph. He rubs his finger gently across the face of the man, through the void between the man and the woman, finally allowing his finger to stop directly on the chin on the image of the woman in the photograph.

RUTH: Ruth stands, head bowed, silently mouths the word "Papa."

RUBY: Ruby stands, head bowed, silently mouths the word "Papa."

RICHARD: Richard turns, stares first at Ruth and then at Ruby. He points at the photograph, but then causes his pointing finger to fold back into his hand, which he clenches now into a fist, beating same, three times . . . against . . . his . . . hip. He relaxes. He silently mouths the word "Mama."

RUBY: Ruby moves to Richard's chair, sits, allowing her skirt to remain pleated open, high on her leg.

RICHARD: Richard notices her naked thigh.

RUTH: Ruth notices Richard noticing Ruby's naked thigh.

RICHARD: Richard notices that Ruth has noticed him.

RUBY: Ruby tugs her skirt down to her knee. With her left hand, she wipes a tear from her left cheek.

RICHARD: Richard moves to the bar. He studies the bottle of scotch whiskey a while before filling five inches of the liquid into a fresh glass. He turns and faces Ruth, lifts his glass to her, then to his lips, drains it of its contents, drinking same.

RUTH: Ruth stares, silently amazed.

RUBY: Ruby bows her head and sobs.

RICHARD: Richard walks quietly to his shoes and socks and collects them. He sits on the sofa, center, and redresses his feet, sitting carelessly atop his sisters' outer garments.

RUTH: Ruth watches, standing straight now.

RUBY: Ruby notices the towel on the floor next to the chair in which she is sitting, rubs and moves same with her toe.

RICHARD: Richard looks up from tying his shoe to watch Ruby nudging his stain with her toe. He stares disapprovingly.

RUBY: Ruby senses Richard's disapproval and stops nudging at the stain. She instead leans forward and rubs the stain with her fingers, returning same to mouth licking them with her tongue.

RUTH: Ruth gags.

RICHARD: Richard is disgusted, completes tying his shoes hurriedly. He stands and tosses on his overcoat.

RUTH: Ruth takes three odd steps backwards, stiffly, stops.

RUBY: Ruby turns in her chair and stares openly at Richard.

RICHARD: Richard walks to the bar, finds scotch whiskey bottle which he raises to his lips and drains, unflinchingly. Richard moves directly to position beneath photograph and stares at same, lifting bottle to image of mother and father.

RUBY: Ruby continues her stare at Richard, amazed.

RICHARD: Richard allows bottle to fall to floor near his feet. He touches photograph, precisely as he did before: man first, then woman. He then bows head, sobs.

RUTH: Ruth bows head, weeps, covering her eyes with palm of right hand.

RICHARD: Richard closes his coat fully now, lifting collar to back of his head. He discovers armband in pocket, removes it, clenching same in fist. He stares at Ruth, arm outstretched in her direction, fist pointing accusingly.

RUTH: Ruth glances up, and then, suddenly, down, averting eyes from Richard's, but then looking up quickly, she stares directly into Richard's eyes.

RICHARD: He waits a moment, watching to see if she will have the strength to cross the room to him.

RUTH: Ruth moves one step toward Richard, not breaking their joined stare. But then she does. She stops. She lowers her eyes.

225

RUBY: Ruby stands, looks at Richard, but remains, unmoving, at the foot of her chair.

RICHARD: Richard watches Ruth a moment and then shifts his stare to Ruby.

RUBY: Ruby smiles.

RICHARD: Richard moves to door, opens same, pauses a moment, turns again into room, unclenches fist, allowing armband to drop to rug, pauses a moment, exits, never closing door.

RUBY: Ruby moves to door and closes same, leaning her back against it. She stares a moment at armband on rug.

RUTH: As does Ruth.

RUBY: Ruby moves to photograph and stares at same.

RUTH: Ruth finds shoes, slips quickly into same, moves to sofa, rapidly collecting her outer clothing.

RUBY: Ruby, suddenly realizing she might be left alone in room, moves quickly away from photograph, sees Ruth; stops, frozen.

RUTH: Ruth races to redress herself in her coat, jamming hat on head, stockings in coat pocket.

RUBY: Ruby has her outer clothing now in her hands but realizes she is too late.

RUTH: Ruth has moved quickly and successfully, assuming an exit position at the door, coat buttoned closed.

RUBY: Ruby is stunned and allows her outer clothing to drop back down on to the sofa.

RUTH: Ruth smiles, touches doorknob.

RUBY: Ruby leans over sofa, her back to Ruth.

RUTH: Ruth stares at Ruby's youthful body, her thighs, her straight back, her rich girl's shoulders.

RUBY: Ruby lifts her face, but cannot turn to Ruth.

RUTH: Ruth glances at photograph, but cannot sustain look at same. She straightens her back, inhales, quietly opens door, exhales. She glances a final glance at Ruby. Exits.

RUBY: Ruby hears the door finally closed.

RUTH: Click . . .

RUBY: She turns quickly. Certain now that Ruth has exited, Ruby stands frozen, sad-eyed, staring at the still closed door. She moves to bar and finds glass decanter on it, which she holds a moment before suddenly smashing same on bar. After shock of glass breaking, there is silence in the room. Ruby moves again to photograph, carrying jagged neck of glass decanter with her; considers destroying photograph, but instead softly caresses same with palm of right hand, touching first the image of the man, then the image of the woman and then again the image of the man. She moves to sofa, still carrying jagged remains of decanter with her. She thinks to sit but does not, instead turns, faces photograph, fully. Leaning forward over sofa, Ruby allows the weight of her body against the final point of the glass, causing the remains of the decanter to enter her body just below the breast, not suicide, but, instead, something more severe. She turns away from photograph, faces front, allows her body to relax on to sofa. Her hand unclenches. The jagged remains of the decanter fall. Blood drops from hand, staining rug. Ruby faces front, pauses a moment. She opens her mouth, screams, but there is no sound.

The lights fade to black.

New York City, November, 1975—November, 1976.

AUTHOR'S NOTE: There are four related plays, of which *Stage Directions* is one, that are designed to be performed in a rotating repertory of two double-bills, under the umbrella-title *The Quannapowitt Quartet*. The title refers to Lake Quannapowitt in Wakefield, Massachusetts, the shared setting of all four plays.

The three other plays are *Spared*, *Hopscotch* and *The 75th*. The latter two plays should be performed in their own evening or bill, in that order. *Stage Directions* is meant to precede *Spared* on the alternate evening or bill.

A company of just three performers may be sufficient to play the entire quartet. I am especially interested in the possibility of the performers who play *Hopscotch* also playing *The 75th*.

Scenic elements designed for all four plays should be minimal, with maximum attention given to the design of lighting and sound effects.

Finally, the entire quartet is related to the trilogy, *The Wakefield Plays*: part one, *Alfred the Great*; part two, *Our Father's Failing*; and part three, *Alfred Dies*. If the seven plays were ever to be played in cycle, they would occupy five evenings: the first, *Hopscotch* and *The 75th*; the second, *Alfred the Great*; the third, *Our Father's Failing*; the fourth, *Alfred Dies*; and the fifth, *Stage Directions* and *Spared*.

227

Gertrude's Easter

THOMAS TOLNAY

Approximate playing time: 25 minutes

Everyone in cast is about the same age—mid forties to early fifties.

Early afternoon.

Lights are dim. Several rows of folding chairs are facing backdrop. Seats in the auditorium, facing in the same direction, are therefore actually rows in the funeral parlor on stage. Ten or fifteen feet in front of the upstage row is a mahogany casket, which is flanked by only a few wreaths of flowers.

The audience is participating in the play as mourners. Of course they are not mourners who knew the deceased previously. They are making a brief appearance here much the way people attend the wake of someone related to a person they work with, for example.

The backs of all players are almost always toward the auditorium. Therefore, whenever feasible, in order to be heard, the player must look at the player she is addressing. The audience is eavesdropping on the conversations.

1.

HENRIETTA, *tall and thin, and her friend* JANE, *average in height and build, are seated in the middle of the upstage row.* JANE *is stage right of* HENRIETTA. *The* ATTENDANT *is adjusting the wreaths near the casket.*

CHARLOTTE, *short and stocky, a black pocketbook looped over her forearm, enters downstage left, but remains at doorway. Hearing* CHARLOTTE's *entrance,* HENRIETTA *turns slightly in her chair, and looks toward the back of the funeral parlor.*

HENRIETTA: Charlotte's come.

JANE: (*turns in her chair to look back*) So that's Charlotte.

HENRIETTA: She's early.

JANE: Doesn't look like you at all.

228

HENRIETTA: One of these days I think her body's going to explode, she's so big.

ATTENDANT, *now noticing the new arrival, stops what he is doing and glides up to* CHARLOTTE. *He nods respectfully to her. Without replying or looking at him,* CHARLOTTE *moves several steps past him into the room, and stops again, far to the right of the chairs. She continues to stare toward the casket, and does not look at the two seated women. The* ATTENDANT *turns to watch her a moment, then moves to the downstage row and sits down on the far-left chair. He assumes a rigid position.*

JANE: Your sister seems to be taking it quite well.

HENRIETTA: She's been waiting for this day a long time.

JANE: (*looks at* HENRIETTA *a moment before speaking*) What's that supposed to mean?

HENRIETTA: It's not supposed to mean anything.

While HENRIETTA *and* JANE *are speaking,* CHARLOTTE *begins her slow march down the side aisle, toward casket.*

JANE: *Pardon me* for asking.

HENRIETTA: Look, Jane. It's just family business.

JANE: You never mentioned anything like that to me.

HENRIETTA: Why should I mention it to you?

JANE: I was under the impression I'm your best friend.

HENRIETTA: Oh, stop it.

JANE: Stop what?

HENRIETTA: (*realizing* JANE *is not going to be satisfied until she gets an answer, she whispers harshly*) If you *must* know, Charlotte despises Gertrude. Always has. Are you happy now?

JANE: (*squirms nervously in seat*) I didn't mean to be nosy.

HENRIETTA: (*immediately appeased*) I know you didn't.

CHARLOTTE *positions herself at the open end of the casket.*

JANE: I'm sorry.

HENRIETTA: That's all right.

JANE: No it isn't. I had no right to ask.

HENRIETTA: Sure you did. You're my best friend, aren't you? (*Smiles faintly at* JANE.)

JANE: I guess I am.

HENRIETTA: I'm just all on edge.

JANE: Is that all it really was?

HENRIETTA: Certainly. You had every right to ask.

JANE: (*pauses a few seconds*) Then you won't mind if I ask you why she hated her own sister?

HENRIETTA: (*Glares at* JANE, *but can think of no way out, so she answers question.*) Gertrude turned Father against us. (*Continues to look at* JANE, *to see if there is any reaction. There is none.*) Charlotte never forgave her for that.

JANE *and* HENRIETTA *grow silent for a few moments. Their attention turns to* CHARLOTTE *up at the casket.* CHARLOTTE *is far enough away so that she can hear the two women whispering, but cannot make out what they are saying.*

JANE: What's taking her so long?

HENRIETTA: It's been a long time for them.

JANE: Isn't she going to say a prayer for the deceased?

HENRIETTA: It wouldn't surprise me if she laughed in her face.

JANE: I think that's terrible.

HENRIETTA: (*nods knowingly*) You wouldn't if you knew everything.

JANE: (*glances at* HENRIETTA) It's really none of my business.

HENRIETTA: (*Pauses, trying to decide if she should say more. At last the silence becomes too noticeable, so she begins to explain.*) Gertrude used to tell my father she was *his* child, and that Charlotte and I were my mother's children.

JANE: Really?

HENRIETTA: My father laughed, but I swear he actually began to believe her.

JANE: What did your mother say?

HENRIETTA: Oh, she told Gertrude she wouldn't go to heaven if she kept talking that way.

JANE *shifts slightly in her chair to look more directly at* HENRIETTA.

HENRIETTA: Why am I bothering you with all this?

JANE: What's a friend for? Especially at a time like this.

JANE *and* HENRIETTA *grow silent again, as if suddenly realizing they shouldn't be talking so much in a funeral parlor. They watch* CHARLOTTE *standing at the casket.*

JANE: It gives me the chills to see your sister staring at Gertrude, now that I know she . . . they didn't get along.

HENRIETTA: I hope you don't think I condone Charlotte's attitude.

JANE: (*Difficult to tell from her tone what she really thinks.*) Naturally not.

HENRIETTA: It's just that I understand how she feels.

JANE: Of course.

HENRIETTA: I can see you don't know what I mean at all.

JANE *looks at* HENRIETTA *blankly.*

HENRIETTA: One year Gertrude was the only one to get a new Easter dress. It was yellow, with little bows on the sleeves. My father said there wasn't money for more, and since Gertrude was the eldest—

JANE: (*interjects*) That can happen in any family.

HENRIETTA: Every day for a week she tried on that dress in front of the mirror. She knew Charlotte and I were watching her, eating our hearts out.

JANE: Children *love* to show off.

HENRIETTA: In the evening, instead of putting the dress away, she'd hang it on the dorknob where we could see it. Just to upset us.

JANE: You don t say?

HENRIETTA: Charlotte couldn't take it any more. Easter morning, she cut the dress to pieces with a scissors.

JANE: Gertrude must've been furious.

231

HENRIETTA: She didn't even cry. She went right down to my father and told him.

JANE: What happened?

HENRIETTA: Oh, he beat Charlotte with his belt, and Gertrude watched.

JANE: (*Leans forward, toward* CHARLOTTE, *and looks her over as if searching for evidence of that beating.*) Even so, do you think it's right for her to take it out on the dead?

HENRIETTA: You can't change the past.

JANE: Course not. Charlotte ought to follow your example.

HENRIETTA: I always tried to be a good sister to Gertrude.

JANE: Course you did.

HENRIETTA: Even after she told my boy friend some terrible things about me. When I was in high school.

JANE: What did she tell him?

HENRIETTA: About another boy. Nothing but lies. (*Pauses.*) Jimmy stopped coming around.

The lights dim slowly, until the stage is in complete darkness. Remains dark for a few seconds, then lights slowly come on to the same intensity as before. The scene remains unchanged.

2.

CHARLOTTE *turns away from the casket, and lumbers slowly to the first row of folding chairs. She sits down beside* HENRIETTA, *stage left of her taller sister.*

HENRIETTA: Did you have a good trip?

CHARLOTTE: (*sighs*) Trains depress me.

HENRIETTA: How's Herbert?

CHARLOTTE: Spring's his busy season. He won't be able to get here.

HENRIETTA: Hope he's not working himself too hard.

CHARLOTTE: Where's Sam?

HENRIETTA: He'll be over this evening. (*Suddenly realizes she forgot to make introductions.*) Oh, I'd like you to meet my neighbor Jane.

CHARLOTTE *nods to* JANE.

JANE: (*respectfully*) Please accept my condolences.

CHARLOTTE, *her face totally devoid of expression, looks at* JANE *but does not reply.*

HENRIETTA: (*Glances at* JANE, *then speaks to* CHARLOTTE.) Seems like it always takes a funeral to get a family together.

CHARLOTTE: (*shaking her head to acknowledge the fact*) Uh huh.

HENRIETTA: I didn't even know she was having trouble with her kidneys.

CHARLOTTE: Neither did I.

HENRIETTA: I got a telegram from the hospital out in Salt Lake, letting me know what happened. They asked where the body should be shipped.

JANE: Guess nobody out there would take the responsibility.

HENRIETTA: (*apologetically*) We're all Gertrude's got. (*Looks away from* CHARLOTTE.) I wired that I'd accept the body.

JANE: What a confused day that was.

HENRIETTA: (*to* CHARLOTTE) Who would've thought, after all the years she's been out West, that you and I would end up burying Gertrude?

CHARLOTTE: Odd how it worked out.

HENRIETTA: Anyway, Sam and I have taken care of all the arrangements. I didn't think you'd mind.

CHARLOTTE: I don't mind.

HENRIETTA: (*indicating the casket*) Gertrude liked mahogany.

CHARLOTTE: Everything looks all right.

JANE: The flowers are *beautiful*.

CHARLOTTE *looks at* JANE.

HENRIETTA: They did a good job on Gertrude.

233

CHARLOTTE: I guess so.

HENRIETTA: You don't think they did?

CHARLOTTE *shrugs her shoulders heavily.*

HENRIETTA: What's the matter?

CHARLOTTE: I don't know.

HENRIETTA: Tell me what it is.

CHARLOTTE: (*Stares at casket a second or two.*) She looks . . . peculiar.

HENRIETTA: I thought so too at first. You'll get used to her after awhile.

CHARLOTTE: I mean the face . . . is odd.

JANE: (*bending forward to look across at* CHARLOTTE) The hospital said your sister, uh, passed away after a long illness. That can take a lot out of a person.

CHARLOTTE: (*She had tried to avoid speaking with* JANE, *but now feels challenged.*) Can kidney disease take a scar out of a person?

JANE *looks at* HENRIETTA *with a puzzled expression, and* HENRIETTA'*s face becomes equally puzzled.*

CHARLOTTE: Gertrude fell down the stairs one Easter, when we were kids. She had to have ten stitches. (*indicating the casket*) There's not a mark on that face.

HENRIETTA: I forgot about that scar.

CHARLOTTE: See for yourself, if you don't believe me.

HENRIETTA: (*hesitantly*) I believe you.

CHARLOTTE: Go ahead. Look.

HENRIETTA *looks into her sister's eyes for a moment. Then she rises and moves slowly toward the casket. At the casket she bends forward to examine the dead face.*

JANE *gets up, sets her pocketbook on her chair, and goes up to the casket. She stands stage left of* HENRIETTA.

CHARLOTTE *rises heavily and, leaving the pocketbook on her arm, moves slowly toward the casket. She stands stage left of* JANE.

HENRIETTA: (*straightens up and gives* CHARLOTTE *a long, steady look.*) It was on her chin.

CHARLOTTE: (*takes a deep breath*) I kept trying to recognize that face. But it just didn't look like her to me.

HENRIETTA: It doesn't look like her.

JANE: This is silly.

CHARLOTTE: (*irritated, but does not look at* JANE) They must have mixed up the names and shipped the wrong body.

HENRIETTA: I guess so.

JANE: You're both just upset. (*Looks back, hoping the* ATTENDANT *can't hear them.*)

CHARLOTTE: (*glaring at* JANE) What about that scar?

JANE: You haven't seen your sister for a long time. People change. Even scars go away, sometimes.

HENRIETTA: It wasn't a scratch, Jane. The scar was long and deep.

The three women grow silent, and concentrate on the dead face for a few moments.

CHARLOTTE: (*to* HENRIETTA) More than likely Gertrude is still at the hospital out there.

HENRIETTA *nods at first, then looks sharply at* CHARLOTTE, *as if something just occurred to her.*

CHARLOTTE: It's possible.

JANE: (*Peers uneasily from* HENRIETTA *on her left, to* CHARLOTTE *on her right.*) What an absurd thing to think.

CHARLOTTE: How do we know she's dead?

HENRIETTA: That's right. We have no way of really knowing.

JANE: But the telegram.

CHARLOTTE: If they thought the body was Gertrude, naturally they'd get in touch with *her* next of kin.

HENRIETTA: (*Tugs at the back of her gray dress nervously.*) Then you think . . . she's alive?

CHARLOTTE: Let me have a look at the death certificate.

HENRIETTA: (*emotionally*) I didn't get one.

JANE: Sh! (*clutches* HENRIETTA's *arm.*) Your voices are rising.

HENRIETTA *bows her head solemnly. Then* CHARLOTTE *bows her head too.* JANE *doesn't know what to do with herself.*

HENRIETTA: Good God!

For the first time, the sisters begin to mourn. CHARLOTTE *sobs quietly, and soon* HENRIETTA *joins in. In a moment, the* ATTENDANT *hears the two women crying, and he stands straight up in the last row, but does not move away from his chair.*

The lights dim slowly, until the stage is dark.

Paradise

STEVEN SHEA

PARADISE was originally presented at the Playwrights Horizons Theatre in New York in June, 1976. It was directed by Paul Cooper, and featured the following actors: Elliott Burtoff, Kathleen Chalfant, John Guerrasio, Greg Johnson, and Jillian Lindig.

Approximate playing time: 60 minutes

1.

D *enters USR pulling a mechanical duck toy on the end of a string. The duck quacks mechanically as it's pulled across the stage.*
D *comes downstage, crosses, walking at a relaxed and regular pace.*
E *enters a beat behind* D, *at the same USR door, pulling an identical duck. Same noise. Same path as he crosses.*

F *enters a beat behind* E. *Same duck, same noise, same path.*

D *crosses downstage of the furniture, passes back upstage, exits by the opposite (USL) door.*
E *follows, one beat behind.*
F *follows, one beat behind.*

2.

A *enters pushing a perambulator.* D *is in it.*
One step behind walk B *and* E. B *holds* E's *hand.*
One step behind them walks F.

They cross at a leisurely pace. D *drops a rattle on the floor.*
The procession stops. A *picks it up, returns it to* D. D *drops it again, on the other side of the carriage.* B *picks it up, returns it to him.*

C *enters USL, from the opposite direction.*
She wears hat, coat, gloves.

237

As she walks past upstage of the others, A tips his hat to her.
She smiles and nods to him.

E: What is the man doing?

F: Is he tipping his hat?

E: Is he tipping his hat to the lady?

F: Is there a lady?

E: Is the lady smiling?

F: Is the lady nodding?

E: Who is the lady nodding to?

F: Why is he tipping his hat?

E: Why is she smiling at him?

F: Is she smiling at him?

C *exits.*

The others exit to the opposite side (SR).

3.

B *enters, nutcracker in hand, comes stage center, stops.*

Beat.

D *enters from the opposite side, a walnut in each hand, held up between thumb and forefinger.*
He approaches B, *stops a step away from her, still holding up the nuts.*
He turns his face away.
B *cracks the nuts, first one then the other, and exits.*

Beat.

D *exits.*

E *and* F *enter with broom and dustpan, sweep up the cracked nuts, exit.*

4.

C *enters to an empty stage.*
She wears hat, coat, gloves. She carries a valise.
She sits down at the table in one of the chairs and waits.

Beat.

B *enters, crosses to* C, *does not sit.*
C *stands.*
B *speaks.*
(During B's *speech* D *enters upstage, stands in the door, watches and listens.)*

B: Do you mind if I ask you a question? There's something I want to ask you. Why have you come here? Nobody wants you here. The boy doesn't want you here. I don't want you here. Nobody wants you here. That's why I'm asking you. Do you want to be here? Is that it? Is it that you want to be here? I don't think that's it. That isn't it, is it? Nobody wants you here at all, you see. That's why I asked you in the first place, that's why I was wondering about it, just what brought you here in the first place, and why you're here, and what brought you here. Well? *(Pause.)* I'd rather you didn't smoke.

Exit B.

C *takes off her hat, coat, gloves.*
D *crosses to her valise, picks it up.*
C *exits.*

D *exits after her, carrying her valise.*

5.

C *enters, sets the table, exits.*
A, B, *and* D *enter, sit at the table.*
A *sits at the head,* D *in the middle,* B *opposite* A.

B *rings the bell.* C *enters, serves, exits.*
A *and* B *eat;* D *does not.*
(E *and* F *enter upstage, stand in doorways, watch, beginning as* C *serves.)*

E: The food is on the plate in front of me, untouched, getting cold. The grease

on the meat is congealing. The potatoes are crusting over. The gravy is forming a skin. The others are eating. There is nothing wrong with the food. The
food is on the plate in front of me. The Chinese are starving.

A: Eat.

E: I'm told to eat, and I comply, mutely. At other times there are other orders
and other instructions, and I comply with all of them. There are countless in-
stances of mute compliance, all identical in principle, all identical to this one.

D *eats, neither rapidly nor slowly.*

E: When the maid is wanted a bell rings and she comes into the room. She brings the food to the table. She serves it, politely, from the left, and we help
ourselves. She stands while we sit. After the meal she clears the dishes, correct-
ly, without stacking them. She waits while we eat and eats her own meal after
we finish.

Beat.

E: We're always polite to each other. We're polite to the maid, who's polite to
us. Nothing is done without please and thank you. There's no cause for
rudeness. We're comfortable. We're sitting down. We're having our dinner
brought to us. It's easy to be polite.

Beat.

E: This scene could be repeated any number of times and it would never
change. I would sit there at the table. I would comply, mutely, when I was told
to eat. Each time the bell was rung the maid would come into the room. She
would serve from the left. She would be polite. She would clear from the right,
without stacking the plates. She would eat her own meal after we had finished.

F: Some things never change. This is bourgeois life.

B *rings the bell.*
C *enters, clears, exits.*

6.

C *enters, goes to the table, sits down.*
She places a pack of cigarettes and a book of matches on the table.

She takes a cigarette out and puts it in her mouth.

D *enters, goes to the table, sits down with her.*
C *offers him a cigarette. He takes it.*
She lights a match, lights his cigarette, lights her own.
They smoke.

C: Take it out of the pack, tap it two or three times on the table or on your thumb nail to pack the tobacco, stick it in your mouth, and light up. That's all there is to it.

Extended moment as they smoke together.

C *puts out her cigarette and stands up.*
D *puts out his cigarette and stands up.*
C *picks up the pack and the matches, exits.*
D *exits.*

7.

A *enters with a bottle of port wine and two glasses.*
He goes to the table, puts the bottle and glasses on the table, and sits down.

Long beat.

C *enters, crosses to the table, sits down.*
A *pours wine into two glasses.*
D *appears in upstage door, watches.*
A *and* C *touch glasses.*

A: Salud.

C: Salud.

They both drink.
Long beat. B *enters by another door into the other part of the stage.*
A *pours some more wine into the two glasses.*
C *takes off her blouse.*
A *and* C *touch glasses again. No spoken toast.*
They both drink.

Long beat.

B *rings the bell.*

C *stands up, crosses upstage without putting her blouse back on, instead*
holding it in her hand, and exits, not at the door in which D *stands.*
D *exits.*
B *exits.*
A *picks up the bottle and glasses, exits.*

9.

Enter A *with a white porcelain bowl, towel, shaving brush, razor, and soap.*
His shirt is off. He wears a sleeveless undershirt.

Beat.

Enter D, E, *and* F, *each with shaving brush, razor, soap, and towel. They also*
have their shirts off and wear sleeveless undershirts.

A *lathers up.*
D, E, *and* F *imitate his actions.*

A *shaves.*
D, E, *and* F *likewise.*

A *rinses.*
D, E, *and* F *likewise.*

A *dries his face with the towel.*
D, E, *and* F *likewise.*

A *picks up his gear, exits.*
D, E, *and* F *likewise.*

10.

C *enters, sits on the table, crosses her legs, runs her finger across her shoulder.*
D, E, *and* F *enter with white condoms in their hands, behind their backs, and*
stand around the table staring at C.

Beat.

Simultaneously A *and* B *enter at side entrance dancing foxtrot, slowly crossing*
behind the three boys and C. *No music is heard.*

D, E, *and* F *blow up the condoms.*

A *and* B, *dancing, exit opposite side from where they entered.*

D, E, *and* F *watch as* C *stands up.*

They let the air out of the condoms.

C *exits.*
D, E, *and* F *exit.*

11.

D *enters pushing* A *in a wheelchair.*
E *and* F *follow, a step behind.*

A: The word *paradise* comes from a Greek word that sounds very much like it, *paradeisos,* meaning paradise or park. In English, the word paradise has several meanings: the Garden of Eden, or a place where souls go after death, such as heaven, or a place of bliss, or a state of happiness.

Pause.

A: The word *paradise* comes from a Greek word that sounds very much like it, *paradeisos,* meaning paradise or park. In English, the word paradise has several meanings: the Garden of Eden, or a place where souls go after death, such as heaven, or a place of bliss, or a state of happiness.

D *exits to the opposite side, pushing* A *in the wheelchair.*
E *and* F *follow them off.*

12.

B *and* C *sit at the table.*
E *and* F *in the usual doorways.*

D *enters, speaks to* B *and* C.

D: Some authorities say that the child is as pure and unblemished as Adam before the fall. Others hold that the child is chaste as the driven snow. Still others liken the child to the first tender shoots of spring. All·of these agree that the child is at one with himself and with the world. All agree that childhood is the sweetest time of life. (*Pause*) Modern critics now regard this view as romantic. Some of them, also authorities in the field, look on the child as a filthy little beast, savage, wild, and malicious. They picture him as a seething sink of rage and lust. Often these modern authorities are silent as to whether childhood is on the whole a pleasant experience, but they imply that it isn't.

Exit D.
Beat.

C: That's an interesting boy.

All exit.

13.

Enter D, E, *and* F.
D *goes to table, rings bell.*
All three lie down on their backs on the floor in a row in front of the SR door.
F *closest to the door, then* E, *then* D *farthest into the space.*

Beat.

Enter C.
She pauses very briefly in the door, then steps over each of the three boys, slowly.
In order to do so, she passes over their heads. They obviously are looking up her skirt.
After she steps over D, *she turns back to the boys, speaks.*

C: They're pink.

C *exits by center door.*
Boys exit.

14.

B *enters pushing* A *in a wheelchair.*
C *follows a step behind accompanied by* D.

C *moves the chair set at the head of the table in order to make room for* A *in the wheelchair.*

C *exits.*

A *is wheeled up to his usual place.*
B *and* D *sit in their usual places.*
B *rings the bell.*

C *enters with a single plate, with food on it, and places it on the table in front of* A.
B *feeds* A *with a spoon, but* A*'s mouth doesn't function and he can't eat. He drools. The food spills down the napkin he has tucked into his shirt front.*

E *and* F *watch from upstage doors.*
B *continues to try to feed* A. *Same as before.*
She continues.
Finally she stops.

D *takes his napkin, stands, goes to* A, *wipes* A*'s chin and mouth, exits.*

A *remains.*

15.

C *enters, sits down in the chair opposite* A.

C: Do you still think I'm beautiful?

A *makes no response.*

C: Do you still think I'm beautiful?

A *makes no response.*

C *takes off her blouse.*

C: Do you still think I'm beautiful?

A *makes no response.*
B *enters center door, looks at* C.
C *looks at* B, *then back at* A.

Pause.

246

C *stands, puts on her blouse without hurrying, exits.*
B *wheels* A *off in the wheelchair.*

16.

D *enters pedaling a tricycle. Slowly. He circles downstage.*
E *and* F *enter, stand together opposite.*
D *stops pedaling, speaks to* E *and* F.

D: How is the situation frozen and how is it fluid? As a child you can't leave the house. There is no way for you to escape. There is no where for you to hide. There is nothing you can do to change anything around you. The people are fixed in their paths. The objects were chosen long before you appeared. The only movement possible is by tricycle.

D *pedals again.*
E *and* F *exit.*
D *exits, pedaling, by same door he came on.*

17.

Enter C, *carrying a white porcelain pan, cloth, towel. There is water in the pan.*

Enter D, *a step behind her.*
D *is barefoot and his pants are rolled up above the knees (unless he's already in shorts, which he ought to be).*

E *and* F *enter, watch from across the stage.*

D *speaks the lines following as* C *washes his legs.*

That feels ok.
It feels nice.
It feels good.
It feels fine.
It feels wonderful.
It feels marvelous.
It feels super.
It feels terrific.
It feels great.

It feels amazing.
It feels fantastic.
It feels fabulous.
It feels tremendous.

C *dries his legs with the towel.*
As C *exits, followed by* D, E *and* F *speak.*

E: I wouldn't mind that at all.

F: No.

Exit E *and* F.

18.

B *enters pushing* A *in a wheelchair.*

C *follows a step behind accompanied by* D.
C *moves the chair set at the head of the table in order to make room for* A *in the wheelchair.*
C *exits.*

A *is wheeled to his usual place.*
B *and* D *sit in their usual places.*

B *rings the bell.*
C *enters with a tray and a baby bottle of milk on the tray. She sets the bottle down in front of* A.

B *holds the bottle for* A, *in his mouth.*
E *and* F *watch from upstage doors.*

A *drinks from the bottle, neither rapidly nor slowly, but continuously.*
When he has finished, B *gives the bottle to* C, *who puts it on her tray and exits.*

B *wipes* A'*s mouth with a napkin.*

19.

B *wheels* A *across the stage in the wheelchair.*
D, E, *and* F *cross, stand in front of them.*
B *stops wheeling, stands still.*

D: Tumors of the brain aren't common. They aren't infectious. They aren't hereditary. They aren't always fatal.

E: If you're young enough you don't understand what's going on in front of you. You can't put what you see into words and you can't grasp hold of it. If you're young enough you don't remember anything at all.

F: Description of myself at the present time: eyes focused, ears open, feet on the floor, hands at my sides, heart beating, lungs breathing, face blank, mind blank, memory blank.

20.

D *enters, leading* C, *brings her to the table, helps her up.*

Enter E *and* F. E *carries black bag with assortment of instruments: rubber hammer, speculum, tongue depressor, stethoscope, pressure cuff.*

The three play doctor with C, *delivering randomly the following lines.*

Breathe deeply.
Any change in your bowel habits?
This won't hurt at all.
Say ah.
Headaches?
Take a breath and hold it.
How's your appetite?
Periods regular?
Does this hurt?
Do you get any exercise?
Cough.
How old are you now?
Headaches?
Take another breath.
Does this hurt?
What about this?
Open your mouth.
Look straight ahead.
Do you ever feel dizzy?
Do you take any medicine?
Got cabbages in your ears?

Bowels regular?
Pain on urination?
Does this hurt?
Take a deep breath.
Shortness of breath?
What did you have for lunch?
Say ah.
Take another breath.
How's your appetite?
Do you have any pains?
Anything bothering you?
Take a deep breath and hold it.
Have you ever been in a tropical country?
Any sensitivity here?
Have you been exposed to any contagious diseases?
Do you have any allergies?
Open your mouth.
Say ah.
Do you sleep well?
How's your general state of mind?
Does this hurt?
Breathe.
Do you use any drugs?
Any pain here?
Try to relax your stomach.
Breathe.

Enter B *upstage. Game ends. All go off.*

21.

D *enters pushing* A *in a wheelchair.*

E *and* F *follow, a step behind.*

A *opens his mouth, but makes no sound.*
A*'s tongue protrudes slightly.*
He makes no sound.

D, E, *and* F *speak the sentences following, not in unison but together, each*

repeating the sentences in a different order. Each may pause during his recita-
tion, occasionally, so that not all three of them are speaking at once the whole
time.

I can't hear you.
I can't understand what you're saying.
I can't hear what you're saying.
I can't understand you.
Why are you talking so softly?
What are you trying to say?
Please speak more loudly.
Please speak so I can hear you.
Please speak so I can understand you.

D, E, *and* F *stop talking.*
A *continues to open his mouth and protrude his tongue.*
Moment as this continues.

A *stops, closes his mouth.*

Beat.

D *exits, pushing* A *in the wheelchair.*
E *and* F *follow them off.*

22.

Enter C, *carrying a white porcelain pan, cloth, towel. Water in the pan.*
Enter D, *a step behind her.*
She sets down the pan and takes off her shoes.

D *kneels, washes her legs.*
He washes higher and higher, gradually.

C: That's enough.

D *stops, exits.*

Beat.

Enter E.
E *crosses to* C, *kneels, washes her legs.*
He washes higher and higher.
She lifts her skirt slightly.

He washes higher.

C: That's enough.

E *stops, exits.*

Beat.

F *enters, crosses to* C, *kneels, washes her legs.*
He washes higher and higher.
She lifts her skirt quite a bit.
He washes higher.

C: That's enough.

F *stops, exits.*
C *dries her legs, puts her shoes back on, exits with the pan.*

23.

B *enters pushing* A *in a wheelchair.*
D, E, *and* F *follow behind.*

B *stops.*
D, E, *and* F *lift* A *out of the wheelchair.*

C *enters opposite side and watches.*

D, E, *and* F *lay* A *on the table.*
B *places a pillow underneath his head.*
His eyes are open and he is awake; merely unresponsive.

B *exits.*
D, E, *and* F *exit.*

C *crosses, stands over* A, *leans down, kisses him on the mouth, straightens.*

24.

C *crosses to chair upstage, sits, takes out a cigarette, smokes.*

Pause.

D *enters on his tricycle, pedaling rapidly, crosses to* C, *stops.*

D: How many pubic hairs do you have?

C: I never counted.

Beat.

D: Can I count them?

C: Yes.

D *backs up half a foot.*
Beat.
C *exits.*

25.

D *pedals downstage to near the table.*

E *and* F *enter, cross to table, stand over* A.
F *has a stethoscope around his neck. He puts it in his ears, listens to* A*'s heart for an extended moment.*
He takes the stethoscope out of his ears, exits.
E *follows him off.*

D *rides off on the tricycle.*

26.

C *and* D *enter from opposite sides.*
They meet face to face stage center.

Beat.

C *reaches under her skirt, takes off her panties, and hands them to* D.

Beat.

C *continues on in the same direction she was walking in before, exits.*

Beat.

D *continues on in the same direction he was walking in before, exits.*

27.

B *enters, crosses, stands near the opposite door.*

E *enters, stops in front of her. She kisses him on the forehead. He crosses to the table, stops near it.*

F *enters. Same.*

D *enters. Same, except that when he gets to the table the three boys lift* A, *carry him offstage.*

B *exits.*

28.

A *lying propped on the table.*
Enter E *and* F *at one door, come to the table, sit.*

Beat.

Enter D, *comes to the table, sits in middle chair.*
D *lectures them.*

D: There are two kinds of fathers, living and dead. Among the living there are good fathers and bad fathers and cruel fathers and kind fathers and generous fathers and selfish fathers and loving fathers and bitter fathers and violent fathers and gentle fathers and happy fathers and frustrated fathers and absent fathers and nice fathers and healthy fathers and sick fathers and dying fathers. There is only one kind of dead father.

D *exits.*

Beat.
E *and* F *exit.*

29.

Music is heard over sound system: Frank Sinatra, singing "Paradise."
Extended moment of song.

C *and* D *enter, dancing, in close embrace.*
Song continues. C *and* D *dance slowly across stage.*

C *and* D *exit as song comes to end.*

CURTAIN

Guide

288 Off-Off Broadway Theatres

EDITOR'S NOTE: *All theatres and addresses off-off-Broadway are subject to fluctuation. Some may be defunct by the time this guide appears. Productions are often staged on a highly irregular basis. All theatres listed are located in Manhattan, unless otherwise indicated. Each theatre was given the opportunity to provide information about its productions and artistic aims by responding to a SCENE questionnaire; that information appears wherever responses were received.*

1. **ABBEY THEATRE,** 136 East 13th St., 598-2401.
2. **ACADEMY ARTS THEATRE COMPANY,** 100 Seventh Ave.
3. **ACSTA,** 251 West 80th St., PL5-5120.
4. **ACTIVE TRADING CO. PRODUCTIONS,** 552 Broadway, 925-3078.
5. **ACTORS & DIRECTORS ALLIANCE,** 321 West 74th St.
6. **ACTORS EXPERIMENTAL UNIT,** c/o Blue Dome, 262 Bowery, 582-4240. Est: 1968. Artistic Director: Robert Capece. Produces both original scripts and classics. Representative productions: "Does A Tiger Wear A Necktie?" by Don Peterson; "Madwoman of Chaillot" by Jean Giraudoux.
7. **ACTOR'S PLACE AT ST. LUKES,** 487 Hudson St., 924-5960. Est: 1968. Artistic Director: Frank Mosier. Established to produce liturgical drama. Representative productions: one-act liturgical dramas produced from sermons at St. Luke's Church. Biblical or philosophical scripts with running time of one half-hour or less considered.
8. **ACTOR'S PLAYHOUSE,** 100 Seventh Ave.
9. **ACTOR'S STUDIO,** 432 West 44th St., PL7-0870. Established 1974. Artistic Director: Lee Strasberg. A workshop for professional actors, playwrights and directors. Representative productions: "Old Times" by Harold Pinter, dir. by Arthur Penn; "Economic Necessity" by John Hopkins, dir. by Arthur Sherman. Audience capacity: 100. Subscription policy: no subscriptions; TDF accepted.
10. **AFRO-AMERICAN THEATRE,** 415 West 127th St., 866-2389.
11. **AFRO-AMERICAN TOTAL THEATRE ARTS FOUNDATION,** Martinique Theatre, 49 West 32nd St. Artistic Director: Hazel Bryant. A community musical theatre with plans for a black musical repertory theatre. Representative productions: monthly Countee Cullen Great Storyteller Series for children; "Ma Lou's Daughters" by Gertrude Greenridge.
12. **AIRLINE THEATRE WING,** Madison Ave. Baptist Church, 31st St., Madison Ave., MU5-1377.
13. **ALAMO PLAYWRIGHTS UNIT,** no permanent theatre.
14. **ALL SOULS PLAYERS,** Unitarian Church of All Souls, Lexington Ave. at 80th St., LA5-5330.
15. **AMAS REPERTORY THEATRE,** 263 West 86th St., 873-3207. Established: 1969. Artistic Director: Rosetta LeNoire. Repertory with a multi-racial theatrical format. Representative productions: "Bubbling Brown Sugar" by Loften Mitchell and Rosetta LeNoire; "God's Trom-

bones" by James Weldon Johnson. Submissions of original scripts are welcome.

16. AMATO OPERA THEATRE, 319 Bowery, CA8-8200.
17. AMDA THEATRE, 150 Bleeker St., 677-5400.
18. AMERICAN ENSEMBLE COMPANY, P.O. Box 5478, Grand Central Sta.; Theatre Off Park, 28 E. 35th St., 571-7549.
Established: 1969. Artistic Director: Robert Petito. Produces new work and work of literary and social value. Representative productions: "Ah, Wilderness!" by Eugene O'Neill, "Break A Leg," an original revue.
19. AMERICAN MIME THEATRE, 192 Third Ave., SP7-1710.
20. AMERICAN PLACE THEATRE, 111 West 46th Street, 247-0393.
Established: 1964. Artistic Director: Wynn Handman. Established, simply, to foster good writing for the theatre, and to provide a home and inspiration for writers of stature and for new writers. Representitive productions: "Old Glory" by Robert Lowell; "Jack Gelber's New Play Rehearsal." Audience capacity: 299 in the main theatre, with a cabaret and basement space for workshops. Subscription policy: 4 plays / $18.-$30. Reads over 1,000 new scripts a year.
21. AMERICAN CENTER FOR STANISLAVSKI THEATRE ART (ACSTA 1), 141 West 13th St. (Greenwich Mews Theatre), PL5-5120.
Established: 1964. Artistic Director: Sonia Moore. Aspires to bring Stanislavski's methods to bear on classic and current work in repertory. Represententive productions: "The Crucible" by Arthur Miller; "A Deed From the King of Spain" by Joseph Baldwin.
22. AMERICAN THEATRE COMPANY, 106 East 14th St., 989-0023.
Established: 1966. Artistic Director: Richard Kuss. Devoted to American theatre from the 18th century to the present. Representitive productions: "The Male Animal" by James Thurber; "Here We Are" by Dorothy Parker.
23. AMERICAN THEATRE LAB, 219 West 19th St., 691-6500.
24. ARENA REPERTORY VII, 277 Park Ave. South, 673-9450.
25. ARENA PLAYERS REPERTORY CO., 290 Rte. 109, E. Farmingdale, L.I., (516) 293-0674.
26. ARTS STUDENTS LEAGUE, 215 West 57th St.
27. ASSOCIATION OF THEATRE ARTISTS, YW-YMHA, Washington Heights-Inwood, 569-6200.
28. THE BASEMENT, 257 Church St., 266-1124.
29. BEL CANTO OPERA, 30 East 31st St., 889-6636.
30. BIG APPLE THEATRE, Presbyterian Church, Lafayette St., Brooklyn. Closed.
31. THE BILLY HOLIDAY THEATRE FOR LITTLE FOLKS, 1368 Fulton St., Brooklyn, 636-1100.
Established: 1972. Representative productions: "Clinton" by Shauneille Perry; "Johnny Moonbeam," an Indian folk tale. Audience Capacity: 218.
32. BACK EAST RESTAURANT THEATRE, 196 Ave. B., CA8-3857.
33. BLACK THEATRE ALLIANCE, 102 West 56th St., 245-8125.
34. BLACK VIBRATIONS, no permanent theatre, 778-4878.
35. BLUE DOME, 261 Bowery, 437-9829.

36. BROODJE CAFE THEATRE, 246 East 51st St., 832-7188.
37. THE BROOKLYN COMPANY, 144 Seventh Ave., Brooklyn.
38. CABARET THEATRE AT NOON, St. Peter's Gate, 16 East 56th St., PL3-4669.
39. CALVARY PARISH HOUSE, 61 Gramercy Park North.
40. CAMPBELL HALL, 455 West 51st St., CL5-7264.
41. CATHEDRAL OF ST. JOHN THE DIVINE, 112th St., Amsterdam Ave.
42. CEDAR PLAYERS, Cedar Tavern, 82 University Place.
43. CENTRAL ARTS, 108 East 64th St., PL8-6327.
44. CHANGING SPACE, 120 West 28th St., 242-6663.
45. CHELSEA THEATRE CENTER, Brooklyn Academy of Music, 30 Lafayette Ave., and 407 W. 43rd St. in Manhattan, 783-5110.
    Established: 1965. Artistic Director: Robert Kalfin. Established to discover new plays and to produce European plays never seen in the U.S.; thinks of itself as able to take chances commercial theatres can't. Representative production: "The Crazy Locomotive" by Stanislaw Ignacy Witkiewictz. Audience capacity: 220 (Academy of Music); 190-250 (Manhattan). Subscription policy: 4 plays/$26. Will read submitted scripts with pleasure.
46. CHICAGO PROJECT/NEW YORK, 79 East 4th St.
47. CHURCH OF THE COVENANT, 310 East 42nd St.
48. CHURCH OF THE GOOD SHEPHERD, 240 East 31st St., 982-3202.
49. CHURCH OF THE HOLY COMMUNION, Sixth Ave. at 20th St., CH3-6262.
50. CHURCH OF SAINT PAUL AND ST. ANDREWS, 263 West 86th St., 873-3209.
51. CHURCHYARD PLAYHOUSE, 342 West 53rd St.
    Established 1975. Artistic Director: Nishan Parlakian. Produces new American and European scripts. Representative productions: "Melons" by Alan Levine; "The Guardian of the Tomb" by Kafka. Audience capacity: 60-70. Subscription policy: none; TDF accepted.
52. CIRCLE REPERTORY THEATRE, 99 Seventh Ave. S., 874-1080.
    Established: 1969. Artistic Director: Marshall W. Mason. A group of six playwrights and seventeen performers presenting American and classic theatre. Representative productions: "When You Comin' Back Red Ryder" by Mark Medoff; "The Sea Horse" by Edward Moore.
53. CLARK CENTER FOR PERFORMING ARTS, 840 Eighth Ave., 246-4818.
54. THE CLASSIC THEATRE: CENTRAL ARTS, Park Ave. and 64th St., 758-6327.
    Established: 1961. Artistic Director: Maurice Edwards. A company entirely devoted to classical works. Representative production: "The Epicene" by Ben Johnson.
55. COLONNADES THEATRE LABS, 428 Lafayette St., 228-6640.
56. COMEDY STAGE COMPANY, 152 West 66th St., 799-7008.
    Established: 1973. Artistic Director: Tim Ward. Emphasis on classical comedies, but looking to find contemporary comedy to produce. Repre-

sentative production: "The Real Inspector Hound" by Tom Stoppard.

57. COMIC BOOK THEATRE COMPANY, 145 West 18th St.

58. COMMON GROUND, 70 Grand St., 431-5446.
Established: 1966. Artistic Director: Norman Taffel. Devoted to theatre as a "common ground" for actor and audience, as simply the progression of physical events. Representative productions: "Analysis Creating a Creche"; "A Hopper Scroll." Subscription policy: none; TDF accepted.

59. COMPANIA DE TEATRO REPERTORIO ESPANOL (Spanish Theatre Repertory Company), 138 East 27th St. (Gramercy Arts Theatre), 889-2850.
Established: 1969. Artistic Directors: Gilberto Zaldivar, Frances Drucker and Rene Buch. A theatre dedicated to modern and classical theatre in Spanish. It has also presented musical works and dance, and has toured abroad under reciprocal cultural agreements. Representative productions: "O.K." by Isaac Chocron; "O Casi El Alma" by Luis Rafael Sanchez; "Teoria Y Juego del Duende" by Garcia Lorca.

60. THE COMPANY, Holy Family Auditorium, 315 East 47th St., 753-3425.

61. THE COMPANY THEATRE, Central Presbyterian Church, Park Ave. and 64th St.

62. CONTEMPORARY DANCE STUDIO, 55 Bethune St., 630A, 989-2250.

63. CORNER LOFT THEATRE, 121 University Place, CH3-5689.
Established: 1957. Artistic Director: Michael Shurtleff. Mainly interested in new scripts of value to American writers, and scripts by established writers little known to audiences. Representative productions: "Home Free" by Lanford Wilson; "The Collection" by Harold Pinter. Audience capacity: 70. TDF accepted.

64. COUNTERPOINT THEATRE COMPANY, INC., 170 West 74th St., 799-6954.
Established: 1974. Artistic Director: Howard Green. The company hopes to establish an ensemble of artists dedicated to distinguished theatre. Representative production: "Miss Julie" by Strindberg. Subscription policy: none; TDF welcome.

65. COURTYARD PLAYHOUSE, 426 West 45th St., 765-9540.

66. CRICKETT THEATRE, 162 Second Ave., 873-6100.

67. CSC REPERTORY, 136 East 13th St. (Abbey Theatre), 677-4210 or 477-5770.
Established: 1967. Artistic Director: Christopher Martin. Representative productions: "The Lady's Not For Burning" by Christopher Fry; "The Maids" by Jean Genet. Considered one of the best companies in the city.

68. THE CUBICULO EXPERIMENTAL/ARTS CLUB, 414 West 51st St., 265-2139, 265-2138 (box office).
Established: 1968. Artistic Directors: Philip Meister and Elaine Sulka. A two-theatre complex devoted to producing new work in theatre, dance and the other arts. Representative productions: "Judas" by Robert Patrick Sword; "Ain't That a Shame: the Saga of Richard Nixon" by Joseph Renard.

69. THE CUTTING EDGE,
   The Cutting Edge serves as a focal point for many women artists, who combine their skills to investigate questions relating themselves to the world. Representative production: "Aroon," a dramatic examination of mothers and daughters.
70. DANCE THEATRE WORKSHOP, 215 West 20th St., 929-8772.
71. RON DENER WORKSHOP AND UNDERCROFT THEATRE, 240 East 31st St., 689-1519.
72. DIGNITY/NEW YORK/ACTING CO., P.O. Box 1554 FDR Station, performing at Good Shepherd-Faith Church, Lincoln Center.
73. DIRECT THEATRE, 455 West 43rd St., 765-2117.
   Established: 1971. Artistic Director: Allen R. Belknap. A permanent company committed to producing new work and interpreting classical plays. Representative productions: "Right You Are" by Pirandello; "Gilgamesh" by Ross Alexander.
74. DONNELL LIBRARY CENTER AUDITORIUM, 20 West 53rd St., 790-6463.
75. DOUBLE IMAGE THEATRE, 250 West 65th St., 874-0861.
76. DOWN STAGE STUDIO THEATRE, 321 West 14th St.
77. DOWNSTAIRS AT BACK EAST, 196 Avenue B, CA8-3857.
78. DRAMA COMMITTEE REPERTORY, 17 West 20th St., 929-8377.
79. DRAMA ENSEMBLE, 1008 Wooster St.
80. DRAMATIS PERSONAE, 114 West 14th St., 675-9922.
81. DRAMA TREE PLAYERS, 182 Fifth Ave., AL5-6353.
82. DRIFTING TRAFFIC, 520 La Guardia Place (c/o Sande Shurin), 673-2802.
   Established: 1971. Artistic Director: Sande Shurin. Emphasis on "strong physical movement" complete with live, original music. Representative productions: "The Satyr Play" by Sophocles; "Sweet Suite" by Leonard Melf.
83. DUMÉ SPANISH THEATRE, 409 West 44th St., 765-3457.
   Established: 1969. Artistic Director: Herborto Dumé. Produces theatre to dramatize "Cuba's sentiments, suffering and passion." Representative productions: "El Robo del Coching" by Abelardo Estorino; "Uncle Vanya."
84. DUO THEATRE (Spanish-English Ensemble Theatre), 94 St. Mark's Place, 730-9319.
   Established: 1969. Artistic Director: Manuel Martin. Duo Theatre hopes to become more stable and cohesive as the group creates its own texts. Representative productions: bilingual works such as "When the Clowns Play Hamlet" by H.M. Koutoukas and "El Pajaro Cu" ("The Cu Bird") by Gloria Zetaya.
85. EAST SIDE THEATRE ARTS, P.S. 19 Auditorium, First Ave. and 12th St., 677-4217.
86. EAST VILLAGE THEATRE, 433 East Sixth St.
87. EASTERN OPERA THEATRE OF NEW YORK, 530 East 89th St., 744-5035.

88. ELBEE AUDIO PLAYERS, 621 West End Ave., TR4-5704.
Established: 1962. Artistic Director: Board of sponsors, including Julie Harris, Frank Capra, Leonard Bernstein. An independent troupe of blind and sighted players performing dramatic readings of major plays. Representative production: "A Raisin In the Sun" by Lorraine Hansberry. Subscription policy: admission is free.

89. EL COYOTE, 252 E. 10th St., OR7-6540.
New and original plays. "Two Dykes and Uxmal."

90 EL GREGO GALLERY, 675 Eighth Ave., 3rd fl.

91. ENCORE STUDIO, 2345 64th St., Brooklyn.

92. ENSEMBLE STUDIO THEATRE, 549 West 52nd St., 541-5460.

93. EQUITY LIBRARY THEATRE, 310 Riverside Dr., 663-2928.

94. EREHAUN THEATRE PRODUCTIONS, at The Cricket and The Gate, 162 Second Ave., 674-9215.
Est: 1974. Art. Directors: Robert Dawson and Brad Lutz. An emphasis on development of original scripts and presentation of older plays of merit. Repres. prod: "Rip" by Julius Adams; "Eros in Exile" by L. Miller. Aud. cap: 170 (Cricket); 150-200 (Gate). TDF accepted for showcase productions.

95. ETC THEATRE CO., 182 Fifth Ave., 924-9418.
Est. 1973. Art. Directors: J.J. Barry, Rae Allen and Frank Bongiorno. Produces both old and contemporary works. Representative productions: "Waiting for Lefty" by Clifford Odets; "Once in a Lifetime" by Kaufman/Hart.

96. EVERGREEN THEATRE, 53 East 11th St.

97. EVERYMAN COMPANY of Brooklyn, 725 Union St., 857-7533.

98. EXCHANGE THEATRE, 151 Bank St., 929-2880.

99. EXPRESSIONS, 350 West 55th St., 586-8604.
Drama, dance, song. "Theatre Offerings."

100. FLATBUSH DUTCH REFORM CHURCH, Flatbush and Church Ave., Brooklyn, 693-5296.

101. FOCUS II, 163 West 74th St., 362-9188, 956-4774.

102. FORDHAM UNIVERSITY AT LINCOLN CENTER, 113 W. 60th St.

103. FORTUNE THEATRE, 62 East Fourth St., 473-9698.

104. THE GENE FRANKEL THEATRE FOUNDATION, 342 E. 63rd St., 421-1666.
Established: 1972. Artistic Director: Gene Frankel. Produces revivals and original work; presents the opportunity for new playwrights to test their talents. Representative productions: "Yin-Yang" by Joseph Walker; "Fight Song," a new musical by Ben Barber and Robert Lamb, with music by John Duffy.

105. FULTON THEATRE COMPANY, 441 West 26th St., 524-6700.

106. GALAXY THEATRE COMPANY, Immanuel Lutheran Church.

107. THE GALLEY PLAYERS, 186 St. John's Place, Brooklyn, 622-1037.

108. GAP THEATRE, 138 Fifth Ave., 478-8262.

109. THE GLINES, 260 West Broadway, 925-2619. Homosexual theatre.

110. THE GOLDEN FLEECE, Studio 17, 18 East 17th St., 691-6105. "A Pushkin Trilogy."

111. **GRAMERCY ARTS THEATRE,** 138 East 27th St., 889-2850.
112. **GRAND THEATRE,** 70 Grand St., 431-5446.
113. **GREEK ARTS THEATRE,** 1 Sheridan Square.
114. **98 GREENE STREET LOFT,** 98 Greene St., 966-7673.
115. **GREENWICH HOUSE,** 27 Barrow St., 242-4140.
116. **GREENWICH MEWS THEATRE,** 141 West 13th St., CH3-6800.
117. **GUILD STUDIO I,** Ansonia Hotel, Broadway and 73rd St.
118. **HAMM AND CLOV STAGE COMPANY,** 35 Jervis Rd., Yonkers.
     Established: 1972. Artistic Director: David Villaire. The company has
     toured with both European and American plays, and aims to share theatri-
     cal experiences with other nations. Representative productions: "Trees In
     the Wind" by John McGrath; "Darts" by Lodewijk de Boer.
119. **HEIGHTS PLAYERS,** 26 Willow Place, Brooklyn, 239-2752.
120. **HENRY STREET PLAYHOUSE,** 466 Grand St., WO2-1100.
121. **HENRY STREET SETTLEMENT'S NEW FEDERAL THEATRE,** 240
     East Third St., 674-1414.
122. **HOTEL BRETTON HALL,** 2350 Broadway, SU7-7000.
123. **THE HOUSE REPERTORY THEATRE,** 413 West 46th St.
124. **HUDSON GUILD THEATRE,** 441 West 26th St., 760-9810.
     Established: 1968. Artistic Director: Craig Anderson. Performs both
     classical and contemporary theatre, as well as dance, puppetry and mime.
     Representative productions: "Days of Wine and Roses" by J.P. Miller;
     "Relief" by George Patterson. Subscription policy: four plays for $10.00.
     TDF accepted.
125. **IMMANUEL THEATRE,** 88 St. and Lexington Ave.
126. **IMPOSSIBLE RAGTIME THEATRE,** 120 West 28th St., 243-7494,
     989-8955.
     Established: 1974. Artistic Directors: Ted Story and George Ferenez. The
     theatre "aims to develop a director's method through his dealings with ac-
     tors, designers, playwrights and the audience." Representative productions:
     "American Stickball League," an original script by Howard Kuperberg;
     "The Hairy Ape." Audience capacity: 98. Subscription policy: $25.00 for 10
     plays, plus extra activities.
127. **THE INTENSE FAMILY TRAVELING THEATRE,** 799-4970.
128. **INTERART THEATRE,** 549 West 52nd St., 246-6569.
129. **INTERNATIONAL ARTS RELATIONS (INTAR),** 508 West 53rd St.,
     246-0984.
     Established: 1966, making it the oldest Spanish theatre group in NYC. Ar-
     tistic Director: Max Ferra. Representative productions: "Caperucta Roja"
     and "Espectaculo" by Valle-Inclan; "La Historia del Zoologico" by Edward
     Albee.
130. **IRISH REBEL THEATRE,** 533 West 51st St. (Irish Arts Center), 757-3318.
     Established: 1972. Artistic Director: James Kennedy. Part of the Irish Arts
     Center, which sponsors poetry and dramatic readings, as well as plays.
     Representative productions: work by Jim Synge, Sean O'Casey and Walter
     Mackey.

131. JEAN COCTEAU THEATRE, 330 Bowery, 677-0060.
Established: 1971. Artistic Director: Eve Adamson. Aspires to produce "the best classical theatre, old and new, to a diversified audience at a low price." Representative productions: "Twelfth Night;" "Endgame."

132. JOSEPH JEFFERSON THEATRE COMPANY, 1 East 29th St., 679-7174.
Established: 1972. Artistic Director: Cathy Roskam. The 1974-75 season included four American plays, one each from the 20's, 30's, 40's and 50's. Audience capacity: 100.

133. JUDSON POETS THEATRE, 55 Washington Square South, 777-0033.

134. KNICKERBOCKER CREATIVE THEATRE FOUNDATION, 929 Eighth Ave., SU7-5400.

135. KUKU RYKU THEATRE LAB, 542 La Guardia Place, 475-9946.

136. LAB THEATRE, All Angels Parish House, 251 West 80th St., UN5-5560.

137. THE LABOR THEATRE, 102 East Fourth St., 477-0993.
Established: 1973. Artistic Director: C.R. Portz. Develops dramatic material relevant to working people's lives. Representative production: "Working Our Way Down" by Bette Craig. TDF accepted.

138. LA MAMA EXPERIMENTAL THEATRE CLUB, 74A East 4th St., 475-7710.
Established: 1962. Artistic Director: Wilfred Leach. La Mama's primary interest is in forms of lyrical theatre, which incorporate music and dance into production of the text; new work and new, conceptual arrangements of old. Representative production: Andre Sherben's Greek Trilogy, with music by Liz Swados. Audience capacity: 90-250. Subscription policy: 6 plays/$25. Seldom considers new scripts submitted.

139. LAMBS CLUB THEATRE, 128 West 44th St., 575-9117.

140. THE LANDMARK THEATRE PRODUCTION COMPANY, 1047 Amsterdam Ave., 850-2425.

141. LENOX SCHOOL THEATRE, 170 East 70th St., CO6-2002.

142. LEVY-SHEA, 100 East 16th St., 677-5690.

143. LIBRARY OF PERFORMING ARTS, Lincoln Center, 799-2200.

144. LIGHT OPERA COMPANY OF MANHATTAN, Jan Hus Theatre, 351 East 74th St., 535-3610.

145. THE LITTLE HIPPODROME, 227 East 56th St.

146. LOEB STUDENT CENTER, NYU, 566 La Guardia Place.

147. LOLLY'S THEATRE CLUB, Commodore Hotel, 42nd St. and Lexington Ave., 832-7404.
Established: 1972. Artistic Director: Mrs. O.W. Bivins. Stresses a setting free of the commercial strains of Broadway and Off-Broadway. Representative productions: works by Agatha Christie, Tennessee Williams and J.B. Priestley's "Laburnum Grove."

148. LA MAMA EXPERIMENTAL THEATRE, 74A East Fourth St., 474-7710.

149. MAMA HARE'S TREE COMPANY, 13th St. Theatre, 741-2796.

150. MANHATTAN PROJECT, 115 Central Park West, 595-2721.
Established: 1968. Artistic Director: Andre Gregory. An experimental theatre producing both traditional plays and new scripts. Representative pro-

ductions: "Alice in Wonderland"; "The Sea Gull"; "Endgame."

151. MANHATTAN PROJECT THEATRE COMPANY, 111 Second Ave., 677-1750.

152. MANHATTAN THEATRE CLUB, 321 East 73rd St., 288-2500.
Established: 1970. Artistic Director: Lynn Meadow. This well-known group presents a variety of new plays, revivals, readings, opera, and musical cabaret. Four theatres under one roof. Representative productions: "Geography of a Horse Dreamer" by Sam Shepard; "Life Class" by David Storey. Subscription policy: $25.00/yr. for all productions in all theatres. TDF accepted. New scripts welcomed.

153. MASTER OPERA, 310 Riverside Drive, 733-2204.

154. MATRIX PLAYERS, All Angels Church, 262 West 81st St., 724-9271.

155. MEAT AND POTATOES, INC., 58 West 39th St., 391-2346.

156. MEDICINE SHOW THEATRE ENSEMBLE, 697 West End Ave., 749-6210.
Established: 1970. Artistic Directors: James Barbosa and Barbara Vann. Ensemble aims "to develop works that juggle incongruities of style and form, mingle wit and high physical energy." Experimental. Representative productions: "Frogs," a group creation with Carl Morse; "Glowworm," structured by Barbara Vann. Subscription policy: no permanent theatre, but TDF accepted.

157 MEMORIAL PRESBYTERIAN CHURCH, 186 St. John's Place and Seventh Ave., Brooklyn, NE8-5541.

158. MERI-MINI PLAYERS, 4 West 76th St.

159. MINOR LATHAM PLAYHOUSE, Barnard College, Broadway and 119th St., 280-2079.

160. MONGOOSE COMMUNITY CENTER, 782 Union St., Brooklyn, 783-8819.

161. MOONLIGHT THEATRE, Broadway and 120th St., 677-2400.

162. MT. MORRIS PARK AMPHITHEATRE, 122nd St. and Mt. Morris Park West, 663-3100.

163. MT. OLIVET CHURCH, 8 G St. and West 12th St., Brooklyn, HI9-2663.

164. MUFSON COMPANY, Elysian Playhouse, 138 Fifth Ave., 758-9427.

165. MULTIGRAVITATIONAL AERODANCE GROUP, 260 West Broadway, Rm. 1103, 966-3894.

166. MUSIC THEATRE LAB, 490 Riverside Drive, RI9-7000, ext. 124.

167. MUSIC THEATRE PERFORMING GROUP, 151 Bank St., 929-2880.

168. NATIONAL ARTS CLUB, 15 Gramercy Park, GR5-3424.

169. NATIONAL ARTS THEATRE, 25 East 4th St., 477-9642.
Established: 1972. Artistic Director: Robert Sterling. Tendency toward the classics and toward plays and playwrights with "big ideas." The theatre is attempting to develop a permanent group. Representative productions: a festival of one-act plays by Shaw; Moliere's "The Miser."

170. NATIONAL BLACK THEATRE, 9 East 125th St. 534-9882.

171. NEGRO ENSEMBLE, INC., 133 Second Ave., 674-3530.
Established: 1967. Artistic Director: Douglas Turner Ward. Produces the works of black playwrights, and aspires to train blacks in all aspects of theatre production. Representative production: "Brownsville Raid." Au-

dience capacity: 300. Subscription/policy: 3 plays/$12. Will read original scripts with diligence.

172. NEW HERITAGE REPERTORY THEATRE, INC., 43 East 125th St., 876-3272.
173. NEW LAFAYETTE THEATRE, 2349 Seventh Ave., 862-2460.
174. NEW REPERTORY COMPANY, 437 West 46th St., JU2-4240.
175. NEW VILLAGE THEATRE, 433 East Sixth St., 475-9506.
176. NEW YORK CITY REPERTORY, 437 West 46th St., JU2-4240.
177. NEW YORK LEAGUE OF PLAYWRIGHTS, 162 West 21st St.
178. NEW YORK LYRIC OPERA COMPANY, 124 West 72nd St., Donald Johnston, TR4-1993.
179. NEW YORK SHAKESPEARE FESTIVAL, 425 Lafayette St., Lincoln Center, 677-6350.
    Established: 1954, has occupied the Public Theatre since 1968. Artistic Director: Joseph Papp. Four separate theatres committed to the presentation and growth of new American writers. Representative productions: "Happiness Cage" by Dennis Reardon; "A Chorus Line" in workshop. Audience capacity: Anspacher, 275; The Other Stage, 108; Martinson and Lu Esther, 150-200. Subscription policy: No TDF, since the number of performances is limited. Scripts are welcomed at the Department of Play Development.
180. NEW YORK SOCIETY FOR ETHICAL CULTURE, 2 West 64th St., 874-5200.
181. NEW YORK THEATRE OF THE AMERICAN, 427 West 59th St., 254-9656.
182. NEW YORK THEATRE ENSEMBLE, 62 East Fourth St., 477-4120.
    Established: 1968. Artistic Director: Lucille Talayco. Both arena and proscenium stages. Ensemble's concern is to provide interesting theatre, to create an acting ensemble, and to promote "life in art." Representative productions: "The Misunderstanding" by Albert Camus; "Tania," a musical by Mario Fratti. Audience capacity: proscenium, 169; arena, 154. Subscription policy: $10.00 for 10 plays. TDF accepted.
183. NEW YORK THEATRE STRATEGY, 1 Sheridan Square, 741-0590.
    Established: 1972. A group of 23 American playwrights interested in forming a repertory company for experimental theatre and touring. Including Lanford Wilson, Charles Ludlam, Sam Shephard, et al. Representative productions: "King Humpy" by Kenneth Bernard; "Gillés de Rais" by William M. Hoffman.
184. THE NIGHTHOUSE, 249 West 18th St., 691-7359.
    Est: 1973. Art. Dir: Gordon Needham. Attempts to provide "truthful, honest, vital, energetic theatre of varied styles." Repres. prod: "The Women's Representative" by Sun Yu; "The Balcony" by Jean Genet. Sub. pol: none. TDF plus $1.00 accepted.
185. NODELDINIS PARK EAST, 1311 Madison Ave., 722-9489.
186. NUESTRO THEATRE, 277 Park Avenue, 673-9430.
187. OCTAGON THEATRE CLUB, 250 West 43rd St., 221-9143.

188. OFF CENTER THEATRE, 2 West 64th Street, 874-5200.
189. OMNI THEATRE CLUB, 145 West 18th St., 581-1810.
190. ONTOLOGICAL-HYSTERIC THEATRE, 80 Wooster St., 260-3328.
191. THE OPEN EYE, 78 Fifth Ave., 243-3880.
192. THE OPEN SPACE IN SOHO, 64 Wooster St., 966-3729.
193. OPEN THEATRE, 423 West 46th St., CL6-7277.
194. OPERA BUFFA COMPANY, 316 East 88th St.
195. ORIBUS THEATRE FOUNDATION, 39 Grove St., 265-4100.
196. THE PAPER BAG PLAYERS, 185 East Broadway, Brooklyn.
197. PARK AVENUE COMMUNITY THEATRE, 593 Park Ave. and 63rd St., TE8-0808.
198. PARK SLOPE CULTURAL CENTER, 186 St. John's Place, Brooklyn, 633-1039.
199. P.A.R.T., 106 W. 43rd St.
200. THE PEOPLE'S PERFORMING COMPANY, 59 Carmine St., 243-1373.
201. PEOPLE'S THEATRE ENSEMBLE, 18th St. Playhouse, 145 W. 18th St., 989-9228. A recent Horovitz festival.
202. PERFORMANCE GROUP, 33 Wooster St., 966-3652.
    Est: 1967. Art. Dir: Richard Schechner and Steve Borst. A well-known, flexible experimental company that stresses environmental theatre, and brings audience and performers closer to problems they share. Repres. prod: "The Tooth of Crime" by Sam Shepard; "The Beard" by Michael McClure.
203. PLAYERS THEATRE, 115 MacDougal St., AL4-5076.
204. PLAYMATES, 346 West 20th St., WA9-2390.
205. PLAYWRIGHTS HORIZONS, 416 West 42nd St., 564-1235.
    Est: 1971; originally housed in the West Side YMCA. Art. Dir: Robert Moss. Experienced theatre people helping unknown playwrights to produce their work. Repres. prod: "Going Over" by Robert Gordon; "Beethoven/Karl" by David Rush. Original scripts welcomed.
206. PORTFOLIO STUDIO, 341 West 47th St.
207. THE PRETENDERS THEATRE, 106 East 16th St.
208. PRINCE STREET PLAYERS LOFT, 228 West Houston St.
209. PROVINCETOWN PLAYHOUSE, 133 MacDougal St., 477-9894.
210. PUBLIC THEATRE, 425 Lafayette St., 677-6350. (See N.Y. Shakespeare Co.)
211. PUERTO RICAN TRAVELING THEATRE, 124 West 18th St., 691-9453.
    Est: 1967. Art. Dir: Miriam Colon. Bilingual theatre in low-income areas in and out of NYC. Repres. prod: "Ceremony for an Assasinated Black Man" by Arrabal; "The Ox Cart" by Rene Marquez.
212. QUAIGH THEATRE, 808 Lexington Avenue, MU7-9040.
    Est. 1972. Art. Dir: Will Lieberson. Concentrates on giving good plays their second chance. Repres. prod: "The Birds" by William Kushner; "One Piece Smash" by Arthur Cainer.
213. RAFT THEATRE, at Title Theatre, Westbeth, 155 Bank St., 924-7790.
214. REPERTORY VII, 427 West 59th St., 245-9656.
215. THE RIDICULOUS THEATRE COMPANY, 53 East 11th St., 477-0504.

216. RIVERDALE SHOWCASE, Broadway Methodist Temple, 173rd St. and Broadway, 222-8788.
217. RIVERSIDE CHURCH THEATRE, 490 Riverside Dr., 749-8140.
218. RIVERSIDE THEATRE WORKSHOP, St. John's-in-the-Village, 218 West 11th St., 666-7170.
219. ROOT THEATRE, 74 Trinity Place, 425-6677 ext. 255.
220. ROUNDABOUT THEATRE, 333 West 23rd St (also, Stage Two at 307 W. 26th St.)., 924-7161.
    Producing Director: Gene Feist. Exec. Producer: Michael Fried. Wide range of work presented.
221. ROYAL PLAYHOUSE, 219 Second Ave., GR5-9647.
222. ST. CLEMENTS THEATRE, 423 West 46th St., 246-7277.
    Est: 1972. Art. Dir: Brian Murray. Performs new works, revivals, classics, and experimental new musicals. Repres. prod: "Figures in the Sand" by Nathan Teitel; "Enter a Free Man" by Tom Stoppard.
223. ST. GEORGE'S CHURCH, 135-32 28th Ave., Flushing, 371-1540.
224. SAINT LUKES CHAMBER ENSEMBLE, St. Luke's Chapel, 487 Hudson St., WA4-5960.
225. SAINT PETER'S GATE, St. Peter's Lutheran Church, 16 East 56th St., PL3-4669.
    Est: 1968 (as Theater-at-Noon). Seeks to bring new, undiscovered and unfamiliar material to audiences (at lunchtime). Repres. prod: "Overrules" by G.B. Shaw; "But Not For Me" by Tom Topor, dir. by John Marquiles. Sub. pol: none. TDF accepted.
226. SAMUEL RUBIN THEATRE, 35 Fifth Ave.
227. T. SCHREIBER STUDIO, 386 Third Ave., 874-7509. Est: 1969. Art. Dir: Terry Schreiber. The production of new works and old deserving a second chance. Repres. prod: "The Trip Back Down" by John Bishop; "Lemon Sky" by Lanford Wilson. Aud. cap: 100. Sub. pol: subscriptions and "mini-subscriptions" available; TDF accepted. Original scripts read by three "incessantly" hard-working readers.
228. SECTION TEN, 115 Central Park West, 254-4850.
    Est: 1968. Art. Dir: Andrea Balis. A community emphasizing the relationship between performer and viewer; physical and verbal assault of the viewer are integral to the theatre's purpose. Repres. prod: "Lulu" by Ron Cowey; "Earth Spirit" by Frank Wedekind. TDF accepted.
229. SEVENTY FOUR BELOW COFFEE HOUSE, 74 Trinity Place, 269-6640.
230. SHADE COMPANY, c/o Valk, 19 Seaman Ave.
    Est: 1970. Art. Dir: Toni Dorfman. Relies on audience/actor interaction, and employs physical means toward this interaction. Repres. prod: "Dr. Hero" by Israel Horowitz; "Till Eulenspiegel" by Don Ferguson. Edward Berkeley, James Milton and Dale Fuller have served as Directors.
231. SHALIKO COMPANY, 425 Lafayette St., 677-6350.
    Est. 1971. Art. Dir: Leonard Shapiro. Seeks to eliminate some of the many paradoxes of commercial theatre. Repres. prod: "The Measures Taken" by

B. Brecht; "Ghosts" by Ibsen, dir. by ROH Fjeldel. Receptive to submission of new scripts.

232. SHELTER WEST COMPANY, 120 West 69th St.

233. SOUTH STREET THEATRE (THEATRE RESEARCH INC.), 16 Fulton St., 265-5997.
Est: 1966. Art. Dir: Michael Fischetti. Performs on various New York piers near the South Street Seaport Museum. Repres. prod: "Moby Dick," "Spoon River Anthology," a "cocktail theatre" on the ship Robert Fulton, a collage of scenes from comic playwrights. Aud. cap: 100.

234. SPACE FOR INNOVATIVE DEVELOPMENT, 344 West 36th St., 947-4671.

235. SPANISH-ENGLISH ENSEMBLE THEATRE, P.O. Box 4357 Grand Central Station, 730-9319.
Est: 1969. Art. Dir: Manuel Martin. Bilingual ensemble devoted to presenting Spanish and Latin-American plays in English, and to performing them in Spanish-speaking countries. Repres. prod: "The White Whore" by Tom Eyen; "Rasputin" by Manuel Martin. Aud. cap: 80. TDF welcomed.

236. SPLINTERS COMPANY FOUNDATION, INC., 52 Greenwich Ave., 924-1422.

237. STAGE 73, 321 East 73rd St., 595-5222.

238. STAGELIGHTS THEATRE CLUB, 218 West 48th St., 929-2181.

239. STAGELIGHTS TWO, 125 West 22nd St., 989-9228.

240. STATEN ISLAND CIVIC THEATRE, Christ Church Parish House, 76 Franklin Ave., New Brighton, Staten Island, 488-2230.

241. SULLIVAN ST. PLAYHOUSE, 181 Sullivan St.

242. TALES, 522 Broadway, 925-3078.
Est: 1973. Art. Dir: Victoria Fales. Produces work by Victoria Fales. Not interested in new material.

243. TEATRO ARENA, 277 Park Ave. South, 362-0330.

244. TEATRO CAROS NUEVAS, 114 West 14th St.

245. TEATRO DE ORILLA, 214 East Second St., 260-2548.

246. THE TELENY THEATRE, 333 Avenue of the Americas, 924-5025.

247. TEN PENNY PLAYERS, 709 Greenwich St.

248. TERRAIN GALLERY, 141 Greene St., WA4-4984.

249. THEATRE DE LYS, 121 Christopher St., WA4-3930.

250. THEATRE EXP-3 EDUCATIONAL ALLIANCE, 197 East Broadway, 475-6900 ext. 40.

251. THEATRE FORUM, 333 Sixth Ave. at Fourth St., 4th fl., 586-4800.

252. THEATRE GENESIS, St. Mark's Place Church-In-The-Bowery, Second Ave. and 10th St., 533-4650.

253. THEATRE OF LATIN AMERICA INC., 344 West 36th St., 628-2814.
Est: 1967. Art. Dir: Joanne Pottlitzer. Founded to bring Latin American arts to the U.S. The theatre has won an Obie for its three-week Latin American Fair of Opinion. It also performs new works in English. Repres. prod: "Chile, Chile" by TOLA (Theatre of Latin America) and Joseph Chaiken; poetry readings.

254. **THEATRE OF MADNESS AT THE BANK,** 1 Front St., Brooklyn, 855-6419.
255. **THEATRE FOR THE NEW CITY,** 113 Jane St., 691-2220.
   Est: 1970. Art. Directors: George Bartenieff and Crystal Field. Produces new plays "toward a return to the religious/mythical element in theatre." Repres. prod: "Day Old Bread" by Arthur Sainer; "Sophia" by Richard Foreman. Aud. cap: 240. Sub. pol: $15.00/play; $25.00/two. TDF accepted.
256. **THEATRE PROJECTS COMPANY,** 161 West 22nd St., LT1-6470.
257. **THEATRE OFF PARK,** 28 East 35th St., MU3-4988.
258. **THEATRE OF THE RIVERSIDE CHURCH,** 120th St. and Riverside Dr., 864-2929.
   Est: 1959. Art. Dir: Arthur Bartow. Aims to encourage new writers and to revive older works with "an experimental frame of reference." Messages for a pluralistic community. Repres. prod: "Short Eyes" by Marvin Felix Camillo; "Have You Now or Have You Ever Been" by Eric Bentley, dir. by Jay Broad. Aud. cap: 250. Sub. pol: reduced rate. TDF accepted.
259. **THEATRE THREE,** Sloane House, 356 West 34th St., OX5-5133.
260 **THEATRE OF THE OPEN EYE,** 78 Fifth Ave., 243-3880.
   Est: 1972. Art. Dir: Jean Erdman. The Open Eye's Concept is based in part on Japanese Noh plays and on the work of W.B. Yeats. Repres. prod: "Hernani" by Victor Hugo; "Moon Mysteries" by W.B. Yeats; "Fire and Ice" by Robert Frost. Aud. cap: 50.
261. **THEATRE UNLIMITED,** 171 West 85th St., 799-2886.
262. **THIRTEENTH STREET THEATRE,** 50 West 13th St., 924-9785.
   Est: 1972. Art. Dir: Edith O'Hara. Produces original musical theatre. Repres. prod: "Park" by P. Cherry. Aud. cap: 72 (proscenium).
263. **TIME AND SPACE LIMITED,** 4 West 76th St., 741-1032.
   Est: 1973. Art. Dir: Linda Mussman. Works with scripts by stripping them of their physical and temporal environment. Repres. prod: Pinter's "Birthday Party;" Beckett's "Endgame." Aud. cap: 80.
264. **TOSOS,** 257 Church St., 226-1124.
   "When Did You Last See My Mother?" by Chris Hampton.
265. **TRIANGLE THEATRE,** Holy Trinity Church, 316 East 88th St., AT9-4100.
266. **TRINITY CHURCH,** Broadway and Wall St.
267. **UNIT 453,** Exchange for the Arts, 151 Bank St., 691-5035.
268. **UNITED NATIONS THEATRE,** Dag Hammarskjold Auditorium, United Nations, PL4-1234 ext. 2413.
269. **UNIVERSALIST CHURCH,** 76th St. and Central Park West, 741-1032.
270. **UNIVERSITY STREETS,** 130 East Seventh St.
271. **URBAN ARTS CORPS,** Church of Holy Communion, 26 West 20th St., 924-7820.
   Est: 1967. Art. Dir: Vinnette Carroll. Repres. prod: "Old Judge Moz is Dead" by Joseph White; "Your Arm's Too Short to Box With God" by Vinnette Carroll and Alex Bradford. Aud. cap: 66.
272. **VENTURE THEATRE CLUB,** 232 Eighth Ave., 924-4791.

273. **VILLAGE CHURCH,** 141 West 13th St.
274. **WALDEN THEATRE,** 1 West 88th St., 724-3311.
    Est: 1974. Art. Dir: Bruce K. Cornwell. Original plays and revivals. Repres.
    prod: "The Night Thoreau Spent In Jail" by Jerome Lawrence and Robert
    E. Lee; "Friends of Mine," an original musical by Robert W. Preston, dir.
    by Bic Goss. Aud cap: 100. Sub. pol: none. TDF accepted.
275. **WAR BABIES,** 163 West 74th St., 675-8939.
276. **WASHINGTON MARKET PLAYHOUSE,** 15 Jay St.
277. **WASHINGTON SQUARE METHODIST CHURCH,** 133 West Fourth St.,
    SP7-2528.
278. **WESTBETH PLAYWRIGHTS' FEMINIST COLLECTIVE,** 463 West St.,
    Apt 402D, 691-0015.
    Est: 1971. Production Dir: Nancy Rhodes. Feminist theatre. Repres. prod:
    the feminist version of "Medea" by Gloria Alvee; "Jumpin' Satty" by the
    collective playwrights.
279. **WEST PARK THEATRE,** 165 West 86th Street, 684-0340. Gorky's "Lower
    Depths."
280. **WESTSIDE COMMUNITY REPERTORY THEATRE,** 252 West 81st St.,
    666-3521, 874-9400.
    Est: 1969. Art. Dir: Andres Castro. Emphasis on reviving the classics with a
    modern viewpoint. Repres. prod: "Arms and the Man"; "The Chairs," dir.
    by Mary Ann Dreir; "Miss Julie," dir. by Patrick Hanratty. Three or four
    plays a year. Aud. cap: 38. Sub. pol: none. TDF accepted. Original scripts
    considered.
281. **WEST SIDE GAY THEATRE,** 37 Ninth Ave., 675-0143.
282. **WESTSIDE THEATRE,** 407 West 43rd St.
283. **WEUSI KUMBA THEATRE,** 393 Dumont Ave., Brooklyn, HY6-4593.
284. **WOMEN'S INTERART CENTER,** 549 West 52nd St., 246-6570.
285. **WPA THEATRE,** 333 Bowery, 473-9345.
    Est: 1968. Prod. Directors: Daniel Dietrich and Harry Orzello. Geared
    toward contemporary audiences and ideas. Repres. prod: "Picnic" by
    William Inge; "Duckling" by Jeannine O'Reilly; "The Ghost Convention"
    by Susan Dworkin.
286. **YORK PLAYERS,** 2 East 90th St., 222-9458, AT9-3402.
    Est: 1969. Art. Dir: Janet Hayes Walker. Produces non-experimental work,
    generally classic or modern. Repres. prod: "Romeo and Juliet"; the plays of
    T.S. Eliot and E. O'Neill. Aud. cap: 100, theatre; 600, church. Sub. pol:
    none; donation. TDF accepted.
287. **YOUNG ACTOR'S COMPANY,** at Prospect Park West, Brooklyn, 622-4926,
    638-5766.
    Est: 1970. Art. Dir: Gail Kriegel Mallin. Also known as "The King's
    Players." Dramatic and musical family theatre. Repres. prod: "Midsummer
    Night's Dream," using 8-19 year old performers; "Rainbow Junction," an
    original musical; "The Adventures of Peter Pan," a rock musical. Aud. cap:
    70-1, 500. TDF not accepted.
288. **YOUNG ARTIST OPERA,** 270 West 70th St., UN4-6177.